THE MONEY SHOT

ANNE DANO

ALG PUBLISHING

Edited by Kristen Weber

Copyedited by Martha Trachtenberg

Cover Design by Elizabeth Mackey

Author Photo by Debora Giordano

Print Edition ISBN: 978-1-942504-70-2

Print Hardback Edition ISBN: 978-1-942504-71-9

Digital Edition ISBN: 978-1-942504-69-6

CHAPTER 1

Sometimes mere mortals must accept that certain things are simply out of our control. Today, as in right now, would be one of those times. And to think, I started the day by trying to convince myself it wouldn't be so bad. That I'm not a morally bankrupt sellout willing to compromise myself to save my career.

That's how the day *started*.

Kevin, one of my three guests, jumps from his seat beside his wife, poking a meaty finger at Kade, seated on Melanie's right. A strategic placement between the two men considering she's married to Kevin, yet having a yearslong affair with Kade.

Her husband's brother.

All of which I knew before this family showed up today.

"You lying son of a bitch," Kevin says.

My name is Dr. Rebecca Matthews. Welcome to my new world.

Taking the cue from his brother, Kade rises, moving in front of Melanie in case Kevin takes this to the level my executive producer, Jenny, recently started yearning for.

She wants it. The anger. The drama. The oohing, ahhing and gasps from our live audience. This is nothing new. Me?

Hate it. Always have.

Every filthy second.

Over the years, we've managed to find the middle ground. The one that keeps our ratings up and my soul unsacrificed.

This, I suppose, is what happens when a show's largest advertiser bails.

Kade's back is to me and I can see by the set of his shoulders, he's ready for whatever his brother intends.

They're both tall, broad-chested men. Farm boys, Kevin had said during our first moments together. Strong and loyal and accustomed to hard work and the occasional brotherly tussle.

Despite my height of five-ten, I'm no match for them and my heart is banging like a high-school band. I'm stunned that the mic clipped to my blouse isn't picking it up.

"Gentlemen," I say, "sit *down*."

Kevin, finger in midair, turns to me. His face is a grotesque mix of red and purple that the camera is probably zoomed in on.

"You," he spits. "You're no better. Orchestrating this whole thing and springing it on me." He gestures to the three hundred folks witnessing this fiasco. "In front of all these people?"

A low murmur cruises over the audience. Kevin isn't the only one duped. This audience came in here expecting the respectable Dr. Becca, winner of nine daytime Emmys.

I've saved countless marriages over the last fourteen years and have given daytime talk credibility. No shenanigans. No circus of emotional ambushes, screaming guests or physical altercations. Just helping people.

Until now. Until the suits told me to spice it up. Walking on set this morning, all I'd hoped for was being able to control the environment. Not exactly my idea of a fulfilling day.

"Don't blame her," Kade hollers. "We needed to get this out. I can't do this anymore."

"Fucking my wife or lying?"

Oh, ouch. *That'll* have to be edited.

In my ear, I hear a chuckle. My stomach twists. I force myself to not look above my left shoulder where, behind the control room glass, someone seems to enjoy this.

We've just humiliated a man, and my staff is *laughing*?

If you hadn't guessed, I'm not a fan of what's known in daytime talk as trash television. Ambushes, I find vile.

And here I am, a willing—sort of—participant in both. In my defense, what is the host of the top daytime talk show supposed to do when ratings slip and her biggest advertiser walks?

What about my staff of two hundred?

And their families?

I won't be the one to tell them our show failed because I refused to "spice it up" when the network suits asked.

"Watch your mouth!" Kade yells and someone from the crowd applauds.

Kevin's skin turns a deeper shade of red and his eyes are giant lasers boring into his brother. I peer down. His hands are fisted, the bones popping like rails.

Oh no.

My executive producer—the EP—will hate it, but it's time to break this up. Calm everyone down before someone gets hurt.

I set my notepad and pen on the table beside me and stand. "Gentlemen." I take a step toward them. "Please, let's all ..."

Kevin's fist connects with Kade's nose. The mic amplifies a horrid crunching sound and a cacophony of hoots and hollers comes through my earbud. The control room. Once again, enjoying this nightmare.

Behind me, the audience, mostly middle-aged suburban stay-at-home parents, roars. My so-called classy audience. I glance back and half of them are on their feet, some waving their fists.

I can't have this. It's disgusting and . . . embarrassing. Years of meaningful work reduced to a circus act. For *ratings*. Shame fills me and my cheeks burn like a four-alarm fire. I turn back to the men, still standing in front of a wide-eyed and clearly stunned Melanie. There's a stain on her blue blouse. Blood spatter.

On my show.

I step forward, shoving my arms between the men, getting into their personal space. "Stop this. Enough!"

Kade, hand over his gushing nose, takes a half step back. Just as I swing sideways to unleash a verbal pounding on Kevin, he cocks his left arm and his giant fist snaps forward.

They say all humans have a fight-or-flight instinct. Mine must be on sabbatical because I have nothing. I'm frozen, my mind numb as—*boom!*—Kevin's fist plows into my face, the blow sending rockets of pain shooting up my right cheek. Momentum throws me backward, teetering on my stilettos as voices explode from my earbud.

I lose my balance, tip sideways and . . .

Crash.

Ow. Ow. *Ow.* Dammit. More pain. This time from my hip that took the brunt of the hard stage, but it's nothing compared to my abused and throbbing cheek.

The shouts of our incensed and hollering audience turn into a muddled *wha, wha, wha* in my head.

Finally, two assistant producers rush the stage, tending to me as Kevin and Kade square off. At least until Kevin peers down at me, the horror of what he's done seeming to focus him.

"My God," he says, squatting down. "I'm sorry!"

"Idiot!" Kade shouts, lowering his blood smeared hand. "You always were a dumbass!"

Fourteen years of taping. Of promising my audience smart,

reflective television that will hopefully help more than just the folks sitting onstage.

And this is what I've become? Sitting on the floor with a throbbing cheek while my show flies completely out of my control.

One producer helps me to my feet while the other stands in front of the audience, urging them to settle down.

I draw a breath, gently touch my cheek, and wince before pulling my hand away. No blood. That's good at least. Back to work. I straighten my skirt and my blouse, then glance at my guests. "Everyone," I say, "please, sit down."

As if that'll cure my problems.

Still on set, ice pack to my cheek, I'm in my chair, phone in hand and killing time by scrolling through endless emails from network execs, assistants, social media advisers, marketing, blah, blah. *On and on they go. Where they stop, nobody knows.*

"So," Jenny, my executive producer, says, her green eyes twinkling as she approaches, "*that* happened. He went total scorched-earth!"

She's wearing loose khaki cargo pants, white Converse sneakers and a white long-sleeved pullover that is somehow more mangled than her normally wrinkled shirts. Jenny has been my EP since we debuted, and she always looks like a harried mom of twelve. As long as she does her job well, I don't care if she dons sweatpants for work.

We've been a team for fourteen years. In that time, we haven't been totally in sync regarding the amount of drama I'll allow on my show. As executive producer, Jenny's rear is on the line with mine. In show business, you're only as good as your last job. Zero security. If my show flops, Jenny will have to explain to future networks why she deserves a shot when, while at the helm, my show's ratings sank like the *Titanic*.

Thanks to Jenny's dedication and talent, we've avoided trash television *and* created the most respected daytime talk show in modern history. No simple feat, that.

And, I've never been attacked. Ever. On-air violence has never been my style. So the twinkle in Jenny's eye?

My professional nightmare.

I've spent years touting my quality show. Ms. High-and-Mighty displaying my Emmys and denouncing the so-called trashy shows. Begging my competitors to rise above all that madness.

Should have known not to get cocky, since I currently have ice and two ibuprofens keeping the throb at bay and I'm afraid to look in a mirror.

My makeup artist will earn her money today.

The audience is gone, sent to the cafeteria where we'll buy them lunch while we figure out if Kade's nose is broken and how to salvage the rest of this taping. With an afternoon show already scheduled and guests about to arrive, it should be interesting.

I've never had a taping postponed because of a physical altercation. At least until being told to *spice it up*.

Well, the suits got their spice.

Anger lurks, lighting up my nerve endings. A guest getting punched in the nose? It's violent and unexpected. Draws all sorts of people to their televisions and gives my nice, professional, sagging show a ratings boon.

Total money shot.

I should be happy. Thrilled even.

And yet . . .

Disgust.

At myself, at my audience, at my guests. My staff members who are enjoying it. The suits who foisted this crap on me.

So much for my doctorate.

Jenny stands over me on the recently renovated stage. A new design of bold reds that were supposed to help my slipping ratings.

Meeting Jenny's gaze, I drop my phone on the side table. "Is he all right?"

"We had a doctor in the audience. Can't stop the bleeding. She sent him for an X-ray."

"Terrific."

As I suspected, there went the day's shooting schedule.

"What's the plan?" I ask Jenny.

"Hopefully, the ER can patch him up and we resume."

I gawk at her, my mouth literally falling open. What is happening today? Mercury must be in retrograde. "With a broken nose?"

She looks at me as if I escaped from the mental health care facility four blocks away. "Are you kidding right now?"

"It's the money shot. I get it. I can still hate it."

All these years, I've been fighting the trash wars. Promising my viewers, my sweet, middle-aged suburbanites, that I won't pollute their world with uncontrolled chaos.

Or violence.

I lower the cold pack from my cheek, scoop up my phone and stand, more than ready for the solitude of my office. My heels tap-tap-tap against the stage, the sound echoing through the space.

Jenny falls in step beside me, her sneakered feet much quieter as we reach the door. She rushes ahead, swings the door open.

"If he can resume," Jenny says, "we'll push the afternoon taping back. It'll be a late night, but what else is new?"

"Fine. Hopefully, I won't have a bruise where he slugged me."

My cheek throbs again. I lift the cold pack to my face and we make a right into the hallway that leads to our offices. Halfway to my office, Jenny breaks off, hustling toward the bullpen where a myriad of assistant producers and interns work the phones.

Kaitlyn, my assistant, appears beside me, reading from her phone as she walks—something I've repeatedly warned her is dangerous—and completely ignores the fact that I'm holding an ice pack to my face.

Am I the only one who thinks this is more than odd? That some monumental shift has just happened?

"I'll call Ryan," she says, "and tell him dinner is off."

Oh, he'll love that. My husband has eaten more dinners alone than either of us wants to admit.

But he signed up for this gig. We both knew the grind. The constant battle for ratings and our responsibilities as public figures.

The rewards that came with it.

Now, with the age of social media and our twenty-four-year marriage the network loves to tout as another of my successes, we're in the spotlight more than I'd expected. Ryan never complains, but all the scrutiny has to get old.

It does for me.

"Thank you," I tell Kaitlyn. "Can you grab me lunch? I need to clear emails."

"Sure. Grilled chicken salad?"

"Perfect."

I've learned to eat a light lunch. Nothing too heavy that will launch my digestive tract into a symphony of noises that a mic will pick up.

I turn into my office, close the door, and head to the attached bathroom. Not ready to face the mirror, I set the ice pack on the sink and slip out of my skirt and blouse. Somehow, they both remained blood free, but will need to be pressed before we resume taping. I hang both garments on the door hook and change into yoga pants and a long-sleeved T-shirt I wore into the office.

Then I do the inevitable. I push my shoulders back, lift my chin, and gather the nerve to step in front of the mirror.

Eh. Could be worse. A splotch of red on my cheek, but thankfully no broken skin. In a day or two, it'll be an ugly bruise.

For today, Steph, my makeup artist, will do her magic and make me, as she likes to say, fabulous.

Right now, I'm anything but fabulous. Inside and out.

I'm a fraud.

On my vanity table beside the sink, I glance at the framed photo of me and Marcia Marshall that I keep as a reminder to be grateful for all things Dr. Becca.

Marcia, the network's executive VP, a total big shot, gave me this show. Literally handed it to me. Marriage in crisis, Marcia and her husband came to me, a licensed clinical psychologist specializing in marriage counseling.

Marcia claims I saved her marriage. I deny it. Recognizing that they still loved each other, they did the work. I simply supplied the materials.

Now, all these years later, after Marcia paved the way for a brief stint as a weekly contributor on a morning show, I'm the star of the Dr. Becca show.

Sounds glamorous. Sounds like a dream come true.

It was.

Looking at my abused face, I'm not sure anymore.

CHAPTER 2

"**B**usted nose," Jenny tells me an hour later from my office doorway.

I sit back in my desk chair, shaking my head. I knew it. Could tell from the odd angle of said nose, but seeing and confirming are different.

Despite the money shot of a bandaged nose, there's no way we can finish. I won't do it.

"Okay," I say. "We'll postpone. Give the audience tickets for another taping."

"Ha!" Jenny enters the office, hands in the air. "Hold on there, sister. Kade says he wants to do it. Total sweeper. Marketing is going *nutso*."

"They know?"

She looks at me as if I've lost my mind. Thanks to slipping ratings and unhappy network executives, we've had a lot of that lately, Jenny and me.

"Of course they know," Jenny says. "I told them. We're *rock stars* right now. I thought you'd be happy."

I won't bother asking if she knows me at all.

The answer is obvious.

"Happy that a man's brother just assaulted him on my show?" I cock my head. "And, yes, I'm aware it's a *sweeper*. I'm allowed to hate it."

A pained noise comes from Jenny's throat. "Becca, I don't understand. The network has been hounding us for months about ratings." She waves her arms in her classic, frenzied way. "This is the *holy grail* of money shots."

"I know that."

"I get that you don't want trash TV."

"Do you?"

For a brief second, she pauses. Checking herself before firing off an inappropriate comment. I respect that she's grown enough over the years to recognize her go-to sarcasm isn't always welcome.

"Yes," she finally says, her voice quiet but firm. "Believe me, I understand what you want. But I'm the one walking the tightrope between you and marketing. I'm trying to make everyone happy."

I don't question this. Jenny is loyal. One of the hardest working producers in the business. She's also a pleaser who hasn't yet accepted that it's impossible to satisfy everyone.

In the war between me and the network, she'll now have to pick a side. Not something I'll ask, but it's inevitable and there will be no winners.

I lean in, resting my forearms on the desk. "Are we truly thinking we can finish this?"

Obviously hopeful, she gives me a quick jerk of her head. "Absolutely. We still have the audience. We'll push the afternoon taping back. Easy."

Easy? Definitely not a word I'd use to describe this situation. Now, I'm stuck. If we air the show, I'll be eaten alive, the meat ripped from my bones by social media trolls accusing me of hypocrisy.

Fed up with the whole situation, I grunt. "Fine. But if I can't make something meaningful happen, I'll burn the building down to keep this show off the air." I gesture to my face. "I need Steph to cover this mess."

"Um." She scrunches up her face. "Don't kill me."

Oh, I know where this is going. "Nope. No. No. *No.*"

"Come on, Bec. We should leave it. Let the audience see."

Now I shoot daggers at her. Before she can speak, I hold a hand up. "Don't bother. I'm well aware that *marketing* will love it. I don't care. It's humiliating. If Steph can't cover it without me looking plastic, I'll have to live with it. But I'm not going out there looking *battered.*"

Jenny takes this in. Seems to absorb it. "We'll see what she can do. And, not to dump on you, but when I called marketing, Devin said he wants to see us after the second taping. Don will probably be there."

Don. One of the many VPs at the network and my boss. Marcia, who gave me this show, is his boss.

"Why do they want a meeting?"

"Probably to congratulate us."

Again, I shake my head, willing myself to stay put and deal with this nonsense when, really? I'm fed up. This career has given me everything. Fame, wealth, credibility. I should be ecstatic. Living my best life.

Instead, I feel . . . ashamed.

With the whole broken-nose fiasco, I've let the network's ratings machine dictate how I run my show. I've betrayed my audience and dishonored them with a format I swore I'd never even dip a toe into.

Total sellout.

Tonight, I'll sit in front of network executives toasting to our success. To the utter collapse of my moral compass.

Won't that be fun?

After being applauded—literally—by Don and the so-called

marketing geniuses, I head home, ready to consume massive amounts of sugar in whatever form it may take.

Hopefully, Ry restocked the Reese's peanut butter cups. The big ones.

I'm a stress eater. I don't keep a lot of junk food in the house for that very reason. Stress and cake are my dynamic duo.

The Reeses? Those are the exception. I always have those on hand.

My driver, Bernie, pulls in front of my building on East Eightieth Street. The coveted East End. We paid mightily for the privilege of living here. All part of the image, I suppose.

The porte cochere in the back allows residents a more discreet arrival, but I rarely need that. There's a musician here, however, who prides himself on his use of it.

The doorman, Al, hustles to open my door.

"Good evening, Dr. Matthews," he says in his normal cheery tone. If he notices the redness on my cheek, it's an Emmy-worthy performance. That, or Steph really did her magic. "You're late tonight."

Al isn't just a doorman. He's a watchtower. Ryan likes to joke that Al has his own missile guidance system that wipes out suspicious people and paparazzi.

"Hi, Al." Before he closes the door, I turn back, bend to peer into the car. "See you in the morning, Bernie. Thank you."

"Yes, ma'am," he says. "Have a good night."

I hate when he calls me ma'am. Particularly since he's twelve years older than me. He's a sixty-year-old retired NYC cop who, three months after his last day on the job, got bored. Since he knew the city like the back of his hand, he signed on with an executive limo service.

Six years ago, my then-driver called out sick and Bernie shuttled me to the airport. We chatted. I liked him and took his card. A few months later, my driver moved to the west coast and Bernie has been my full-time driver since.

He says he enjoys it. The consistent schedule. Not dealing with, as he claims, assholes.

Al closes the SUV's door and escorts me to the building entrance. Ryan and I have a three-story condo starting on the twelfth floor that comes with every amenity imaginable. We've spent a small fortune decorating it, and yet, something is still missing. I try not to think too hard about it.

I ride the elevator to twelve and step into the hallway separating our unit and the one across from us. We looked at that one but preferred the lighter neutrals of ours.

Once inside, a large foyer with a grand staircase and hand-welded iron chandelier Ryan found in Greenwich Village welcomes me home. I drop my keys in the dish on the entry table. Ryan's voice streams from his man cave at the end of the corridor. The room is complete with a humongous, wall-mounted television, a bar, card table and slot machines, that Ryan has grown to love. He considers it his little paradise.

Considering the time he spends alone while I'm working, I love that he loves it.

My shoes squeak against the marble, alerting him of my arrival. He sits on the sofa, one foot propped on the coffee table, and he wears his normal evening attire of athletic shorts and a T-shirt. Overhead lights illuminate his white earbuds.

At forty-seven, he hits the gym regularly, and his muscled arms and shoulders prove it. The bright white of his shirt emphasizes dark hair that's a week overdue for a haircut and falls haphazardly over his forehead. He's blessed with chiseled features and thick hair that curls adorably in the humidity.

Have I mentioned my husband is gorgeous? I often tease him that I'm forced to chase women off with a stick.

He meets my gaze and holds his phone up as if I don't see him talking.

I take the hint that he'll be a minute. Or fifty.

I leave him and ascend the staircase leading to the second

floor. By now, he's probably eaten. Takeout, he'd told Kaitlyn when she'd called to tell him our dinner reservations needed to be canceled.

If my husband was upset, I wouldn't know. Somehow, it doesn't seem right to me that my career dictates our social schedule. Ryan? Total gamer. He understood when I climbed on the daytime TV treadmill that he had climbed on with me.

Twenty-four years we've been married. Operating together, building a life, sacrificing our privacy, but enjoying the rewards. This residence alone is a testament to it.

Me? I'd rather be in our beach house, sixty-five miles south in Deal, New Jersey.

I hit the last step and stare into my chef's kitchen with the ridiculously expensive light gray cabinets and stove that I can barely operate.

Around here, Ryan does the cooking. He claims it's a creative outlet that lets him experiment with flavors and textures. A few years back, he'd pondered culinary school, then realized his hobby would equate to a full-time job, which he already has.

Ryan is the CEO of a nonprofit that helps families dealing with tragedy. Whether it's sudden death, a fire, storm damage, whatever, Living Hope is at the ready. The job came about eight years ago, after we'd attended a holiday gala. We'd met the chairperson of the board who'd mentioned they were in the market for a new CEO. Ryan, then unfulfilled in his role of running a tech start-up, threw his hat in the ring and found his calling.

He gives me a lot of credit for his success. My connections mean introductions to insanely rich celebs more than willing to open their wallets.

Together, my husband and I are a force.

On the counter near the stove are the promised takeout containers from the Italian restaurant down the street. If it's lasagna, my husband's love for me will be obvious.

I pop the container open and—yep. My Ry. Total gamer.

He knows me. Understands the struggle I'm currently dealing with.

Retrieving a plate from the cabinet, I slide the square of lasagna from the container, the hefty weight of it already making my mouth water as I pop it into the microwave.

A minute later, the microwave dings just as I'm contemplating a weekend trip to the beach house. In a few weeks, Memorial Day will bring a surge of tourists to the shore. When I was a kid, my parents owned the house and my shore friends had a nickname—Bennys—for people who drove down from north Jersey and New York and crowded the beaches. My friends who lived full time at the shore excused me from that distinction since we owned a vacation home there.

Even as a part-time resident, I resent the crowds. Yes, I'm definitely a hypocrite that way. I like quiet beaches and not having to dodge cars parked bumper-to-bumper on my street.

For that reason, early May and late September are my favorite times at the shore.

Ryan prefers city chaos over the roar of the pounding Atlantic. If I can't talk him into the weekend at the shore, I'll have to go alone. I need it.

I take my plate and settle in at the island, the aroma of fresh garlic and Romano cheese sending my system into a fog of delirium.

"Hey, you."

Fork in midair, I turn to my husband, who has just cleared the top step. "Hi."

He kisses my head and wanders to the refrigerator as I shove the first bite of lasagna into my mouth. The rich sauce and Italian spices interact with my serotonin receptors like a hit of acid.

Not that I'd know what a hit of acid feels like, but I've heard enough to wager a guess.

I sit back, close my eyes and chew slowly. "So good," I say.

Ryan snorts. I open my eyes. He's standing across from me, his hands braced against the counter, the long sinewy muscles of his forearms on display. An open bottle of Modelo sits in front of him.

"You know," he says, "another guy might be jealous of the way you react to Tony's lasagna."

I know he's joking, but the comment hits me a certain way. A certain way that's probably more a product of my pissy mood and rotten day than anything else.

Ryan has never been the jealous type. I know this. He might be the most emotionally secure individual I know.

Early in our relationship, I was the jealous one. Who could blame me? Everywhere we went, women flocked. Steel to a magnet.

Pushing the thought away, I conjure a smile. "Maybe you can get Tony's recipe. You're pretty good in the kitchen."

He winks and blows me a kiss that ten years ago would've made my clothes fall off.

We're good. Both of us knowing what buttons—good and bad—to push on each other. It comes with history. Years of intimacy, talking and observing.

He takes a slug of his beer, then points the tip at my face. "What's that about?"

His voice holds no heat. Just concern over his wife's marred features. Ry is maddeningly levelheaded. Sometimes, I love it.

Sometimes, I want fire.

Now? I love it. I simply don't have the energy for fire.

We have a routine, Ryan and I. I come home and we sit in the kitchen. Rather, I sit—in this exact spot—while Ryan tests some new recipe he found somewhere. Or sometimes I eat takeout and he watches.

Either way, we hash out the day.

"Oh," I say, wagging my fork toward my damaged cheek. "*That.* A brawl broke out on set today."

Not much shocked Ryan. He's heard enough of my stories that he's built up a resistance. Now, his mouth flops open, his jaw hanging there as if its weight is too much. "Someone *hit* you?"

There's that fire I sometimes want.

I shovel more lasagna and immediately swallow. "Relax. It was an accident. Love triangle gone wild. He was aiming for the other guy. I got in the way."

"*That* was your first mistake. Never get in the middle of a dogfight, Becca. Let your crew handle it."

Seriously? That's what he has to say after I got popped in the face? It shouldn't have even happened.

Not on *my* show.

He takes another slug of his beer. "Are you okay? Did the doc look at you?"

"I'm fine. And yes, a doctor looked at it. It'll probably bruise. Luckily, I only have to get through tomorrow's tapings and I'll have the long weekend for it to heal."

"What happened?"

I set my fork down. At the rate I'm going, I'll polish off the entire meal in record time and be sick all night. Add the bloat to it and I'll look a mess tomorrow for another two tapings.

"Aside from the husband breaking his brother's nose?"

Ryan's mouth flops open again. "His *brother*? No way."

"Yes, way. On my show! In front of a live audience. There was blood. I mean, come on? Dr. Becca is turning into a fight club and marketing loves it."

"Of course they do. It'll be a sweeper."

Even Ryan knows the lingo. "Yeah. And I'm stuck. As soon as the suits heard about the broken nose, they set up a meeting. Then they stood and applauded when I entered the room. Not because I'd convinced them all to apologize to each other and got them acting like adults. No. Never that. They're happy about the violence I allowed to take over my set."

My stomach lurches—probably the result of eating too fast. Or maybe stress. Who knows? I press my palm against my aching middle. "I'm dying, Ry. Seriously. I can't do this. I've worked too hard."

"But they're happy, right? You gave them what they wanted. Now they'll leave you alone and you can go back to doing what you do."

What was he talking about? If I get a ratings spike from this fiasco, they'll never leave me alone.

After the elation I witnessed in that meeting today, I'm screwed.

Despite my aching belly, I pick up my fork again, ready to dive in.

I can't do it.

As much as I want to, I can't shovel another bite. I drop my fork, let it clatter against the marble countertop. "You don't believe that any more than I do. When they see the ratings boost, they'll want more. And more."

"So, tell them no."

At this, I have to laugh. My husband needs to look around. Take a gander at the Viking range he loves so much. The double wall ovens.

The man cave.

He makes decent money, but a nonprofit CEO can't afford a twelve-million-dollar condo on the Upper East Side. Never mind the cost of decorating it.

"Kinda hard to say no when my ratings are slipping, and I have two hundred people to worry about. Not to mention," I gesture to the room, "all this."

His head snaps back. "What's that mean?"

He knows. We both do.

We don't talk about it. We're partners in this deal. Without

Ryan and our seemingly perfect marriage, I wouldn't be the nation's top-rated talk show host. The super-marriage-fixer.

"I've spent years promising my audience I wouldn't pollute their world. I've built my reputation on it. And now, I'm supposed to abandon that? All to make my advertisers happy?"

At this moment, I don't give a fig about marketing or advertisers or ratings. All I care about is being stuck. I can't quit and I can't stomach—literally—what happened on set today.

Where does that leave me?

Powerless, that's where.

And I can't accept that.

Ryan lets out a long sigh. "What do you wanna do?"

Jump off the treadmill.

The words are right there. Ready to slip from my mouth. I've sacrificed so much of myself over the years. My personal goals, dreams of babies and play dates and snack times, all traded for money and fame.

I shove my plate away for good and sit back on my stool. "Why didn't we have kids?"

Clearly puzzled by the change of subject, Ryan's eyebrows draw together. "What?"

"You heard me. Why?"

"Well, I'm not . . ." He shakes his head. "I don't know. Your career, I guess."

"You're fifty percent of this equation. At any point you could have said, 'hey, Becca, how about busting out those babies we always talked about?' You never did. Why?"

He stops. Just stands there staring at me, the silence of the room humming around us. There's something there, hidden behind his beautiful blue eyes. Something he's thinking, but I can't quite read.

"I suppose," he says, "after a time, I liked our life. Just us. Freedom to do what we wanted when we wanted. You said nothing." He shrugs. "I figured you felt the same."

"I didn't."

"It's my fault now?"

Lord, I'm in a mood. How can I blame him? I'm a grown woman. I should have said something. "No. It's both of our faults. We let my career dictate how we lived. *We* should run our lives, Ry, not my career."

How did I let this happen? All of it. The trash TV, the lack of babies. It's like I've been on autopilot.

I stand, grab my plate, and walk around the island. This conversation will get us nowhere. Particularly in my mood. I'm famous for saving marriages. I should know not to discuss sensitive topics when I'm churned up.

"I shouldn't have brought it up. Not now. I'm tired. I need a hot shower to scrub off the filth."

Ryan remains in his spot as I step around him and toss the rest of the lasagna into the garbage, rinse the plate and shove it into the dishwasher.

When I close the dishwasher, he gently clasps my arm. "Is that what you want? Kids? Will a baby fix your problems?"

My problems? "Seems to me my career affects your life too."

"It does. But if giving it up will make you happy, do it. Go back to private practice. I don't give a shit. We have enough money to last us a lifetime."

I peer down at the floor. Some fancy tile I can't even remember the name of. The decorator suggested it and I couldn't have cared less. I draw air into my lungs and let it out. Amazing how one deep breath can settle the mind.

I meet Ryan's gaze again, allow myself to get lost in those deep blue depths. "I'm . . . having a day. Can we hit pause? Let me wind down and get some rest before we have this conversation?"

"Of course."

"Thank you. Would you be up for a trip down the shore this weekend? Maybe leave Thursday morning?"

The joy of taping two shows a day over three days means no tapings Thursday and Friday and the ability to work remotely when necessary.

"We have that benefit this weekend," Ry says. "The flood relief one."

Shoot. His company was hosting a fundraiser for victims of flooding because of a nor'easter that slammed the coast last month.

"You're right," I say. "I'm sorry. I forgot. The benefit is more important."

He squeezes my arm again. "Hang on. *I* have to be here this week, but you don't. Go to the shore. I'll stay here."

My husband. So good. But I've dragged him to every function known to man in the last fourteen years. He's done it with enthusiasm and a definite lack of complaints.

I owe him this. I reach up, cup my hands around his cheeks. All that good Ryan warmth slips right into me. "I want to be there for you. How about I leave Thursday morning and come back for the benefit on Saturday?"

He whips off a smile. "I'd love that. Perfect compromise."

"Good. It's settled. Now, I'm taking a shower and putting today behind me."

CHAPTER 3

The soft swell of classical music draws me from nothing short of combative sleep. The war between mental and physical fatigue has always been a challenge. My brain won't shut down, but my body begs for rest.

I've tried herbal remedies, prescription drugs, vitamins, all of which leave me with nightmares or a hangover.

Thus, the war rages.

I open my eyes, steal a look at my phone, sitting on the dock on my bedside table: 6:01. Tapping the screen, I silence Fauré. "Après un rêve" (Op. 7, No. 1, to be exact). I glance over my shoulder at Ryan's broad back and the familiar smattering of freckles on his shoulders. As usual, his soft, steady breathing relaxes me. Helps me ease into the morning.

I gently fold the quilt back and work my way out of bed. As someone who doesn't sleep well, I'm not only envious, I'm careful not to wake others who do.

Another reason I insist on two tapings a day. By Wednesday, my body and mind are . . . worn. Still functioning, but not nearly as sharp as I prefer.

I need to get through today and then I'm off to the shore. After yesterday's fiasco, how bad could it get?

I proceed to the en suite bathroom where my bare feet hit the tile and cold shock shoots straight into my calves. Our interior designer, although excellent, was all about the marble. My house has more marble than the Met.

Personally, I hate it. I prefer wood that doesn't feel like a barefoot trek through the Antarctic.

After washing up, brushing teeth and scooping my hair into a ponytail, I do my normal morning evaluation. Botox still holding. Roots coming in. Some of them gray. I'll need to restore the honey blond I've been for the last ten years. When I was younger, my hair was a cross between sandy blond and light brown. I never minded it.

At least until I got to television and was told it had no "life" on camera. Thus, color after color experiments began until we landed on this apparently perfect shade of honey blond.

Whatever. All I know is the older I get, the more frequent the touch-ups.

I cross to the closet and change into my favorite navy running shorts and paisley sports bra.

Five miles on the treadmill starts my morning. Every day. Unless we're at the shore, then I run on the beach. Just not at six a.m.

I tiptoe out of the bedroom, closing the door behind me. My goal of not waking Ryan is, I'll admit, as much for my benefit as his.

I'm rarely alone.

There's always someone, somewhere, needing, expecting, demanding my attention. My morning run is my quiet time when I watch videos or the news or a home show.

Since yesterday turned into a dead loss, I'll catch up on emails while on the treadmill. Not exactly the break I enjoy, but if I can clear my inbox, it'll be less I have to do tonight.

I walk through the third-floor hallway and spot a scuff on the otherwise pristine baseboard. Vacuum cleaner, no doubt. I'll take care of it later. I keep a can of white trim paint on hand for just these occasions.

When we moved in here five years ago, we converted one of the four bedrooms to my office. The door is ajar and I stride in, grabbing my iPad off the solid wood, live edge writing desk I treated myself to. I spotted it in a store window. Every item in the place was handmade by the extremely talented owner. There's something about the imperfections, the slight scarring on the weathered top combined with the fancy scrollwork on the legs that called to me.

Ryan and the decorator told me the rustic style more suited the beach house than the modern vibe we had going here.

My office.

My desk.

Besides, perfection is overrated.

Ignoring the folders sitting on the otherwise paper-free desk, I unplug the iPad from the charger and hop on the treadmill.

Yes, it's in my office.

Ironic, since lately all I can think about is the treadmill of my career.

I shake off the annoying thought. Mentally, I need to get with it. Take my own damned advice and greet the day as a new chance to correct whatever needs correcting. To live in the moment.

Blah, blah, blah.

I let out an exaggerated gag as I set the iPad in the holder, tap the treadmill's auto program button, and choose a workout. I start with walking, then a light jog to warm up before the belt pushes me faster.

The walk gives me a few minutes to scan my emails. Four hundred from yesterday. It's difficult to type while running, so I typically clear the easy ones first. Those are usually FYI only and require little more than a got-it response.

The belt speeds up. My legs pump and I focus on quieting my upper body to save energy.

Hanging on the wall in front of me is a framed photo I took of the Atlantic from the deck of our shore house. My daily reminder that life is good.

My heart rate kicks up. I draw a breath through my nose, exhaling slowly. Part of a good run requires controlled breathing. I like the challenge of it.

Of succeeding where most fail.

Following the advice I'd give any of my show guests, I take a second to enjoy that. To remain present and appreciative of my strong, healthy body.

Then I get back to the dreaded emails. Next up: credit card bill forwarded by Ry. Since he pays our bills, a task I'm more than happy to forgo, he sends me the credit card statement every month for review.

My right knee aches. *Too hard.* My feet are pounding the ramp. It happens when fatigue sets in and I lose my form. I refocus and lighten my steps before clicking the attachment. A pdf of the bill pops up and I swipe at the screen, zooming down to the list of charges.

Since everything is on one bill, separated by card number, I rarely bother checking the total or Ryan's charges. I don't need the added pressure.

All I know is we have enough to cover whatever it'll be. Another thing I'm grateful for.

Still, I wouldn't mind Ry curbing his spending. I don't mind him treating himself, but there's always some new phone or gadget or kitchen item he needs. Last month, it was a ten-thousand-dollar espresso machine.

The belt speeds up, and I push myself, keeping my pace

steady and feet light. My ponytail thumps against my back, the rhythm soothing me.

I go back to the bill. For whatever reason, there's only one page. Odd, since it's normally at least three.

My eyes lock on a charge for La Perla. *La Perla?* The high-end lingerie shop?

In the years Ry's been sending me these bills, I've found maybe two mistakes. Maybe.

Still running, I move down the statement and see a restaurant charge from Connecticut and a hotel charge.

Definitely not mine.

Did Ry even look at this? Obviously, the credit card company sent someone else's bill. I scroll to the top. Check the name. Yep. Wrong person.

No idea who Laurel Shelton is.

Has to be a mistake.

Dismissing it, I go back to my emails and deal with whatever I can in my remaining time.

When I'm done, I stand on the belt, sweat dripping everywhere. I dry myself with a towel from the stack I keep on a shelf next to the treadmill, then give the machine a quick cleaning with a disinfectant wipe.

Five miles.

Done.

And I didn't trip while clearing emails.

Win.

Win.

I grab water from my mini fridge and head back to the bedroom. Ry should be up and out of the shower by now, leaving it available for me as we get ready for our workday.

"Good morning," I say, leaning against the bathroom doorjamb.

A towel around his waist, he's slightly bent over the sink, dragging a razor over his cream slathered face. I love this about him. That he doesn't bother with electric razors and takes the time to do it the old-fashioned way.

It's a closer shave, he's always said.

I take a second to enjoy the view of his bare chest and arms. Truly, he could be a cover model. Albeit a middle-aged one. He's the glorious combination of rugged elegance that certain men perfect as they grow older.

Water droplets fall from his thick hair, dotting his shoulders and the wisps of chest hair across his pectorals.

"Morning," he says between strokes. "Good run?"

"I suppose."

He smiles. "I know you hate that thing."

I do indeed. "I saw your email. The credit card."

After dipping the razor under the faucet, he tilts his head. I instinctively mimic the head tilt as he takes another long, precise stroke down his cheek and navigates his jawline.

"Yeah," he says. "Got it yesterday. Assuming it's ready to go?"

He begins a new stroke on his left cheek.

"It's not mine. They must have sent you the wrong bill. Surprised you didn't catch that. The name on it is Laurel Shelton."

For a brief second, an *infinitesimal* second that to anyone else would be meaningless, he pauses, then finishes clearing the row of cream. He sets his razor down and faces me, his face still half covered.

"Huh," he says. "I didn't open the attachment. Sorry. I was rushing. Trying to get done. I'll call them. Tell them they sent the wrong bill."

He peers at me for a second, his gaze direct. His features remain relaxed, his shoulders loose. Not an iota of tension.

My husband, I believe, is hiding something.

It's all there.

Including the earlier pause.

It's what's *not* there that bugs me.

With Ryan's charm and looks comes an innate ability to operate on the fly. To storm ahead, pulverizing any obstacles in his way.

He's good. Really good.

I'm better.

I've spent years studying body language. My husband's is no exception.

My mind ticks back twenty-six years to when we were still in college and dating. Exploring our new love and learning each other's quirks. Our *tells*.

My roommates drooled over my perfect, perfect, perfect boyfriend. My stunningly handsome, smart, and kind lover who bought me gifts for no reason.

Perfection indeed.

Except for that one night. The first dent in his armor.

I SWING through the exit of the university's television studio and tilt my chin to a starlit sky. Cool, spring air nips at my cheeks, but I breathe it in, savoring the excitement that comes with the final edit on a piece for my media class. I *love* this class. Not so much the news reporting, but doing interviews. Learning about people. Analyzing them.

The assignment meant interviewing someone on camera. Piece. Of. Cake. I enjoy talking to people. A good thing, too, since I recently changed my major to psychology.

Riding the high of finishing, I walk the path to my dorm. I never enjoy walking alone late at night, but the path is well lit, and the studio is only a short distance from the dorm. Still, it's nearly midnight, so I pick up my pace, staying in the brightest parts of the path.

A woman's laugh sounds behind me. I glance over my shoulder. A couple in the shadows moves closer to me. I don't mind;

safety in numbers and all that. I slow down, letting them catch up a bit.

Then I hear it. The man's voice. My heart squeezes. First with that burst of excitement that happens every time he enters my orbit and then . . . wait . . .

A mere four hours earlier, he told me he'd be studying. Prepping for his International Business final.

And here he is, walking with a woman.

Could Ryan be . . .?

No.

I'm not going there. Not allowing my thoughts to overwhelm me and send me down a rabbit hole that will paralyze me.

Their voices come closer. I sneak another peek over my shoulder. Thirty yards behind me, the streetlamp illuminates the face of the dark-haired love of my life. Mr. Perfection.

I turn and halt, staring straight at him as they close the distance. He's laughing at something the girl said. She's blonde and tall, nearly the same height as Ry. Just like me, is all I can think. She's wearing an unbuttoned spring coat that flaps open as she walks, revealing jean-clad legs that go on for miles and thigh-high stiletto-heeled boots.

Aside from her height, she's everything I'm not. Curvy, yet trim, with large breasts under a tight sweater. Me? I'm more lean, with a 34A cup size. Not exactly voluptuous.

This girl? My boyfriend is staring down at her, laughing at something she's said while my stomach squeezes to the size of a pebble.

They're almost on me now, the love of my life clearly so enthralled he doesn't notice me.

"Ryan?"

At the sound of my voice, his head snaps up.

For a split second, under the glow of the streetlamp, his face freezes, his surprise evident. His mouth instantly spreads to a wide smile as he abandons the woman beside him and hustles toward me.

"Becca," he says, "what the hell are you doing out here at this hour?"

Ah. The art of the spin.

I glance over his shoulder at the woman, who is standing stock-still, her eyes boring into the back of Ryan's head.

Good.

"I was at the studio," I say. "Taping that segment. I told you earlier."

"Yeah, but this late?"

"We ran long. There were others before me."

"I don't like you walking by yourself."

I glance over his shoulder again. At the blonde.

"Who's she?" I whisper.

"Ah." He lightly clasps my forearm and angles sideways toward the woman. "This is Carrie. She's my study partner. We were at the library."

His study partner? Seriously?

I burst out laughing. But inside? Panic is a jackhammer fracturing my ribcage.

He's lying.

I'm not sure why or how I'm so positive, but I am. I *feel* it.

"The library," I tell him, "closed an hour ago."

"Well, yeah. We went for coffee. Carrie, tell her."

"We went for coffee," she says, her tone more than a little pissy. "Look, Ryan, I've gotta go. We'll talk later."

She pushes by me on her extremely high heels and clickety-clacks her way across the cement sidewalk. Good riddance.

"Wait," he yells. "Let us walk you."

Us? Really?

She gives him a backward wave. "I'm good. Talk later."

He turns his attention back to me, his smile firmly in place.

"The *library*," I say, my mind conjuring visions of what might have happened if I hadn't caught him.

Ryan taking her to bed. Ryan sliding inside of her, as he'd done with me just hours ago.

His tongue on her.

A generous streetlamp cuts the darkness, allowing me to see his narrowed eyes. "You don't believe me? Are you kidding?"

More gaslighting. Fantastic.

I shrug. "You failed to mention the tall blonde study partner."

"Maybe because I knew you'd be suspicious."

"No. Sir. You don't get to do that. When have I *ever* acted suspicious?"

"How about now?"

I stab both hands in the direction the blonde just went. "And with good reason. Did you lie to me?"

"I did not."

"Are you seeing her?"

"I am not."

"Can I trust you?"

"You can."

Boom. That fast, his speedy answers dice right through my anger and jealousy. I take solace in that. Anyone who can answer that quickly has to be telling the truth.

Right?

He lifts his hand, drags it over his face. "Becca, why would I risk what we have? You're amazing. And kind. You're brilliant and funny. The total package. I'd be an idiot to cheat on you. And I'm not an idiot."

Maybe it *was* just studying and coffee.

Maybe I have jumped to the wrong conclusion.

My God. What is wrong with me?

I've got this perfect guy my friends love. Every one of them. When does that ever happen?

If Ryan is a liar, surely one of us would have pegged it.

And there's no way I can tell them about this episode. It looks bad. If I tell my friends, it might change their opinions of him. It'll tarnish the image.

Let them see something I don't want the world to see.

My mom's constant warning loops in my head. *Don't share your business, Becca. It never amounts to anything good.*

He's telling the truth. He has to be. Doesn't he?

BACK THEN, I convinced myself he hadn't lied. Now, I continue to stare at my husband while contemplating that singular incident all those years ago.

"Who is she?" I ask.

His mouth opens, and I put up my hand. "Before you say anything, think about what I do for a living. I know you, Ry. I know when you're doing a snow job. Laurel Shelton. Who is she?"

My God, I want this to be a mistake. I want Laurel Shelton to be some unknown woman in some unknown town that has nothing to do with us.

"She works for me," he tells me.

My body sags, my legs nearly coming out from under me. I catch myself, bracing against the doorframe.

"Whoa!"

He reaches for me and I flinch.

My reaction backs him up a step. "Don't get crazy," he says. "I get copies of all employee credit card bills. We use the same company for our personal cards. I was busy yesterday. Distracted and moving too fast. I saw the email from our credit card company and sent you her bill instead of ours. No big deal."

No big deal.

I want to believe him. I do. Knowing how he reviews financial matters, I could see him dealing with all credit card statements at once and then moving on.

But . . .

"There's a La Perla charge," I say. "She shops at La Perla with her company card?"

"If that's true, she shouldn't be. She probably used the wrong card. She'll have to reimburse us."

He delivers this line with such ease that I have to wonder if I'm paranoid. Making too much of it.

He swivels, picks up his razor and continues shaving, alerting me he's finished with this topic.

The side eye he gives me can't be missed. He might be done, but I'm not.

"Getting late," he tells me. "Your driver will be here in thirty."

His tone is casual. As if I haven't just implied he's betrayed our twenty-four-year marriage.

Lucky me, all I need to do is hop in the shower, tie my hair back and throw on joggers and a pullover. I have hair and clothing stylists and a makeup artist at the studio who will make me camera ready.

Simplifies my life tremendously when trying to get out of the house.

Particularly when I fear my husband is having an affair.

CHAPTER 4

On lunch between tapings, I sit at my desk, staring at my phone. Specifically, the credit card statement Ryan emailed me.

Laurel Shelton.

I mutter her name over and over, willing the letters to spit out more information.

Underneath her name is an address. Tenafly, New Jersey. Ritzy town. One of the most expensive in Jersey. I looked at it before buying our place. In the end, we decided Manhattan would be easier.

Dropping my phone, I drag my laptop from the corner of the desk and fire it up. My grilled chicken sits next to me. Can I tell you how sick of grilled chicken I am? I ignore it, my mind bent on Laurel Shelton.

Associate producers have taught me a thing or two about spying, so I go incognito on my browser and type in Laurel Shelton's name. A second later, there are links to Facebook and LinkedIn profiles and a collection of images. All different.

Who knew there were so many Laurel Sheltons?

I try again, tapping in her name and Tenafly, NJ.

A fresh batch of results pops up. Now we're talking.

My eye immediately goes to the photo of the stunning—I mean, ridiculous—blonde with bright green eyes. Her hair is shoulder length, like mine, but poker straight and parted down the middle. Few women can pull off that center part, but she does it flawlessly.

I already hate her.

Plus, she might be banging my husband.

I concentrate on her face, the curve of her cheek, the way her upper lip is a tad larger than the lower.

Is it weird that she sort of looks like me? Well, the younger, more stunning version of me. Kinda like the girl from our college days.

My stomach spins and I eye the chicken before nudging the plate away. Back to the computer. I click on LinkedIn. Over ten Laurel Shelton profiles. Scrolling, I find the ridiculously stunning blonde and click.

Her smiling face greets me. She appears to be all of thirty years old and her amiable smile and lack of wrinkles adds to my irritation. I've been Botoxing for ten years and still have crow's feet.

Instinctively, I lift my hand to the spot between my eyebrows and run my fingers over my frozen skin.

Back to Laurel Shelton, marketing Rep for Cara, an athletic apparel company. So much for her working for Ryan. Then again, I might not have the right person if this Laurel works for Cara. They were one of my sponsors a few years back, but bailed because our demographics skewed too old.

As much as it stung, I agreed. Cara's target was an up-and-coming thirty-something, yoga-obsessed female who made enough to spend $150.00 on a sexy sports bra and leggings.

In short, Laurel Shelton was their target. Not my middle-aged suburbanites.

A knock sounds and I glance over the top of my computer.

Jenny stands outside the glass wall. She's wearing her typical baggy jeans paired with a wrinkled white button-down. Her dark hair is stacked on top of her head, probably secured by a pencil. A few wisps bust loose and combined with the wrinkled shirt, it gives her the usual frenzied-mom look. I wave her in.

She hustles in, drops a stack of folders on my desk. "Next week's tapings. It's a good lineup."

What that means, lately, is suspect. Who knows what kind of nonsense the folders contain?

"Thank you. Are we set for this afternoon? Everyone is here?"

"All good. They're in the green room. We're working with the wife on wardrobe. She showed up in stripes. God help me."

Wardrobe mishaps were common when dealing with untrained guests. What looked good on the street could be a disaster on camera. Our mini makeover was one perk of appearing on the show. Hair, makeup, clothes, the works. But occasionally, guests simply wanted to be in their own clothing. The adult form of a security blanket.

"I'll stop in and say hello."

"They seem like a pleasant couple."

Meaning, no one will punch me. I hope. So far, today's shows are akin to my regular format. A calm, middle-class family unlikely to break into a brawl on my set.

"Good."

Jenny eyes me, her gaze zooming to my cheek. "How's the cheek?"

"It's fine. A little sore."

"Can hardly see it. Steph is a magician."

"She sure is."

"I spoke to Devin," Jenny says.

Devin. My marketing archenemy.

Jenny doesn't know it, but she has a tell. When she says those four words and stops, it's her unconscious warning that I should brace myself.

Which I do. I sit back, wait for the bomb—whatever it might be—that'll blow up my day. "And?"

"We're moving yesterday's scorched-earth show up. They want it to air on Monday."

Monday.

"That fast?"

Our compassionate marketing team can't even give me a week to absorb it. To ready myself for the blast of criticism that will come from my faithful viewers, the ones who've kept us at number one for years now.

I did my best to salvage that situation, but social media will still eat me alive.

And I'll deserve it.

"Ratings, baby," she says. "I'm sorry."

Really, she's not. At this moment, Jenny is the queen of sorry not sorry.

I shake my head. "Fine. What else?"

"That's it. You're taking it well."

"Actually, I'm not. I'll deal with it."

"Anything I can do?"

"Other than convince marketing not to air that show?"

Recognizing my sarcasm, Jenny gives a perfunctory nod and spins on her sneakered foot, leaving my office and closing the door.

Huffy Jenny.

She wants me to open up. To tell her what will make me feel better about the current state of our programming. Well, I just did. She doesn't realize it, but that's about as touchy-feely as I get. I don't share my business. She's been with me long enough to know that.

What does she want? For me to break down in tears? To be *vulnerable?*

Not happening.

I bring my attention back to one Laurel Shelton. I need more on her. Enough to figure out if she's Ryan's mistress.

Our life isn't easy. I'm a celebrity. With that comes media pressure and his involuntary participation in having our privacy invaded. He knew that going in. Plus, maybe after twenty-four years, things aren't as exciting as they used to be.

I've felt it. The routine of daily life. The lack of sex because we're both too tired and are just as happy to sit in bed and watch television or read on our tablets.

Even if we *are* in a rut, I haven't betrayed our vows.

What a pisser that would be. A woman renowned for fixing broken marriages with a two-timing husband.

Another knock sounds—will these people not leave me alone? I glance up and see Molly, one of our assistant producers, standing in front of the glass. Some hosts prefer not to interact with staff, choosing a solid hierarchy system for communication. Me? I don't mind staffers coming directly to me with questions. As a result, the APs aren't afraid to knock on my door.

I wave and Molly opens the door, pops her head in. "Hi. Sorry to bug. The wife for the next show isn't loving wardrobe. She wants her stripes back. Do you have a sec to drop by and talk to her?"

I nod. "I told Jenny I'd pop in."

"Thanks. You're awesome."

She backs out of the doorway. "Molly, hang on."

For a second, an internal warning flashes. From the time I was young, eleven years old to be exact, my mother conditioned me to not share my business. To never let people know what's going on.

The lesson came full circle when I told a friend I'd gotten my period. That friend, my *best* friend, told someone else, and I suddenly had tampons hanging from my locker. Humiliating.

Mom was right.

I shouldn't share my business.

Except I needed help. And Molly, of all the APs, is a magician at digging up dirt. And, hello, she appeared at my door at the exact time I was gathering intel on Laurel Shelton. If that's not a sign, I don't know what is.

Molly stares at me, her mouth dipping into a puzzled frown. "Becca?"

"I'm sorry," I tell her. "My mind wandered." Thinking quickly, I point to my laptop. "I'm doing research on a potential guest. Um, a friend suggested her. I'm not ready to reach out, though, and want some background."

"Ah. You want to keep it on the down low?"

"Exactly. If I give you her name and address, would you please get some background?"

She steps into my office. "Sure. Whatcha got?"

From the glass holder on my desk, I grab a piece of the fancy notepaper with my name embossed in gold. A gift from Don after the last Emmy win.

I write Laurel Shelton's name and address and pause for another second, my mother's warning coming back to me.

It's only a name and an address. Not as if I'm slicing myself open.

I hand over the note. "Don't spend too much time on it. I'm not sure there's anything there."

The afternoon taping goes blessedly smooth. No catfights. No stripes, after a quick visit with the wife. No one assaulting me. Just your run-of-the-mill husband installing spyware on his wife's devices.

Let's just say the spyware isn't their only issue.

With the lack of communication between them, it'll be a miracle if they make it. If they do, in six months, we'll have them on the show again, celebrating my brilliance and telling the world how happy—*happy, happy, happy*—they are.

For now, I do the best I can with limited time and send them on their way.

After cleaning up some loose ends, I text Bernie. We have the timing perfected. He texts when he's about to pull up, opens my door and I hustle out of the building.

Tonight is no exception. I step off the elevator just as Bernie hops out of the car, umbrella shooting up to shield me from the rain.

Seconds later, we're dodging other umbrella-wielding pedestrians on the crowded sidewalk, some of whom notice me, and say hello.

It's not unusual for folks to stop me. Typically, I'll take the time to engage them. They're fans and without fans, I can't make a living. They deserve my attention.

Tonight, the steady rain keeps everyone moving.

Back in the car, Bernie glances back. "How was the day?"

"Uneventful," I say, once again thankful for a normal day of tapings.

He pulls into traffic, earning a horn blast from somewhere behind us. "Staying in tonight?"

Apparently, what with worrying about my husband cheating on me, I hadn't told Bernie about my plans and the fact that he'll get a few days off since I drive myself to the shore.

"I apologize," I say. "I forgot to tell you I'm heading down the shore. You've got the weekend off."

He meets my eye in the rearview. "Really?"

His voice has an excited lilt that makes me chuckle. "Yes. Really."

"I mean, not that I mind working the weekends, but my grandson has a T-ball game. They're in Connecticut."

"Perfect. Go see your grandson. I won't need you until Monday."

Once home, I don't dawdle. Ryan texted me earlier, announcing he'd scheduled a donor dinner since I'd be gone.

Fine with me. Given my spying mission on Laurel Shelton, I'm not sure I can face my husband right now.

Guilt settles on me. He'd been nothing but supportive and patient when my work took precedence over . . . well . . . everything.

Is it fair to him? This suspicion?

If he's cheating, yes, it's fair.

If not, he'll never know of my 007 activities and I can put it behind us.

I head to the bedroom where I slip into a lightweight cashmere sweater, leggings and ballet flats. I'm off the clock now and in my ready-to-relax attire.

Quick change complete, I grab the weekender I packed last night and leave the house, heading to the underground garage for my SUV.

I'll hit the end of rush hour traffic and my GPS tells me it'll take two hours to the shore. Might have to stop along the way for food.

My phone dings. Incoming text. Molly's name lights up the dashboard screen. Ooh. Maybe she has news. I hit the button on my steering wheel and a chipper female voice informs me Molly is still gathering info on Laurel Shelton.

My momentary excitement vanishes. All I have so far is what I knew this morning. Name, address, employer.

Address.

I drum my fingers on the steering wheel. It's not too late. I could take the GW bridge to Jersey, rather than the Verrazano. Maybe do some reconnoitering in Tenafly. Sure, it would take me miles out of my way, but ... Tenafly.

No-brainer.

I head for the George Washington bridge. Just a peek at her house, her neighborhood, that's all I want.

Forty-five minutes later, I turn onto Laurel Shelton's street.

Dusk has slid into evening, offering shadowy darkness for cover that eases my death grip on the steering wheel.

I cruise the block, slowing down when my GPS friend tells me my destination is on the left. A white, two-story Craftsman with blazing coach lights. The driveway is empty, but the interior lights are on.

It's a pretty house, not oversized like some others on the block, and appearing recently renovated. I drum my fingers on the steering wheel.

This woman is thirty years old and can afford Tenafly? There's currently nothing for sale under a million. Yes, I checked.

How much did a thirty-year-old marketing gal make at Cara?

Maybe she comes from money.

It's quite the rabbit hole my obsessed mind takes me down. I shake my head. Really, why do I care?

All I need to know is if she's sleeping with my husband.

I cruise to the end of the block, do a quick U-turn and park three houses down on the opposite side of the street.

If someone comes along, I'll pretend I'm on the phone. Very important call. *Very* important.

What the hell am I doing? Literally staking out this woman's house. Totally letting my imagination get the best of me. I don't even know if she's the same Laurel Shelton who works for Cara.

This Laurel Shelton might work for Ry and he might have indeed sent me the wrong credit card statement.

This is a fool's errand. It has to be. I shake my head, disgusted with myself. My work issues are wearing me out, making me think too hard about too many things I have no business thinking about.

I need to get to the shore and put this week behind me.

Headlights shine from the opposite end of the block and I sit, waiting for the car to pass. If it's Laurel and she works for Ry, I don't want to be seen. I'll simply wait here until she goes inside.

The car slows, then stops at the curb in front of Laurel's. My scattered mind freezes and hyper-focuses on the vehicle. Could this be her? Arriving home by Uber or another car service?

The rear passenger door opens and a tall man steps out. The rain has stopped, freeing him of an umbrella. His back is to me, the streetlight illuminating his dark hair.

My gut clenches.

My entire body clenches.

It's like one long hunk of steel locking me up as I ponder the man's broad shoulders. I've run my hands over them thousands upon thousands of times.

Damn him.

He turns, his handsome face fully visible to me as he bends low, telling the driver something. Unlike me, Ryan doesn't have a full-time driver. He has a service he uses when he chooses not to drive himself.

So much for a donor dinner. Unless, of course, said dinner is taking place at this residence, that happens to be the address on a credit card statement with purchases from La Perla.

Damn him.

He pays no attention to the expensive white SUV just down the street. In this neighborhood, it's probably not an uncommon sight. Plus, it's getting dark and I'm once again thankful he most likely can't see me.

The car moves past me while Ry heads for the front door. He digs into his pocket for something—his phone, maybe?

My world starts to crumble as my charming, reliable husband sticks a key in the lock and enters Laurel Shelton's house.

CHAPTER 5

I sit frozen in my seat, the reality of what I'm seeing sinking in.

Panicking won't help me. Breathe. That's all I need to do right now. Breathe and focus and not jump to conclusions.

Reasonable Dr. Becca. That's me.

But really? A key to someone else's house? Reasonable is one thing. Foolish is another.

I play back this morning's conversation. His nonchalance about Laurel being an employee and his sending me the wrong bill.

So easy how the lies slipped from his mouth while he looked right in my eyes. Still, knowing him as I do, I sensed it. Recognized the signs.

Maybe I didn't want to believe it.

Maybe? Why would any woman want to accept that her husband of twenty-four years is cheating? Particularly when that woman is famous for saving marriages.

Fury pummels me, heartbreak dismantling me from the inside.

I close my eyes and draw deep breaths. *Do something.* Sitting here won't get me answers.

Leave. I could simply drive off, wait for Molly to finish her inquiries on one Laurel Shelton and then confront Ryan. Show him whatever evidence I've gathered and wait for an explanation.

Evidence, however, could take a couple of days and there's no way—no way—I can stew that long.

I scoop up my phone, ready to call him and see if he has the nerve to answer. What then? *Hi, honey? What are you doing?*

I shake my head. That won't work. The man looked into my eyes and lied. Doing it over the phone? No-brainer.

The answers I want are right in that house. Just three doors down from where I'm sitting.

Before I lose my nerve, I yank on the handle, kick the door open and formulate a plan. I'll ring the bell and . . . surprise!

But, God, what if it *is* an innocent meeting? Rational Becca again. She's persistent that way.

He has a key.

I shake my head, instantly scolding myself for all the second-guessing. If I'm about to embarrass myself, so be it. At least then I'll have answers. I focus on Laurel's door. Black with a window —no curtain—at the top. An interior light illuminates the entry. I can see it as I march up the path. If I wanted, I'm tall enough to peep right in that window.

Not ready for that. For what I might see.

Adrenaline keeps me moving, my focus on the door. The doorbell. My hand shakes, my muddled thoughts and simmering anxiety stirring me up. I press the button.

From inside, I hear the simple *ding-dong,* but it's like a gong going off, banging around inside my skull.

I hate this. Dr. Becca, marriage expert, spying on her husband.

"It's dinner," a female voice calls from inside.

He did say he'd scheduled a dinner. I put my head down, staying out of sight through the window.

The front door swings open and . . .

Ryan.

His gaze connects with mine and I suck in a breath, hoping the ground will open up and swallow me. My temples throb, the pressure, the all-out pounding blurring my vision. Seconds stretch on. It may have been five or thirty or even a full minute. I don't know. All I know is that for once in his schmooze-filled life, Ryan has been silenced.

"Babe?"

A woman's voice. From behind him.

Babe?

Reasonable Becca retreats, totally gives in while my body succumbs to the emotional beatdown I've fought off these last minutes. I let out a soft, guttural moan.

How could he do this to me? To *us*?

No time for that. He did it. I'll need to deal with it. Deal with the heartbreak, the feelings of inadequacy and the fallout. Later.

Blessed fury blows away heartache. What the hell has he done? I straighten up, grit my teeth because, my *God,* he may have ruined us.

Ruined *me.*

"You son of a bitch," I finally say.

I push by him, inviting myself into Laurel Shelton's house, storming inside. At the end of the hallway, the stunning blonde from the photos I'd found comes into view. She halts. Literally skids to a stop, arms wide, mouth hanging open in horror.

Or guilt.

Too soon to tell.

I jab a finger at her. "You're Laurel?"

"Becca!" Ryan says from behind me. "What are you *doing?*"

Ha! I spin back to him. "Me? What are *you* doing? I *knew* you were lying. An *employee?* Really? Do you think I'm that stupid?"

He takes a few steps, clearly gathering his thoughts, then stops two feet from me. His arms are loose at his sides, his body seemingly relaxed.

Gifted liar.

"You don't know what you're talking about," he says.

"Don't I? Then why do you have a key to this house?"

"What . . ."

"I saw you get out of the car and walk to the door. I *saw* you open it with a key."

"Calm down."

Calm down?

He's kidding, right? Has to be. I flap my arms. "Oh, please. In the history of calming down, there has never been a worse time for someone to calm down."

I turn back, checking on Laurel. Gone.

Coward.

She'll give my husband a key to her house, but she won't face me.

Fine. I'll deal with Ryan. I spin back. "You told me you had a donor dinner. And, no, I didn't follow you. I had her address from the credit card bill. I took a detour on my way to the shore. Just to see. And who shows up, but you. Jesus, Ryan!"

"Lower your voice."

Oh, now I'm told to lower my voice. Classic stalling tactic.

I poke him in the chest. "I'll never forgive you for this."

Behind him, the front door is still wide open, beckoning me to storm out. The answers I came looking for are confirmed. Maybe not verbally, but I've seen enough to know, without question, Ryan has a . . . what? Girlfriend? Mistress?

I storm by him, through the open door and take a few steps on the path before turning again. "I gave you everything! And this is how you repay me?"

From the doorway, Ryan slaps the overhead light off, plunging me into darkness. "Lower your voice."

The neighbor's porch light goes on, then the front door opens. An older man stands there. He cranes his neck, staring at me. "Laurel? Everything all right?"

Ryan turns, waves to the man. "It's not Laurel. We're fine. Thanks."

The man lingers, then nods, returning to the house. No doubt he'll be watching from inside.

Terrific.

"You're causing a scene," Ry tells me. "Is that what you want? For someone to recognize you?"

He's right. Damn him.

He looks around, sees our car parked down the street. "Let's go to the car."

"Absolutely not."

"Pardon?"

"If you want to get off the street," I point to Laurel's house, "we're going inside."

"Have you gone mad? You don't even know this woman. She's a donor."

"Then why do you have a key?"

That stops him cold. My husband is once again silent.

I push my shoulders back, lift my chin and turn from him. The man I've loved, trusted, for more than half my life. I walk away, focused on each step that takes me farther from him. From the life I thought we had.

CHAPTER 6

t 9:37, I turn left off Ocean Avenue onto Paradise Lane, the side street leading to our home. After lowering the window, I stick my hand out. Moist, salty air fills the car. There's something therapeutic there. The saltwater cleansing my foul mood.

I wish.

Drawing my hand back inside, I swipe it over my damp face, thanks to ninety minutes of body-racking sobs while driving eighty miles an hour on the Garden State Parkway. Everything hurts. My head, my heart. Everything. My entire body feels bulldozed.

"Helluva week so far," I mutter.

All around me, once-tiny beach cottages have morphed into bloated homes built on lots the size of a napkin. A dessert napkin.

All, that is, except our house. *Ours* is the original cottage we bought from my parents. Built in 1925, it has a wraparound porch that extends to the back and overlooks the ocean. We've updated the interior and kept a fresh coat of paint on the exterior, but compared to the rest of the McMansions, our baby looks . . . puny.

Worn.

Might be time to do something about that.

Up ahead, my mother's Mercedes is in the driveway and my already fatigued body closes in on itself. My parents live five minutes away and the security system lets us know when Mom comes here to decompress after a fight with my father.

My mother either hasn't realized or doesn't want to discuss the fact that I'm aware every time she steps into the cottage.

I don't mind. The house has long been our refuge.

But I must have missed the alert for this visit and was hoping for quiet tonight. Ryan has been blowing up my phone since I left Laurel's house. I finally pulled into a rest stop, sent him a text telling him to leave me alone and he eased up on his efforts to contact me, but has still texted.

I can't deal with one more thing this week. My personal life and my career have gone bonkers. Let's not throw fighting parents into the mix.

Parking beside the Mercedes, I shut the engine. Since I didn't tell her I was coming, I fire off a text letting her know I'm about to walk in. Scaring the hell out of her and causing a stroke would only add to the drama of the week.

I slide from my SUV and pause for a second, listening to the crash of the ocean behind the house. Tomorrow, I will sit up in my bed and stare out at the waves. We're lucky that way. A reminder to be grateful. To appreciate the blessings.

So, Ry had an affair. Plenty of men do. I should know. I've built a career on it.

But . . . *dang it,* it's a hot sword straight through me. I'm now the fool who missed her husband having a side piece.

Does he love her? Is he leaving me? Will I wind up alone?

These thoughts. Too much.

I open the rear car door to retrieve my weekender.

"Becca," a man's voice calls, "hello."

Startled, I spin back and let out a hard breath. My neighbor, Danny Engles, is dragging a garbage can to the street. He leaves it midway, veering in my direction.

Danny is a movie producer who relocated from California in November. I wouldn't call him a friend. I don't have many of those anymore. An anchorwoman I worked with years ago told me something happens when you become famous. Noncelebrity friends can't make the climb with you. She was right. Whether it was jealousy, my limited time or just plain not being interested in the chaos that comes with having a celebrity around, I've lost friendships due to my career.

Neighbor Danny has been kind to us, inviting us to his holiday party in December that was nothing short of spectacular. Even my husband, who hates home parties because the buffet skeeves him, raved about the lobster tails and shrimp. The pasta with a variety of sauces. The steak kabobs.

The guests too, were incredible. A-list actors including the young woman from Danny's most recent Oscar-winning film.

Since then, we've regularly gotten together for drinks. Nothing organized. Just a simple text from one of the three of us saying, "Hey, come over for a drink."

"Bubby," Danny says, "let me help you."

Danny cracks me up. He's fifty-three, four inches shorter than me and calls everyone Bubby. A habit, he once told me, he'd picked up from his grandmother because he found it funny. He has a rash of kids running around from, I believe, two or three different women. His oldest son is married. Meanwhile, Danny's youngest child is five and in kindergarten here in Deal.

Whatever the man has, it's something charismatic. People are drawn to him. Good-looking in a salt-and-pepper way, his dark eyes and sculpted face support craggy lines that make you believe he's experienced life in all its forms, good and bad. With that comes a presence, a comfort in his own skin, that intrigues me.

The spotlight on his garage illuminates him as he hustles toward me in khaki shorts and a white T-shirt. His dark hair is, as usual, freshly cut and neat and he already appears to be sporting a tan.

"Hi, Danny," I say. "I've got it."

He peers up at me and points to the Mercedes. "I talked to her when she got here yesterday. Said she was helping you with a project."

A project. Good one.

"Yes. I thought I'd surprise her."

"Holler if you need anything." He winks playfully and offers a grand smile. "Always up for a threesome with two beautiful women."

"My God, Danny, you are a pig."

Having worked in show business and seen the power men have wielded over the years, I wonder if there are a slew of women ready to slap a sexual harassment suit on him.

He laughs and heads back to his garbage can, the darkness swallowing him. Innuendos aside, I've found Danny to be an okay guy. He enjoys chasing away people who think it's okay to walk up the stairs from the beach and peep in windows.

My phone dings and I immediately stiffen before I realize it's not Ryan's assigned tone. He's been calling and texting since I left him. All of which I ignored, aside from that one text demanding that he leave me alone.

Ignoring him might be childish.

Passive aggressive, even.

Too bad. I need a minute to contemplate what he's done to me. Personally and professionally.

I check my phone. Mom.

No sooner do I reach the front door than it swings open. My mother stands there in pink silk pajamas that might be mine and a smile spreading wide. Her expertly dyed ash blond hair is tucked behind her ears, her normal subtle makeup washed away.

I love my mother. She's always happy to see me. I have a momentary slap of guilt over my thoughts just a few minutes ago.

It's not that I don't want her here. Never that. I simply know *why* she's here and that bothers me. That my parents, after fifty-some-odd years, don't know how to communicate.

"Hi, lovey!" she says, waving me inside as if I'm a guest in my own home.

"Hi, Mom."

I drop a kiss on her cheek, and stand in the entry, letting the energy of the cottage seep in. Whether it's the light grays and whites, the easy beach vibe or the stillness, this house is my savior.

"I'm sorry," Mom says. "I didn't know you were coming."

I toss my weekender and tote on the sofa. "Don't apologize. You know you're always welcome. Everything alright?"

She nods, attempting to minimize her presence, but truth is in her eyes. That dullness I've seen countless times.

"Of course!" she says, her voice too loud, too chipper. "Everything is fine!"

My stomach lets out a grumble. Dinner. I missed it apparently. I head to the fridge. Like the kitchen in the city, we've outfitted this one with stainless, high-end appliances that Ryan has prepared fantastic meals on.

I glance at the counter stools where I've sat testing spice levels as he fed me food from a pan. Or when we've shared takeout from containers while drinking beer or wine or whatever cocktail we whipped up.

Another shock wave hits me, tears bubbling up. Thankfully, Mom is behind me, oblivious.

Exhaustion. That's all this is. I need rest. Tomorrow, when I'm fresh, I'll be able to buck up.

I open the fridge and find what looks like foil-wrapped pizza along with two bottles of white wine and fresh vegetables.

How long would Mom be staying?

"Help yourself," she says. "I felt like Amico's for dinner."

Our favorite Italian restaurant with to-die-for brick oven pizza. I help myself, popping a slice onto a plate and into the microwave. Typically, I hate pizza in a microwave. It never heats evenly. Tonight, I'm too tired to care.

"I bought vegetables," she says, still laying on the faux cheer. "Help yourself!"

"I see that." I brace my hands against the island and give her my best stern look. "Mom, knock it off with the peppy. What's going on?"

"What? Nothing. I'm fine! *Just* fine."

"You're using the Stepford voice."

Growing up, it was all about putting on a show, making sure what the neighbors saw was nothing but wedded bliss. Happy, happy, happy.

Inside our home?

Not so much.

As an adult, I occasionally informed my mother she sounded like a Stepford wife when using that high-pitched, chipper voice.

She meets my gaze and her shoulders droop, the weight of her life apparently landing too hard. I know the feeling.

The two of us? We're what Jenny would call a hot-ass mess.

The microwave dings and I drag the pizza out. Otherwise, the reminder dinging won't cease. Despite my howling belly, I set the pizza down and reach across the island, squeezing her hand. "What happened?"

She shakes her head, makes a show of rolling her eyes. "You know your father. Came home yesterday in a mood."

My parents. Complicated people. Complicated relationship.

At seventy-two and still one of the northeast's top spine

surgeons, my father's ego barely fits through their front door. And it's an enormous doorway.

Thankfully, I'd inherited enough of his arrogance to call him out on his nonsense, but my mom? Although formidable, she wants peace. Always. At all costs.

A nice thought, of course, because who wouldn't want serenity? As an adult, I've admired her willingness to sacrifice herself for her family, but she gave too much.

She'd groomed my father to believe she'd always go along with his wishes. In turn, he's taken her quest for peace as weakness. An inability to assert herself and set boundaries.

"You guys had a fight?"

Mom shrugs one delicate shoulder.

A fight, in my parents' world, meant my father stating what he expected to happen and my mother saying "yes, dear" before telling him she'd be sleeping at my house.

Zero communication skills between these two.

I take a bite of my pizza, my mind ticking back to my childhood. I swallow and set my slice down. "I remember when we still lived up north, you'd bring me down here for weekends after I'd hear you guys *discussing* something. Dad never came."

She nods. "I needed space. Why do you think I was so insistent that we keep this house when we bought the bigger one? Your father moaned about the expense of two shore houses."

"He was right. Why have two houses so close together?"

Unless, of course, you needed a spare to save your sanity. I guess my mother and I aren't all that different.

"You saved me by buying this one."

We'd never voiced it, but I knew. Down deep, I was aware that my mother needed a refuge. So did I. As a teenager, after I'd gotten my license, I'd lie to my parents about studying and sneak down here just to sit on the beach for an hour.

To this day, I've never shared that with them.

I look around, taking in the soft gray walls, the photos of the beach scattered about. "I love this house. In a lot of ways, it's my haven too. When I walk in the door, stress vanishes."

"Rough week?" Mom asks.

"You could say that."

"Are those marketing folks still insisting on trashy segments?"

"Trash sells, Mom."

She cocks her head, studies me. "Where's Ryan?"

With his girlfriend.

And, cripes, I don't have it in me tonight to explain. Besides, my mother, the one who'd put up with my father's antics all these years, would tell me to work it out. That we'd been married so long, there had to be a way to fix it.

Did I want that? To make my marriage work? To forgive him? *Could* I forgive him?

Or did I, someone known for fixing broken marriages, want to walk away and make my cheating husband social media fodder?

There are times I miss being a private citizen and having my own practice. Back then, I worked with couples for longer than a few hours and made a meaningful impact.

Back then, I didn't need spin-control for my husband's affair. If I leave him, the world will know I'm a fraud. A certified con artist famous for saving marriages when my own is failing.

Ryan's little tryst—if that's what it is—has the potential to incinerate my already suffering ratings. If this keeps up, with only another year on my contract, my run might come to an end. Which leaves my staff out of work.

The choice isn't really a choice. I have to save the show.

Perhaps I'm not all that different from my mother. She hid behind the illusion of a happy marriage simply to avoid gossip. Me? I'm sheltering behind my number one show. Here we are, both of us running from our husbands.

"Ryan is home," I tell her. "Had a meeting."

I pop the last bite of pizza into my mouth and place the plate in the dishwasher. "I'm beat. Can we talk more tomorrow?"

"Of course, dear. I'm in the guest room. I'd never sleep in your bed."

"Even if you had, it's okay. But thank you. One of my favorite things is the view from my bed."

"It's peaceful."

"It is indeed."

CHAPTER 7

$\mathcal{M}$y ringing phone drags me from what some would call sleep. I'm not sure all the tossing and turning qualifies.

Eyes closed, I drop my hand on the bedside table, feeling around for the device of doom and finally landing on it. Before I can pick it up, it goes silent.

I blink against the sunlight streaming over the top of the shades on the oversized windows and slider. The shades are adjustable from both ends and I have them open at the top. Unless someone stands on a ladder or a chair, they can't see in.

Widening my eyes, I stare at my phone. Missed call from my cheating husband. The one who knows I like to sleep late at the shore.

Not only does he have an affair, he wakes me up at 8:00 a.m.

A text fires in. Also Ryan. Letting me know he's on his way.

Now he wants to barge in here and force a confrontation?

Before reacting, I ponder a response. That's what he wants. For me to engage.

I'm not ready. Am I freezing him out? Maybe. I hate being that person. It's insanely passive-aggressive and Dr. Becca would advise against it. Right now, I'm not Dr. Becca. I'm one of the betrayed spouses I've counseled thousands of times. I'm hurt and angry and . . . devastated.

Overwhelmed.

None of which is a delightful combination for a *talk*.

I drop the phone on the bed beside me. Would Ryan really show up here? He's a creature of habit. Breakfast at the Bridge Café down the street before work, then straight to the office, or so I'm told. After last night, I can't be sure what's fact or fiction.

I'll call his bluff though. Why not?

If I don't respond, the worst that'll happen is he'll show up. At which point, I'll inform him I'm not ready to talk. Not without risking spousal homicide.

Besides, knowing me as he does, if I don't engage, he'll take the hint that driving all the way down here will be a fool's errand.

He's a lying cheat, but no fool.

Ignoring my phone, I hit the button on my remote and open the shades the full depth of the window. Sunlight glitters off the ocean's whitecaps and a sailboat bobs in the distance under a clear blue sky.

I needed this. A time-out.

In a matter of days, my world has imploded and sitting around in bed won't help me. I eye the treadmill in the room's corner. I positioned it in front of the sliding door so I could watch the ocean while running on days I choose to stay indoors.

Today won't be one of those days. I need to get outside, clear my head with fresh air and come up with a plan to deal with Ryan.

And his girlfriend.

The thought is another hot stab—*stab, stab, stab*—to my chest. I lift my hands, pressing them against the spot where pain shoots in all directions. My stomach pitches and I draw a breath, force myself to release it slowly.

Move forward. That's all I need to do. Figure out how to compartmentalize the stress.

One step at a time.

I throw back the quilt and head to my dresser, pulling out running shorts, a T-shirt and a long-sleeved pullover in case the morning air has a chill.

A run on the beach will do me good. Fresh air. Room to move. Time to think.

Or, maybe, *not* think.

There's a concept.

As soon as I open the bedroom door, I'm welcomed by the rich aroma of fresh-brewed coffee that already awakens my senses. Mom getting us started.

"Mom?"

No answer.

I check her room and the guest bath. Nothing.

Back in the kitchen, there's a note on the fridge. My mother's perfect script informing me she's gone back home.

In Mom speak, this means she's over my father's transgression and will never speak of it again. No conversation on how to fix the problem, no admitting her pain—or his. Just pretending it never happened.

Dysfunction at its finest.

By now, I'm used to it.

I can't worry about it. I have my own issues. Leaving the coffee until after my run, I swing through the back door, ready to feel the warm sun on my skin.

An HOUR LATER, I've cooled down and settled my breathing as I hoof it toward the wood stairs leading to my back deck. Sweat drips everywhere and I drag an arm across my forehead.

Good run.

I suppose.

It's such a love-hate relationship, this running thing. I like the feeling of accomplishment, the juicy endorphins that make me feel strong and alive. The act itself?

Torture.

Before I reach the steps, I spot Danny, on his own deck, sitting in a chair, mug in hand. Not in the mood for a chat, I wave and detour toward the front, away from my chatty neighbor.

Yes, I'm being rude. I convince myself it's a necessary evil if I want some alone time. The pace at the office is unrelenting, and it typically filters home where I catch up on emails or return phone calls. Busy, busy, busy.

So busy that my husband had an affair? I wince and immediately stop myself. Correct my thinking. For years, Dr. Becca has assured wounded partners it's not their fault that their significant other betrayed them.

If Ryan was unsatisfied, he should have voiced it.

Talked to me. Maybe I've been distracted the last few years, that's on me. I'll own it.

A mistress?

No.

That's his fault.

I reach the driveway just as a horn honks. Hoping it's not said cheating husband, I swing my gaze up to the silver sedan.

Jenny. My EP.

What on earth is she doing here?

Rather than parking in the driveway, for whatever reason, she makes a K-turn and pulls in front of Danny's house where the garbage men have left his empty can.

She hops out of the car. She's wearing tattered baggy jeans, a Henley and her signature checkered Vans. Her dark hair is loose, falling over her shoulders.

"Hey," she says.

"Hey, yourself. This is a surprise."

"Yeah. Sorry. I tried calling, but you didn't answer."

I jab my thumb over my shoulder, then wipe sweat from my forehead. "I was running."

"I see that." She looks around and tips her head to the sun. "It's a nice day. Figured I'd take a ride. Maybe walk on the beach and grab lunch before I head back."

There's no invitation there. She knows better. In a way, it saddens me. In a way, not. Yes, I'd love to have Jenny as a confidante. Given our business relationship and the fact that her job is to amp up the drama on my show, I don't think sharing my personal—and exploitable—issues is a smart move.

We've had lunch together hundreds of times. Always business. Always in the city. Except once. On hiatus. She was on her way back to Manhattan from visiting a friend in Atlantic City and stopped to discuss staff moves.

She stayed an hour, we ate lunch and took care of business.

Done.

Ever the watchdog, Danny appears in his driveway, his arms wide.

"Whoa!" His gaze swings from Jenny's car to me. "*Bubby, please.*"

"What?" Jenny asks.

"He's mad," I mutter. "You parked in front of his house. It's a quirk."

"Sorry, Danny," I call across the lawn. "She didn't know. This is my EP, Jenny."

He keeps walking, moving straight for us. "A pleasure," he tells her, "but *really*? Becca's driveway is available. And the spot in front of *her* house."

Danny, Danny, Danny. Gotta love him.

"Jesus," Jenny says. "Is this for real?"

I snort. Can't help it. "Yep." I point to her car. "Do me a favor and move it. Otherwise, I'll never hear the end."

"Hey," Danny spits. "When I have a guest, I tell them to park in front of my house. Courtesy to my neighbors."

Jenny holds up her keys and heads back to the vehicle. "My apologies," she says. "Didn't know."

Can't make this stuff up. And I host a daily talk show.

I shake my head, chuckling because three blocks down is a public beach with only street parking. When summer hits, this block will be packed with cars.

"Danny," I gesture to our nice, peaceful road, "come Memorial Day, it'll be bumper-to-bumper cars every day."

He gives me a look, his dark gaze steady. "Not if I can help it. I'll put cones out."

Oh, my ornery neighbor might be just what I need right now. A little comic relief. I let out a snort. "You know you're funny, right?"

"Bubby, you have no idea."

Car drama done, a satisfied Danny retreats to his house while Jenny accompanies me inside. I am desperate for a shower and more than likely reek of sweat, but it'll have to wait. I wave Jenny to the sofa while I fill a pitcher with filtered water and some lemon wedges I keep in the freezer.

I set the tray with the pitcher and glasses on the coffee table and pour. "What's up?"

"Sorry to barge in on you."

Actually, she's not. After all these years together, I know her. This impromptu visit is one of her sorry not sorry moments.

"Couple of things," she says. "The week was so busy. After what happened, I wanted to see how you were feeling about everything. I know the shore always gives you clarity."

After finding my husband with his mistress, I have zero clarity.

"Honestly, Jen, I haven't thought too hard about it. We both know I hate that format. I don't foresee a time when I'll be comfortable with . . ."

How to describe it without sounding bitchy?

"Trash TV," she offers.

I turn my hand palm up.

She scooches forward on the sofa. "I get it. Just so you know, I'm trying. My goal is to find the happy medium where there's enough spice to satisfy the suits, but you're not getting punched."

Spice. I hate that word. It's marketing's word. And, as much as I appreciate their hard work lining up sponsors, I don't want them dictating my content.

Yes, I'm naïve. Sue me.

"A happy medium would be nice."

She takes a sip of water and sets the glass down. "By the way, who's Laurel Shelton?"

My head snaps back, my spine stiffening. How does Jenny know that name?

Her hands fly up. "Whoa. Sorry. Didn't realize it was some big secret. I needed Molly to jump on something yesterday and stopped by her desk. I asked her what she was working on. She said you had a potential guest for her to vet. That stuff usually goes through me."

She meets my gaze. There's no heat there, but it's loaded with meaning I'd be an idiot to miss. This is why she's here. She thinks I'm circumventing her.

Helluva week so far. Punched by a guest, my husband is banging a thirty-year-old and I've pissed off my EP.

I shake my head. "I'm sorry, Jenny. It was something I wanted Molly to check into for me. Quietly."

"So quietly that the EP shouldn't know about a potential guest?"

I should have expected this. That having an assistant producer doing research might get out.

"I wasn't keeping it from you."

"Weren't you?"

I blow air through my lips. I'm not thrilled with her tone. However, she knows I've been unhappy. To her, this must feel like I no longer trust her when there is simply no other executive producer I'd rather have. I lean in, holding eye contact. "You've been fantastic through this ratings mess. I know how hard you're working. Trying to keep everyone happy and moving in the same direction."

Now, she's the one who snaps back. "Are you firing me?"

Firing her? After all these years together, *that's* what she thinks? How have I, generally a competent communicator, botched this so badly? "No!" I say with a wee bit too much force. "There's no one else I'd rather do this with."

Still seated, she doubles over, slapping her hands over her face. I've done this to her. Made my tough-as-nails EP feel … vulnerable.

Dispensable.

Guilt slams me. I've been so damned caught up in my own issues, I inadvertently caused her stress. "Jenny, I'm so sorry. I … it's nothing about you. Not at all."

She drops her hands and blows out a huffing laugh while staring at the floor.

If she's crying, I'm not sure what I'll do. She and I? We're the strong ones. We hold everyone together.

That's our job.

She lifts her head. Her eyes are clear, her relief evident. "I was scared."

I reach my hand out, set it on the table in front of her. "I wish you'd have called me yesterday. I feel terrible I put you through this."

Waving me off, she rests back, her shoulders sinking into the deep cushions. "What's going on? Why won't you tell me who this mystery guest is?"

The last thing I want is to talk about this. To admit Laurel is

Ryan's girlfriend. That the so-called relationship expert is a fraud. Her *marriage* is a fraud.

Humiliating, that.

But I owe Jenny an explanation. "She's not a guest. It's … personal."

Jenny shakes her head. "I'm not following."

Oh, for the love of humanity. This entire conversation is torture. "I wanted Molly to get me information on Laurel Shelton for personal reasons. It has nothing to do with the show. I was doing it myself, but only got so far. Molly came by and I asked her for help with," I roll my hand, "Laurel."

Finally, she bobs her head. "Okay. Now that I'm not freaking out over losing my job, is there anything you need from me? Can I help with this Laurel Shelton thing?"

"I wish you could. Believe me."

She holds up her hand. "Understood. But, you know, if you need to talk …"

"I know. Thank you."

"If something's going on that could, say, affect the show, I can help. My loyalty is to you and our staff and keeping everyone employed."

She's right. My marital issues could implode on us. Put people out of work. If anyone would know how to save my show, it's Jenny. She has the rapport with marketing. Devin in particular.

"Laurel Shelton," I say, the name absolute acid on my tongue, "is Ryan's mistress."

For a few seconds, Jenny doesn't move. She's frozen, letting the words bully their way into her brain.

I know how she feels.

"Wow." Her eyebrows lift. "Didn't expect *that.*"

"You and I both. On Tuesday night, I suspected something. Yesterday, I asked Molly to help me and last night I confirmed the affair. I confronted the two of them and immediately drove down here. Since then, I haven't talked to him. I'm trying to figure out what to do."

"Well, yeah. I mean, divorce isn't exactly a good look for someone who's built a career on saving marriages."

Ouch. Good old Jenny. Never one to mince words.

"It sure isn't." I hold my arms wide. "Thus, I'm hiding at the beach."

I could count on one hand, less than one hand, how many people I confide in. There's a therapist, but I haven't seen her in a year. My mother is one. Ryan is the other.

My mother, whom I'm not ready to admit this to, and Ryan, for obvious reasons, are not options.

I meet Jenny's eye. We've been coworkers for years. She's as much responsible for the success of our show as I am.

She's been grinding, not only to produce a quality show, but day in and day out, dealing with the staff and the guests, some of whom have horrendous stories of abuse. We've all become … numb … to it.

We have to.

It's survival.

Becoming emotionally attached to every guest, and their heartaches, would hospitalize us.

Now, I'm faced with following my mother's edict of not sharing my business, and possibly insulting the woman who helped me become Dr. Becca, or I can have faith in someone unrelated to me.

In many ways, I owe Jenny my career. She deserves better than to be treated like an outsider when Ryan's affair could cost us the show.

Time to break my rule. "I don't know if I want a divorce. I'm not sure of anything right now."

"Understandable. Can I ask another question?"

Enough. Either we're having this conversation or not. "Of

course." I smile. "My marriage is, unfortunately, part of my career. That makes it, for today, your business too."

"Thank you. Just say if I go too far. You know me. I ask questions. I really want to help you through this. And not because of the show. I respect and admire you. And that's saying something in this business."

"It sure is." I sit back, readying myself for the barrage of questions. "Fire away."

"This woman. Do you think it's serious? Or," she flaps her hand, "a fling."

"No idea. I wasn't there long enough to find out."

"What made you suspicious?"

"She has a credit card. He accidentally sent me the bill—I assume he pays it." I let out a sigh, feel the punch to my solar plexus. "Which probably means it's more than a fling."

What a thought. What if he leaves me for her? Not that I can't be without a man. I can. There's this pesky thing called love. Despite the devastation he's leveled, I love him. The bastard.

"Eh," Jenny says, "he could be trying to impress her. The rich guy who'll buy her anything if she puts out."

My stomach flips and she immediately winces. This results from what we do each day. The emotional self-protection that comes with focusing on ratings rather than the human element of heartbreak.

"It's alright," I tell her when we both know it's not.

"Do you think this woman might go public?"

I'd been up half the night wondering that very thing. The tabloids would eat me for lunch then dinner. Maybe a snack, too.

I lift one shoulder. "I don't know. From what I've found, she's a professional. A marketing exec at Cara. She lives in Tenafly, for God's sake. She's no bimbo."

"Tenafly is pricey."

Indeed. I circle a hand in the air, working the problem. "Let's assume she won't blow up her life by going public. I don't think her fancy Tenafly neighbors are gonna like a bunch of paparazzi on their street."

"I agree."

Jenny slouches back, clucking her tongue the way she does when she's mulling something. She finally bolts back up, her eyes wide. "I have an idea."

"Will I hate it?"

"Maybe."

"Excellent."

I roll my hand, urging her on.

"What if you go public? Just put the affair out there and admit your marriage isn't perfect."

Horror mixed with a dose of fear and humiliation smothers me, literally paralyzing my lungs. I open my mouth, let it hang there for a second while I try to breathe. *In, out, in, out.*

Her hands fly up. "Just an idea!"

I'm trying to think like a talk show host and not a betrayed wife. The host in me knows I'd be shark bait.

"You'll take a ton of heat," Jenny says, "and then some celebrity will screw up and—bam—attention shifts. My thought is, by you releasing a statement, you control the narrative. Not Ryan, not the girlfriend and definitely not the social media vultures."

She has a point. Some of the tension locking my shoulders releases.

I may not hate this idea.

It definitely frees me from the pressure of always appearing happy. Happy, happy, happy. Always having to live up to the Dr. Becca image.

Sorry, folks. Nobody's life is that perfect.

It might work. I mull it over, considering the benefits of simply admitting my marriage isn't perfect.

"It's not the worst idea," I admit. "I make a statement. Ask for privacy and let the circus begin."

"Would Ryan go for it?"

I cluck my tongue. "I don't care what he wants."

That might be the only thing I'm sure of.

Jenny hops up from the sofa and begins pacing, snapping her fingers as she goes. "We'll get your publicist on it. Something about how all marriages have ups and downs. You want to be open about your struggles and help other people, blah, blah."

This is the magic of Jenny. She's brilliant with spin control.

Unfortunately, it's my life she's spinning.

She stops pacing, just halts right in the middle of my living room, all her contained energy crackling.

"What?" I ask.

"Wow. Wow, wow, wow." She starts walking again, wagging a finger at me. "You're going to despise this, so, you know, take a minute. Let it sink in."

"I think I know what —"

"What if we did a show on it? On you and Ryan? We get a guest host—a therapist—to come on and help you." She stops walking again, slams her hands on the sofa cushions. "Talk about a win-win. You guys get counseling and you're being *totally* transparent. Our entire marketing team may pee themselves."

At that, I laugh. The vision of Devin, my archenemy, standing in front of me, his perfectly pressed suit pants saturated, gives me a moment of professional satisfaction.

Except, how far am I willing to go for ratings?

I've loved Ryan since college. We've built a life. Some would call it an amazing life. Now, he's made a mistake, a huge one. If I agree to this stunt, it'll humiliate us both.

Have I really become that person? That vile woman who would sacrifice her loved ones for ratings?

Maybe.

Sickness fills me, sticking right at the base of my ribs. Impossible situation.

"What are you thinking?" Jenny asks.

"Oh, I'm thinking a lot of things."

Now I'm the one who stands. I walk to the sliding glass doors that lead out to the back deck and peer at the ocean's glistening whitecaps.

If I did this, it would mean outing myself—sharing my business—in a way I've never done before.

Ryan would hate it, and possibly me. Then again, he should have known better. It's not as if he didn't know what I did for a living. He's half of this team and has a responsibility to uphold the image. The one that earned him the life he has.

Not to mention the Maserati.

The Maserati should have been a clue that my husband might be in the midst of a full-blown midlife crisis, and I was too busy to notice.

I turn back to Jenny. "My head is exploding. I need time."

"Of course," she tells me. "Take the weekend."

The *weekend*?

I must have made a face or given some sort of outraged body language because she throws up her hands. "Or you know, however much time you need. It's your marriage. I just don't want someone to leak it. Then you lose all control."

Meaning, someone like Laurel Shelton.

Who even knew how long this had been going on? Or how careful they'd been? As we speak, some paparazzi might be trying to sell a photo.

"A couple days," I say. "Give me a couple of days."

CHAPTER 8

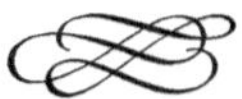

$\mathcal{I}$'m sitting on my back deck, an open book in my lap and early afternoon sun streaming across my cheeks. I'd like to report I've read pages and pages and pages in the ninety minutes I've been out here, but if I did, I don't remember a single thing. The book is a prop, abandoned an hour ago so I could explore the vastness of the ocean.

The Atlantic requires no thinking. And that makes it a lovely distraction.

"Hello!"

Danny.

I give up on the ocean and peer across the deck rails separating our property. He's in his normal T-shirt and sunglasses and holds up a pitcher of something fabulous looking.

"Margarita?"

At 2:00 in the afternoon? When I have a load of emails awaiting my already limited attention span?

Eh, why not?

"Absolutely." I point to the beach. "Chairs on the beach?"

"You got it."

I pop in the house, grab my big hat and sunglasses, hoping

beach-walkers won't recognize me. I love talking to fans. They got me where I am. They put me in a position to buy this house when my parents would have sold it to strangers.

My fans gave me my life. Truly.

I spend most days reminding myself of that. To be grateful and kind when I meet people who want to chat even though I'm already late. No matter where I need to be, I remind myself.

After discovering my husband has a mistress and my EP wants to put it on national television, I can't face admirers. Not when I'm a fraud living a lie.

Rather than carry my chair down the thirty steps, I fling it over the railing, making sure it clears the rocks under the deck and hits sand. I've lost a few chairs with my shortcut, irritating Ryan enough that he created a pulley system so I could tie the chair to the rope and lower it.

I don't even have the patience for that today. Plus, I'm not sure I care about his irritation.

Danny meets me on the beach and I glance around. A dozen or so walkers and a few doors down a couple reading under an umbrella.

All in all, fairly quiet. Danny hands me the acrylic pitcher—no glass on the beach—while he sets up his chair and the folding side table that has a hidden cooler under the top.

"Look at you," he says. "You're in full Jackie O mode with the hat and glasses."

I crack a smile and drop into my chair, kicking off my flip-flops so I can dig my feet into sand that sends warmth shooting up my calves. "I'm incognito."

"Ha. Is it an issue down here? People bugging you?"

"Occasionally. I don't usually mind. Today? Not up to being Dr. Becca."

He tilts his head, considers that for a second. "I get that. Been around enough movie stars to see the downside of fame."

"With social media, it's a slippery slope. Celebrities post

their every move and then rail about their lack of privacy. What do they expect? I try to give my fans access, but not to where I can't leave my house without being bombarded."

"It's smart."

Ten yards in front of us, waves crash, the foamy water rolling onto the beach and receding. There's a light wind and I rest my head back, opening up to sun on my cheeks.

Danny hands over a nearly full tumbler adorned with seashells. I haven't been drunk in… I don't even remember the last time. A while.

Looking at the tumbler, today may be the day.

"Love these tumblers." I hold it up to read the bottom. Nothing.

"My ex-wife gave them to me. I'll ask where she got them." He stares out over the ocean. "Days like this make me miss California. Sunshine. Not too hot. Quiet beach."

I take a sip of my margarita, the lime and tequila pleasing my taste buds. I smack my lips together and make a popping noise. "Helluva cocktail."

He grins. "My specialty. I'll teach you."

"That would be fun."

He turns to me, his eyes hidden behind his Maui Jims. "Listen, I'm sorry about the thing with your producer. People in my private space? No can do. Like I said, I've been around actors who can't even walk out of their house without being bombarded."

"Not a big deal. This will be your first summer here though and trust me, the traffic gets insane. You'll be lucky if your driveway isn't half-blocked by a parked car."

"I'll get it towed."

"Every day, seven days a week, bumper-to-bumper cars. You get used to it."

"I doubt that."

At this, I snort. "Guess you didn't know there was public

beach access three blocks down?"

"Funny how the realtor left that out."

We both laugh and then I angle toward him. "Why the parking quirk? It's not like they're in your driveway. It's a public street."

"But it's my house and I don't want strangers near it." He shrugs. "Bubby, I got a ton of hang-ups. Ask my three ex-wives."

Another rumble of laughter escapes. After the week I've had, it feels … good.

Calming.

Danny, I'm realizing may not be as quirky as I've thought. He simply has different boundaries.

"Three ex-wives," I say. "What's that like?"

Tipping his glasses down, he peers at me. "Are you head-shrinking me, Dr. Becca?"

"Not at all. I'm curious."

Particularly since I'm contemplating the future of my marriage, and my producer expects me to flay myself open to my viewers.

Danny sips at his margarita and rests the tumbler on the arm of his beach chair. "Would I prefer not being divorced three times? Absolutely. Then again, I wouldn't have my kids."

"Do you have children with all of them?"

"My first and third. The second ex—lovely woman—was a rebound. Totally unfair to her. I screwed up a lot those couple of years."

Fascinating. In my experience, I haven't known many men able to admit their mistakes. Whether it's a reflection of the company I keep or not, I'll have to analyze later.

I shift my chair sideways, facing him. A couple walking by glances over. If they've recognized me, there's no indication. "How did you screw up?"

"Aside from rushing into marriage with a woman who deserved better?"

"Aside from that."

"You're head-shrinking me."

Again, I laugh. "I'm not. I'm … working through something … and need input."

"Trouble in paradise?"

I say nothing. He takes the hint I'm not ready to open up and pulls his gaze away, giving his full attention to the crashing waves. "My first wife, she deserved better too. I'll love her until the day I die."

Exactly my fear. That I'll divorce Ryan because I'm angry and then mourn the relationship until my last breath.

"My fault," he continues. "I fucked every woman who showed interest. In Hollywood? There was a lot of interest."

My stomach clenches. Men. Why was it so hard to keep it in their pants? "Ouch," I say.

"Eighteen years of marriage. We literally had it all. I let my ego destroy it."

The psychologist in me appreciates his candor. "You're amazingly self-aware."

"After three marriages? You'd hope so." He waves it off. "I was a mess after Melissa—first wife—left me. We were living in LA. She kept the house. I moved a few blocks away to be close to the boys. We made it work."

"How many sons do you have?"

"Three. And a daughter with Kelly. You've probably seen her. My oldest is thirty. He's married now. No kids. The other two are twenty-eight and twenty-five. They're still single and smart enough to take a lesson from their dad who apparently sucks at marriage."

I shake my head. "Practice makes perfect?"

"Ha! I'm a shitty husband, but all three of my exes tell people I'm a good father. I think that's generous."

"In my opinion, it's the greatest compliment there is. I've seen many couples use their kids as pawns. Or worse, weapons."

"In Hollywood, marriages come and go. The kids always suffer. Didn't want that. That's why I moved here. The boys were adults and Kelly, she's a Jersey girl and wanted to move back to be close to her family." He jerks a thumb over his shoulder. "She's five minutes from here. What could I do? Let my baby grow up without a dad? I relocated. Work remote when I can, fly when necessary."

"It had to be easier in LA."

"My daughter is here. It's a no-brainer."

I wish I had a no-brainer. Everything feels … heavy. An elephant sitting on my chest, the pressure paralyzing.

He rolls one hand. "Come on. Tell me."

"What?"

"You're stewing on something. Tell Daddy what it is."

Daddy? I laugh again. "Now, that's just weird."

"I'm a weird guy."

"Hadn't noticed."

This time, it's his turn to laugh, and it fills me with … something. Who was the last person, a nonbusiness acquaintance, I sat around talking and laughing with?

Not my husband. Lately, it's been all about work stress. Sure, there's been conversation, but not a lot of fun.

That stings.

No wonder he went looking elsewhere. Not that I'm blaming myself. There've been cracks, tiny fissures, that we didn't address. Talking gave them oxygen, and we were too busy and too short on energy for emotional upheavals.

It was simply easier, for me anyway, to ignore our marital rut.

The thing about fissures?

They expand, leaving giant canyons.

I peer back at Danny whose eyes are hidden behind sunglasses. I wouldn't call him a friend—so to speak. Until now, he's been our neighbor. An acquaintance.

My other so-called friends revolve around either my career or Ryan's. Some of these people, we've known for years. Double digit years where they've talked of fights with loved ones, financial difficulties, estranged children.

I *know* them. At least I think I do. Whether or not they've noticed, that honor only goes one way.

I haven't allowed them in.

With me, it's surface stuff. Frustrations with the network, aging, my sagging neck on camera and the pros and cons of plastic surgery. All of which could be found on the Internet.

"I don't have confidants," I blurt.

"Of course you don't."

My head snaps back, the shock halting me. I may have even gasped. How the hell does he know if I have friends or not? "Excuse me?"

"Honey, in this business, you gotta watch everybody. What's their angle? What do they want? Are they users?" He waves it off. "Seen it a hundred times. People breaking the trust."

He gets it. My goofy neighbor. Go figure. I pick up my margarita, take a healthy slug before setting it back down.

A wave crashes, its white, foamy wonder rolling in. It retreats and I wait for the next, all of it a stalling tactic. My version of ignoring the obvious mess my life has become.

No friends, crummy ratings and a two-timing husband.

Yay.

Me.

I face Danny again. "Do you have go-to people?"

"Outside of my exes, I have a few."

A few. "That's it?"

He slides his glasses down his nose, peering at me over them as if he's about to make an important point that requires my seeing his eyes.

"That's it," he says. "They've proven themselves to me. Everyone else has broken the trust. Talked to a reporter, leaked something. You know the drill. Once that happens, they're out."

He understands. Relief rolls over me like one of the crashing waves. I've spent the better part of my life closing myself off. Making sure I didn't overshare. As a teenager, it left me lonely. Downright bereft. As an adult, even more so. My problems got bigger, my loneliness and isolation more acute.

Until Ryan.

Who has now betrayed me. A dull ache settles in my chest. Tears fill my eyes. I try to blink them away because heaven forbid my neighbor should see me crying. It would mortify my mother.

The tears overwhelm and drip free. I reach up, swipe at them under my sunglasses and shoot a sidelong glance at Danny who's doing his best to study a seagull in flight.

I take another slug of the margarita. The sun has melted most of the ice and the almost-lukewarm liquid hits my tongue, the lime flavor somehow sharper.

I set the tumbler down and clear my throat. Danny peers back at me. "You okay?"

"Good." I lie. "I don't have friends. I think I used to, but I got so paranoid that I let them go."

"Then," he says, "you must be one hell of a lonely woman."

I want to argue. I open my mouth and something catches in my throat again. This guy, my neighbor who doesn't let people park in front of his house, understands me.

"Listen, Dr. Becca." He waggles a hand at me. "I feel like you have something on your mind. Something you need to talk about. Probably the noticeably absent Ryan."

I don't respond. Just sit there frozen.

"So," he continues, "let's play a game. I'll give you information only shared with two people. Something I've guarded with every fiber of my being. I'll let you into my circle of trust if you let me into yours. Deal?"

It's a lifeline. Danny is giving me an opportunity to open up. In a safe space.

I nod.

"My youngest son," he says, not skipping a beat. "Great kid. Funny. Generous. Well-liked. Every parent's dream. Except, he's a raging drug addict. Been in rehab three times. Just got out of the last one. So far so good, but heroin is his weakness, and he lives in Hollywood. I'm not confident."

Here I am worried about ratings and my cheating husband when my neighbor's child has life-threatening issues.

I shake my head. Maybe at myself, maybe at Danny's plight. I'm not sure. All I know is something has to change. "I'm so sorry, Danny."

"Thank you. Me too. Now, time for you to live up to your end."

I consider this for a few seconds. I've made a deal, and I don't renege on deals.

Panic slithers inside me. A warning, perhaps. The snake about to bite. Admitting my personal business? Putting it out there and possibly having him share it?

Worse than a snakebite.

But, oh, he's a smart man. He's told me something equally personal. Even damaging. Hollywood gossips would love to grab hold of it. After all, he's a big shot producer with a few Oscars to his credit.

I take my glasses off, fold them and set them in the side pocket of my chair before meeting his eye again. "Ryan is cheating on me."

The words slip from my mouth. Just sort of flop free. No stuttering or the usual stab to my chest when I think about it.

Just … bam. Done. Said it. I might even feel a bit of relief. Dr. Becca would say that's good. That by confiding in someone, I've released it and am no longer carrying the secret.

Secrets are weighty.

"Ach!" he says. "Now I'm the one who's sorry."

"Thanks, but you're not the one who should be apologizing. Plus," I roll my hand, "it's not a good look for a woman who's built a career on saving marriages. My EP wants to do a show on it. Her argument is that we'd control the narrative by making a statement before the press or social media folks pile on."

"It'd be a sweeper."

I poke a finger at him. "If I never hear the term sweeper again, it'll be too soon. I got socked in the face during a taping the other day and all anyone could say was it'll be a *sweeper*."

He sits forward, whips his glasses off and studies my face. "Holy hell. Are you okay?"

I turn my head and point to the bruise I covered with makeup. "He wasn't aiming for me. I got too close."

"First rule, Bubby, never get between two pissed-off men."

"You sound like Ryan. Two great armchair quarterbacks."

The couple who walked by is back, both of them eyeing us. Instinctively, I slide my glasses on and ignore them, completely shifting in my chair so my back is to them. Everything about my body language is a giant stop sign.

"Look," Danny says, his gaze on the couple, "men can be assholes. In a variety of ways. I'm sorry you got sucker punched."

"The network suits aren't sorry. They love it. It's what I've been fighting against for months."

"Not your style."

The statement is so matter-of-fact, I nearly weep. Finally, someone recognizes it.

Not even Ryan said that. All Ry had to say was that maybe it wouldn't be the worst thing.

"You might get a short-term ratings spike," Danny says, "but you'd abandon your audience. The tried and true. Once they're gone, you have to find new viewers. Vicious cycle."

"Exactly. No one seems to care that my middle-aged, upper

income viewers aren't interested in trash TV. It's not that hard, right? I mean, you're not even my producer—you don't even do television—and you understand."

He shrugs. "It's easier to see when you're outside. They're gone, by the way. The couple." He points down the beach. "What about Ryan? What are you doing about that situation?"

"No idea."

I roll through the same synopsis I gave Jenny. It's easier this time. As if the earlier rehearsal flushed some of the emotional sewage.

Danny stands, picks up his chair to face me and then sits down again. For a guy in his fifties, he's in good shape. Not super muscled, but his lean body is toned and, like his face, already showing the kiss of sun. In a few weeks, he'll have the bronzed look of die-hard beachgoers.

"Make sure you wear sunscreen," I tell him.

He offers a thumbs-up and runs his foot through a pile of sand. "Do you want to save the marriage?"

Again, I don't know. I'm too … hurt. Too angry and humiliated to make logical choices. All the good years are collapsing under the surge of one error.

"I'm still absorbing." I plaster on a faux smile. "When I'm done hating him, maybe I'll love him. In the meantime, I have to decide if I'm going to allow my network to prostitute my personal issues."

"Take the personal out of it. Look at it like any other show. How do you decide what makes the cut?"

"We discuss if there's an angle that hasn't been done before. And could it help people? I'm not interested in a circus. My producers sometimes hate me for taking the high, moral ground."

"Lean into that. Outing your husband will give you a ratings boost. Will it help people?"

I close my eyes, tip my chin to the warm sun and picture

myself on set, standing in front of the new furniture I had no say in, announcing my husband's infidelity.

Having carefully chosen the parts of my life I allow the world to see, I despise this idea.

"Oh, Bubby," he says, "your reaction says it all. You're screwed."

I lean forward and bang my fist—thump, thump, thump—against my chest. "It's nauseating. I mean, who willingly goes on television and admits they're a fraud?"

"Who said you're a fraud?"

"Um, news flash, I've built a career on fixing marriages and my husband has a side piece. I'd say I'm a fraud."

He flashes a smile, all white teeth against dark skin. He's the quintessential rich guy I normally don't like. But there's something down-to-earth about him too.

Maybe Danny is my friend.

He picks up his margarita, then shoves it in the sand. Opening the top of the table, he retrieves ice for both of us and then tops off our glasses.

After storing the pitcher, he comes back to me. "*I'd* say you're a heartbroken spouse. Big difference. You think because you specialize in marriages that you should have known? Are you a mind reader? Take it from a cheater. We buy into our own bullshit. Convince ourselves if we don't think we're doing anything wrong, our wives don't either. Plus, you're a busy woman."

"So it's my fault?"

"Hell no. Being busy gave him an opportunity to hide it. *He* did this, Becca. Not you."

I think back on the last few months. The tension with the suits. The stress of increasingly difficult shows as we tried to "spice it up."

Danny isn't wrong. I've been busy. And distracted.

"That's the angle," I say. "I'm a busy, working wife, who

thought everything was okay, when it wasn't. That this could happen to anyone."

I could almost buy that. Almost. I've known for a while, maybe even years, my marriage had lost its spark. That we'd become better friends than lovers. Not that I, Dr. Becca, could admit it. I liked the image the world saw.

Even if I knew it wasn't real.

"Bingo," he says. "I'd lay odds a lot of smart, successful women have dealt with it. They were just too scared to tell anyone. Can you embrace it and ride the hell known as social media?"

"I stay off social media."

"Brilliant move. Is this powwow helping you at all?"

"Actually, yes. It's zooming in on the important things. The rest is mental bedlam."

He holds up a finger. "Have you done the topic before?" A second finger. "Will it help people?" A third finger. "Are you ready for it?"

The answer to all three questions: No, yes and no.

CHAPTER 9

I spend the rest of the day alone, at first clearing emails—margaritas and all—and then curled up in various chairs with a book. I've silenced my phone, checking it every hour in case work needs me or Ryan has decided to, once again, ignore my request to be alone. So far, he's complied.

As for work, nothing can happen in sixty minutes that can't be dealt with on the hour. It's a silly argument, but one that allows me to put the phone down. To ignore the device of doom that I'm rarely two feet away from.

I need this. The isolation. The quiet.

At 7:00, I grab a slice of the leftover pizza my mother ordered. I pop it in the oven while checking my phone..

A call and text from Ryan. I click on the voicemail message, wanting to hear his voice, the familiarity and comfort of it, yet bracing myself for the heartbreak that's shattered our relationship. I can't quite rationalize all the sides of my emotions.

All I know is it stinks.

"Becca." His voice carries the rough edge I recognize as exhaustion. "Please. Talk to me. That's all I ask. I'll give you your space, but please, call me back."

What my husband doesn't realize is that giving someone space means not calling and texting.

I shoot him a text, telling him I'll be home on Sunday and we'll talk then. Period. End of it.

A knock sounds on the front door just as the oven timer beeps. I check the app on my phone and see my mother standing at the door, waving at the camera.

She knows me too well.

"Come in," I say into the phone and hit the button to unlock the door.

Seconds later, she's walking into the kitchen wearing a black sheath with a fuchsia wrap and heels. "Hi, dear."

"Hi, Mom." I open the oven and slide the slice out. "I'm eating the rest of your pizza. Have you eaten?"

"Oh, yes. Your father and I went to the club."

The beach club they're members of is one of the better ones, with sleeper cabanas bigger than some of the area's cottages. There are two restaurants that my folks seem to like equally. One is fine dining and the other beachy casual. Based on my mother's attire, they went fine dining, the two of them getting all dolled up. Not so much for themselves, but for their acquaintances at the club who will see the happy couple.

Happy, happy, happy.

Smoke and mirrors. All of it.

"I should have asked if you wanted anything," she says.

"Nah." I smile and hold up the slice. "I'm kinda enjoying this."

Mom slides onto one of the barstools and motions to the door. "Your father says hello. He was going to come, but he got a call from the hospital and dropped me off."

"I'll take you home when you're ready."

"Thank you. How was your day?"

"It was good. I sat on the beach with Danny."

"Neighbor Danny? The producer? He's a little odd, no?"

"He is. But it's refreshing. He's very self-aware."

Mom smiles. "Whatever *that* means."

She wouldn't understand. My mother might be the least self-aware person I know. Or maybe she simply chooses not to go there.

"It means he's honest with himself and because of that, I find him easy to talk to."

"Lord, Becca, please don't tell me you're *attracted* to him."

Mom. All high-brow haughtiness. I hold back the eye roll I'm dying to level on her. "Uh, no. But I enjoy talking with him. He helped me figure some things out."

Once again, I brace myself. It's not so much admitting to my ultra-private mother that I'm considering splashing my husband's infidelity across the television screen. It's anticipating her blowing right on by my emotional upheaval and warning me not to do it. To keep up the facade, no matter what.

I set the pizza down, slide the plate to the side and lean in on my elbows. Now or never. "Ryan is cheating on me."

Her lipsticked lips—sheer pink—form a perfect oval while she takes in the words. "The *bastard*," she spits.

That about sums it up. "I found out the other night. Thus, the impromptu trip down here. I needed time alone."

"The *bastard*. You've given him *everything*. Everything! And he does this? Did he not even *think* about what this would mean for your career?"

Mom is no slouch when it comes to drama. Her random emphasis on certain words is her signature.

"I'm guessing he wasn't thinking about my career."

"Well, you're probably right." She holds both hands up. "Let's face it. He's a fool. You'll get over it."

"I'll get *over* it?"

Now I'm doing it. The emphasizing thing.

"Of course," she chirps. "You don't throw twenty-four years of marriage away over some bimbo. Please. With a man who looks like Ryan, women are a tuna sandwich. He can find them anywhere."

Tuna. *Sandwich?* "Mom! What a thing to say."

A gulf of silence lands between us and I study her like I would a patient I'm considering a forty-eight-hour hold for.

By now, my mother's casual attitude toward a marital crisis shouldn't be a shock. Yet, here I am, gobsmacked and wondering what planet we're living on.

Wondering if my mother has experience in this area that might help me. "Mom." I pause. Is it fair to put her on the spot? She's my mother. He's my father. If the answer isn't what I hope, will it change my love for him?

I can't imagine that. Not loving my Dad. Literally the first man I ever loved. Still, over the years, I've seen—and mostly ignored—the warning signs of a marriage in trouble. Dad working seventy hours a week, Mom disappearing at times when he *was* home.

"What?" Mom asks.

Their marriage is dysfunction on steroids. Major issues. But they've stayed together all these years. They care enough to work through the rough patches.

"Has Dad cheated on you?"

Barely missing a beat, she scoffs. "As if I would know? He's gone so much, I'd hardly be able to tell."

Not exactly the emphatic no I'd hoped for. She didn't even take a second to think on it.

"Does it shock you that I asked?"

"Honestly, Becca, what does it matter? Our marriage is far from perfect, you of all people know it. But I've loved him forever. Sometimes it seems longer than forever. Even if he had an affair, multiple affairs, where am I going? I could never leave him."

Yes, you can.

I don't dare say it. I know better. When I was a kid, I walked in on them having a brutal, terrifying argument. I haven't thought about that day in a long time. Years. Which is interesting since it shaped so much of my thinking about my parents.

It was May—just like now. Coincidence? Maybe. Or maybe I'm simply someone who learns life-altering lessons in the spring. Whatever it is, the sun had been shining that day too. The sky bluer than I could describe. I was ten, anticipating my birthday just a few weeks away. That day, though, was about my parents and their wedding anniversary and going big with a party in the backyard of our new house. We'd moved into the house, a giant one with a bowling alley in the basement, six months earlier and Mom wanted to show it off. Particularly the yard with the lap pool for Dad and then a bigger one alongside with a rock waterfall and a slide.

Everything about the day had to be exceptional. After all, it was in honor of the day my mom married her prince. She'd tell me that all the time. About when she looked at my father all she saw was perfection. Her husband. The handsome doctor.

I'd come home from playing at the neighbor's house. Before I could make it inside, my father's voice boomed through the closed patio door.

Until that day, I'd never heard my dad yell.

Why this is bumping up against me now is not a mystery. That day was the one that changed everything for me. Literally spun me on my axis, crumbling the foundation I'd been living on. *That day* taught me that perfection, as much as my mother yearned for it, was a mirage.

It simply didn't exist.

The memories rush back at me. My sliding open the door, hearing my mother and father screaming at each other in the oversized butler pantry.

"Oh, Donald. Just shut the fuck up and go back to your calls. That's all you ever want anyway."

"Those calls gave you this house, you ungrateful bitch."

The swearing alone rocked me. At that point, I'd never experienced those words coming from my parents. Sure, I'd practiced them, alone in my room, whispering them, thinking I was cool.

But my parents? Speaking to each other that way? No. Not okay.

All these years later, I peer at my mother across the island. "Do you remember the day I walked in on you and Dad fighting?"

"The anniversary party?"

She remembers. "Yes."

"How could I forget? That was horrendous. It took me months to get over you witnessing that."

Months. Wow. "You told me marriage is hard and that plenty of couples argue, which, of course, is true."

"It is."

"And then you told me not to tell anyone what I saw. That you wouldn't want it to get out."

My mind reels as I replay my mother's words from that day. *"Sometimes marriage is hard. It's a normal thing. Plenty of couples argue."*

My first introduction to how dysfunctional a relationship could be.

I keep still, giving her no body language. Not a shake of my head or a frown. Nothing.

Dr. Becca in full talk show host mode. "Mom, I need to ask you something. I'm desperate and need help. I honestly don't know what to do."

"Honey," she says, her blue eyes softening, "you're my rock. You can ask me anything."

I nod, choke back a flood of emotion because I have to go there. I have to ask her how she's managed to stay married all these years, when I know—I *know*—what goes on between them.

"Are you satisfied with your marriage? With loving him when there's drama that sends you here to escape?"

Again, she doesn't flinch. "I'm satisfied when he acts like the man I love."

"And when he doesn't?"

She lifts one shoulder. "I've learned to deal with it."

I don't want to *deal* with it. Ryan and I have been in a rut. Now, with this affair? I don't know what to think.

Maybe his own boredom drew him to Laurel Shelton. I don't know and I refuse to make excuses. To give him a pass for breaking our marriage vows and humiliating me.

"Mom, I'm not sure I can get past this."

"Becca, you *can't* be considering divorce."

"Why?" I hold up a hand. "And don't tell me it'll be a scandal. I'm well aware. I'm tired of pretending I have a glorious life. Being afraid that people will see that my marriage isn't perfect. The pressure is relentless. "

"And what? You'll let everyone know your business? Let the gossips skewer you? All because Ryan slipped?"

Slipped. She can't be serious. Then again, this is my mother. "This wasn't an oops!"

Whoa. Too loud. My mother's head jerks back. I shut my mouth, clearing my throat for a second, corralling my temper. "I'm sorry I yelled. This wasn't a one-night stand. Wasn't him getting drunk with his buddies and losing his sense. He gave her a credit card. That's how I found out."

"I see," Mom says. "Is he in love with her?"

There's that question. The one nagging at me. Silently lurking in the back of my mind. This, in fact, might be the reason I'm refusing to speak to him. Maybe I don't want to know my husband has fallen in love with a younger, more beautiful version of me.

"I have no idea," I say. "We haven't gotten that far. He's been calling and texting. Apologizing."

"Talk to him. See what you're dealing with. Then you make a plan. Please, don't be rash."

I cock my head. "When have you ever known me to be rash?"

"This is an extreme situation. You have your future to think about."

I'm too worried about the present to worry about that. "You may have missed it, but I'm the breadwinner. I'd say it's Ryan who should be worried about *his* future."

CHAPTER 10

On Sunday evening, I walk into our apartment, dropping my keys in the bowl on the entry table. The familiar clink of metal against glass suddenly slaps against a nerve. Odd that. I've heard that sound countless times, but now? It's all different. Everything. What I know, what I thought I knew. My habits are attached to a life that's a sham.

"Hello?" I call.

Ryan's car is parked in the underground garage, but that doesn't mean he's home. He could have taken a car service.

Perhaps to his girlfriend. Maybe out for dinner. Maybe making love in her Tenafly home that I now wonder if I helped pay for.

Smoke and mirrors.

I shake it off, refusing to be leveled by treacherous thoughts. "Hi."

I peer up. Ryan is at the top of the stairs, his head poking over the railing. "Hi."

"I was about to start dinner. Skirt steak. You hungry?"

After a morning run, I'd whipped up an omelet at eleven and then sat on the beach alone until mid-afternoon, killing time, putting off my return to the city. After that it was a rush of cleaning up, showering, throwing on running shorts and a long-sleeved T and flip-flops before heading back. I'd forgotten a snack for the drive and hadn't bothered to stop, so, yes, I was hungry.

Starved.

"I am," I say, ascending the stairs. "We need to talk."

"I know."

Ryan remains at the top of the stairs, waiting for me. When I reach the landing, he makes a move toward me. My body stiffens, ready to retreat. I can't help it, I back up.

I'm simply not ready for him to touch me. I've spent an entire weekend imagining his hands all over Laurel Shelton. How does he greet her? Does he hug her? Press his body into her? Kiss her? Slide his tongue into her mouth playfully as he does with me?

"I can't," I say.

For a few seconds, he stares at me, his eyes searching mine. What he's looking for or expects, I don't know. If it's forgiveness, he'll be waiting awhile.

He turns, moves back to the island where he has ingredients scattered. I settle onto my usual barstool, a silent heaviness pressing me down.

Nothing feels right anymore.

Ryan returns to his food prep, pulling ingredients from the fridge and doing his best to sell the idea that he hasn't blown up our lives.

It all seems so normal. So ... us. My chest locks up, the damned punch that comes with knowing what I know.

He glances at me, then turns, abandoning his task and leaning against the counter. "I'm sorry."

"I'm sure you are."

"Becca, she's —"

I raise my hand. Whatever he's about to say will wait. I need to set boundaries. Being a therapist, I've learned that certain spouses need all the details. Times, places, how long. For others, less is more. They simply can't emotionally tolerate too much information. I'm in the latter group. "I don't need details. Just tell me if it's serious."

His shoulders droop and he cocks his head, looks at me with his blue eyes that I always thought gave so much away. Guess I was wrong.

"No," he says. "She's—"

"She has a credit card we're apparently paying for. You have a key to her house."

For a few seconds, he doesn't answer. I've got him there. He knows it.

"It was a mistake," he says. "I was playing big shot."

Ryan always did like the good life. And people seeing it.

He and my mother. They're a pair. I just never realized it until this very second.

"Becca, it's over. I swear to you. I ended it the other night."

Good to know. "And how long have you been seeing her?"

He winces, and my stomach shrivels. Damn it. Broke my own edict of not wanting details. I close my eyes, readying myself for the blow that comes with being a fool.

"It's been on and off."

Ohmygod. Total nonanswer that doesn't bode well for Becca-the-fool. I force my shoulders back, sit a little taller and will my brain to stop. To simply slow down. One question at a time. That's all I have to focus on. "How long?"

"Six months. Maybe seven."

At least it hadn't been years. That, I couldn't have handled. At all. I set my hands on the marble, let my skin absorb the cool surface for a few long seconds. Anything to buy time and get my thoughts in line.

"Okay," I say.

"Okay? That's it?"

"Not by a long shot. Your inability to keep your pants on has betrayed me *and* our marriage. It's put my career at risk. I don't think I need to remind you that if my career goes, so does our lifestyle." I wave my arms, gesturing to the room. "Our twelve-million-dollar home."

His eyes deaden. Just … bam. Ryan has never liked being threatened. Who does? Maybe he should have thought about that before he had an affair.

"No one needs to know," he says. "We'll work it out."

Will we? I'm not so confident. "If you were unsatisfied in our marriage, you should have respected me, *loved* me, enough to discuss it. Ry, you know what I do for a living. How could you risk it? How do you know your girlfriend won't go to the press?"

"She won't."

"Well, forgive me for questioning your judgment right now. Clearly, you haven't been discreet enough. What with the credit card statement mix-up. We have to get ahead of this."

"What are you talking about?"

"I talked to Jenny the other day."

His eyes bulge. "You told *Jenny*? Have you lost your mind?"

I point at him. "Watch it. You're in no position to question me. Yes, shockingly enough, I told my executive producer. The one who, along with two hundred staff members, will lose her job when my career goes bust because I'm a *fraudster*, claiming to be a marriage expert while my husband is cheating on me."

At this he scoffs. "A tad dramatic, no?"

Oh, that's brilliant. I drop my hands to my lap, curl my fingers into fists and let the rage boil inside me while I ponder his spectacular selfishness. I uncurl my fingers, flexing them in and out. In and out.

"Ryan," I say, keeping my voice level while my brain goes haywire again. "Are you ready for the storm this could create if we try to hide it? I'm not. I've spent four days imagining all the ways you've made love to this woman. The things you've said and shared and *experienced* with her. You selfish prick!"

Whoa. Where did that come from? Dr. Becca would tsk-tsk me. *Fuck off, Dr. Becca.*

Ryan puts his hands up. "Take it easy. Calling me names won't help."

On that, he's right. I'm not about to apologize though.

He lowers his hands. "Tell me what you want."

What I want is to turn the clock back. Figure out where we went off the rails.

At a complete loss, I shake my head. "I don't know. I'm so pissed at you I can't think straight."

"Then what? What do you need from me?"

"We're doing a show on our marriage."

It flies from my mouth. Part of me wonders if I'm taking enjoyment from it. His punishment perhaps?

I'd hate to believe I'm capable of such pettiness. But I *am* a woman scorned.

He gawks at me. I can't blame him. I'm the one who's insisted on keeping our personal life private all these years.

"Spin control," I say. "Doing a show lets me admit to the world that I'm human. That Dr. Becca has problems too."

"Do you realize how humiliating that will be?"

"No more than me standing in your girlfriend's home. Or being outed by the press or on social media."

Touché. Got him on that one.

With no defense available, he rolls his eyes. "So this is how it'll be? You giving me daily whippings until you're over it?"

Now it's my turn to gawk. "Get this straight, Ryan. I will never be over it. *Ever.* But I'm not ready to throw twenty-four years of marriage away. If you want to stay together, it'll be on my terms. If that's not good enough, I'll make a statement that we're divorcing and we'll hash out a settlement."

His skin turns a greenish hue, his mouth hanging open. If he vomits on our pristine counter, I'm not cleaning it up. I'm already knee-deep in his mess.

Although, I honestly can't blame him. Part of me is feeling the same shock. I'm not sure I even want a divorce and I've just used it as a weapon.

It's the stark reminder that without me, the good life goes away. Sure, he earns decent money and he'll get a nice settlement, but I'll fight him over spousal support until we're both bloody. I'll quit my job before I give him one red cent more to spend on his girlfriend.

He meets my gaze, clearly measuring my resolve. "You can't be serious."

"As serious as a heart attack." Having had enough of him, of this conversation, I push off the stool. "I'm not feeling much like skirt steak. I think I'll go out for something while you consider your options. You've got until I leave for work tomorrow to decide. You can sleep in the guest room tonight."

WHILE I'M in makeup and hair getting transformed for our morning taping, Jenny pokes her head in.

"Morning," she says. "Good weekend?"

Attempting not to move my head while Steph, our makeup artist extraordinaire does her magic, I meet Jenny's eye in the mirror. After what I admitted to her at the shore, we both know there's no chance I had an enjoyable weekend.

The question, I surmise, is habit. Our usual routine of small talk before getting down to business.

"Good enough," I say. "Can you talk a second?"

"Sure."

Jenny comes toward me and leans against the vanity strewn with Steph's tools.

I meet Steph's eye in the mirror. "Would you give us the room? I promise we'll be quick."

She sets down her bronzing brush and jabs a finger at me. "*Don't* touch your face."

Tough crowd I work with. "Yes, ma'am."

While she exits, I simply stare at my executive producer, knowing full well that after this conversation my marriage will no longer be private. It'll be fodder. A commodity to be manipulated by the network.

Jenny waits for the door to close, then faces me. "You okay?"

"Yes. I wanted to let you know I thought about our discussion on my … situation. I agree. It might be smart to do the show."

Her features remain neutral, the words somehow suspended between us.

Did she hear me? Is her mind wandering?

I wave one hand. "Jen? Hello?"

She shakes it off, lets out a hard breath. "Sorry. I'm—are we talking about the same thing? About you going public about Ryan's affair?"

I wince. Lord, even the words are painful.

"Sorry to be blunt," she says. "Making sure I understand."

I believe her. Knowing how intensely private I am, this conversation is probably no easier for her than me. She'll be the one navigating unknown terrain. Figuring out a way for me, not to mention my family, to salvage our dignity.

Throughout my ratings battle, Jenny has been my sounding board and a significant support. Without her, I'd be a wreck.

"I'm tired, Jenny. Mentally worn out. The idea of carrying on like nothing has gone wrong feels like an elephant on my chest. I'm counseling others on how to save their marriages when mine is a mess. If Ryan's mistress goes public, I'll be a laughingstock. I can't risk it. Not so much for me, but for our staff."

"I hate it for you, but I agree. I feel like coming clean is the …" She curls her lip. "Not right choice, but the appropriate one.

I suppose. Plus, if you release a statement, it's your news to share, not someone else's."

"Agreed. I'll talk to Don today and let him know what's going on and that we have a plan. I'm sure marketing will be involved."

"No doubt."

"Once I talk to the suits, we'll do a staff meeting. I'd like to do that before we leave tonight. I don't want anyone blindsided."

Jenny nods and slides her phone from her back pocket. "I'll call Arnelle. See if she can get us on Don's schedule before the afternoon taping. That one should go smoothly."

The second taping included a divorced couple in their thirties fighting over custody of their three small children. After studying the notes these last couple of weeks, I have what should be a solution. If they're willing to cooperate.

So far, neither of them has put their children first in this mess and that has to stop.

Motherhood may have eluded me, but these cases—the ones involving innocent kids—drive me to madness. How can people not realize the damage they're doing to their children when they're supposed to be the ultimate protectors?

A knock sounds and Steph pokes her head in. "Sorry, guys, but we're behind schedule."

"You're right," I say. "Come in."

Jenny boosts off the vanity table and waggles her phone at me. "I'll talk to Arnelle."

She's trying to play it cool, but there's a certain energy about her, that glow she gets when she knows she has a sweeper.

Whether that sweeper will destroy me is the only question.

AT 12:30 I walk into Don's office and find him in the wingback chair he prefers in the sitting area of his office. He claims he likes that chair because it faces the doorway and he can see who enters.

Across from Don on the sofa is Devin, my marketing arch-enemy. Why he's here, I have no clue since I requested this meeting and didn't include him. Patience already strained, I'll now have to find a nice, professional way to tell him to get out.

"Devin, hello."

"Hey, Becca. Hope you don't mind me sitting in."

Bless his cold heart, he's given me the perfect intro. "Actually," I say, "I have a private matter to discuss with Don. Would you please give us a few minutes?"

Don meets his eye and Devin lets out a soft huff. As if the little lady is being a nuisance. Well, his job exists due to the revenue this little lady's show brings in.

The mood I'm in? He can kiss my rear.

He gets to his feet, moving slower than a geriatric patient with a new hip before pausing to adjust his jacket sleeves. It takes every ounce of my self-control not to roll my eyes. This is what the VP of marketing has resorted to in order to control the situation.

I offer a pleasant smile and check my watch. "If you don't mind, I have a taping in twenty minutes."

At this Don laughs. It's one of the things I appreciate about him. He doesn't suffer fools.

Devin? Total fool.

Don jerks his chin toward the door. "I'll call you when we're through."

My enemy leaves, closing the door behind him just as I claim his seat. "Thank you for seeing me. I won't keep you."

"No problem at all," he says. "I always enjoy our meetings. What's up?"

He holds out a beautifully manicured hand, then lets it drop. That's the other thing about Don, his appearance screams big shot. At nearly fifty, his skin glows—probably some work being done there—and his weekly haircuts keep his more pepper than salt hair perfectly groomed. Throw in the three-thousand-dollar suits and Don is more camera-ready than me on my best day.

"I wanted to alert you to a situation. A personal one."

His eyebrows lift a smidge. "Is everything okay? You're not sick, are you?"

Physically? No. Emotionally? Different story. "No. I'm …" I pause. Smooth my hands over my skirt and think about how to say this. How to make it sound not as bad as it is. Not like it has the power to tank my show.

Finally, I give up. As my dad likes to say, no one should ever be afraid of the truth. He's right. I should have considered being authentic and open about my personal life earlier in my career. Not being so determined that the world see us as gloriously happy when we weren't. Yes, we've loved each other, but we're human. We fall into ruts. We disagree. We argue over money and family and everything else couples disagree on.

If this situation is enough to ruin me, I'll have to face it eventually. Might as well get it over with. I lift my chin, let out a soft breath. "Ryan is having an affair."

Don's head dips forward. He immediately catches the slip and recovers. "Becca, I'm so sorry."

"It's a shock, to be sure."

"Are you …"

The intended question hangs there, unspoken yet so full of power, my big shot network executive can't say it.

I'll help him. "Am I divorcing him? I don't know. I feel it would be wise for me to take control and make a statement."

"I agree."

"I've spoken to Jenny and, as much as I hate it, we're kicking around the idea of me doing a show on it. My situation, specifically."

Now his mouth flops open, which is saying something about my boss. "Wow," he says. "Forgive me, but I'm shocked."

"You're not the only one. But, if I continue on national television, counseling couples on their marriages when my own is in trouble, I'll look like a hypocrite. If I allow people to see that Ryan and I are doing the work, I'll appear more authentic."

Don narrows his eyes, a habit he's developed when pondering an idea. Finally, he nods. "I give you a ton of credit. I'm not sure I could do it."

Neither am I. But I've offered and now I must follow through. "Thank you."

The alarm on my watch chirps. Time to go. I stand and Don does the same.

"Taping in ten," I say. "I'll craft a statement and keep you updated on ideas for the segments on my marriage. If you could keep this between us until I have a statement ready, I'd appreciate it."

"Whatever you'd like." He holds an arm to the door, walking me out. "Becca, I really am sorry you're going through this."

His voice is low, with that soothing lilt I've heard only a few times when there's been some crisis in the world.

I nod, force a smile because my husband cheating on me should never—ever—rank up there with a world crisis..

Compared to that? This is a breeze.

No one is dead. No one is physically injured.

At least not yet.

CHAPTER 11

*B*efore I even reach the studio door, my phone rings.
Devin.

How lovely.

I continue down the hallway where laughter carries through the studio wall. Various pictures of me with celebrity guests line both sides of the corridor, my fourteen-year career on full display. Randy, an up-and-coming comedian, is warming up the audience by telling jokes. He's also giving instructions on when to applaud, when to ooh and ahh and advising them on what I deem inappropriate behavior. Whether or not marketing likes it, physical violence is now at the top of the list.

Speaking of ...

"Devin," I say into the phone. "I'm walking on set, can this wait?"

"Don called me about your show idea. This is great stuff. I'll get the team on it."

Dumbstruck, I halt. Had I not just requested that Don keep this between us? Had *he* not agreed?

I stand in front of the studio door, my gaze locked on a black smudge as anger prowls inside me.

"This is *great?*" I say, my sarcasm sharper than Lizzy Borden's ax.

"Your viewers will love it."

My life is falling apart, and he's celebrating? Should have expected it. All he sees are dollar signs.

"Devin, I don't have time for this."

"Becca, we need to move on this. Your ratings could use it."

Oh, that … *fucker*. Weaselly little man who has never, ever, managed a show, let alone hundreds of people. He has no idea what it feels like to sit in front of guests who abuse one another, including their children, and try to help them. Some of them I'd like to lock in a cell.

Now, weasel Devin thinks he's going to make a circus out of my public humiliation?

"I have a show to do. I'll set a meeting when we're ready."

"Becca—"

"No! This is my *marriage*! I'm about to open up my private life for public consumption. Marketing doesn't get to decide how I'll do it. I'll walk out of here before that ever happens."

And then I do something I'd never have dared before.

I hang up on him. A network VP.

No goodbye. No have a nice day. No cooperative, reasonable Becca.

I look up, see a bunch of staffers, a mix of producers, APs and interns, gathered at the end of the hallway, all of them obviously on their way to the studio. They must have heard the yelling and hung back, unsure how to handle Becca-gone-wild.

They're all wide-eyed and staring like I'm tripping on acid. I may very well be.

And, thanks to Devin and Don, my plan for telling the staff before I release a statement sent has just been blown to bits.

So much for controlling the narrative.

My phone rings again. Jenny's ringtone. Given the time, she's no doubt looking for me.

I tap the screen. "I'm in the hallway. Give me two minutes."

Then I hang up and face my staff, still huddled like a bunch of ducklings waiting for their mama.

"Well," I wave them forward. "Come on down. We have a show to do."

Show or not, I don't move. Three feet from me, they stop, their puzzled gazes shifting left and right and then finally at me.

"Obviously, you heard my conversation with Devin. For those of you who don't know him, he's the VP of marketing." I want to add he's the bane of my existence, but after my outburst, I'm trying to maintain some sort of professionalism. "We don't have time now, but I'll be calling a staff meeting this afternoon. I intended on letting you all know about this today before I made a statement. I've just found out my husband is having an affair."

A few of them let out loud breaths. One of the senior producers shushes them.

"It's all right," I say. "I had a similar reaction."

My phone rings. Jenny again.

I ignore her. Don't even bother taking my eyes from my team. The precious schedule will have to deal with unexpected situations. God knows I have.

"I'll give you more information later, but we'll be doing segments on my marriage. On Ryan and I working through our issues."

"Whoa," Niko, one of the newer hires says, earning a glaring look from those around him.

"What?" he says, then looks straight at me. "You're badass. Seriously brave."

A rush of something … pride maybe … fills me. Millennials. Sometimes they make me insane with their lack of filter. Today? I admire it. The boldness, the willingness to say whatever is on their minds.

The freedom.

I could learn a few things.

"Thank you," I tell him. "Now, let's have a good show."

AT SIX O'CLOCK, after the second—and completely nonviolent—taping, I'm still sitting at my desk, fiddling with the dreaded statement about my two-timing husband. I really need to get this thing released, but I'm stalling. Afraid to face the barrage of fraud accusations that will come.

My door is open and a few producers are down the hall, engaging in their usual one-upping over guests they've booked for future shows.

I may be the host, but the producers are the ones working the phones, talking to guests, doing whatever it takes to get them on the show. After listening to the heartbreaking and sometimes traumatizing stories, they have to convince these folks, many of them victims, that yes, they should share said victimization with the world.

Only to have the segment sometimes scrapped four days before taping.

You can't do this job for years without an emotional toll. It's drama, drama, drama all the time. A staffer once joked that we have enough cortisol in our office to flood the building.

To combat stress, producers resort to gallows humor. I'm convinced it's their own version of therapy.

"Eat your heart out," Heather says. "I've got a fifty-year-old, three-time divorcee with abandonment issues who does hard drugs and prowls clubs at night picking up twenty-year-olds. Oh, and she's screwing her son's college roommate."

"Ew!" someone—Jasmine maybe—hollers. "That's just gross."

"Oh, man," one of the guys says. "That was seriously my fantasy when I was at Berkley. My roommate's mom. Totally hot."

At this, I have to laugh. The differences between men and

women always amaze me. Heck, I've made a fortune on that amazement.

Jenny appears at my door in a T-shirt submerged in wrinkles. Her hair is tucked up with a pencil that's falling down on the job.

"Hi," she says. "How's the statement coming?"

I glance at my laptop screen and the dreaded statement that I've been tweaking. I wrote it, sent it upstairs and received a nearly unrecognizable draft back. It's a maddening process.

What the PR team doesn't realize is this is *my* personal life. I'll word my statement the way I want. Thus, they're not getting another crack at it.

"Eh," I say. "PR had some suggestions. Most of which I hate. Some, I'll keep."

"Does Ryan know it's going out?"

"He does."

She nods, but otherwise offers no reaction. "FYI, after the staff meeting, a few of the producers stopped to see me. They may pop in. To thank you."

I cock my head. "For?"

"They realize this is hard. Rather than going public, you could have quit, put us all out of work and gone to your beach house to hide. You've got the balls to admit what's going on and do a show on it. It's admirable."

Maybe to them. For me, it's hell on earth. "I appreciate that, but no need for anyone to thank me. Please let them know. This entire episode is awkward enough. Once I'm done tweaking, I'll have Kaitlyn send out the statement. I'll make no further comment and we'll get back to work."

"The press will be all over you."

"Over *us*."

I have a loyal, hardworking staff, but some of them are entry level and earning wages to match. All I can hope is that when the offers come in from bloggers, podcasters, and tabloids, they'll resist. I trust my staff, but money gives people loose lips.

"Taken care of," Jenny says. "I told everyone if they comment, I'll fire their asses."

Good old Jenny. Always managing to say what I won't.

"I heard you ripped Devin a new one. Serious case of hero worship going on there."

"Well, there shouldn't be. I reacted out of frustration. Not my finest moment."

She waves it off. "You have a lot going on."

A long silence envelops us. Apparently, Jenny came in here for a reason. And it wasn't to check on my personal well-being or the status of my statement.

I sit back and rest my hands in my lap. "You look like you have something on your mind."

She drops into the guest chair across from my desk. "I guess you know me."

After all these years? You betcha. I hold my hands out. "It's what I do."

I brace myself, settling my shoulders against the cushioned desk chair.

"Devin called me an hour ago."

If I hear that man's name again today, I may fly into a homicidal rage. "He *is* relentless, isn't he?"

"I guess, in all of his infinite free time, he's dreaming up ways to do the show on you and Ryan."

"Excellent. He's a producer now as well as a marketing whiz. Lucky us."

Although I doubt the whiz part.

Jenny curls her lip. "He asked my thoughts on how we should structure the show. I told him you and I hadn't discussed anything at length, but we'd floated the idea of a guest host working with you and Ryan."

Internally, I cringe. Another psychologist stepping on my stage chips at my already ravaged nerves.

I've given everything I have—energy, time, love—to this show. Turning my chair over to someone else?

Please.

"It's a lot to think about," I say. "I'd be handing off my show."

"Nuh-uh. Never. You'll still be in charge. We'll write a script, even more detailed than what we already use."

My team has been together long enough where we've forgone detailed scripts, opting instead for outlines they review with guests. No ambushes or confusion.

At least, that's how we've done it in the past. Recently? I'm not sure we're sticking to the plan.

In the case of my life being splayed across television screens, we'll lock in details. I'll know exactly what questions will be asked. Assuming we go with this idea of a guest host.

As much as I despise it, I don't see another way. I can't exactly offer counseling to myself or my cheating husband.

I shake my head, clearing my spiraling thoughts. "How did Devin feel about a guest host?"

"Hate to say it, but he loved it. He even has someone in mind."

I know who he wants. "Let me guess. Marley Ren?"

Marley. The network's newest star. Too opinionated and brash for me, but tearing it up on the morning show as a guest contributor twice per week. Then, of course, she appeared for big stories that required a psychotherapist's opinion.

She is me right before I got my big break. Only Marley's style is more combative, more challenging. I gently coax, Marley demands.

Frankly, I have trouble watching her. The damage she could inflict on an emotionally unstable guest might be beyond repair.

Given her ratings, the network doesn't seem concerned.

And now, the VP of marketing, after harping on me for

months about *my* plummeting numbers, wants to put her in my chair.

Talk about ambush television.

I sit forward, pulling myself closer to the desk and prop my elbows on it, leaning in. "What do you think?"

"About Marley?"

I lift one shoulder. "About anything."

"She's not my favorite choice."

"But?"

"She has a following. And the morning show viewers are your demographic."

"Some of them."

"True."

"I don't want that crowd. Not interested."

My stomach seizes, and I breathe through it, hoping the pain will subside. Breathe. That's all I need to do. Just breathe.

"We can control her," Jenny says.

"Marley? Good luck."

"So, tell Devin no on Marley?"

"That's a definite. No Marley."

Ever.

No sooner do I step into the condo does my phone ring. I check the screen. Don.

I set my purse on the bench and sit beside it, resting my head against the stair rail behind me. Across from me is the water-color Ryan had to have despite the half-million-dollar price tag.

These are the moments when I'm so tired of my phone and the never-ending emails and pressure that I want to stop. Just walk away from it all.

Maybe I should have stayed at the shore a few more days. The shore feels … easier.

Less complicated.

I tell myself I can go back to private practice part-time and then volunteer somewhere. Help the underprivileged who are lacking adequate mental health care. That would be a worthy existence.

We've been smart with money. Without a salary, we'd be comfortable for the rest of our lives.

We.

If I can't move beyond Ryan's affair, we may become an I. A

life without Ryan, I never expected or even considered. Two weeks ago, I'd have said it was unfathomable.

Now, all I want is peace. To slow my brain down and find a way to save two hundred jobs while not sacrificing myself to gossips.

The ringing phone echoes through the vaulted entry, and I pick up before the call goes to voicemail. "Hi, Don."

"Becca, hello. Sorry to bother you at home. I'll be quick."

Sorry not sorry. "I just walked in. What's up?"

I have no—zero—doubt why he's calling. The second I nixed Marley being the guest host on my show, Jenny relayed that message to Devin who immediately whined to Don.

The men in this industry? They stick together.

"Listen," he says, "I understand you're not comfortable with Marley Ren, but please, think it over. It could be great for your ratings."

Again with the ratings.

And, frankly, I'd like to bust his behind on not keeping his word by sharing the news of Ryan's affair.

I'm seeing a trend with the men in my life. Maybe it's me. Not that it's my fault, any of it, but maybe I've let them slide. Took things in stride too much. Tried to always be reasonable and not a "hormonal" woman. Because, yes, if a man in my position fights back, he's strong. Ambitious, even.

Me?

Hormonal bitch.

I draw a slow breath and exhale, refocusing myself. "Don, I've been thinking about Marley since Jenny left my office."

A total lie, but my boss doesn't need to know that. What *he* needs to know is that I'm still a team player who cares about saving my show.

"Good," he says, "I don't want us to be rash."

Ha. When has Becca Williams Matthews ever been rash? I *dream* of being rash.

"Of course not," I say, keeping my voice even. "My concerns about Marley are simply that she and I have different approaches. I'm about to put my life out there for viewers to pick apart. If I didn't have a show, I'd find a therapist to counsel us and handle it privately. Marley's style wouldn't be a fit for us. That's all."

"Understood."

"As for the ratings, I agree, it would be a boon. However, whatever bump we get will be short term. I've spent fourteen years building my audience."

"You're worried about the demographics."

"Damn right I am. My viewers will hate her."

"You don't know that."

"Actually, I do. I got a report when my ratings started slipping. Marketing did a focus group comprised of my viewers. Everyone said they didn't like overt conflict. They don't want the screaming and yelling Marley has built a platform on."

That group is my lifeline.

"We'll tell Marley to tone it down," Don offers.

My right temple throbs and I press my fingers against it in a futile attempt at relief.

These men. Just can't admit it's a bad idea. Fascinating. "And alienate her own viewers? I don't see it working."

The front door opens and Ryan steps in. He meets my gaze, the look hard and cold enough to freeze Hawaii.

He's pissed at me. Too bad. It'll get worse when our so-called joint statement about his infidelity is released. He should have thought about consequences before he dropped the Cucinelli pants he loves so much.

When he marches up the stairs behind me, I watch him go. His broad back, the wavy dark hair a week overdue for his thirty-day cut.

Gorgeous.

Somehow, I still love him. And I hate that about me.

Between my pounding head and the pain ripping through my torso, I might vomit.

"All right," Don says. "Can we at least consider it? Take a couple of days? Would you do that for me?"

If I say no, I'll be defying him. Possibly violating my contract —I'll have to refresh myself on the verbiage.

"Sure," I say, once again lying. "Let me think it over."

"Excellent. That's all I ask. Now, I'll let you go."

"Thank you. Have a good evening."

Disgusting, this civilized talking. I disconnect and jab—*jab, jab, jab*—my middle finger at the phone. Childish, yes, but whatever. It makes me feel better.

Still holding the phone, I linger on the bench. I'd like to stay here. All night. Not face my angry husband, not face the humiliation he's foisted on me.

Somehow, in barely a week, my life, the day-to-day of what I thought I had, is rubble.

Demolished by the wrecking ball known as infidelity.

Leaving my purse and tote, I haul myself up the stairs that might as well be Everest.

As usual for this time of day, I find Ryan in the kitchen. Making a sandwich at the island.

No dinner tonight. No cooking for the wife who's forcing him to admit to a nation that he stepped out on her.

"That was Don," I tell him, completely ignoring his passive-aggressive tactics. "The suits are pushing for Marley Ren to be the guest host."

Turkey in hand, he meets my gaze, his eyes blazing. "Marley Ren? Noooo. The woman is a vampire."

On this, at least, we agree. "I've already said no. Don asked me to think about it, and unless I come up with someone good we might be stuck with her. She has the ratings."

He sets the turkey onto his half-complete sandwich, wipes

his hands on a dishtowel and folds his arms. "This is our life and you're worried about ratings?"

I cock my head. Funny how before I knew about his little affair, he was all about keeping my ratings up. "My ratings gave us this life."

"Ratings didn't. You and I did. I'd like to think our marriage is more than material wealth."

Oh, please. Now he wants to spin it? Make it my fault?

Apparently, he's forgotten what I do for a living.

"Ry, be careful here. Your poor judgment created the problem. I'm trying to control the narrative."

He gawks at me. "Are you *listening* to yourself?"

His voice booms through the quiet house, lighting up my nerves and taking me back to my childhood and the yelling my parents tried to hide from me.

"You sound like Don and your buddy Devin," he rants. "I don't give a crap about the narrative, Becca. I care about saving our marriage."

That's rich. *Now* he wants to save our marriage? A vision of my gorgeous husband, his toned body naked and standing in front of an equally gorgeous and naked Laurel Shelton is seared into my brain. It's like an all-day X-rated film playing in my mind. All the ways he makes love to her. Touches her.

The places his mouth goes.

I dip my head, press my hands into my eyes so hard pain shoots through my orbital bone. Tears clog my throat and *no, no, no* . . . Not doing this.

If I let go, I may never get the pieces glued back together.

"Becca —"

His fingers gently wrap around my forearms. I drop my hands. He's reaching across the island and something snaps inside me.

I leap backward, yanking free of his grasp that just days ago I welcomed. "You don't get to touch me."

He sets his hands on the island, leaning into them. "Am I supposed to wait until you decide to let me out of purgatory?"

Probably.

Even to me, it sounds harsh. But he made a promise. He broke it. I shouldn't have to work overtime trying to keep it off social media and live with the threat of public embarrassment.

I straighten up, lift my chin and meet his eyes. "I guess you should have thought about that before you slept with Laurel Shelton."

And then I do the thing I've been wanting to do since I walked into the house. I walk away.

CHAPTER 13

After barely three hours of sleep, I pull myself from bed at my usual time, head to the bathroom to wash up and pull my hair into a ponytail.

In my closet, I lift running shorts from the drawer, a nice pair of pink tie-dye ones with a coordinating solid tank top Ry gave me for Christmas.

I love this outfit. It's fun and pretty. I stare at my perfect-fitting shorts for a few long seconds. Did he buy the same ensemble for Laurel?

I drop the shorts. *Damn him.* My favorite running shorts and I'll never be able to wear them again without that nasty thought worming in.

No running today.

Running is physically demanding, brutal even, and I'll need every bit of energy to get me through two tapings today. Plus, Devin will pounce on me with spreadsheets and PowerPoint presentations on the benefits of Marley Ren.

The idea of that woman on my stage terrifies me. Ry is right, she *is* a vampire. A total loose cannon. She can demoralize me with the killer combo of making me look like an idiot for not suspecting my husband was cheating *and* for being a professional fraud.

Classic one-two punch.

For the thousandth time, I roll through everything I know about infidelity. The increasing lack of physical contact, his constant phone use, not letting said phone from his sight, the work dinners that ran late.

Sure, our marriage had gotten fairly routine, but we still made love. Maybe not as much, but …

Wait. Could he have … Had he been leaving our bed and making love to her?

Or vice versa.

Were there days when he slept with both of us?

Hot, nasty bile pools in my throat.

I can't torture myself this way. I've counseled endless couples on this very topic. On not thinking too much. On controlling spiraling thoughts.

Leaving the shorts on the floor, I grab tights and a long-sleeved pullover to wear to the studio. I then hit the shower, text Bernie that I'll drive myself to the office today. I'm heading to the shore tonight, anyway.

Decided that at three a.m. when more visions of Ryan and Laurel testing sexual positions filled my mind.

This experience gives me another level of empathy for heartbroken spouses struggling to trust their partner. If nothing else, it'll make me a better therapist.

Hard work, this.

Bernie texts back thanking me for the day off and letting me know he'll be around if I need him. A good man, my driver.

I head back to the closet, pick out a dress and a pantsuit for the two tapings today, assemble my necessities for another weekend at the shore and head out before Ryan is even out of bed.

. . .

Between tapings, I sit at my desk reviewing emails. Given the drama of my life, this normally irritating task is oddly soothing. Click, read, respond, delete. Click, read, respond, delete. Over and over and over.

My customary salad sits beside my laptop and just as I shove a forkful into my mouth, someone knocks. Marley Ren stands in my doorway in a slaying red dress that hugs every inch of her curvy body. Her platinum blonde hair shines—probably recently touched-up—and her green eyes glow.

She is, as the song says, a girl on fire when I'm charred rubble.

I force the food down and take my time setting my fork in the bowl. "Marley, hi," I say, not bothering to hide my surprise.

Marley has never visited my office before. Ever.

"Hey there." She sashays in—does anyone say sashay anymore?—and sits in one of my guest chairs before being invited.

This is Marley.

Bullish.

Rude.

I ease back and cross one leg over the other. Casual, relaxed Dr. Becca. Nothing but a social call.

Even if I know better.

I hold my hand out. "What can I do for you?"

She glances at the Emmys perched on the shelf on the side wall. "Thought I'd come say hello."

Cocking my head, I smile, letting her know she's not fooling me. "That's very kind, but since I have a taping in thirty minutes, let's cut to it. You want a shot at my show."

She flashes her trademark smile that somehow doesn't offend me. "Actually," she says. "I want a shot at my *own* show. If I can get there using *your* show, I'm happy to do so."

I'll give her points for honesty. "At least I know where you stand."

"Look, Becca. We're different animals. You don't need to be threatened by me."

"I'm not." I gesture to the Emmys and various other industry awards. "You may have missed it, but I'm the gold standard."

"Oh, I'm aware. I've learned from you. Thank you for that. You've opened doors for people like me."

I certainly have.

"My show isn't a fit for you, Marley. I'm sorry."

"What if I promise not to get amped up?"

Interesting. "Why would you do that? Doing my show will alienate your audience. It'll be career suicide."

I could say the same about me if I let this woman on my set.

She leans in, drilling me with her vibrant green gaze. Off-putting, those eyes.

"What makes you think I can't make *both* our audiences happy?"

"Because, no offense, I won't let you bully me on my show. *I* won't let you raise your voice and poke your finger. That's what your audience loves about you."

"I'm willing to risk it."

I let out a soft chuckle. She's persistent. I don't mind. This business requires grit. In the daytime talk wars, it's essential. Particularly for women.

Suddenly, Marley doesn't seem all that different from me. Here we are, two women, battling for our seat at a table full of men.

Still, she's too abrasive. If I let her do this and she goes rogue, I'll be ruined.

"Come on, Becca. We can help each other. Give me a shot, and I promise, I'll play it straight. No antics. I'm smart enough to know when to tone it down. You have to believe that."

I do believe it. You don't succeed in this business without intelligence. And instincts.

The alarm on my phone chirps. Fifteen minutes until taping.

I tap the screen, silencing the phone. I don't have time to negotiate with her. But I sense something—integrity—in her words. In her promise.

Shoot. I don't want to like this woman.

Meeting her gaze, I nod. "Give me a day to consider it."

"Ha!" Her smile is wide enough to fit a 747. She pumps a fist.

I can't help the snort that escapes. Her enthusiasm is admirable. "It's not a yes, Marley. If, by some miracle, I decide to let you do this, at the very least there will be ground rules."

"I can do ground rules. No problem."

We'll see about that. "It'll be scripted. If you veer right when you're supposed to go left, I'll nix this entire thing. This is my life. You will not humiliate me."

She forces a huff that's disguised as a laugh. "Jesus," she says. "I should be insulted. Why would I humiliate the queen of daytime talk? Your viewers would put me in front of a firing squad."

Before I can speak, she holds up a hand.

"Please, let me prove to you I can be a team player. Between the two of us, with our combined viewership, it'll be a sweeper. The network mucks will love us. We'll own this place."

Jenny appears at my door and I glance up. When Marley peers back, Jenny's eyes do a cartoonish pop that makes me bite my bottom lip to stifle a laugh.

"Hey," Jenny says to Marley, then meets my gaze. "Steph is waiting on you."

I stand. "Right. Sorry. Marley, I need to get to makeup. Give me a day."

Then I stroll from my office, leaving behind the woman I may have been wrong about.

Could I possibly like Marley Ren? The vampire?

. . .

A LITTLE BEFORE NINE, I pull into the driveway of the shore house. I must truly be out of my mind because I'll have to drive right back to the city tomorrow morning and the Parkway traffic is horrific. Never mind trying to get through the Lincoln Tunnel at rush hour.

The other, more pleasant option is to drive thirty minutes to Atlantic Highlands and take the ferry. No. Not the ferry.

The other one. The boat Mom told me about in the fall that I nicknamed the Snooty. A retired Navy captain mortgaged his house, found an investor and went all in on a mega yacht for transporting VIPs to the city. The round-trip cost? Ridiculous. The limited capacity of twenty? Fantastic.

Throw in the idea that all passengers are prescreened, and no press allowed and it's calling my name.

Anyone paying that much for a boat ride is a celebrity or too much of a big shot to care about me.

Plus, just in case, I could test wearing a wig to see if anyone recognizes me. Maybe sit on the upper deck. The yacht would shave a good half hour to forty-five minutes from my commute.

As soon as I get inside, I'll check availability. Plan in place, I open my rear passenger door and grab my weekender. Danny's house is lit up, so I pause for a few seconds before marching to my front door, unlock it and toss the bag in the foyer. Locking up again, I walk next door, but before I can even press the bell, the door swings open.

Danny appears in his typical shorts and T-shirt, phone in hand. "Bubby, hi. Got an alert from the security system. You okay?"

"Can I come in?"

His eyebrows hitch, but he steps back, waving me through. "Sure."

He points beyond the great room to the kitchen with the giant marble island. "Grab a stool. I'll pour some wine."

"Thank you. I could use it. I'm sorry about barging in."

"No problem. I was watching a game. Always have time to listen."

Thankful for the invitation to spew, I nod. Danny might make movies, but he's a producer and deals with the same personalities I do.

He slides a glass of white wine in front of me that I'm guessing is a pinot grigio. He's good that way, remembering what his guests like.

I raise my glass to him. "Cheers."

"Bottoms up."

I take a long sip, savoring the lemony undertones. I can't drink too much. Taping tomorrow and the wine will dehydrate me and turn my skin leathery on camera.

Danny sets his glass down and props a hip against the island. "What happened?"

"I have to release a statement about Ryan's affair."

"Have to?"

"If I want to," I make air quotes, "control the narrative, I need to beat everyone else to it."

He pulls an eh face. "You don't want to?"

"Would you?"

"Point there."

I wave it off. "Then there's Marley Ren. She came to see me today."

"Should I know her?"

"She's a psychotherapist and a contributor on the network's morning show."

I give Danny the rundown on Marley, trying with every fiber to remain neutral in my summary.

"You're telling me," he says, "that she's the anti-Becca."

"Exactly. *She's* the one throwing gas on a fire I'm putting out."

"And she wants a crack at guest hosting your show and

fixing your marriage." He grabs his glass and holds it up. "Here's to ambition."

We clink and take another sip. "I'm not her biggest fan. Never have been."

"But?"

"She promised me she'd go easy and not bust out her flamethrower."

"Do you believe her?"

I shrug. "Maybe. There's something almost likable about her."

"Maybe the set of brass balls she's carrying?"

I laugh. He might be right. It takes a strong woman to deal with the boys' club. "She has gumption. Clearly, she knows I nixed her guest hosting."

"And what's the problem?"

"Her ratings are fantastic. She could bring viewers over."

"She has different demographics. You said it yourself."

He drums his fingers on the counter, twists his lips. I don't know him well, but I know enough about people to get that he's noodling something.

"Spit it out, Danny."

"I have a question. It's personal."

I've already told him my husband is cheating. How much worse could it be? "Go ahead. I need help and you know the business."

"Don't freak when I say this. I mean no harm. Does part of you want to put her in front of Ryan and let her have at him?"

Part? How about all? The thought annihilates me. Am I that vindictive?

I ponder this for a good thirty seconds. I can't deny it but won't admit it either. My emotions are too twisted, too coiled inside me. I'm using my show to save my marriage, and my marriage to save my show. It's … slippery. And, do I even want to save my marriage? Will I ever trust Ryan again?

"Could be," I tell him.

He tilts his head, gives me another eh face. "That's honest."

"What would *you* do about Marley?"

"I'm not risk-averse. If she gets me ratings, I'd give her a shot. Short leash. Really short."

"Good. I'm not crazy. Before today, I despised everything this woman stood for. She's the do-whatever-it-takes image I'm at war with. She'll go scorched earth and not worry about the human toll. I don't want that. Yet, I'm tempted to give her a shot."

Danny shrugs. "Her aggressiveness might help. How hard are you—and Ryan—willing to work? When my first wife caught me cheating, I had no interest in digging deep. I know that now. At the time? Clueless. This Marley sounds tough. She'll go there."

"I'm sure she will."

"But is she the lightning rod you need?"

My phone rings. Ryan's ringtone. I stand and dig into my pocket. "Speak of the devil." *That* saying never rang more true. "I need to tell my husband he's about to get run over by Marley."

"Bubby, good luck with that."

I tap the screen before the call goes to voicemail and tell my husband to hold on before peering across the island. "Thank you for the help."

He smiles. "Anytime."

I leave the wine and Danny, heading for the front door. "Hi," I say to Ryan, trying to keep my voice even. "What's up?"

"Hey," he says, his voice a little sad. "Nothing. Where are you?"

As if he had the right to ask? "At Danny's."

I'd like to say it was an off-the-cuff comment. I'd like to, but I knew he'd wonder why I'd be at Danny's at this hour.

Maybe it's good for him.

"Danny's? Why?"

"I needed advice, and he's a producer. Not that you have a right to ask me."

Silence fills the line. I keep walking, inhaling the salty, moist air that instantly knocks the edge off.

"You there?" I ask as I unlock my front door and step inside.

"Yeah. I was just … thinking … about you. About the mess I—"

"I can't do this with you. Not yet. You've apologized. A thousand times. I appreciate that, but you need to give me a minute."

"I get that."

"Then why won't you leave me alone?"

The words spill out, seemingly too fast for me to stop, yet I don't regret it.

I want Ryan and his affair to go away. Not necessarily to not have occurred because, as corny as it sounds, I believe everything happens for a reason. What this reason is, I'd love to know and may never, but I need to process it.

Figure out where it takes us. Where it takes *me*.

"I'm scared, Bec."

Whoa. I stop in the living room, my mind reeling, my body frozen. It's an odd mixture of energy and paralysis.

Ryan has never, not once, uttered those words. He's been my strength. My steady, logical supporter. When I can't see the finish line, he drags me across.

I love him for that. Always will.

Finally, I peer down at my feet, run my toe over a frayed edge on the area rug. "Ry, I'm scared too."

It's all I can say. I'd love to wax on about not knowing who he is, but he showed me this side of him twenty-six years ago on our college campus when I found him with another woman.

Foolish, foolish Becca.

Now, I'm caught in this trap. Loving him for what we've had together and hating him for shattering the trust we'd built.

I clear my throat, pick up my weekender and head down the

hallway to the bedroom. "Ry, we've—" No. I won't make the network suits the bad guys in this thing. "*I've* decided. Marley Ren will be the therapist working with us for the show."

"Marley. *Ren.*" He lets out a grunt. "You're punishing me."

Amazing how Danny and Ryan both came to that conclusion before I had. Maybe cheaters knew how to cut through the muck faster.

"Maybe," I say.

"No maybe about it. If you were thinking logically, you'd see that."

I move into the bedroom, tossing my bag on the bed. "Kinda hard to think logically when my husband simultaneously implodes our life and my career."

At the window, I peer up at the sky, search for the moon. A few stars. Anything to remind me of the beauty in life.

Nothing but blackness.

How appropriate. "Ry, I'm tired. Let's talk later."

"You drop this bomb on me and now you don't want to talk?"

"I can't. Not yet. You screwed up. Own it."

With that, I hang up.

Quickly, I power down the phone, avoiding any chance of him driving me crazy with calls and texts.

All I know is I need sleep. I have a ferry to catch in the morning.

"You're in."

I'm sitting in my office, still dressed in jeans and the long-sleeved cashmere pullover I wore on the Snooty. Snooty or not, it's a nice way to travel. Due to a morning chill, I spent most of the ride inside on the upper deck, staring out at the water while a couple of Wall Street looking guys worked on their laptops or messed with their phones.

No one talked.

No one stared.

No one asked for autographs.

My test-drive of the wig proved successful as I seemed to go unrecognized. Either that or the Wall Street guys humored me. If the other passengers are that uninterested in me, I may be able to forgo the wig entirely.

I ditched it as soon as I hopped into the back of Bernie's SUV. He laughed at me and I joined in. As silly as it was, I enjoyed being a blonde. Or perhaps it was being anyone other than Becca Matthews.

Now, I'm at my desk sitting across from Marley, in full-on Dr. Becca mode.

Marley, once again, is in a body-hugging dress—this one a bright magenta—that shows off her curves. If I had that body, I'd do it too. I'm more tall and lean. Not a curve to be found.

She eyes me from her spot in the same chair she'd claimed yesterday. "I'm in?"

"Yes. If you want a chance to help me save my marriage, you've got it."

Her glossy lips slide into a wicked, satisfied smile. *Easy there.* "You have *zero* slack," I say. "Before every show, I expect, in writing, the topics to be discussed. No ambushes. No stoking the audience. No slimy tactics for the money shot."

"*Nothing* organic? You can't be serious."

"Organic is fine. What you won't do is turn my show into a circus. If you need examples of what I'm talking about, give me an hour and I'll pull some of your segments."

She curls her lip. "Wow. No need for insults."

In my quest to keep her focused, perhaps I'm being harsh. "No offense intended. You know what I'm talking about." I lean in, resting my elbows on my desk. "I'm giving you an opportunity. If you do this right, I can help you get your own show. Don't blow it by making me unhappy. My ratings may not be what they were, but you said it yourself, I'm still the queen of daytime talk. I can make you the star you want to be."

By the time this is over, I may have handed her the keys to my kingdom. If it gets my ratings up and saves two hundred jobs, I'll risk it.

It might even be the spark Ryan and I need. The thing that cuts us so far down we have nowhere to go but up.

"Okay," Marley says. "We'll do it your way. Will you at least allow me to say if I think it's not working?"

Being emotionally connected to this topic, I'm a dead loss for neutrality. I'll be useless in judging its value to an audience.

"Of course," I tell her. "Privately though. You and me. Not even Jenny. Once we make a decision, we'll bring her in. Agreed?"

"I can live with that. When do we start?"

"Next week. Every Friday will be Becca and Ryan day. We'll air one show each week."

"How many shows?"

I shrug. "As many as it takes."

Jenny appears on the other side of the glass wall of my office, her eyes wide enough to fit a freight train.

It's a look I don't see often, and my nerves sizzle. My EP is a pro. Not a lot rattles her. An excellent trait in this business. Plus, as she's grown into her job, she's developed a hard outer shell. One that keeps her from emotionally sliding too far one way or the other. I like to tell her she's like an Alaskan fishing vessel. Small but mighty enough to take on a violent ocean.

This look?

Panic.

I wave her in and the door flies open. She ignores Marley and locks her laser focus on me. "I need a minute."

Not a request. Whatever is happening is big. I just hope it's not what I think it is.

I peer across the desk at Marley, offer my best on-camera smile. "I'll be right back."

Leaving my office, I close the door and Jenny pulls me a good ten feet in case, I suppose, Marley has bionic hearing.

"Where's your phone? I've been texting you."

"It's in my drawer. I silenced it for the Marley meeting." Now my panic is rising, my heart slamming against my chest. "What is it?"

If she tells me my husband has killed himself, I'll … I'll …

No.

This is Ryan. He'd never.

"Page Six has it," Jenny spits.

Page Six. The *New York Post*'s enormously popular gossip column. Before my imagination spirals down all sorts of rabbit holes, I hold my breath. Let it out slowly, readying myself.

"The affair?"

"Yes."

Oddly enough, a rush of calm washes over me. I'm in what my staff calls maintenance mode. It's a gift inherited from my surgeon father. My brain takes over, lining up solutions before my emotions create chaos.

I can do this. Work the problem. I should have sent the statement out already. Instead, I've put it off. Convinced myself I should let it sit in case I wanted to tweak it this morning. The entire plan for controlling the narrative?

Toast.

Charred toast.

My offensive position has been obliterated. Can't worry about it now. All I can do is get the statement out.

I push my shoulders back and lift my chin. *I can do this.* "I planned on sending the statement this morning. What do they have?"

"That he's having an affair."

"Photos?"

"No."

That's good at least. Not that any of this could be considered favorable optics. It is, in fact, the nightmare that has stolen my sleep.

I nod. "How do they know?"

"Unnamed source."

"Someone leaked it."

Given the handful of people who knew, it wouldn't take a seasoned investigator to figure out who. I cycle through the list. My boss, Devin, probably Devin's team, and the PR department.

My staff.

Marley Ren.

I swing my head to my office door. No. She wouldn't. What benefit would it be to her? She wants the guest hosting job. Pissing me off doesn't win her any favors.

Same goes for the network. They want the shock factor in this thing. They're not about to give up the ratings triumph.

Laurel Shelton?

Danny.

I told Danny. Confided in him. Could he?

My mother's warnings about not sharing my business nag at me.

But Danny isn't a stranger. We had a deal. He told me about his son. Armed with that information, I could inflict enormous pain.

And no one willingly surrenders that kind of firepower.

Each second convinces me Danny isn't the source. That confidence, that all-out knowing? Another gift. One I have only felt a few times in life.

"Becca?" Jenny snaps her fingers at me. "Hello?"

I shake off my chaotic thoughts. "Has Page Six released it?"

"Yes."

I start walking, hustling to my office, hollering for Kaitlyn.

As usual, she instantly appears, scurrying toward me. She's like a genie out of a bottle.

"I'm about to send you a statement," I tell her. "I'll post it to Facebook. You need to blast it out everywhere else. Then call Devin and April in PR. Tell them I need them. Now."

Marley is still sitting in the chair, scrolling her phone.

She meets my eye as I storm through the door. "Guessing you just heard about Page Six?" She holds up her phone. "I got the alert."

I corner the desk, drop into my chair and fire up my laptop. "I drafted a statement. PR helped."

"PR. They're maddening."

"Agreed. I'm sending it out now, but my intent was to beat everyone else. Entire plan blown."

I open the latest draft of the statement, copy it and head straight to Facebook.

Marley leans in, catching my eye. "This is going to sound patronizing. I'm truly sorry for that, but relax. We can deal with this."

We? We're a *we* now?

"It'll be chaos for you," she continues, "but we're in good shape. You've just offered me the job as guest host. If you're sure about that, we can capitalize on the attention. We'll immediately tell everyone about me helping and—*boom*—we've instantly shifted everyone's attention. All they'll be talking about is the two of us teaming up. Sister, you and me? We'll be rock stars. The Dynamic Duo."

I pound the return key. Done. Statement posted.

Collapsing back in my chair, I stare at the screen a second. My so-called private life has just become enormously un-private.

Can't think too hard about that. It was bound to happen.

"Lawdy, lawdy," Marley says, her voice way too gleeful for

my liking as she scrolls on her phone, "will you look at this? Devin will shit himself."

A vision of Devin soiling himself flashes. I might be losing my mind, but a gurgle of laughter shoots straight up my throat.

I sit taller, meeting my new partner's gaze. Me and Marley Ren.

Never saw *that* coming.

Total trust in her may never happen, but for now, we're in this together.

And it's time to play defense.

CHAPTER 14

*A*fter a hellacious day, Bernie eases to a stop in front of my SUV parked in the ferry landing lot. The network's version of supporting me was to send me—and my adulterous husband—to a black-tie charity event in place of Don and his wife.

Get out there, Devin had said. Let people see you. Talk about the new show with Marley. Great PR.

Blah, blah, blah.

Ryan, being Ryan, complained for all of thirty seconds until he realized that Manhattan's wealthiest would be in attendance and he could squeeze donations as eight hundred snobs openly gossiped about us.

No one could ever accuse Ryan of not being able to focus.

Me? Wrecked. Nerves completely blown. But I kept my smile in place and made my network happy until the dinner plates were cleared. Then I was out.

Having missed the last Snooty, I called Bernie. He was kind enough to drive me to the shore, so I could hunker down for the long weekend.

All I can hope for now is that I don't have a collection of paparazzi in front of my house.

Too bad I can't make my street private. Danny, Mr. Don't-Park-in-Front-of-My-House, would love that. Particularly with Memorial Day and tourists looming.

Halfway home, my phone rings and Danny's name lights up the screen in my dashboard.

I tap the button on my steering wheel. "Hi."

"Where are you?"

His voice is rushed. Panicked even. Which isn't exactly alarming. Danny has a bit of drama merchant in him.

"On Ocean Avenue," I say. "About fifteen minutes away. Something wrong?"

"You bet there is. Our street is *smothered*. News vans. Camera crews. The damned spotlights have everything lit up like Broadway. One guy from TMZ just knocked on my door. Can you imagine?"

Actually, I can.

My stomach drops.

"I'm so sorry, Danny. Page Six ran Ryan's affair. Social media blew up."

"I saw it. I'm sorry."

"It was bound to happen. What did you tell TMZ?"

"To get the fuck off my property and tell his buddies the same. My daughter is here, and she has school tomorrow. I don't need this."

Guilt pummels me. Danny has been nothing but kind—aside from yelling at my EP—since he moved in.

"I'll fix it," I say, completely unsure how to do that.

I owe this to my neighbors. They don't deserve the intrusion.

"Bubby, please. You can't fix this. You need to ride it out. How the hell are you going to get to your house? You don't have a garage! I keep saying you should renovate."

Seriously? *Now* he wants to start on my *cottage* messing with the real estate comps?

Unfortunately, he's right. If I had a garage, I'd drive right in and close the door behind me.

Maintenance mode kicks in, my brain spitting out options. My parents' house? Hotel?

Considering I have no clothes with me and I'm in an evening gown, the hotel won't work. Nor my parents' house, since I don't have clothes there and I'm six inches taller than my mother.

I can't run from this. Danny is right, I'll need to ride it out.

"I'll deal with them," I say. "I'll ask them for privacy and to be respectful of my neighbors. Of course, the fact that Ryan isn't with me will send up a whole new round of speculation."

What a mess.

I check the dashboard clock. If I turn around, I could be back at the townhouse by twelve-thirty. Maybe closer to one.

"Call me when you turn onto the street," he says. "I'll open my garage and you pull in. Maybe you can get inside before they realize it's you. Then you sneak over to your house through the back."

This is what my life has come to. Lurking in the dark to enter my own home.

Get off the treadmill.

I shake the thought away just as tears threaten. No way. No crying.

This is what I, *we,* signed up for. We've been on top of the world for years now. Almost too lucky that scandal hasn't set its nasty sights on us.

Now? Our turn in the barrel.

My tiny miracle is my neighbor throwing me a lifeline. "Danny, thank you. You have no idea what this means to me."

"Please," he says. "If they know you're down here, word'll get out and we'll have a nation of YouTubers crowding the street. Maybe I'll call the cops. Or see if we can hire private security to keep people off the block. Yes! That's an idea. Gotta go. Call me when you're close."

He hangs up. I can't help but pity the dispatcher who's about to receive a call from my anxious neighbor.

The people on the block must hate me bringing this madness to their sanctuary. I'll be sending gift baskets, nice ones, to each of them. This might even warrant a personal delivery.

Ten minutes later, Danny's plan goes off without a hitch.

Before the crowd even realizes it's me—they're busy with the two police officers who apparently just arrived—I'm in the garage, parking beside Danny's Cadillac. As soon as my tail is clear, he closes the door behind me.

Mission accomplished. Danny stands in his mudroom entry, one foot holding the door open.

"Cops showed up two minutes ago," he informs me in a smug tone. "I told them to make sure everyone stays off private property. Good thing we don't have sidewalks. They're relegated to the street and *that,* my friend, is a safety issue." He hacks his hand through the air. "Done! Let's have a drink."

I climb the steps to the door. "It's late."

"Honey, if anyone needs a drink, it'd be you. Let's go. By the way, helluva dress. Versace?"

"Yes. The network thought it would be appropriate for Ry and I to sub in for a black-tie thing. I wanted to kill myself."

Once I'm inside, he closes the door and strides to the kitchen. I dutifully follow, sliding onto the same barstool as my previous visit, and place my purse on the one beside me. "Pour me something good."

"Pfft, all I have is good."

He delivers the line with such ease, I can't help laughing. Danny isn't the prototypical leading man, but there's an unconfined energy about him. Confidence without arrogance that's endearing.

After the last week, I may sort of love Danny. Not in a happily ever after way. Ryan is—was—my happily ever after and look where that got me?

Danny is more than that.

Friendship.

Or what I perceive friendship should be. Someone to confide in. To share secrets and laugh with. Trust, I've never quite had. In the past, all trust ever brought was disappointment.

Across the breakfast bar, Danny whips up what looks like a couple of dirty martinis, adding three olives to each. He hands one over and holds up his glass. "To kicking the shit out of reporters. Most fun I've had in ages."

"Cheers." I take a healthy sip and the vodka sears—literally makes my eyes water—my throat. I let out a short cough and slap a hand over my chest. "Whoa. You weren't kidding about it being good."

"Told ya. Chopin Reserve. Worth every penny."

I make a mental note to pick up a bottle I will happily share with my vodka-loving father. "Is your daughter sleeping?"

"Yes. Abby—Abigail—is upstairs. Her mom had something tonight. I told her I'd do school drop-off."

"Look at you, all domesticated."

"With my kids? Bet your life."

"Is drop-off fun?"

Still on his side of the bar, his gaze wanders to the staircase leading to the second floor. "I like it. Good car talks. I warn her off boys and she does the customary eye roll. Sometimes she laughs. She's got a great laugh. It's not a giggle. It's like," he circles a hand, a wistful smile lighting up his face, "full-blown from the belly. Every time. It's fantastic. You'll meet her this weekend."

He says this as if it's a given. As if he's allowing me access to his beloved child.

"I'd like that."

"How come you never had kids?"

I run my finger along the stem of my glass, considering my answer. "I wanted them. Ran out of time, I suppose."

"Bullshit."

I shoot him a back-off-guy look. He raises one hand. Gives me a finger wave. "You can give me dirty looks all you want. I still call bullshit."

To think, I thought I liked this man.

But he's … well … right. Again. Total nightmare to admit.

With the wonders of fertility treatments and surrogates, plenty of women my age raise children. And, eh-hem, ten years ago, thanks to my gyno who informed us if we weren't planning on having kids soon, it'd be a good idea to freeze my eggs, I did just that.

It's not too late. I could still do it. With or without Ryan.

I sip my martini and set my glass down again. "When we were first married, we talked about kids. My career took off, and it never happened." I shake my head. "No. We *allowed* it to never happen. Ry told me last week he didn't want kids anymore. Guess he forgot to mention that along the way."

"Men are dicks. But, come on, you're an independent woman. You don't need him. It's not like you can't afford daycare while you're working."

"Um, Danny?" I hold up my left hand. The one with my wedding ring. "Still married. Can't force kids on him."

He cocks his head. Stares at me for a few seconds.

I don't need to be a rocket scientist to know what he's thinking. My life—my marriage—might be over. I can decide it's over. This is my opportunity to walk away.

To *quit* and have a baby on my own.

I ponder that while Danny sips at his drink.

In the adjoining living room, dolls and various other toys are thrown about. A pink, fuzzy blanket and a stuffed dog sit on the top of the sofa cushion. I can picture Danny and his daughter, sitting there, watching television together.

I can still do it.

What if the supposed super-marriage-fixer walked away from her own marriage?

"I'd end my career."

"By having a baby? Doubtful."

"Um, in case you missed it, my success is based on fixing broken relationships. The marketing department would have a collective stroke if I divorced Ryan."

He shrugs. "Forget marketing. Forget ratings."

"This from my movie producer friend?"

"Who better? I understand the pressure. The necessity to score big. I was chasing the high that came with success and it cost me everything."

He gets it. Which is good because he'll understand why I have to save my marriage *and* my show. Thanks to my cheating husband, my personal life is now wrapped up in a nice package with my career.

"Daddy?"

We both turn. An adorable girl, five, I think Danny said, stands at the base of the stairs in a pair of *Frozen* pajamas. Her dark curls have exploded into a ball of frizz that makes me giddy. She's clutching a doll whose hair is no better.

My God, she's cute.

Danny points at her. "Young lady, what are you doing up?"

She eyes me for a few seconds, and I sense something. If I'm any good at my job, which I know I am, she's wondering why I'm in her father's house.

I've heard it a million times. Children not wanting to share their parents.

Danny marches to her, scoops her up and smacks a kiss on her cheek. "Go to bed."

"You're so *loud,*" she tells him, heavy emphasis on the last word. "How am I supposed to sleep?"

Her tone is pure exasperation. Similar to Danny's the day he yelled at Jenny in front of the house.

Danny's mini-me.

"Love it," I mutter. "She's totally your child."

We both laugh and she offers a perturbed, pouty face. I roll my lips in, trapping the smile.

"I'm sorry," he tells her. "We'll be quiet. Now go to bed."

Still in her father's arms, she peers back at me.

"That's Ms. Becca," Danny says. "She lives next door."

"The one who's never here?"

"She's coming more often. She's also my friend, so, you know. Be nice. Have a little respect, got it?"

Abby lowers her head, snuggling into Danny's neck and a burst of something shoots around inside me. Whatever it is, isn't good.

It's . . . raw and ugly and . . . Vicious.

Loss.

I missed all of this. The familiarity, the connection, that comes with having a child.

"Back to bed," Danny tells her. "I'll tuck you in. Can you say goodnight?"

"Goodnight, Ms. Becca," she says. "Bye-bye."

"Goodnight, Abby. I hope you have wonderful dreams."

Danny turns to me. "Don't go anywhere. Be right back."

I nod and return to my cocktail. Two minutes later, he's back, laughing to himself. "She's a pip."

"Sure is. Your mini-me."

"I know. My ex can't stand it. I think she's the funnier, kinder version of me. Not the idiot one." He waves it away. "Anyway, where were we?"

"You were telling me about your obsession with work."

"Right. I left Hollywood to raise my kid. I knew what *I* wanted. I had to strip all the bullshit away and figure that out." He meets my gaze. "What do *you* want?"

Easy. "I want my husband to not have cheated on me."

"Beyond that. No offense, Bubby, that's surface crap. Dig deeper."

Sigh. What if I don't want to? What if it hurts too much? "I want to save my show."

"Wha, wha, wha. You're talking, but not saying anything."

Oh, come on. Seriously? How much of this do I need to take? "Wow. I guess men *are* dicks."

Readying for my grand exit, the great storming out that will show that my nosey neighbor has gone too far, I slam the last of my martini. The expected vodka burn doesn't materialize. Instead, it's a smooth balm on my throat that somehow cools my anger.

I set the glass down and stand.

"I'm being an asshole," he says. "You need an asshole right now."

"Do I?"

"Yeah. Because the people around you won't push. Your EP? She's worried about her job. The suits at your network? Forget it. You're their cash cow about to do a show on her failing marriage."

I open my mouth, but he holds his palm out. "All I'm saying is you're working really hard doing what everyone expects. You're putting *your* problems out there. Is it what you want?"

This man. Maddening. Obnoxiously so. What do I want? It's been so long since I thought about it.

I open my eyes again. Meet his gaze. "I don't know."

Except, I do. I just can't admit it. I have it all. Success, wealth, fame. And I want to give it up? No. That's insane.

Danny reaches across the bar, squeezes my hand. It feels … good. Comforting when there's been a lack of it lately.

"Bubby, you could lose years of your life working at something you don't want. Been there. It sucks. Do you want this segment on saving your marriage? Or is it about saving the show?"

Marital crisis aside, it's too late. I lift my hands, let them drop. "Marketing is already working on promo."

"So? You'd piss people off. Big deal." He grins. "I do it all the time."

I let out a snort. "Don't I know it?"

"I've beat you up a little here. It's late, you're tired and, well," he waggles his eyebrows, "I have school in the morning."

"I have to think." I swirl a finger around my head. "It's all muddled in my brain."

The vodka isn't helping.

"You're trying to fix everything at once. Doesn't work that way."

He's right. I constantly advise people to break down the issues into manageable parts. I should follow my own advice.

"Not that my opinion matters," Danny says, "but if it were me, I'd focus on," he holds up one finger, "do I want my shit out there?" Another finger goes up. "Can I get past what my spouse did to me?" Another finger. "Do I have to save the show?"

Wow. In three sentences, my neighbor, my friend, has summed up my life. As complicated as it all feels, it might all come down to those three not-so-simple decisions.

Finally, I grab my purse. He walks around the bar to escort me to the back door. I pause for a second, meeting his eye. Given my heels, I basically tower over him. I take a chance and hold my arms out.

"Bubby needs a hug," he says, leaning in. "That's okay. We all do sometimes."

I squeeze my eyes closed, thankful for the unexpected kindness and pleasant surprise that is Danny. My nutty neighbor.

"Thank you," I tell him. "You have no idea."

"Unfortunately, I do." He steps back and squeezes my hands. "Whatever you decide, you'll be okay. I promise."

CHAPTER 15

On Monday morning, Jenny comes breezing into my office, her face lit up like Times Square. What she's so happy about, I cannot fathom. Maybe she has inside intel on a ratings boost I'm unaware of.

She pokes a finger at me. "You're going to love this."

This is the environment I've fostered. I've never told my staff *not* to engage in small talk or inquire about my personal life, but my actions, my walking straight to my office and lack of lingering in the bullpen to chat, made it clear.

Don't ask, don't tell, let's get to work. It's been my unspoken modus operandi. All to protect my privacy.

I sit back and hold my hands out. "I could use good news."

Considering I spent my entire weekend contemplating the destruction of my marriage *and* my career.

Is walking away from all of it—the show, my staff, my marriage—the answer? Or is it a short-term fix that looks good now because I'm overwhelmed and exhausted?

I'm not in the headspace to make that decision, but I've been hasty on agreeing to the segment on my marriage. Yes, it's allowing me to stop hiding, to live a so-called authentic life, but will it destroy me altogether?

Talk about throwing the baby out with the bathwater.

"Becca," Jenny says, "did you hear me?"

I snap out of my fog. "I apologize. What's up?"

"Remember the plug I told you about after Friday's show?"

As a way of finding guests, we often run messages asking viewers to call in if they've had experience with certain topics. They're called plugs and generally result in a flood of messages that interns and associate producers screen.

I nod. "The one about successful women and adulterous husbands?"

"Yes!"

Obviously unable to contain her enthusiasm, she smacks her hands against my desk "The phone lines went nuts. It'll take the staff all day to get through those messages."

I might be drained, unacceptable on a Monday after a long weekend, but I'm not seeing why this is such a grand event. "That's ... good."

"Good?" she laughs. "Are you feeling okay? It's *fantastic*."

On any other topic, I'd recognize the positive aspects. After all, we might get any number of shows out of those calls. Fresh shows. Something I can really dig into.

Without getting slugged in the face.

Who'd have guessed *that* would ever be a goal?

"Sorry," I say. "I suppose this topic is too close."

Jenny's shoulders fly back, her mouth falling open. "Oh, no. So sorry, Becca. I'm a jerk. I was so excited, I just barged in here without ..."

"Hey, it's fine. You're doing your job. It's what makes you good. I appreciate that more than you know."

"Next time, I'll," she circles a hand in the air, "I don't know. Tone it down, I guess. Something."

Which, honestly, I don't want. Jenny, my star EP, should not have to dial her energy back because my husband cheated on me. For her, even if she doesn't realize it, that would be soul crushing.

"No. No toning anything down. I'd hate that. Anyway, I'm glad the plug worked."

"It sure did. Once we get through the messages, we'll see if there's anything promising. I'll keep you updated."

Oh, goody. Just what I want. A briefing on how we can milk Ryan's cheating into better ratings.

Kaitlyn appears at my door. Unlike me, she appears well-rested, and her face has that youthful glow I never appreciated at twenty-five.

"Sorry to interrupt," she says. "They're ready for you in makeup."

"Got it." Thankful for the reprieve, I nearly leap from my chair.

"I'll see you down there," Jenny says, hustling out of my office.

I move toward the door and Kaitlyn falls in step beside me as we head to the makeup room. "I have lunch with Marley today," I tell my assistant. "Would you see if we can reschedule that for tomorrow or Wednesday?"

The last thing I need is Marley pressuring me. The lunch was to be a working one where we'd sketch out my expectations for the segments. In short, it would be my opportunity to set boundaries.

Marley needs boundaries.

My husband, I suppose, is entitled to some input on what those boundaries should be and since I haven't spoken to him since the black-tie dinner the other night, I need more time.

I may be the betrayed spouse, but is it fair to force Ryan to sit on my stage and air to my millions of viewers why he'd let the little brain run the show? Then again, if he hadn't had an affair, none of this would be necessary.

I keep ruminating on that. As if it justifies flaying myself—and our loved ones—open for the world. All of them will suffer the humiliation right along with us. And for what?

Ratings?

No. More than that.

Jobs. Two hundred of them.

"I'll reschedule her," Kaitlyn says, typing into her phone. "Anything else?"

Did she have a week? It would take that long to list all the things I need right now. "No. Thank you."

When we reach our destination, Kaitlyn breaks off and I find Steph leaning on the vanity, scrolling through her phone.

"Morning," I say.

She peers up at me, then sets her phone down. "Good morning. All set?"

Hardly, but that's not her problem. I climb into the chair, stare at myself in the mirror, taking in my sagging cheeks and shadowed eyes.

Something has got to give. I sit back, surrendering to her magic. "All set."

AFTER A LONG DAY, not to mention facing the swarming paparazzi at work, I trudge through the front door. The incessant beeping of the security system sounds, and I walk to the keypad hidden behind a graphic print hanging in the entry hall.

Apparently, Ryan wasn't expecting me, as he'd already set the alarm.

At 7:30.

Or he has someone here and wanted to be warned if I showed up. Would he do that? After all the nasty press? Bring a woman to my bed?

The roiling sickness that has attached itself to me this last week assails me. Bile rises in my throat, and I slam my eyes closed, breathing through it. I force my shoulders down and focus on loosening my limbs. Stress will do that. Tighten everything up.

I drop my tote and toss my keys in the bowl on the entry table. "Hello?" I call, just in case.

Ryan appears at the top of the staircase. "Hi."

"Hi."

"Wasn't expecting you."

Was I supposed to call now? I start the climb, my cement feet struggling with each step. "Got done late. We need to talk."

"Ya think?"

Sarcasm. Excellent.

He turns from his spot at the top of the stairs and walks away. By the time I reach the landing, he's at the refrigerator, dragging out eggs and chicken.

"You hungry?"

Hunger isn't something I've felt in the last week. Especially after my stomach just rebelled, but I need food. Another sad development, since Ryan and I have spent countless hours in this kitchen. Him cooking while I sampled and applauded his culinary wizardry.

That too, it seems, has fallen victim to adultery.

"I should eat," I tell him.

He jerks his head to my usual stool and gets to work pouring breadcrumbs—homemade no doubt—into one of the rectangular trays he uses for coating meat.

There's an open bottle of wine, something red, airing on the island. He spots me eyeing it and turns to the cabinet behind him, grabbing an extra wineglass.

Usually, he'd pour. This time, he simply slides me the glass.

His own act of rebellion, I'm sure.

This is what we've come to. A few weeks ago, we'd laugh over my office war stories and the retaliatory things I witness couples doing. Now we're participants.

I pour myself half a glass, set the bottle down and look up at him just as he lifts an egg to crack it. "I have a meeting with Marley tomorrow."

He freezes, hand in midair. "That's fast."

"I can't put it off any longer."

He pounds the egg against the bowl, the shell disintegrating and oozing its contents all over his hand.

"Dammit!"

Whoa. He drops the shell in the garbage and slides to the sink, washing his hands before returning to the fridge for an additional egg. Hopefully, he won't continue to take his frustrations out on our eggs.

He tries again, this time with more care.

"Ryan, we're taping next week."

"Un-huh."

"You agreed to this."

He pounds another egg, manages to not destroy it and tosses the shell in the bowl. "Um, no. I didn't. You *told* me we were doing it. The network wanted it. I do what I always do. I went along."

"Let's not do this."

Finally, he meets my gaze, his blue eyes darkening with heat generally not directed at me. "*This* being humiliating me on national television?"

Did he seriously just say that to me? "Ha!" I bark out a forced laugh. "Now it's my fault you couldn't keep your dick in your pants?"

And wow! *You go, girl.*

"Jesus, Becca! Real nice."

Crass language, coming from Reasonable Becca, must not be agreeable.

Too.

Bad.

"You may not have noticed," I say, "but I don't currently care about nice. If you'd been *nice,* I wouldn't be the one publicly humiliated."

"So, this is what? Revenge?"

There's that word again. "This is me saving my show and two hundred jobs. Saving the style of living you seem to enjoy."

My success has allowed Ryan to do whatever he professionally and personally chooses. It's not something we've ever voiced. It's simply been an understanding of our partnership. He's put up with the nonsense that comes with fame and has been rewarded appropriately.

Now, I've hurled it at him like a flaming ball.

He lets out a soft huff. "And there it is. You finally said it. All these years, I've been the freeloader."

His words sting. I'd like to defend myself, but what's the point? I wanted to hurt him.

Period.

I shake my head. Draw a long breath and look away, fighting a rush of tears. I hate what I'm becoming. All this anger and heartbreak? It's acid on bare skin. I blink away the moisture in my eyes, push my shoulders back and face him again.

"I don't want to do this. It's why I've stayed away. I need to work through my feelings and being here stirs me up. I'm hoping we can fix it."

"On national television?"

His continued sarcasm isn't lost on me. "Yes. On national television. I don't like it either, but maybe it'll help us."

"Why can't we do therapy on our own? Why do we have to do a show?"

I don't bother responding. At best, they're rhetorical questions. He's been married to me for twenty-four years. He knows having both of us on set, having him admit what he did to my millions of viewers, makes for good drama.

At my silence, he shakes his head, picks up a fork and

scrambles the eggs with the force of a jackhammer. Apparently satisfied with his egg massacre, he dips chicken in the egg wash.

"Anyway," I say, "I've told Marley she has a short leash. If she wanders off-script, I'll pull the plug."

"You know as well as I do, the network won't allow that."

No. They won't. I could refuse to do the segments. Call out sick for a week. All of which might get me fired and then what happens to my staff?

"I don't think it'll be an issue. She's promised me."

At this, he rolls his eyes. I can't blame him. He's heard my endless complaints about her ambush tactics.

He sets his fork down and rests his hands against the island, peering down at them.

In body language speak, this is Ryan pondering his next steps. Resignation, on my confident, charming husband, is ugly.

Eventually, he peers at me. "Boundaries. Hell if I know. I mean, I'm not getting into specifics on the … um … on *Laurel*. It has nothing to do with her."

This makes me laugh. An honest to God chuckle. It has everything *and* nothing to do with her. She's the woman he had an affair with. Not necessarily Laurel Shelton, but any nameless existence in our obviously fractured marriage.

"For our purposes, Laurel isn't relevant. We need to get more into the why of it."

"Why I had an affair?"

"Yes."

"What if I don't know?"

Now he expected me to coach him on this? "That's why we're doing therapy. To figure it out."

He shakes his head again. "Not on television. Counseling, yes. I'll sit in an office and admit everything if it saves us. I'll do the work, Bec, but I can't do it on TV. No way."

He loves me. I know it. I can see it. In his eyes. Despite the fading harshness, there's that blue-gray softness that's helped me through countless career difficulties.

Me and Ry. A killer team.

"I'm sorry," I tell him. "Too late to back out."

I rise from the stool, no longer feeling the urge to eat one of Ry's amazing meals. Those meals came with the old us. An *us* that had routine and laughter and trust.

Now?

I'm not sure what we have.

I cock my head. "I think I've lost my appetite. You go ahead. Before I meet with Marley, is there anything else I should know?"

"Like what?"

I shrug. "I don't know. Just … anything. I'd rather not have any surprises during taping."

He stares at me for another long moment, his mind clearly working. Lord, I hope he's not hiding anything.

Finally, he shakes his head. "There's nothing."

I so want to believe that. "You're sure?"

My asking is a joke. Even if there's more, he's already said there isn't. He can't walk that back. He can't say *"Oh, right, there is something more since you've asked me twice."*

Still, relief washes over me, shattering the tension that's locked my shoulders. "I'll give Marley a strict outline. Do you trust me on that?"

He waves me off. "Of course."

"Thank you."

I slide the stool in, the brush of felt pads intensifying the silence bouncing off the walls.

"Bec?"

I look up at my husband. The man who, until two weeks ago, had been my only complete confidant.

My best friend.

"Yes?"

"I love you."

His voice shatters like glass hitting pavement and my chest caves in. Just disintegrates. I still love him. I know I do. Always will. I'm too torn up to say it. I'd rather claw his eyes out. Rail on him for wrecking a perfectly decent life.

He clears his throat. "I want to work this out."

I swallow, ready to share the sentiment, to tell him we'll get through this, but … nothing. All that emerges is the strangled mix of betrayal and heartbreak.

"I'll sleep in the guest room tonight," I say.

ON WEDNESDAY, after my second taping, I emerge from my private bathroom where I basically chiseled off my makeup. It's not lost on me that as I get older, it takes more and more effort to get me camera ready. To hide the tiny lines that are no match for Botox and fillers.

If this keeps up, there may be a facelift in my future.

I drop into my desk chair, opening the laptop to deal with the endless emails. Before I dig in, Jenny appears at my door, her face long, her cheeks hollow. A definite departure from her usual frenetic energy.

"Hi," I say. "Why do you look like someone stole your puppy?"

It might be worse than the puppy since my comment doesn't even garner half a smile.

I wave her to her usual chair and close my laptop, intending to give her my full attention.

"Sooo," she says, "we have a development."

Lately, I really hate developments. Whatever this is, she's not happy. Anticipating an issue, I rock back, cross my legs, and fold my hands in my lap while Jenny slides into her chair and squares her shoulders.

Another spurt of anxiety floods me, and I brace myself. I just hope it's not another…

No. I'm not going there. Not even putting it out into the universe.

"I mentioned yesterday about the tremendous response to the plug we ran. We've had extra people reviewing voicemails. Including the APs."

Typically, our interns handle phone duty. Not assistant producers.

"And?"

She holds her hand flat, tilts it back and forth. "Most were a bust, but there are possibilities for future guests."

"Good."

"There are a lot of cheaters in the world." She waves it away. "Anyway, there was one message that Molly retrieved."

Molly. The AP who helped me with intel on Laurel Shelton. "It must have been an interesting one if you're here."

She winces and I know I'm sunk. Just … dead. Whatever this is, it's about me.

Or Ryan.

Knew I shouldn't have put that thought into the universe. Last night's conversation, my asking Ryan if there were any other secrets and that brief hesitation, slips through my mind.

"Please don't tell me there's another one."

Jenny holds my gaze, her eyes somehow vacant yet completely focused.

"I'm sorry," she says.

I spring forward, my back rod straight, a blood rush scorching my veins. He could *not* have done this to me.

Again.

Wait. This could be a hoax. Happens all the time. Scammers and opportunists looking for a few minutes of fame. It wouldn't be the first time someone lied to get on a top-rated daytime talk show. That's why our producers run background on everyone. To weed out the fakes.

But what if it's nothing about Ryan? I've already leaped to a conclusion when I haven't heard the issue.

I roll my chair closer to the desk and tap the edge. "Tell me what you've got."

"Molly returned the call. It's a woman from Queens. Her name is Tiffany Ambrose. She's twenty-eight."

Younger than Laurel.

When I don't respond, Jenny continues. "She's a server at a café on the Upper East Side."

My stomach knots so tight I might vomit. Our townhouse is on the Upper East Side. Ryan hits the Bridge Café, right up the street, every morning before heading to work.

"What café?"

Jenny checks the legal pad she walked in with. "The Bridge? Do you know it?"

The name is an assault. Total bombing of my system that fires my temper while simultaneously paralyzing my lungs.

Later, I can lose it. Right now? Focus. Work the problem. I clear my throat. "It's a few blocks from my house."

Jenny's nose wrinkles. It's painful even for her, but she keeps her gaze steady on mine. "She, the woman, says she and Ryan." Jenny rolls her hand. "Well …"

I nod like one of those stupid little bobbleheads from Yankee Stadium that Ry loves so much.

"They had an affair," I say. "When?"

Please, please, please, don't let this be a long-term thing. Let it be a fling. A one-night stand that happened years ago. A mistake.

She's only twenty-eight. How many years ago could it have been? Instinctively, I know I'm grasping. Looking for any excuse to what …? Make it not matter? Oh, that was ten years ago, we're in a better place. But ten years ago, this woman was only eighteen, which is a lot worse than my husband screwing a twenty-eight-year-old.

I may puke all over my desk.

And assuming this woman is legit, could there be more?

Jenny looks down at her notepad. "She, um, says it started in November. Not this last one. The year before."

Somehow, this is a relief. That my husband, hopefully, wasn't simultaneously carrying on multiple affairs.

"How long?"

Again, she checks her notes. "He ended it in March."

At least *he* ended it. Not that it makes me feel any better, but I'm thinking damage control. About meeting with Marley, who will absolutely salivate over this.

One thing at a time.

"Okay." I jerk my head. "Let me talk to Ry. See if she's lying."

"Will he admit it?"

After lying to me the night before about having no other secrets? Who knows? He, however, is not stupid. Understands that if we don't give her the audience she apparently wants, since she called in, she may beat us to the press. We won't control the precious narrative.

If I never hear that phrase again, it'll be too soon.

I pick up my phone, nudge my chin to the door. "Give me a minute. Please."

Yes, I was just insanely rude to Jenny. All of this practicing self-control is frying my brain cells. "I apologize."

"For what?"

"I was rude. Kicking you out of here."

"For fuck's sake, Becca. Don't worry about it."

She's on her feet now, but not moving. Again staring at me with that spooked—pitying?—look she came in with and I know. Feel it with every ignited nerve ending.

There's more.

"What . . ." I croak, then stop to clear my throat and close my eyes for a brief second before trying again. "What is it?"

She lifts a hand, lets it drop. "I don't know how to tell you this."

"If there are more women, just say it."

How much worse could it be? Does my husband have a harem? That might be more of a scandal than my career could sustain.

"The woman. She says she has a … baby. Ryan's baby."

CHAPTER 16

$\mathcal{M}$y own brand of hell. That's what this is. Someone has to be playing a joke. Right? Messing with me?

Stunned stupid, I shake my head. "Did you say she and Ryan have a *baby*?"

"I'm so sorry."

Fury mixed with agony rips through me.

After all the years together. His knowing I wanted children. His indifference to my career taking precedence over starting a family when he knew, *knew*, I'd wanted kids. All that time he'd stayed silent. Let me get old, almost too old, for children.

All. These. Years.

And then, not two weeks ago, he'd told me he was okay with us not having children. That *he* liked the freedom. Something that would have been lovely to know ten or fifteen years ago.

Except, oh, wait, he has a *baby* with another woman.

I can't do this. Can't take it. It's too much. The show, the staff, my rotten husband. I'm simultaneously losing everything.

Tears bubble. I slam my eyes shut, dig my heel into the floor and spin myself to the wall. At least I have enough sense left to hide my meltdown from Jenny.

I open my eyes, swipe the tears from my cheeks as I peer out the window. Across the street is another office building. A man, phone to his ear, is pacing in front of the window parallel with mine. Back and forth he goes. Back and forth, back and forth.

"Becca?"

Jenny. What am I supposed to say? I'm … lost.

Total devastation and it occurred in front of one of my staff. There appears to be no end to the humiliation Ryan will inflict.

"I need a minute," I tell her.

"Of course. Let me know if I can do anything."

The swish of fabric, her jeans as she walks, fills the silence, then abruptly stops. I don't move. Just sit watching the man pace while I remain paralyzed by how little I know about my husband.

"Becca?"

Jenny. Still here. Why, why, why won't she go away?

"Yes?" I manage, my back still to her.

"I know I'm your producer, but I'm also your friend. I hope you know that."

How pathetic am I that my EP has to offer herself up as my friend? She knows I don't have anyone. Of course she does. I never get calls from besties or talk about fun outings.

How pathetic.

I can't look at her. Can't. We're coworkers and my husband has betrayed me in ways I cannot fathom. I give Jenny a backward wave. "Thank you. I'm okay. Just need to catch my breath."

The click of my door closing sounds and relief drops on me like a lead blanket. I'm alone, behind a closed door and it would be so easy to just let loose. Have a good cry and scream. Pound the *shit* out of something.

But that glass wall is a fishbowl. *Everyone* can see in here.

Giving up on the guy across the street, I stalk to the bathroom, shutting the door and grabbing a thick, fluffy hand towel from under the sink. I roll it up and my stomach cramps. A vicious knot that doubles me over.

I shove the towel against my mouth and let out a roaring howl, the fabric taking the brunt of the noise. I'm not even sure what this pain is. My stomach or my heart disintegrating?

Maybe both.

Either way, I let it out. All the roiling hate and venom eating me from inside out.

How, how, how could he do this to me?

I don't understand. Won't ever. I pound my fist against the sink. Bam, bam, bam, the smack of skin against porcelain fills the tiny bathroom.

I gave him everything. Houses, clothes, cars. Social status. Literally handed it to him while I navigated the battlefield known as daytime talk wars.

Wait. My scream dies in my throat, and I lower the towel. *Wait, wait, wait.* I uncurl my hand, toss the towel aside and brace myself against the sink. I've been hosting my show for fourteen years. The shenanigans I've witnessed?

Mind-numbing.

The producers are so immune they crack jokes, one-upping each other over who has scored the most interesting guest.

All that experience, and I fell for the oldest trick there is. Maybe she *is* a server at the Bridge. Easy enough to confirm. But she could be lying about the affair. People do it all the time. Create alternate realities for attention.

Her word against ours. A lie that juicy would land her on any number of celebrity gossip sites.

I blow out a hard breath. Force out a laugh. Clearly, the stress of the last two weeks has gotten to me.

You're okay.

At least that's what Dr. Becca would say. *Give yourself some grace.* My tagline. Literally. I've said it so often, marketing has put it on coffee mugs, T-shirts, pens. It's on my show's web page and billboards. *Give yourself some grace.*

Finally, I stand tall, lift my head, and peer at the blotchy mess that is my face. At least I'd scrubbed off the makeup prior to my crying jag. Still, black smudges loom under swollen, red eyes. I can't leave my office looking like this.

No way.

I'll have to sit in this damned bathroom until I can clean myself up. Slapping the faucet on, I run the hand towel under cold water, saturating it and squeezing out the excess before sitting on the lowered toilet seat and throwing the towel against my face.

The cold is a shock. A good one that draws heat from my cheeks. My mother's words from childhood come back to me. *"Put a cold compress on your eyes, Becca. Don't let anyone see you like this."*

There's a weird sort of comfort there. Something routine and familiar to latch on to when nothing feels routine and familiar.

I channel my mother, the one who is an absolute ace at showing the world only what she wants them to see.

I need a plan. I press the towel harder against my closed eyes and breathe. I can do this. I know I can.

Plan.

Go home. Confront Ryan. Get the truth, no matter what.

Deal with the carnage.

My emergency stash of makeup and skin supplies under the bathroom sink helps me hide most of the red blotches from my crying jag, but my puffy eyes? I'll need at least fifty tubes of inflammation reducer for that mess.

If anyone looks close enough, they'll see the remnants of my meltdown. Nothing to be done about it.

By now, rumors must be flying amongst my staff about my husband's secret baby. Talk about the makings of trash television. A sweeper for sure.

Shoulders back and head high, I emerge from the bathroom. If anyone in the corridor looks through the glass, all they'll see is me in full Dr. Becca form.

Never let 'em see you sweat.

At my desk, I gather my laptop and planner and call Bernie, alerting him I'm leaving early. Fifteen minutes, he tells me.

Then I call my husband.

"Hey," he says, his voice carrying that tone that means he's occupied.

His tone irks me. As if I'm nothing but a bother. I grit my teeth, force myself to stay focused. I'd love to rip him one. Right now, just unload my anger and heartbreak and … hatred.

At this moment, for the first time, I hate him, the man I've loved more than half my life.

"Hello," I say, my voice unusually formal. "I need you to meet me at home."

A brief pause ensues. I can picture him, at his desk, lifting his head, staring straight ahead in that squinty way he does when thinking. "What's wrong?"

"We have to talk."

Again.

"Now? I'm working."

And I'm not? *"Now."*

Not bothering to wait for a response, I hang up. Prior to the last two weeks, I've never summoned him home. He never gave me reason to.

I shove my laptop and planner into my tote, grab my purse and head to the door, breezing by the bullpen offering a good night to the staff. Zero eye contact.

All I'll see is pity and I won't tolerate that.

Jenny's door is ajar. She's meeting with Emily, one of our

producers, but I pop my head in. "Hi, guys. Sorry to interrupt." I shift my gaze to Jenny. "Please send me your notes on . . ."

What? My husband's baby? I don't even know the sex of the child. I slide a glance at Emily, then come back to Jenny. "The Bridge Café."

"Of course. Do you want them typed up?"

"No. Just snap a pic and text it to me. ASAP, please?"

She jerks her head. "I'll do it as soon as we're through here."

"Thank you."

By the time I reach the lobby, Bernie is idling at the curb. Since it's early in the day, the sidewalk appears free of loitering paparazzi. A blessing, considering I'm having a lot of trouble keeping my head in the game.

Bernie hustles around the car, takes one look at me and frowns.

"Whoa," he says, opening the rear door. "Are you all right?"

My driver knows me well. Has listened to thousands of personal and business phone calls and, unlike my husband, has never violated my trust. At least that I know of. I'm sure, given recent events, tabloids and podcasters are blowing up his phone with offers. I couldn't blame him if he did cash out.

Most would.

I slide into the rear seat and meet his eye. "I'm okay. Thank you for getting here so quickly. Just so you know, I'm giving you a ten-thousand-dollar raise."

His head snaps back. "What?"

I wave him away before onlookers recognize me and pounce. Understanding my issue, he closes the door and I flip the lock, just in case.

One minute later, he's merged into traffic and eyes me in the rearview.

"Becca, I don't know what this is about a raise, but forget it. You pay me enough."

Bernie. Such a good guy. He has no idea what's about to

happen. The hounding we will endure whenever I leave my house or office. He'll have to deal with swarming photographers and manage not to run them over and get us sued.

He'll be a bodyguard and driver. The human fly swatter chasing away bugs.

"Given the storm about to come down on me—on us—it's not nearly enough."

He rolls to a stop at a traffic light, glances over his shoulder. "What happened?"

"I'm sorry. I can't talk it about it yet."

I peer out the window, blindly staring at an aquamarine dress in the Saks window I don't need but would love to hop out and buy.

Retail therapy. Something I often advise against, but now fully understand the need for.

Ignoring the dress, I look back at Bernie. "I'm going home to talk with Ryan. Then I'll tell you."

A horn honks and Bernie checks the light. Green. He hits the gas and remains blessedly silent for the rest of the drive.

When we reach my building, he opens the car door, and meets my eye. "All clear. I don't see any photographers. Should I wait? Do you need me?"

"No. I'm fine. I'll drive myself to the shore and take the Snooty in tomorrow."

I slide out and give his forearm a squeeze. He glances down, his brows drawing together. Have I ever, in the years he's worked with me, touched him?

Given that I'm not the touchy-feely type, probably not. Sure, there have been hefty bonuses, extravagant birthday and Christmas gifts, but have I ever once told him how much he means to me? This man who has been at my disposal, no matter the hour. He's safely carted me around, avoiding paparazzi and making sure I'm on time regardless of traffic.

Anticipating the pounce of a photographer, I take a peek at

the passing pedestrians. No one in sight. This whole coming home early thing has thrown everyone off.

"I'm sorry," I tell Bernie.

"For what?"

"For never telling you how important you are to me. You've been extremely loyal, and I owed you that."

A sad smile drifts across his lips. He sets his hand over mine. "You've been great to me. Whatever is going on, I'm here for you. I've got you, Becca."

Emotions flood, rising in my chest and stealing my breath. Between Danny and Bernie, support has come from the oddest places. It's not lost on me they're both men. Protecting me in a way my husband hasn't.

I regroup, send Bernie on his way and enter the townhouse, dropping my bags by the staircase. I don't intend to be here long and will grab them on my way out.

Behind me, the front door opens and Ryan steps in. His dark hair is slightly disheveled, a few wisps falling across his forehead, giving him that rugged look that takes some men from handsome to stunning.

Damn him for that.

He shuts the door behind him. "What's this about?"

I spin and march toward his man cave. "Lock the door."

Yes. I'm paranoid. The last thing we need is someone bypassing building security and sneaking in our front door. He's lucky I don't make him set the alarm.

Inside the man cave, my eyes lock on the giant television that took three men to hang. I thought—still do—it was ridiculous. A phallic symbol, I'd joked, but Ryan had to have it.

I turn away from it, facing Ryan as he strides into the room. Gone is his usual easy gait. All I see now are stiff shoulders and limbs. Readying himself for battle. He halts three feet from me and folds his arms. "I'm here. What is it?"

My phone.

On the way home, Jenny texted me the promised photo of her notes, but I left the phone in my purse.

Didn't matter. What little details I have are seared into my brain. A cancer I may never get rid of. "Tiffany Ambrose," I say, then shut up and wait.

He gives me *nothing*. No wide-eyed horror, no squinty eyes, no tight lips or head shake.

There it is. The sharp lesson I learned years ago and was recently reminded of when I confronted him about the credit card bill.

Ryan, my charming Ryan, is an exceptional liar.

Finally, he forgoes his defensive stance, unwinds his arms, and lets them fall to his sides.

In the barely half a second it takes for him to respond, he's given me no sign he recognizes the name.

Could he …

Is this …

Wait. Maybe it *is* a hoax. Someone trying to create chaos. Which she has. What am I doing?

I draw a breath, close my eyes for a second, and put my thoughts together. The only way to do this is to spit it out. I open my eyes. Meet his gaze.

Would I even know if he was lying? Two weeks ago, I'd have thought so. Now? Anyone's guess.

"We ran a plug the other day," I offer, "asking for people who have experience with adultery. A Tiffany Ambrose responded. She works at the Bridge, and she says she's the mother of your child."

Boom. Said it. *Purged* it like bad shellfish. It's oddly calming.

Ryan finally—finally—gives me something. His head drops forward, and he flops his mouth open. Classic shock.

That's good. *Good, good, good.* Maybe we're okay, relatively speaking.

"Please." My voice catches, the sound too squeaky and strangled. "Tell me it's not true. Do you have a child?"

"Bec, this is *ridiculous*."

I step forward. I want him to convince me there's no baby with someone else after we'd never had children of our own. So far, he hasn't. All he's done is avoid my question.

"Do you know," he begins, "how many women I meet every day? Now you think I'm screwing every female I trip over?"

"I didn't say that. She called in. Said she's a server at the Bridge and you're at the Bridge every morning. Her baby is six months old. She gave us specifics. When the affair started and ended. *Everything*."

"What do you expect me to say?"

Now I'm the one who's shocked. What kind of question is that? "How about that she's lying? That we'll sue her for slander, and I have nothing to worry about. That, when Marley grills us on television, this woman will have no grounds to publicly humiliate me. *That's* what I expect you to say. Answer my question, Ryan."

He shakes his head. Hard. "What question? You're throwing a lot at me."

Oh, please. Now he's deflecting. "Answer the question. Please."

"Becca!"

Rage spews, the intensity lighting my body up like a volcano. I spin away and stalk the room, tears filling my eyes. It's all too much. The anger and heartbreak and … disappointment.

I have to get out. Just run. Go to the shore and stick my head right into that beautiful sand. Pretend none of this is happening. But no … I can't. I'm not foolish enough to believe I can avoid the destruction of life as I know it by hiding at the beach.

"Damn you!" I roar. "How could you do this to me?" I turn back to him. Tears pour from my eyes, saturating my cheeks. I don't bother swiping at them. What's the point? "I've loved you from day one! You're the only person, the only damned person, I've shared my life with. My *secrets*. I *trusted* you."

For the first time, I want to physically strike another human being. Just beat on him until all this hurt and anger and rage exhausts itself.

"I'm sorry," he mutters, dragging a hand through his hair. "Again."

Those three paltry words slap me from my rant. No denials, no trying to convince me.

It's true. He's all but admitted it.

Devastated, I drop onto the sectional. I prop my elbows on my knees, throw my head into my hands and wet tears seep into my fingers. "Tell me everything," I say. "And this time, tell the truth. If you even know how to do that."

CHAPTER 17

Ryan stands in the middle of his man cave, the phallic television behind him. Isn't that the ultimate symbol of our life?

There's always something more he needs. Wants. How the hell big does a television really need to be?

Bigger. Better.

Younger. Prettier.

How many women will it take to satisfy him?

I'm not sure I want to know.

"Becca, it didn't …"

I bolt upright. "No. You don't get to tell me it was meaningless. Not this time. You had a *child* with this woman. Am I that blind? How have you been co-parenting without me even knowing it?"

"Hang on." He shakes his head. "The baby. She's not in my life. In *our* life."

She. Ryan has a daughter. Somehow it hurts even more. A boy would have been easier. At least that's what I tell myself.

"Well," I scoff, "I know for sure she's not in *my* life. Considering I didn't know she existed. You met her mother at the Bridge?"

"It started out harmless. A mild flirtation. Then I ran into her one day after her shift. I took a few hours off and was walking past the café. She came out. I bought her a coffee across the street. Harmless."

Coffee with another woman he'd had a "mild flirtation" with is harmless? Either my husband is an idiot or in total denial.

And he's not an idiot.

I peer up at him, dumbstruck. "I don't need the details. Besides, your girlfriend gave them all to my producers."

He winces. "It only lasted a few months. I could count how many times we were together."

"Is that supposed to make me feel better?"

"I wasn't sneaking out every night to see her. It wasn't often."

"Often enough that she wound up pregnant."

"I always used protection."

Lucky me. I snort, the sound so pathetic, I can't believe it came out of me. "Well, it *failed*. You just said you're not in the baby's life. You've abandoned a woman who has your child."

"No, I haven't. Come on, Bec, you know me."

Do I? "Apparently not as well as I thought."

"I pay child support. Every month. If she needs extra, I give it to her. She's not greedy. She's not *blackmailing* me."

Anger and heartbreak whip up another dose of sarcasm, and I whirl my finger in the air. *Whoopdee fucking doo.*

"So, *we've* been giving her money every month?"

How could I have been this naïve? This checked out of our finances, our marriage, that I didn't know he'd been siphoning child support money?

Not only am I a fraud, I'm a fool.

He runs his hand over his face and sighs. "I pay the bills. It wasn't that hard."

I guess not.

My mind spirals. All those nights I worked late or went to functions without him. He's had plenty of opportunities for affairs. Do I even want to know if there are more?

I made it easy enough.

Analyzing my foolishness might take all night. Self-flagellation, I tell my guests, is a useless endeavor. All I can do is move forward.

Damage control.

I take a breath. "Okay. Do you speak to her? Tiffany?"

He shakes his head. "No. She left the Bridge when she was out on maternity. She works nights now. Steak place on Fifth."

Fifth. I just saw a dress at Saks on Fifth. Have I driven by this restaurant, completely unaware that the mother of my husband's child works there?

I shake it off. Doesn't matter now. "Did you get her that job?"

"I helped. The money and hours are better."

He'd always been good that way. Using his connections to help others. I'll give him credit for that. It's one of the things I've loved about him. I try to hang on to that. To that little piece of me that loves this man.

"So, you have a child you don't interact with. Ever?"

He lifts one shoulder, lets it drop with a casualness that eviscerates me. If I don't beat him to death, it'll be a miracle.

"Ryan, did it occur to you that this child might need a father?"

"Tiffany knew from the start I wasn't interested. I told her I'd never leave you. That I loved you."

He *loved* me. Unbelievable. I wrap a hand over my forehead, dragging my fingers across it in a gentle massage. Helluva headache.

"Bec—"

Still seated, I shove my palm at him. "Just ... *don't*. If you loved me, you wouldn't have done this."

"Think whatever you want, but I do love you."

When I drop my hand, he continues. "Tiffany called me. When she found out she was pregnant. I had to ask her if she was sure the baby was mine. I mean, we'd only been together a handful of times. How would I know who else she was involved with?"

A last morsel of hope springs inside me. "Did you do a paternity test?"

"Yes."

There went that morsel. Exhausted, I double over, resting my elbows against my knees again, letting my fingers dangle as I stare at my shoes.

Every inch of me aches. It reminds me of four years ago when I had the mother of all flu attacks. In bed for days, my body ravaged and unable to hold food, I'd lie there, hour after hour, sweating and shivering, wondering if my organs were breaking down. If I was slowly dying.

That's how I feel now.

Dying a slow, agonizing death.

"What's her name?" Devastated, I peer up at him. "Or don't you know?"

He spears me with a look. "Really?"

Maybe that was a cheap shot. He deserves it. "What's her name?"

"Calle. Calle Ambrose. Tiffany wanted her to have the same last name as her. I guess for school, doctors and such. Plus, you know, it wasn't as if ..."

If he tells me one more time how he'd walked away from his own child, I really will murder him.

"You financially support the child, but don't have a relationship. Have you met her?"

"No."

My head lops forward. The hits just keep coming. "You can't be serious."

"Bec! Are you not listening? I didn't sign up for fatherhood.

If I didn't do it with you, I certainly wasn't doing it with a woman I barely knew. It was casual, Bec." He cuts his hand through air. "That's it."

"Until it wasn't," I shoot back. "A baby isn't *casual*."

Blowing air through his lips, he shakes his head. "I'm doing the best I can, given the situation."

"Then why is she calling my show?"

"I don't know."

"Are you current on child support?"

"Absolutely."

"Well, clearly she wants more."

"It's not money. She knows I'll give it to her."

How very generous of him. "Then it's notoriety. Her fifteen minutes of fame."

"I'll call her. See what it's about."

Oh, he'll *call* her? How generous. I slap my hands over my thighs. "Excellent. You do that." Having heard enough for one night, I stand. "We're not done, but I need to think about this."

"Nothing has to change."

Now who's naïve? I wag a finger at him as I stride by. "I'm going to pretend you didn't say that. How do you expect me to act like this hasn't happened? That my husband hasn't had multiple affairs, one of which produced a child and, oh, right, I'm reportedly this super-marriage-fixer. You've not only annihilated my trust and our marriage, you've taken my career with it."

CHAPTER 18

*C*ompletely wrung out, I navigate the New Jersey Turnpike and then the Garden State Parkway at eighty miles an hour. No easy feat on a normal day, never mind between intermittent bouts of hysteria.

At Ocean Avenue, I lower my window. As a kid, I'd do the same. Open the window the second we hit Ocean Ave. Moist, salty air fills the car and I inhale, fully drawing it in. I love it. Always have.

For me, there's really nothing like it.

I hang the left onto our block where the McMansions are lit up and dwarfing our cottage. Danny is home, his car in the drive instead of the garage.

And, thank God, there are no reporters or paparazzi milling about. At least that I can see. Danny's efforts with the police department have clearly worked. Perhaps his schmoozing skills are even better than Ryan's.

I pull into my driveway and shut the engine, looking around just in case. All I see is a couple, lit by a streetlamp, strolling on the next block.

Resting my head back, I close my eyes and crave rest. A lot of it. I may have an emergency Xanax or two in my vanity. A gift from my mother who regularly indulges.

I've never been tempted. Never had the desire. I consider it an accomplishment, given the stress and chaos of maintaining a quality show.

My phone rings. Danny. This can't be a coincidence.

"Bubby, you all right?"

Does he sit in his front window keeping watch? "I'm fine. Just pulled in. Catching my breath."

"I wasn't sure why you were sitting there. Coast is clear. Cops have been chasing vultures away all day."

"I'm sorry," I tell him.

"For what? Being famous?"

"Pretty much."

"You sound tired."

I let out a snot-filled laugh. "Danny, you have no idea."

"Want a drink?"

"Not tonight. Tomorrow, definitely. And, Danny, sorry to say, things might get a lot crazier around here."

"Uh-oh. New development?"

"Yep. I'll tell you about it tomorrow."

"Okay. Go inside. I'll stay on the phone until you get in. Just in case."

A good man. A good friend.

I sure need one right now.

AT NINE A.M. I'm hoofing it down the beach for the last half mile of a five-mile run. Beside me, the ocean waves break and slam the shore with the same violence roaring inside me. I could run ten or a hundred miles today and it wouldn't tame the monster devouring me.

I focus on breathing—in, out, in, out—and sidestep a hole in the sand that's big enough to break my ankle. Between children digging and folks putting up umbrellas, it's a hazard I've grown accustomed to.

The jutting turret on the house a block down from mine draws my attention. That turret is my motivation. The landmark representing the end of this torture I put myself through.

Pain shoots up my hamstrings through my glutes and settles in my lower back. It'll stay there until I stretch. And stretch and stretch.

I do this torture to stay in shape. Keep my legs strong and shapely with zero fat so they look good on camera. Age is kicking in, so I take enough collagen that I haven't experienced the loose, crepey skin many women do.

Yet.

It'll happen. At which point, I'll consider surgery. Yes, I'm that vain. It's not only about my career and looking good on camera, although, that's part of it.

I like shorts. I like my legs to look a certain way in those shorts.

I'm self-aware enough to admit it.

I shake it off. These thoughts? Who cares? My life is coming apart and I'm worried about loose skin?

I blow by the turret, slowing to an easy jog until I reach Danny's house. Sunlight glimmers off the glass that stretches from the first floor to the top of the house. The back of Danny's house is amazing. Glittering glass from end to end in all directions.

The upkeep must be brutal, but it's stunning.

Beside Danny's stunner is my single-story cottage with its wraparound deck and weather-worn steps.

I halt. Just stare at the two homes as if it's the first time.

Every house on this block—every one of them—has been torn down and rebuilt. Gone are the four-room cottages with clanging screen doors and rickety outdoor showers. All of them rebuilt to represent wealth.

Prestige.

All but mine. Mine is the has-been. The throwback to a simpler time when people only wanted an escape from the weekly grind and would drive down for a few days of salty serenity.

My family has owned this home my entire life. There is not a memory of the shore that doesn't include it. Sure, I've updated it over the years. New kitchen and paint, repaired steps, all of it an attempt to leave the footprint unchanged.

To hang on to my childhood.

I'm sentimental that way, I guess.

What I've called my adorable cottage has somehow become the ugly little sister to Danny's beauty queen and I'm suddenly seeing it from my neighbors' eyes.

I've heard the chatter, the casual questions about when I'll give the house a refresh.

I head up the stairs, taking them at a light jog. At the top, I'll run through stretches and then feed my ravenous system.

I realize that I never had dinner last night. Not that digestion would have been possible after finding out I'm a … what? Step-mother? No, that wouldn't be accurate.

Really, I'm nothing to that child.

I'm the wife of her father. Something, when this goes public, I'll have to figure out how to explain.

"Good morning, dear."

Whoa! I halt, my heart slamming.

Behind me, my mother lounges on our outdoor sectional. I let out a hard breath. The other thing I'm able to admit to myself in a completely non-judgy way is that my mother is the last person I want to see right now.

I'll have to tell her about Ryan's child. So not ready for that, but she's here, and it's as good a time as any.

"Hi, Mom. I didn't see you there."

"I'm sorry I startled you. On my way back from the bagel

place, I saw your car. I bought breakfast sandwiches. Are you hungry?"

A bagel sandwich. The carbs alone will bloat me straight out of my jeans.

"Starved, actually. Thank you. I need to stretch first."

"That's all right. I put them in the warmer."

A breeze kicks up, and she tilts her head back, allowing, for just a few seconds, the sun to splash over her face.

My mother is beautiful. Always has been.

Her face untouched by needles or scalpels, she's fought aging with every product available. She's the one who turned me on to taking collagen. As much as she loves the beach, she's always worn hats and sunscreen. Both of which have allowed her skin to remain supple with only laugh lines and slight crinkling around her eyes.

I want that. To be comfortable with wrinkles.

The network would have a fit.

"How was your week?" she asks.

Ha. My week. "Well, Mom, it actually *sucked*."

My mother's face distorts comically, her nose wrinkling. *"Well,"* she says. "That's quite blunt. Are you fighting with Ryan? Is this about the girlfriend?"

Shock factor complete, I prop one foot on the deck rail, stretching my hamstring, focusing on the pull and sudden release, and leaning into it. "It's about girlfriend number two."

A long pause ensues.

I can't look at her. No way. I keep stretching, focusing on the top of my foot for a few seconds before switching legs. "There are two women," I continue. "Not simultaneously. I guess we can give him credit for that."

"That's *one* way of looking at it."

"This one comes with a bonus. She has a baby."

"A *baby!*"

My mother, the drama queen.

"Yes. Ryan's."

Lowering my foot, I switch to a quad stretch and stare out at the ocean, ignoring the humiliation gutting me.

"Ryan has a *child*? After the two of you decided *against* it."

If my mother doesn't stop with the heavy emphasis on certain words, I might lose my mind. As if it's not horrible enough, she needs to amp it up a decibel or twelve?

"That's the kicker," I say. "We never decided against it. We simply didn't pursue it. I'm angry about that."

"That *bastard*. Men are *pigs*! Every last one of them. They're all alike. They want their wives at home, keeping their beds warm. Putting meals on the table, playing the perfect host to their social circle and family while they go out *carousing*. I'll say this, maybe wives should start doing that instead of staying home alone all the time."

Finally, I glance over at her and switch legs, stretching my other hamstring.

"I swear," my mother continues, "it's like we're supposed to fulfill all the roles that men want us to. What about *them*? When do *they* fulfill their roles?"

Giving up on the stretch, I stand tall, lean one hip against the railing and face her while she prattles on.

"When do *they* give us what *we* want? All these years …"

She stops talking. Whips her head up and squares her shoulders. The pulling-herself-together posture.

Ah. She's not talking about me and my cheating husband who suddenly has a child. She's talking about *her* husband.

My father.

Whom, for the most part, she's done a great job of not complaining to me about. She's protected him.

And me.

I've known though. I'm not blind and I'm certainly not stupid, recent events notwithstanding.

"Mom, are we talking about you right now? Or me? Because,

no offense, you've had choices. You could have walked out anytime."

She waves her hand, her elegant, coral-tipped fingers floating through the air. "Please. And wreck your life?"

My life? I'm forty-eight years old. I can only assume she means when I was a child. "Plenty of my friends had divorced parents."

"Oh, I know. Believe me."

"What does that mean?"

"The gossip, of course. You don't think people talked about those women? *Divorcees.* And worse, we had to make sure our husbands didn't fall for them. No way was I getting divorced. I liked my life."

At that, I laugh. "You liked the image of your life. Your actual life, the part you didn't let people see, wasn't so great, right? I mean, what about your friends?"

"What about them?"

"Did you ever share with them about the problems in your marriage?"

"It's nobody's business."

"Do you even have friends, Mom? I'm not talking about the country club folks that you meet for dinner once a month. Those are acquaintances. I'm talking about people you connect with on an intimate level."

Her glacial look should be enough to flash freeze me. "I have friends, Becca."

"Who are they?"

She gasps.

Yes, I'm being awful. Can't help it. For years, she's pressured me to keep my private life out of the public eye. To make sure no one saw anything but happy, happy Becca.

Even when my marriage fell into a rut, all the world saw was the country's top-rated talk show host who not only saved everyone else's marriage, she had a great one herself.

In short, I've turned into my mother. Letting people see only what I wanted. Not connecting on an intimate level. Too risky. If I allowed myself to open up, I became vulnerable. A story to sell.

"Mom, all these years you've said," I mimic my mother's sweet, high voice, "'Be careful who you get close to, Becca. Don't get too friendly, Becca. Don't share too much, Becca.'" I shake my head, cross my arms. "My paranoia runs deep. Do you know that? I'm terrified, Mom—*terrified*—to form relationships. I'm constantly worried everyone will disappoint me."

"It's not a bad thing."

"It's a horrible thing!"

My mother, clearly having had enough of me, finally stands. "Your relationship issues—marital or otherwise—are not my fault, Becca. Don't take it out on me."

I watch her walk toward the slider.

She's right.

I can't blame her for the things I've allowed to control my life. I'm an adult. Fully capable of making choices. Breaking whatever cycle I'd like.

Isn't that what I tell my patients?

No. Not patients. Show guests. That's all they are to me. They come and go. No long-term commitment. No ongoing sessions.

Just done.

If they're lucky, we have them back to tout their—and my—success at saving their marriage.

I follow my mother through the slider. "Mom, I'm sorry. I shouldn't have spoken to you like that."

She grabs her purse off the counter stool. "You're right. Maybe you have more of your father in you than I thought."

With that, she waltzes out the front door, closing it gently behind her, the soft click of the latch echoing in the silent house.

My mother isn't the door-slamming type. She doesn't need it. Her power, her rage stays hidden, vibrating just below skin surface, where only she knows about it.

I suppose that's the problem with my father. He sees the rage, but doesn't care anymore because he knows she'll come back.

And now, she's done to me what she typically does to him. She's walked out, stewing.

Only she usually comes here to stew. Where will she go now?

I run to the door, whipping it open and bolt to the driveway where Mom is backing out.

"Mom! Wait."

She simply puts up her hand. A wave or the classic stop sign? Gotta give it to my mother, I'm not sure.

I catch up, smacking my hands on the hood of her Mercedes. "Wait!"

She keeps going, backing out, letting me know she doesn't intend to stop. She's that mad.

A first for us.

Makes me wonder if this is what it's like with my father. Did he chase after her the first few times? Then, when she came back, he knew this was how it would be. They'd fight, she'd leave, she'd come back.

Dysfunction at its best.

I halt at the end of my driveway, watch her brake and then shift the car to drive. I could leap in front of the vehicle. Block her path. Make her listen to me.

Won't do any good. Not now. She's angry and I know her. It takes a bit to cool off.

I stand in the driveway and watch her go.

"Bubby! What the hell are you doing?"

I turn and spot Danny marching across his driveway, hands

flying. The garage door is open. Chasing after Mom kept me busy enough not to have noticed him.

My mom drives down the street at her typical leisurely pace. *Nothing to see here!* After an argument, she takes on a mystical, calm demeanor.

It's a gift, really.

I flap my arms at Danny. "I just had a fight with my mother."

"No kidding. I heard you yelling from inside. Half the neighborhood heard you."

Great. Excellent. Not only do I have a scandal brewing, I'm causing a scene. *On a roll, Becca.*

Well, so what?

I've spent years controlling my emotions. All that stress locked inside? It's tearing up my organs. I've dealt with ulcers and stomach cramps. Migraines that left me in a dark bedroom, barely able to move for days.

All so the world could see happy, happy Becca.

Happy Becca is the pits. Humans aren't built for that. My life is falling apart. I deserve to be a menace to my neighbors.

"You know what?" I say way louder than my mother would approve. "I. Don't. *Care.* Have you eaten? Mom brought breakfast sandwiches I probably don't deserve, but I'll be damned if I'll let them go to waste. Carbs and all!"

Danny scurries up beside me, his shorter legs double-timing to keep up as I storm back to the house.

"Ooh-eee," he says. "Have I mentioned you might be crazy?"

Might be? Please.

The two of us tromp through my front door and I point to one of the counter stools, head to the oven and tap the warmer off while I get coffee going. I'll take the sandwiches out once I have an espresso in hand.

"Espresso? And, please, don't lecture me about the caffeine amping me up more. After the week I've had, I want full throttle."

"Oh, hey, if you're making it, I'll take one."

"Milk?"

"No. Black. What can I do?"

I point to the cabinet. "Plates are in there. Silver is in the drawer below."

Something about the step-by-step process of crafting the beverage relaxes me. If my career goes bust, I may have a future as a barista. I go to work, scooping beans into the grinder and then smack the button. The whirring sound gives me something to focus on other than my argument with Mom. Once the beans are thoroughly demolished, I move on to filling the water reservoir on Ryan's insanely expensive espresso machine.

Only the best for Ryan.

Only the best.

I remind myself that I like this machine and the process that goes with it. That I find it *soothing*.

After measuring out the precise amount of coffee—I have it down to a science—I set to work making two double espressos, then grab one of the hand-thrown cups from the stand. Like my husband, there are certain things I'll splurge on. Custom-made espresso cups big enough to hold a double are one of them and these are fantastic.

Danny does a decent job of setting out plates and silverware and takes a seat at the island. "What happened with your mom?"

I don't bother looking back at him. "I was a jerk." While waiting on the coffee, I shake my head and fiddle with the frother. "I didn't know she was coming and wasn't prepared to have a conversation. I knew it and did it anyway. I'm a *therapist*. Should have known better."

"Listen, you may be famous, but we all mess up sometimes. You've had a rough couple of weeks. She'll forgive you."

The coffee drips, so I turn to the wall oven where I grab three bagel sandwiches. Why three, I have no idea since my father is probably working. Maybe Mom wanted to give me a choice. She's good that way. Always fussing over the people she loves. That realization slams me with a fresh round of guilt.

The foil is warm to the touch, but not hot and I carry them to Danny, setting them on the island. "Take your pick. I'll eat anything."

He surveys the choices while I tend to our coffee and hand him the first cup. "Sugar?"

"No."

Wow. He's good. Espresso is bold. Particularly this blend. I need sweetener.

I start in on the next coffee, but glance over my shoulder. "Don't wait. Eat. I'll be right there."

Against my orders, he waits, but takes a sip of the brew.

"Fantastic," he says. "You'll have to teach me."

"It's easy. It's not the process so much, but the beans. Gotta do fresh-ground. There's a coffee and tea shop in Long Branch. They have the best beans around."

I finish crafting my latte and join Danny at the island, unwrapping one sandwich and taking a bite before even bothering to see what it is. It hits my tongue and I nearly groan with pleasure at the gooey cheese and greasy pork roll that sends my taste buds into euphoria. "My God, that's good. A heart attack waiting to happen."

"You just ran your ass off."

He's right. I take another bite, force myself to chew slowly, savoring it before swallowing. I shift to face Danny before taking another bite of my sandwich. "You asked about my mother. I told her about my latest development and we went off the rails."

"What development?"

I shift front again and take a gargantuan bite of my sandwich. Stress eater much? I chew once, attempt to swallow the whole thing and the wad gets stuck in my throat. My eyes bulge and I swallow again and again, slamming a gulp of my coffee while Danny smacks me on the back.

"Easy there," he says. "You okay?"

Nodding, I set the sandwich down. Stress eating almost just got me the Heimlich maneuver, so I'd better take a break.

Back to Danny I go. "The fight with my mom. Vegas rules?"

"Vegas rules."

For good measure, he holds up his pinky and we do a pinky swear. The gesture makes me smile. Danny has that way about him. He knows how to disarm a situation, suck the tension right out with a silly pinky swear.

Which is good because I need advice. I could try my agent, the one I normally speak with twice a year for the obligatory, you're-my-client-so-I'm-calling-you effort. She left me a voicemail when the Page Six story ran, but I haven't called her back yet. Really, she can't help me now. Not yet anyway. I need a friend and with pissing off my mother and my current hatred of my husband, Danny is the closest thing I have to a confidant.

"There's another woman," I blurt.

Danny's eyebrows shoot up. "Two women? At *once?* Ambitious."

"No. This one was before Laurel. A server at the coffee shop where he eats every morning. Now she works at a steak place on the Upper East Side."

Danny lifts his sandwich. "She upgraded."

"She had to. She had a baby."

Bagel in midair, mouth open and ready to bite, he halts. "Don't even."

I lift my mug in toast. "Here's to Ryan and his amazing sperm."

The sandwich plummets from Danny's hand, landing so hard on the plate that the top half slides free. He wipes his fingers on his napkin and reaches for my arm, giving me a squeeze. "Bubby, I'm sorry."

The gesture is so soft, so pure and heartfelt, it stuns me. In this business, I don't run into a lot of that. Doing what my staff does, it's numbing. Makes people jaded.

Secret babies? We see them all the time. Total sweeper.

Except, this time, it's Ryan's secret baby, and that takes a sweeper to another level.

What Danny offers now? Kindness. No gallows humor or crass jokes?

I'm not sure what to do with that.

I catch my breath as an image of Ryan, my beautiful, supportive Ryan, holding his child takes residence in my brain.

Tears bubble up and I set my mug down, slam my eyes closed. A strangled sob erupts from my throat. Talk about humiliating.

Panic floods me. I reach for my napkin, frantically swiping at the now-flowing tears. "I'm so sorry."

My mother would be mortified. Her words ring back. *Don't share your business, Becca. It never amounts to anything good.*

Danny releases my arm, waves me off and sits back. "What are you apologizing for?"

What *am* I apologizing for? For being hurt by the so-called love of my life?

I finish blotting my face and toss the napkin down. "I don't know what to do. Laurel, the mistress, was one thing. Plenty of men have affairs. It let me parlay trying to save my marriage with a ratings boon. It checked every box for keeping my career intact while being transparent about our issues. This? Too much. Too degrading. And worse, Ryan knew about this child and still went along with doing a show on us. How does a man who says he loves me let me make a fool of myself like that?"

Still facing me, Danny drums his fingers on his thighs. "One thing at a time here. Tell me about this baby. Has he taken responsibility?"

I give him the rundown on Ryan paying support, but having not met the child.

"Okay," he says.

Just okay. No commentary on what a jerk my husband is. For that, I'm thankful. We both know it's true, but knowing it and hearing it are two entirely different things.

I lift my hand, palm up. "Okay, what?"

"We know where he stands on the whole thing. At least he's not living some kind of double life."

Isn't he? "He says he told these women he'd never leave me. I guess he simply likes *variety*."

Sarcasm. The ultimate salve for a broken heart.

"Anyway, when my mother showed up here this morning, I wasn't prepared for a conversation. I hadn't sorted out how to tell her and I kinda snapped."

"Why?"

With my parents' business, I have to be careful. Sharing details of my bad marriage is one thing. My parents' marriage? No. "There are things in my life, ways I conduct myself that are my mother's doing. Bad or good, she's drilled it into me. I've grown to resent it and I lost it. I was unkind."

Danny tilts his head. "Honey, you gotta give yourself a break. You're stressed. Lost your temper. Last I checked, you don't own the corner on screwups. You'll apologize and talk it out. She knows you love her."

That's true. She does. I tell her. A lot. Some of my shoulder tension melts away. As a therapist, I should appreciate the act of talking things through, yet the relief I'm experiencing somehow surprises me. "I hope so."

"What are you thinking?"

"About?"

He holds his hands out. "Your marriage? Do you want to save it?"

"I can't even look at him, how am I supposed to stay married to him?"

"I understand. I put my first wife through this. Not the child part, but the affair. It took her two years before she could have a non-kid-related conversation with me."

Two years. Wow. "Really?"

"Truth. My therapist says she was grieving."

"You have a therapist?"

"Bubby, after three failed marriages? Bet your life."

The grieving thing makes sense to me. I've told guests the same. Grief isn't only about physical death. It comes with all forms of endings and takes a good couple of years to work through.

Whether my marriage is over or not, I've suffered a massive ending to the life I thought I had. To the *man* I thought I knew.

"Even if I want to save the marriage," I say, "clearly this woman intends to go public. I mean, why would she call the show?"

He shrugs. "Ask her. She reached out to you—"

"To my show."

"Yes. Knowing the message would get to you. Why'd she do that when she could have called Ryan?"

"Ryan says he gives her money. She either wants more or she wants something else. Figure out what it is."

"And, what? I call her up, we talk and then I tell my network there's a secret baby we're adding to this shitshow? I'm not doing that."

"Whoa. I didn't say add her to the show. I wouldn't rush into *that* decision. An affair is one thing. A child is another. He'll be crucified on social media."

"I know! That's why I don't know what to do. I can't go on television, claim I want to fix my broken marriage, but gee folks, I only want to fix the part about the woman he didn't have a child with. This other woman? The one with Ryan's *baby*?

We're not talking about that. It's ridiculous. Beyond ridiculous. I'll be a laughingstock. And worse, I have the next three days to figure it out."

"Why three days?"

"Um, I have to be back at the office on Monday."

Again, he shrugs. "Why?"

"I have a taping! I can't just call in sick."

"Cancel it. You're the host. You've had an emergency. A personal issue. The world already knows about Ryan's affair. It's the perfect excuse. Put out a statement that you're taking a few weeks off to focus on your personal life. Boom. Done."

"The network expects us to tape the segments on my marriage next week."

"Tell them no."

Tell them no? Has he lost his mind?

He must see the horror on my face because he laughs. Literally laughs at me. "Hear me out," he says. "You probably have a couple of weeks of shows in the can, right? Run those. You'll have to catch up when you get back, but it's doable. You're a strong woman, Becca. Room to breathe is what you need to figure out what you want for your life."

A few weeks off.

That sounded heavenly. And in May? Right before tourist season goes full blown and I can enjoy the serenity and space.

Danny might be on to something.

"I'll think about it," I say. "One thing is a definite though."

"What's that?"

"I'm calling her. I want to know what this woman wants."

CHAPTER 19

I take a quick shower to wash away the sweat and rotten energy from my argument with Mom before I call one Tiffany Ambrose. Dressed in shorts and a long-sleeved T-shirt, I head to the kitchen, lining up my mental to-do list. I have emails to deal with, notes on future shows and the dreaded outline for Marley.

Although, after this latest development, I'm not sure segments on my imploding marriage are wise. I'm just not sure how to get out of it without pissing off the suits.

I grab my laptop and phone from the table where I left them, ready to take both out on the deck where I can watch the waves and recharge after the emotional morning.

Arguing with Mom has never been a thing. Maybe once a year I'll disagree with her, but never spewing emotional vomit.

For years, I've kept myself in check. Always burying my feelings. I'd been bred for that. From the time I'd witnessed that nasty fight between my parents, my mother has drilled into me not to overshare.

I turn, peer around my house where I've hosted countless dinners and barbecues for acquaintances.

None of whom I'd call a friend. Not in the genuine sense where we share secrets and gossip about silly things like sagging skin, weight gain and husbands.

Prior to me dumping my problems on Danny, there's been no one I'd allow myself to be vulnerable with. That I'd expose myself to.

Too much risk that they'll leak some juicy bit to a tabloid.

Mom and Ryan. That's it. Not even my father.

These thoughts. I don't need them. Keep moving. That's all I need to do.

I head out to the deck with my laptop, phone and leather portfolio, the Gucci one Ryan gave me for Christmas, and settle into my favorite chair.

Before contacting Tiffany Ambrose, I do a quick check of my emails to make sure there's nothing new I should know.

I click on a message from Jenny sent first thing this morning. Despite my telling her it was unnecessary, she transcribed her notes regarding Tiffany. I do a quick skim, finding Tiffany's number. It might as well have been a neon sign the way my attention locks on to it.

This woman has reached out to me. She wants something. Probably my husband. Or money. The shakedown I see celebrities fall victim to while trying to hide their secrets.

Not happening. I'll tell the world about Ryan's child myself before I'll be blackmailed.

That alone stiffens my spine. My career and marriage might be collapsing, but I'm still me. There's comfort there and I soak it up.

I scoop up my phone, enter the code that will display "restricted" on the other end and then dial the number from Jenny's email.

Three rings in, someone answers. "Hello?"

Her voice is ... nice. Higher than mine with a sweetness that's not sugary.

Young. How old is this girl? Wait. I know. I check Jenny's notes to be sure. Twenty-eight.

"Hello," I say, my voice steady thanks to years of on-air work. "This is Becca Matthews."

A long pause ensues. "Oh," she finally says, the word breathy and scraping my last nerve. "Hi. Thank you."

"For?"

"Um, calling? I guess. Didn't think you would."

Neither did I, honey. I shake it off, channel Dr. Becca. "You should know, I've spoken to Ryan. He confirms what you told my producer."

"I'm sorry about that. Telling the producer. I tried asking for you, but they wouldn't put me through."

She's sorry, but not for screwing my husband. Something unleashes inside me and my ribs ache. I stare out at the blue of the Atlantic and the sun glistening off whitecaps. I can do this. I know I can.

"What is it you want?" I ask.

"I'm not sure."

"Pardon?"

"I . . ."

"Tiffany, if it's money—"

She gasps. Either she's a talented actress—I've seen plenty of those—or she's truly horrified.

"It's not," she spits. "I have enough. I work. And Ryan helps. He's good that way."

My lying, adulterous husband deserves brownie points? He won't get them from me, but at least we're not being black-mailed. Relief washes over me.

"You did a show awhile back," Tiffany says.

Something about her watching my show completely creeps me out. "I do a lot of shows."

"Right. The one with the husband who was living a double

life. He had children and his wife resented his kids. You made the point that the children were innocent. Did you mean that?"

Where was *this* going? I could balk. Tell her it's television and we say a lot of things for good ratings. But that? True. Children shouldn't be held responsible for their parents' unacceptable behavior. They're the innocents.

"Yes," I say, even though it'll probably haunt me. "I meant it."

"That's nice. Important. Kids are, you know, they can really get screwed up. Anyway, my daughter. Her name is Calle."

"I'm aware."

"Right. Well, I saw the posts about Ryan's affair. His other one. And I thought, now that he's been … outed … I guess, it was time."

And here we go. I draw a breath. Wait for whatever demand is coming. "Time?"

"Calle doesn't have anyone. I'm an only child. I left home when I was sixteen and haven't been back. Ever. I don't even talk to my parents."

How this is my problem, I'm not sure. "Look, Tiffany, you'll need to just spit it out because I have no idea what you want from me."

"Ryan is her father."

"Ryan doesn't want children. And you've just assured me he's provided for …" The baby's name is stuck. Right there on my tongue. "Her."

I can't say it. If I do, she becomes real. Yes, it's ridiculous. I know she exists, but somehow, if I don't actually speak her name, I can pretend Ryan hasn't done this to us.

"That's why I called you," Tiffany says. "I don't really talk to Ryan. He's not interested."

"And?"

"Well, I was watching the news the other night. They had this family on. Divorced parents. The dad, turned out, was gay.

He was in a relationship with another man and they had a baby. The two families were, like, blended, I guess."

It hits me so hard I collapse back in my chair.

This woman wants a … a …. *Family?* Shock paralyzes me. She should have asked for money.

Money was easy. I have a ton.

Gobsmacked, I draw a breath, concentrate on keeping my tone even. "You want us to …"

"It's not like I want to spend every weekend with you. Or have Calle spend the weekends. I know that's not possible. Ryan was clear. Crystal. No. Kids."

It sounds harsh. More harsh than I've known Ryan to be, yet, when he locks on to something there's no wiggle room. I can hear it. His indignant tone that can scrape me raw. Had he used that tone with Tiffany regarding his own child?

If so, for a brief second, she has my sympathy, and it knocks the edge off my ire. "Then what is it you want?"

"Maybe a get-together? I don't know. Just so she knows people love her."

We don't know her, how can we love her? It's not her fault though, this baby whose only offense is existing.

That tears it. She wants her child to be loved. What good mother wouldn't?

The simple fact is so unexpected, and so clearly from the heart, I have no reply.

Damned Ryan.

Not only does he cheat on me. Not only does he lie and secretly support his mistress and child, he walks away from them.

And now I have to clean up the mess. I could sit here and rail on her. Scream about her immense nerve expecting me to accept her child into my world.

Not a child. Not yet. We're talking about a six-month-old *baby.*

"Hello? Dr. Becca?"

Dr. Becca. The name of my show. I suppose it's better than Dr. Matthews. Or worse, Mrs. Matthews.

I sit up, clear my throat. "This is a lot."

That much, I can admit.

"I know. I'm sorry. For everything. I'm so, so sorry. I was stupid and naïve."

For whatever reason, I believe her. I also need to end this call. It's too much. Ryan, my mother, Tiffany. The day from hell.

"Um," I say, "I need to think about this and talk to Ryan."

"Right. Sure."

"Give me a couple of days." *A year or twenty, maybe.* "I'm assuming I can reach you at this number?"

"Yes. It's my cell."

"All right."

"Dr. Becca?"

Again with the Dr. Becca. "It's Becca."

"Oh, okay. Yes. Becca, thank you."

"For what?"

"Calling back. Being decent. Most wouldn't."

On that, I know from experience, she's correct. "I can't promise you anything. Especially where Ryan is concerned. But I'll consider this. That's the best I can offer. In the future, please don't call the show. Call Ryan."

I hang up without saying goodbye. There is only so much of civilized Dr. Becca inside me. I sit for a few long minutes, staring out at the ocean's whitecaps and the sun glistening off the water.

What am I supposed to do?

I glance over at Danny's house. I've dumped enough of my personal life on him. At some point, he'll get irritated. Won't he?

Or was that part of friendship? Being there for each other. No matter how annoying.

No clue.

Another sad realization in a day filled with them. I have work to do. On myself. On my relationships.

People talk all the time about having a tribe. I never, even doing what I do, quite understood it. I had my mother and Ryan. They, I suppose, were my tribe.

Both are currently unavailable to me.

I'm alone and must fix that. Eventually. Now, I have to decide what to do about Ryan's child.

Two hours later, I'm still sitting on my deck, doing nothing. Zippo. When was the last time that happened?

Even if I'd tried dealing with emails, my attention span ranks in the negative. In the time I've been sitting here, I've decided to tell Ryan I spoke to the mother of his child. For a brief few minutes, I'd considered keeping him in the dark. Retribution for all the secrets he's held. Unfortunately, or fortunately, depending on how one looks at it, I don't have the energy to carry all that weight around.

I scoop up my phone, tap the favorites icon and then Ryan's name. This time of day, he'll be at his office.

Well, I think.

Given what I've learned, he might be out screwing a server.

He immediately picks up. "Hi."

Not screwing a waitress, I guess. "Can you talk?"

"I'd love to. Hang on. Let me close my door."

I wait, hear the snick of a door latching on the other side.

"I'm glad you called. I was going to, but … Jesus, Bec. How did we get here?"

Really? *He's* asking *me*?

"No," he says. "Don't answer. I know how we got here. It's my fault. All of it. I promise, it'll change. I'll do whatever you want. Just, please, don't leave me."

Something in his tone, that defeated rumble, makes me believe he means it. That he loves me.

"It can't be what I want," I say. "*You* have to want it. We can do therapy for the next ten years, but if you're not willing to work, don't waste my time."

It may be cruel, but honesty often is. From where I'm sitting, I've spent years thinking my marriage was something altogether different. Were we in a rut? Sure. A lot of couples are. Did I think there was a baby with another woman? *Uh, no.*

"I'll do the work," he says. "I swear."

I don't respond. I'm not ready. Still processing what I've learned. I'm not even sure I want therapy. And that terrifies me.

"Ry, I called Tiffany."

His only response is silence. I know he's still there. I can hear him breathing, so I wait him out.

"You spoke to her?"

"I did. It was awkward, obviously, but I wanted to know why she called."

"And?"

"It's not money."

"I told you that. I give her …" He trails off, realizing he probably shouldn't share that he gives another woman anything she needs.

I grip the phone tighter, force myself to stay focused. "She's concerned about her—about *your* daughter."

"Why? Is she sick or something?"

The way he says "she" snaps my head back. Sucker punched. His child isn't some random stranger he saw on the street. Her name may be stuck on his tongue, as it was on mine. Buried under the weight of his mistakes.

"No, Ryan. She's not sick. Tiffany has no family; I assume you know that."

"She has family. They're estranged."

"Whatever. They're not in … Calle's … life." There. Said it.

It's oddly freeing. "She wants *Calle* to have a family. And since you've made your position clear—"

"She came to you, thinking you could talk me into it. I can't believe this."

He can't believe it. That's almost comical. "Well," I say, "it's not about you. For once."

"Nice, Bec."

Sure is. "This is a courtesy call to tell you I'm going to meet your daughter. Whether or not you approve."

"Why would you do that?"

I'm lost for an answer. "I honestly don't know. However, Calle shouldn't be punished because her father—"

Is a lying asshole?

I shake it off. "Whatever."

"Bec, please don't do this. The arrangement is working. If Tiffany needs something, she contacts me. That's it. She knew from the start what it was."

Foolish, foolish man.

"Perhaps," I say, "but your poor decision-making led to a child. I will not allow that child to feel alone. To feel that, if her mother isn't available, she has no one."

To feel like I feel at this very moment because my mother isn't speaking to me.

And there it is. An absolute wrecking ball to my head.

The line goes silent again. I'm not surprised. Ryan isn't accustomed to being called out. Frankly, I never had reason to.

Foolish, foolish woman.

"So." I let out a breath. "I'm going to call her back and set something up. I'll do it quietly and in a discreet location where we won't be seen."

"Where?"

"I'm not sure. It won't be here. Probably in the city."

"If that's what you want, I can't stop you."

No. He can't. I note he hasn't offered to accompany me on what he has to know will be a painful meeting.

"All right," I say. "I'll keep you posted."

For the second time today, I hang up without offering a goodbye. I can't think too hard about that.

I'm entitled to my anger. I'm also entitled to a weekend of peace while I contemplate the recent addition to my life.

CHAPTER 20

On Friday morning, I roll over, stare out at a hazy gray sky over the tops of the shades in my bedroom.

I usually don't sleep with them open. Too risky, that. After all, the paparazzi aren't exactly kind when it comes to selling photos of celebrities who aren't camera-ready.

Last night, however, a blanket of stars glittered, so I slipped on the Boss Lady nightshirt Jenny gave me for Christmas, crawled into bed, hit the remote on the shades and lowered them enough to watch the light show.

I managed to fall asleep and apparently stayed that way because here it is—I glance at my phone in the dock beside my bed: 9:30.

What?

It's been daylight for hours and I've been snoozing away. Heaven help me. Still, if someone *had* put a ladder or chair in front of my bedroom window, I'd have heard them.

I hope.

Scrambling, I shove covers off and get to my feet. The room whirls—stood up too fast—and I hold my arms out, grasping at nothing but air.

Slow down. It's Friday. I'm down the shore and have nowhere to be. Not even a Zoom meeting to attend.

What's the rush?

My run. That's the rush. Way behind schedule. Even on my relaxed shore schedule. Time to log my miles. Keep the legs and body lean. The idea drops like a lead balloon, the heaviness pushing me back a few steps to the bed where I perch on the edge.

What if I stayed here?

Binge-watched Lifetime movies from bed while my world, the one outside these windows, spun wildly out of control. No Internet. No social media. No emails. I wouldn't be the first person to escape and hide from life for the day.

Run.

It's like an incessant pecking in my brain. Run, run, run. As if I'm committing some crime by not logging those miles.

I've done this to myself. Created this routine, this uncompromising exercise schedule that now feels wrong if I vary it.

But I'm so freaking tired. I glance at the treadmill in the corner.

That blasted thing. It's become a symbol for my existence. Each day, the treadmill of my life dictating what I should or shouldn't do.

I shove my shoulders back. My life. My routine.

I decide.

Hitting the button on the remote, I fully open the shades. Cloudy, but not raining. The ocean looms, the whitecaps from yesterday gone, leaving an odd sense of calm. The Atlantic is never quiet. It likes action. The hard break of waves, even on calm days.

This, I think, is what I need. Action, but calm. As much as I'd love to curl into bed and pull the covers over my head, it's not me.

I'd be bored in four—maybe three—minutes.

I get to my feet again, slowly this time, setting myself. When the room stays put, I head to the closet for running shorts, a tank and a long-sleeved running shirt. This time of year, the morning, considering the clouds, probably still has a chill.

My sneakers sit dutifully on the closet floor. I bypass them, opting for my slides that I'll kick off at the base of the stairs.

No running.

Today, I'm doing my version of crawling under the covers. Slowing down, giving my brain a rest, taking time to be grateful for the beach and sand. The ocean that settles me.

For this life that, although it is in turmoil, allows me these moments.

As I walk.

ON MONDAY MORNING, after not running for four solid days, I take the Snooty into the city. After a weekend of soul-searching, I didn't come to any concrete conclusions on my marriage. I largely spent the time alone, even avoiding Danny. Not for any reason other than simply needing to hibernate and block out the noise.

Given my lack of decisions regarding my marriage, I'll be commuting again this week. It'll be an extra few hours out of my days, but I'll be in my happy place. All I know is I can't be under the same roof as Ryan.

One thing at a time.

I spot Bernie standing next to the idling SUV and hop in, pulling my wig off. When I'd boarded the yacht, the young guy checking me in located my name on the list and then asked for my ID. I'll give him credit because he handled it like a champ, basically ignoring the blonde wig, rather than the honey-blonde on my driver's license photo.

He had the whole I-see-this-all-the-time vibe.

Bernie glances at me in the rearview. "How was the weekend?"

"Quiet," I tell him. "Yours?"

"Good. Saw the grandkids."

This is our Monday routine. I get in the car, we exchange brief pleasantries and then fall into silence while I bury my head in my phone.

Every Monday.

Same, same, same.

I pick up said phone, run my finger over the darkened screen until it lights up with the photo of Ry and me all glammed up at the Met Gala.

My rib cage does that weird collapsing thing and I'm reminded, not that I could forget, that the life I knew, the one of the smiling couple in that photo, was a facade. A fake. A knockoff of what a good marriage should look like.

I tap my password in, change the photo to the one of the beach I took on my morning walk yesterday.

Then I drop the phone into the cup holder. "Bernie, tell me about your grandkids."

He eyes me again, then goes back to the morning crush. "My grandkids?"

"Yes. Tell me what they love. Anything."

From my spot in the back seat, I see his puzzlement. The way he rolls his bottom lip out, cocks his head sideways. Probably wondering who I am and what happened to his boss.

"It occurs to me," I say, "we've fallen into a routine. To be honest, I blame routine for my current situation. I've gotten so caught up in the day-to-day of living that I'm screwing up."

"Screwing *up*? Are you kidding me?"

"Serious as a heart attack. I've been checked out, Bernie." My mother's warnings about oversharing crash into my thoughts like a pickaxe.

My mother who, by the way, still hasn't returned my calls, is giving me fits. I believe she knows that and I find it a childish manipulation.

Bernie honks at a taxi, lets out a muffled swear. "Checked out of what?"

"My marriage for one. I missed the signs. No. I can't even say that. I knew we were in a rut."

"Whoa, a rut isn't an excuse to—"

Bam, he stops talking. Just smacks his lips together and holds up a hand. "Sorry. I overstepped. Not my business."

There's that imaginary line I've drawn between myself and the people surrounding me. Bernie? Different. Not a staffer or an intern. He's so much more than my driver.

"Bern, you overhear everything I talk about in this car. Of all the people in my life, you've probably heard more of my personal business than anyone. You've never once betrayed me. In return, I've given you nothing."

"Pfft. You give me plenty."

"I'm not talking about bonuses and gifts. I'm talking about things that matter. Conversation and caring about what you do outside of this car. Tell me about your grandkids."

Yes, he probably thinks I've lost my mind. That I'm reacting to Ryan's infidelity. Maybe I am.

But I'm also sick of living my life in fear of getting close to people.

Sick to death of it.

"*Well,*" he says. "Wendy is the oldest." He laughs. "She got screwed. Poor kid. My son is a sports nut. I guess it's my fault. We all are. Even Evelyn. She says if you can't beat 'em, join 'em."

I smile, enjoying the easy way he speaks of his family. He's never done this before. Probably because I hadn't given him the opportunity. I don't think I ever acted uninterested, but I certainly never encouraged it.

Never wanted to blur the lines between personal and professional.

"My son has three girls," he says. "No boys. He's shoving every sport imaginable at Wendy. I tell him all the time, leave her alone. She's an artist! My middle granddaughter likes books. The little one? She's four. Forget about it. She's nuts. Always on the go. Massive energy to burn. Loves to wrestle with her sisters. He might have a shot at an athlete with her."

I can't help but laugh. "I'd like to meet her. I love a girl who goes against the grain. Bring her along sometime. All the girls. We can give them a tour of the studio."

He perks up, meeting my gaze in the rearview. "Really? They'd love that."

"Of course. Why didn't you ask? I'd have gladly set it up."

"I didn't want to overstep."

There's that word again. Obviously, I have given him the impression I've been uninterested. *Becca, Becca, Becca.*

He eases to a stop at a light, the midtown traffic the typical snarl of a Monday rush hour. I lean forward and the seatbelt tugs across my neck. It'll probably leave a burn mark Steph will have to cover, but who cares?

I touch Bernie's elbow, but he keeps his focus on the road. "If I ever made you think you'd be overstepping, I'm sorry. That was never my intention."

He lifts his left hand from the wheel, covers mine with his. "Not at all. I knew it wasn't personal. People in your position can't let random folks in. Good way to get taken advantage of. I get that."

"Yes, but you're not random. I hope you know that."

He gets quiet for a second, clearing his throat. Have I choked up the tough, retired cop?

I believe I have. I kinda love it.

"Thank you," he says. "That means a lot."

The light turns green and Bernie shoots through the intersection. I sit back, stare out the window at the skyscrapers and storefronts and turn my attention to the day ahead.

On the Snooty, I sent Don a text about a quick meeting today. I'm taking Danny's advice and requesting a couple of weeks off. My battered brain and heart need the rest, and I don't have the energy for Marley's verbal swordplay.

Or, frankly, other people's marital issues. I'd be even more of a fraud by trying to help others when I can't even help myself.

I peer back at Bernie. I owe him an explanation. Of course, he'll be paid for the weeks I'm away, but he deserves to know this latest potential scandal.

"Bern," I say, when he brakes for another light half a block from the studio. "I'm hoping to take a couple of weeks off. An unplanned vacation."

"You should," he says. "You work hard. Plus, the last couple of weeks. The photographers and reporters? I'd get the hell out of Dodge."

If only it were that easy.

The light changes and he zooms through it, pulling to the right and stopping at the usual spot at the curb. He slides the gearshift to park and swivels to face me.

"There's more drama," I say. "I want you to hear it from me. I found out last week that Ryan has a child with another woman. It's a second woman. Not the one we knew about."

He gives me the same wide-eyed shock I'd seen on Danny, then rearranges his face into a neutral, non-judgy expression. "Becca, I'm so sorry. I … don't know what to say. And that's a first."

I do my best at a smile. "There's nothing to say. Obviously, it's devastating. The woman called the show last week. I won't get into that, but I've spoken with her. I may actually decide to meet the child."

"Wow."

I let out a sigh. "Well said."

"Thanks for telling me." He shakes his head. "It has to be

brutal. If you need anything—anything at all—I'm here. I've got you."

He's got me. Lord, that sounds good. Too good. But I believe it. Am absolutely sure of it. I jerk my head. "Now *that* means a lot to *me*. It might get a little crazy in the next few weeks. So, thank you."

He nods, then hops out to open my door while I fluff my hair and ready myself to face the world as Dr. Becca, number one daytime talk show host.

CHAPTER 21

*B*efore I can even fire up my laptop, Jenny strides into my office bringing her typical frenetic energy with her. She's like a rubber ball ricocheting off the ceiling.

She's wearing slacks and a button-down cotton shirt. Her hair is stacked on top of her head, secured with a pencil. Another of her habits. Why she doesn't keep a supply of hair ties in her desk, I'll never know.

Habits. Hard to break.

Really hard.

The psychologist in me knows this.

Thankfully, I'd already had coffee on the Snooty because there's no way, after the last couple of weeks, I could face Jenny's interminable stamina without a caffeine bump.

"Morning," she says.

"Good morning. How was the weekend?"

"Good."

Once again, as with Bernie, this is typically the extent of it. No prolonged conversation about who did what, unless of course, it somehow pertained to work.

Kaitlyn appears at the window, then swings her head around the doorframe. "Starbucks run. Need anything?"

"I'm good," I say. "Thank you."

She peers at Jenny, who shakes her head, and Kaitlyn is gone. That fast, on the move again.

"So," I say, "the weekend. Did you do anything fun?"

For a second, she eyes me. Yes, I'm breaking protocol. It's about time. Jenny has been with me since my morning show gig and I barely know her.

That has to change.

She draws her eyebrows together and scrunches her nose.

Really? Is it this bad that she's completely perplexed by my asking what she did over the weekend?

"Um," she says, "a new gallery opened down the street from me?"

She poses this more as a question than statement, something I can only surmise results from her not being sure what exactly is happening. I stifle a laugh. "That sounds like fun."

"It was actually. We met a new artist. Eclectic. Sort of modern with a little surrealism thrown in. If that makes sense."

The "we" she's referring to is Jenny's significant other. They've been together, hmm… ten years? Fifteen?

Another thing I should probably know and don't.

I relax in my chair, cross one leg over the other and settle in. I don't mind starting the day this way. No drama, no crisis right out of the gate. "Did you like the artist's work?"

"Loved it. Brant wasn't a fan, so we won't be putting any of it in our place anytime soon. There was one piece. I couldn't get enough of it. It was," she circles a hand, as if searching for the right word, "vibrant, I guess. I loved it. I'm considering it for my office."

An idea strikes me, but art is such a personal thing, I want to be sure. "What's to consider? You just said you loved it."

"I know."

"The cost?"

She goes silent, which rarely happens and only confirms my suspicions.

I sit forward and tap my hand on the desk. "I want you to have that painting. Call the gallery. Tell them which one it is and I'll buy it. Will they deliver?"

At this, she lets out a strangled laugh. "Uh, I'm sure they will, but you're not buying me that painting. It's unnecessary."

"I want you to have it. You *deserve* it."

She holds up her hands. "Whoa, whoa, whoa. You don't even know how much it is."

"Is it over fifty grand?"

"No!"

"Excellent. Case closed. Call the gallery. Now, we need to get to it. What's up?"

She shakes her head, twists her mouth this way and that. I've completely knocked her off her game, and it's oddly satisfying.

Fun.

And when's the last time I actually had fun at work? I may be on to something here. Not that I'll buy expensive gifts for my entire staff, but breaking up the monotony once in a while might not be a bad thing.

I make a mental note to have Kaitlyn come up with ideas. Happy hours, dessert days. Something.

"Don't take this the wrong way," Jenny says, "but what's going on with you? We're totally off-script."

I let out a soft laugh. I've stymied my nearly unstymie-able EP. "I'm trying something new."

She gives me an exaggerated sigh. "Please don't."

"It's nothing earth-shattering. At least *I* don't think."

She sighs. "What is it?"

"Getting to know people."

"We've been together all these years. You know me. And I sure as hell don't expect you to buy me expensive paintings."

"Do I? Know you?"

That brings her up short and her head snaps back. "Of course. I mean, yeah, we talk business most of the time, but I consider us friends."

Interesting. I'm not sure I agree with her definition of a friend, but I'm also not inclined to argue.

"Good," I say. "I don't want this to look like …" What? Buying loyalty. Ugh. Completely not my intention. "Whatever. But if that painting moved you, maybe even inspired you, we need it around here. We'll consider it a business expense for my hard-working EP."

I give her a toothy smile that lets her know I'm done debating.

She shakes her head, laughs softly at her predicament, then sobers, meeting my gaze. "Thank you. It's an amazing gesture. I'm so grateful."

"Hey, without you, I wouldn't be where I am. You've done the heavy lifting. I've always known that. I don't tell you enough."

She puts up a hand. "Ho-*kay,*" she cracks, "gettin' kinda sappy here."

Good old Jenny.

The two of us share a smile, our cue to get back to business. "Are we all set for today?"

"We have the Eckersons in the green room. Emily and Cole. That woman is *emotional.* Might be a rough one."

On the ride into the city, I reviewed my show notes. Tragic story. The Eckersons' three-year-old son drowned in their swimming pool on Cole's watch nearly two years ago.

Emily blames him.

She's fighting it, but it's always there, quietly lurking and that growing resentment is destroying their marriage.

There are no ambushes here. No setups. This is heart-breaking stuff.

"We need to help them," I say.

"You will," Jenny says. "They want it. They're willing to work."

"Let's hope it's not too late."

She cocks her head. "So, you're good?"

"Pardon?"

"For today? That's why I came in here. Just wanted to make sure," she rolls her hand again, "you know, that after last week you were okay."

Ah. Time to cut the nonsense. We don't have time and I certainly don't have the energy. "After finding out about Ryan's daughter? No. I'm not okay. Not in the least."

For a second, I consider opening up. To Jenny. Friend or not, a secret baby is a sweeper.

A big one.

Marley will drool. She'll carve the meat right off Ryan's bones to get to his issues. To get to why he not only had affairs, but a child he never informed me of.

That terrifies me.

"Anything I can do?" Jenny asks.

"I wish there was. I did phone her. Tiffany."

"Wow."

"I didn't want her continuing to call the show. And, let's face it, I was curious."

"What did she want?"

At this, I shrug. "I'm not ready. I guess. To talk about it. I'm still processing."

Jenny holds up her hand. "Understood."

Now, I have to ask what's been haunting me since I left on Wednesday. I sit forward, meet my EP's gaze for a few seconds, holding my breath as anxiety kicks my pulse up. "Does the staff know?"

"About the baby?"

"Yes."

"Don't think so. Molly is good. She's smart. She also enjoys working here. I can't imagine she'd gossip. I certainly haven't told anyone."

"I didn't mean to …" I shake it off. "I apologize if I offended you."

Jenny leans in, puts her hand over mine and a weird tension fills me, buzzes straight up my arm.

We don't do touchy-feely around here.

Ever.

Still, I cracked the window open. I force myself to be still, but Jenny hasn't survived twenty years in this business without instincts.

She senses my discomfort and eases back before standing. "I'm unoffendable. I'll check in with Molly. Make sure we're keeping Tiffany and the baby on the down-low."

"Thank you."

She turns to leave, then spins back, snapping her fingers. "Devin left me a voicemail asking where we are with Marley. They want us taping this week."

"It's not happening," I say. "I asked Don for a meeting today. After this latest development, I need to figure a few things out before we start taping."

She bobs her head a little too emphatically. "Totally get it. Would you be willing to make Tiffany part of the show? I'm guessing that's what she wants."

I cock my head and realize this is why Jenny came in. It plays in my mind, scenes in a movie all coming together.

Jenny received a call from Devin and let it go to voicemail because she had an idea. She wanted to talk to me first though. To see if I'd flay myself open on national television by putting Tiffany—and perhaps Calle—on the show.

Sweeper, sweeper, sweeper.

This has always been my concern about revealing too much of my private life to Jenny. She's the executive producer of the country's biggest daytime talk show. That prohibits her from truly being my *friend*. Creating drama is part of her job. Right now, I have exploitable drama.

It's not her fault. She's been groomed to chase ratings, and I've benefitted from her relentless pursuit of the money shot.

"I'll talk to Don about the taping schedule," I tell her.

She stands still, almost frozen, for a few seconds. Probably waiting for me to give her something she can tell Devin.

Which I won't do. Devin will have to wait.

THREE HOURS LATER, after my morning taping, I'm sitting in Don's office. Me on the sofa, he in his usual chair. My timing may not be good. The grooves between his eyes are deeper than the Grand Canyon. A sure sign he's stressing. I've noticed this about my boss, how he draws his eyebrows into a hard pinch when aggravated.

Plus, he's already announced he's squeezing me in before lunch. Meaning, I'm interrupting his day.

"Come again," he says, cocking his head.

He heard me. I know he did. Don has this thing he does when trying to control his temper. He'll always use some variation of "excuse me," "pardon me" or "come again."

The psychologist in me believes it's his way of slowing things down, giving his brain a few extra seconds to get itself in order.

I lock my shoulders back and lift my chin. "I need to take a couple of weeks off," I repeat, hoping my boss actually processed it that time.

"*Now?*"

I nod. "It's bad timing. I'm aware."

He bolts out of his chair, strides to the windows overlooking Times Square and begins pacing. He wants to scream. I know he does.

If the roles were reversed, I would.

However, I have never—not in fourteen years—taken unexpected time off. When Ryan's appendix exploded? I hired nurses to be at the house when I taped and then handled administrative tasks remotely.

When my gallbladder decided it wanted to secede? I taped until I couldn't stand the evil sickness any longer. I had surgery the Friday before Labor Day and was back taping on Tuesday. Still don't know how I managed it, but that's me, the company gal setting an example for my team.

Don stops pacing, turns back to me and leans against the windowsill behind him. He runs a hand through his thinning gray hair, then folds his arms before meeting my gaze. "You realize the money we've spent plugging these segments? Not to mention getting Marley on board. Her agent? He's a greedy son of a bitch. And now you want to bail?"

"I'm not *bailing*. As you're aware, I'm having personal issues that need tending."

I don't feel the need to share the latest bombshell about Calle and keep it to myself. Plenty of time later for that announcement.

"Come on!" he waves me off. "You of all people know how many people have cheating spouses. Is this some kind of power play? Because you're pissed about Marley?"

I gawk. My lower jaw literally flops open. After all these years of being his go-to talent, the one he called on when others *bailed* on him for last-minute fundraisers or events or guest appearances.

I did it. Every time. Whatever he asked. I think back on the fights with Ryan when I chose the network over our personal plans. The shows he gave away tickets for or attended alone.

No wonder the man had an affair. I was MIA.

I lean forward, propping one elbow on the arm of the chair. "If I had a problem with Marley, you'd know it. In the beginning, I didn't like the idea. But I'm doing it. After everything I've done for this network, I'm offended."

And *pissed*.

How dare he tell me I can't take time off? I'm willing to prostitute myself by putting my marital problems on the air—all for ratings—and this is what I get?

I let out a sarcastic snort, then stand, smoothing my slacks as I do. "I'm here as a courtesy. I could have sent you an email. I'm entitled to a certain amount of personal leave. It's in my contract."

His eyes narrow as he studies me. That line about the contract—the subtle threat that I'm not afraid to make this a legal matter—may not have been in my best interest.

After all, I'm fairly certain I'm required to give a certain amount of notice. Still, I've thrown that fireball and I'm not backing down.

"I'm well aware of what's in your contract. Including the clause stating you need approval for time off."

I hold my arms out. "So, what? You won't approve it and when I take the two weeks anyway, you'll fire me?"

I don't think so.

My ratings may be slipping, but I still have the top-rated daytime talk show. And my remaining sponsors love me.

Boom.

The revelation, the reminder to myself, buoys me. The suits would never admit it, but I hold power in this relationship. Not all of it, but enough.

I hold my head a little higher. "Don, I'm taking the next two weeks off. I'll tell the staff and deal with rescheduling my tapings. I'll also call Marley." Won't that be fun? "I'll make sure we're as buttoned up as possible. Beyond that, I'm not sure what else is expected of me."

"How about not taking a vacation when we need you?"

A *vacation?* Hardly.

Enough already. I turn and head for the door.

"Don't you walk out! We're not done!"

"Well, guess what? *I'm* done. Fire me. I don't care anymore." For kicks, I pull out my most powerful weapon: my relationship with his boss. "I'm sure Marcia will understand."

I march from the office with my boss screaming about insubordination and suing me. Don's assistant is at her desk, eyes wider than manhole covers.

"He's upset," I tell her.

"No kidding."

I reach the elevator. Press the button. Don't look back. Again, I press the button. *Come on. Hurry up.*

"Becca!" Don hollers.

The elevator dings, and the sound sends a wave of relief whooshing inside me. The doors open and I hustle on, jabbing at the button, willing the doors to close before Don sticks his meaty arm between them.

Please, please, please, don't let him step on this elevator.

The doors start to move, get halfway there before Don appears and then they close, sheltering me from my raging boss. Alone in the elevator, my heart slamming like a jackhammer, I lean against the side wall. Let out a heavy breath. Holy cow. This stunt might get me canned.

If I melt down in here—and believe me, I want to—the security camera will capture it. The video of me dropping to the floor and screaming will run through this building like wildfire.

Stiffening my legs, I stand still, staring at the doors. Focusing hard on the long seam down the middle just for something to distract me from the brewing panic ready to pummel me. I can do this. I'll get through the second taping and then tell the staff I'm taking the next two weeks off.

It'll be a scheduling mess, but they're good. They'll handle it.

All I know is I need out of this building. Away from curious looks and gossip over my cheating husband.

Damned Ryan.

Our marriage wasn't perfect, but I have never cheated on him. So, yes, I'm laying this one on him.

The one who single-handedly dismantled our marriage and my career.

CHAPTER 22

At seven o'clock, after dealing with as much as I could before leaving for two weeks, I step out of my office into the hallway. The bullpen is quiet, everyone gone by now.

The silence is odd. Foreign.

Almost wrong.

It hits me that I'm never the last one here. My staff works hard and typically outpaces me, staying long after I've left.

Today, they all cleared out an hour ago, off for drinks at the bar down the street. Good for them.

A clunking noise draws my gaze. The door at the end of the hallway swings open and Marley glides through it, hair flying, hips swinging. She's bearing down on me like a category five hurricane.

This is what dawdling got me. A confrontation.

"Becca," she calls, her voice echoing down the long corridor. "Hang on."

I paint a smile on. "Hey, Marley. I was just heading out." I make a show of checking my watch. "Catching the last ferry."

She continues toward me, the overhead lights illuminating

her face. Somehow the harsh glare accentuates her perfect face. On me, those lights are a nightmare. Her? Total goddess.

"I can walk with you," she says. "I got your message."

Covering my rear, I'd called her after my argument with Don. I wanted her hearing the news from me since I can't trust the suits.

I reach back, flip the light off in my office and close the door. I don't bother locking it. There are enough security cameras in here to keep the president safe, never mind the Emmys.

"Girl," Marley says, "you sure know how to cause a dustup! Don is losing his mind."

Typical Marley. No pussyfooting around. "I'm aware." I motion her to the elevator and the two of us fall in step, her spiked heels tip-tapping against the tile, while my flats make zero noise.

"I'm sorry," I tell her. "Hopefully, you know my reputation. I'm a pro. I despise wasting others' time. I am, however, smart enough to know I need a break."

"You need to think," she says. "I get that."

Here I was, expecting Marley to rage at me and . . . nothing. Just calm understanding.

Huh.

We reach the elevator and I tap the button. A whirring noise sounds, the elevator coming to life from—I glance up—the first floor.

Might be a minute. Great. I face Marley again.

"Look, Becca, I'm not the enemy. You and me? We have different styles. Doesn't mean I'm not a woman who under-stands heartbreak. I'm divorced."

This, I didn't know. At least, I don't think I did. I must give her some sort of facial expression that indicates my surprise.

"I was young," she continues. "He was my high-school sweet-heart. We went to the same college and got married. It was over before graduation. We didn't have the longevity you do, but I love him to this day. More than that, I *miss* him. When I drink too much? Total nightmare. I text him and tell him I love him."

That's rough. If I were her, I'd quit drinking.

"I never got over it," she continues. "Probably never will. And, frankly, I can't imagine going through that now with social media being what it is. Under the circumstances, you're a rock star for what you're dealing with."

Wow. A compliment from Marley, one known for being stingy with praise. The elevator dings, knocking me loose of my half-stunned state. "I appreciate that, Marley."

"You expected me to yell? Scream at you like Don?"

I step into the elevator, hold the door for her and press one. "That's exactly what I expected."

"I wouldn't do that. Not only do I respect you, but we're women. We need to have each other's backs or the boys' club will destroy us. The entire building is chattering about you basically telling Don to go fuck himself. Personally, I love it. It's about time this network started treating women like the powerhouses we are. You do what you need to. I've got your back here and when you return, we'll start taping. If that's what you want."

If that's what I want.

Have I said something that led her to believe I didn't want to save my marriage?

After learning of baby Calle's existence, maybe I don't.

Could be too big of a hill—an absolute mountain—for me to climb. Given the lies, how could I ever trust Ryan?

The elevator glides to a stop, the doors whooshing open. We step out and stand in the empty elevator bank. Not twenty yards away, the evening security guard sits at the U-shaped desk, his eyes glued to his computer screen.

Here I am, with my so-called archenemy, my competitor, shocked to my heels. Who'd have guessed Marley Ren would come to my aid?

Not me.

Beyond the glass entry doors, Bernie stands beside the SUV, waiting for me. I gesture to him and face Marley again. "My driver is waiting. I'm glad you came to see me. You have no idea what the support means to me."

"Yeah, I do." She waggles her finger between us. "We've got this, Becca. You and me. We've *got* this."

We say our goodbyes and I hustle by the security desk, offering a good night. I always say good night and good morning. Always. I learned that from one of the network anchors who got lambasted in the press by a disgruntled guard telling the world the anchor was a conceited jerk who didn't pay any mind to the "help."

Lesson learned. Be nice.

Outside, Bernie moves from the vehicle to meet me at the front door. I keep my head up, my eyes on the SUV as a swarm of photographers falls in and Bernie ushers me through the pack.

Flashes blind me and shouts rattle my ears, the voices working hard to carry above the others.

"Becca! Are you divorcing Ryan?"

"Becca! Who's the mistress?"

"Becca! Have you hired a divorce lawyer?"

Becca, Becca, Becca!

We reach the car and Bernie swings the door open. He huddles behind me, blocking the photographers as I hop inside.

"Beat it!" he yells, shoving the door closed behind me.

I immediately lock it and put my head back, breathing through the adrenaline rush.

Bernie jumps into the driver's seat muttering about vultures. Poor guy. I warned him this would get worse.

"Ignore those jackasses," he tells me.

"It's fine, Bern. I'm getting used to it."

Not really, but a girl can dream.

We pull from the curb and I glance back through the lobby

glass. Marley is gone. More than likely heading back to her office, determined to prove her ambition just as I used to. Can I trust her? She's aggressive and, well, mean. Get in her way and she'll eliminate you.

No question.

The list of producers and guest contributors she's mowed down on her way to her regular spot on the morning show is proof of it.

Frankly, she terrifies me. And that's not easy to admit. I'm not exactly a wilting flower.

Up to this point, literally to this very second, I've considered her my rival. Treated her with a cool indifference that let her—and anyone else at the network—know I won't go without a war. When it comes to Marley, I've operated under the belief that if I slipped up, she'd not only snatch my time slot, she'd spit on my bloody carcass while stepping over me.

This Marley?

The nice one?

No idea what to do with her.

I let out a breath, exhaustion finally taking hold. Movement from the front seat draws my gaze. Bernie throws a quick glance over his shoulder.

"You okay?"

"Tired. Bern, I'm just so *tired*."

Something in my chest tightens. A giant, punishing fist stealing my air. I close my eyes, count down from ten, inhaling slowly and letting the oxygen recharge me.

Lately, all I'm doing is fighting. Fighting, fighting, fighting. Whether it's the suits or the Ryan revelations, anger and heartbreak are constant.

Zero relief.

Privately, I've cried enough tears to fill a swimming pool. Maybe a river. I'm sick of it. The weakness and lack of control.

How could Ryan do this to me? Adultery, I might be able to

find my way back from, but a *baby*? After knowing I'd wanted children. How could he let the years slip away while never—ever—sharing he'd changed his mind?

My eyes water. I blink, then blink again, forcing the tears away.

But, damn him, he'd never said a word and then had the nerve—the absolute disregard for me—to father a child with someone else. The disrespect alone is enough to bring a fresh bout of waterworks and the blasted tears pour out of my eyes. An absolute monsoon that I don't even bother trying to hide. What's the use?

I let out a sob. Where did *that* come from?

"Becca? You okay?"

Nope. Not okay. At all.

I suck a hard breath, jamming my palms into my eyes. "I'm …"

Another sob. I'm a mess.

"That's it," Bernie says, gunning the gas. "I'm taking you to the shore. There's no way I'm putting you on the boat like this. Not when people will see you. Probably take pictures that'll wind up on Page Six. Not doing it."

"It's the Snooty," I tell him. "And I can wear my wig. I won't have you driving all the way to the shore and back. I'm fine."

"You're not fine," he says, his voice so soft, so gentle, I can't believe it's coming from him. The hardened, former New York City cop.

He waves a hand in the air. "You're crying. Rightly so. Sit back and relax. Or throw a fit and scream. I don't care. It's only us. You're safe."

Safe.

The one thing I've always wanted. Security. Loyalty. All things I thought I had with my husband.

"Thank you," I tell Bernie. "I so appreciate you."

He heads toward the tunnel, waves a hand again. "Whatever. Just relax."

Following instructions, I rest my head back and stare out at the buildings, the pedestrians, everyone going about their normal lives while inside this car, I'm giving in to heartbreak.

On Tuesday morning, I wake to sunshine blaring through the tops of the partly open shades.

I blink, then blink again, the brightness nearly splitting my skull in two. There are things I remember from last night. Arriving home after nine, pulling the cork on my favorite pinot, drinking straight from the bottle and then heading to my room where I sat on the bed, downing the last of the wine before curling up and apparently falling asleep.

Still in my clothes.

With the bottle beside me.

A great look for Dr. Becca.

Considering my behavior, I'm probably having a nervous breakdown. I'm not sure I mind. Anything to escape my life.

I'm a fool. An *idiot*.

Well, idiot might be harsh. At the very least, I'm an intelligent woman who allowed herself to ignore the obvious.

"Trust," I grumble, my throat raspy from the endless tears and exhaustion. "Always dangerous."

I roll out of bed, walk to the slider and step out on the deck into the unusual warmth of an early May day. I don't even know what time it is. Based on the position of the sun, it has to be nearing noon.

Noon! When have I ever slept until lunchtime?

I spot Danny on the beach, tucked into his beach chair. He's shirtless and reading a book. Tromping down the stairs, I head straight for him.

My mouth feels like day-old gum. Probably should have brushed my teeth.

Oh. Well.

I hit the beach, my toes curling into the grains. By July, the sand will scorch unprotected feet.

"Danny," I call as I approach.

He swings his head around, tips his Maui Jims down and peers at me over the top.

"Bubby," he says, "you look like you were rode hard and put away wet."

I take a moment, consider the usual condition of my hair first thing in the morning. The heavy makeup I didn't bother removing after taping yesterday.

"Trying something new," I tell him, coming to a stop.

At this, he laughs. Still, he rises from his chair, tosses his book in it and waves me to my deck. "Well, you've aced it. You're a mess, Becca. Let's get you off the beach before some bloodsucker sees you."

He's right.

Anyone these days could make a million dollars just by snapping a cell phone pic.

Instinctively, I try to smooth my long hair, tying it into a loose knot behind my head while I tromp up my steps with Danny in tow.

My back to the beach, I slump into the sofa, hiding behind the deck rails.

Danny sits across from me and holds his hands wide. "Since you're not in the city, I guess you took time off."

"I did. Two weeks."

"Good." He points at me, then circles his finger. "I don't recommend the hungover look."

"No kidding. I need to talk."

He sits back, settling in. "Go for it."

"Well," I say, "I spoke to the mother of Ryan's child."

His eyebrows rise, but beyond that, his features remain neutral. Total non-judgment I'm immensely thankful for.

My aching head throbs, the pain shooting straight to my stomach. I focus on taking even breaths. The fresh air hitting my system offers some relief.

Or maybe it's just being able to talk about this. To *admit* it.

I meet Danny's gaze. "She's estranged from her family. She wants me to talk to Ryan, see if Calle—that's the baby—could spend time with us."

I dip my head again, jam my palms into my eye sockets. Between the wine, lack of decent sleep and crying, I'm cooked.

Physical and mental ruin.

I grit my teeth and hold my breath, forcing away the chaos fogging my brain. The child isn't mine. Why should I feel this responsibility?

Clearing my throat, I drop my hands. "She wants her child to know people love her."

"Holy shit."

"Well said."

He tips his head back against the cushion and stares up at a cloudless sky. "Just … wow."

Danny, speechless? I should get an Emmy for that alone. "I want to meet her."

He peers back at me, his dark eyes filled with a sort of shocked wonder. "Seriously?"

"I've been thinking about it since I talked to her. It's not fair to the baby. Her parents might be irresponsible, but it's not her fault, right?"

"Obviously. But," he rolls a hand, "can you get past the irresponsible part?"

"No idea."

I really don't know. Absolutely clueless. I do know what a lonely childhood looks like. Learning the hard way that my mother had the right idea and that so-called friends weren't immune to gossip. To letting me down.

Yet, here I sit, sharing my business.

"As a father," Danny says, "I understand. I'd want to at least meet her. There's Ryan's shared DNA there."

I poke my finger. "Exactly. Does she have his eyes, his crooked smile? It feels silly, but I can't stop wondering."

"It's not silly. You're human. We're curious beings."

"So, I'm not crazy?"

He snorts. "No. I'd do it. But I'm not the nation's top-rated talk show host. Are you ready for the storm if someone finds out?"

I point to my face. "Does it look like I'm ready? I can't continue like this. It's not healthy. Maybe meeting her will help. I don't know."

"You'll have to be careful."

"I'll find a private place."

"I'd let you use my house, but considering I'm your neighbor …"

"Too close," I tell him.

I puff out my cheeks. This would be a great time to have people I could ask a favor of. Actual friends whom I trust not to call the press when I want to meet my husband's child.

Danny narrows his eyes. "Your parents?"

Gah. "I'd sooner poke my eye out. Besides, my mother is still ignoring me. Right now, it might be a good thing."

You're safe with me.

Bernie's words from the night before stream through my embattled brain. Could I ask him? No. I shake my head. Too much.

You're safe with me.

"My driver," I blurt. "He's been with me for years. Never sold a photo, a story, nothing. He's a steel trap. It's too much though, right? To ask him to let me use his house? It feels …"

"Ballsy?"

"Yes. It's not his problem."

"But you need a friend."

"Would you do it?"

"Hell, yeah. But that's me." He gives me a wolfish grin. "I'm pushy."

Pushy. Something I've never been. Always agreeable Becca. Reasonable Becca.

Screw off, reasonable Becca. I need to take control of this situation. Quit letting the circumstances dictate my actions. If Ryan doesn't like it?

Too.

Bad.

I poke a finger. "You're right. Bernie told me if I ever needed anything—"

"There you go. You need something."

I sure do.

CHAPTER 23

*A*s usual, Bernie has come through for me.

I'm not sure what I expected when I so boldly asked if I could use his home to meet Ryan's mistress and her daughter, but his hesitation was zero.

Not one second. Now, twenty-four hours after speaking with Danny about this meeting, it's about to happen.

We cruise a tree-lined street in the Williamsburg section of Brooklyn until Bernie parks the SUV in front of a tidy three-story brick home.

Bernie has told me he grew up in this house, living here his entire sixty years. Upon Bernie and his wife getting married, his parents moved into the basement apartment where they stayed until their deaths twenty years later.

In some ways, I imagine living in one house is a blessing. To not want more. To be satisfied and comforted by the sameness. To not feel the pressure for bigger and better. More and more and more.

Before I can ponder this longer, my door comes open and I slide from the rear seat, meeting Bernie's eye. "Thank you for this. You'll never know how much this means to me to be able to do this in private."

"Happy to help. I couldn't be more flattered. Thank you for your trust."

He waves me forward, closes the door and hits the button to lock the car. I follow in silence as we walk to the front stoop.

We're early.

Tiffany and Calle aren't due for another forty-five minutes, a strategic plan on my part in case we were followed, or I was seen by a fan.

In which case, I'd simply say Bernie invited me for a family gathering. Our cover story is that Tiffany and Calle are part of Bernie's world.

Not mine.

Sometimes the universe really does throw a bone.

Bernie unlocks the front door, gives it a gentle push when it sticks and ushers me inside where I pause in front of an oak staircase leading to the second floor.

To my right is a spotless living room—not a pillow out of place. Long, pinned back drapes hang over the double windows where shades are pulled low. The extra layer of privacy relaxes me, loosens the tension in my neck.

I can do this.

The house is quiet except for the tick-tick-tick of a clock coming from another room.

"Evelyn is out," he says.

I nod. "She didn't need to do that. This is her home."

"She went shopping with her sister. Believe me, she doesn't mind. Her sister can spend money like nobody's business."

Thinking of Ryan, I smile. I'm not a big shopper. My husband? It sounds as if he and Evelyn could do damage together.

The thought brings a mix of emotions. All the jokes I've

made about Ryan being worse than a woman when it comes to his spending suddenly fall flat.

I am no longer amused by the way he handles our money. Had I been paying attention, maybe I'd have known he gave his girlfriend a credit card. Maybe I'd have known he was supporting a child.

Maybe he'd be here supporting me—*and* his child—while I do the work that comes with processing his mistakes. Instead, I'm alone.

His choice, not mine.

Before setting up this meeting last night, I called and invited him along. He chose to decline. Which shouldn't have shocked me. Ryan, I'm realizing, is all about Ryan. Doing whatever is necessary to protect himself no matter the wreckage he leaves behind.

"Have a seat," Bernie says. "What can I get you? I picked up ginger ale."

He knows my guilty pleasure. I tend not to drink soda. If I indulge, I go straight for the refreshing bubbles of ginger ale, drinking it from the can.

Right now, I could use it. "I'd love one."

I scan the seating options, my mind fast-forwarding to Tiffany and Calle's arrival. If I settle into the high-backed sofa, it leaves an opportunity for Tiffany to sit with me.

Then there's the upholstered beige side chair to the right of the sofa. That allows distance and it's a solitary seat.

Side chair. Definitely. I might be working on my issues surrounding trust and letting people into my life, but I'm not ready to get cozy with Ryan's mistress and their child.

Bernie returns with the ginger ale, and a glass filled with ice. "Wasn't sure if you wanted the glass," he says. "You usually don't." He sets them both on the coffee table and points. "I wiped the can."

Yes, he knows me well. Who knows what filth has touched the top of that can? "Thank you."

I pop the top and take a long drink, the carbonation tickling my throat.

"My thought is," he says, "when she gets here, I'll go up to the bedroom. Watch television. I won't be able to hear you. Or I could leave. Not a good option, I don't think, since it's my house. If someone saw us and I leave, dead giveaway you're having a meeting."

Guilt lands on me. Here I am, shooing his wife away and now relegating him to a bedroom in his own home. "I agree," I tell him. "I'm sorry you'll be hiding upstairs."

"Not a problem. You need privacy."

For the next thirty minutes, he sits with me while my nerves and mind crackle. I need to relax. Just a meeting. I've done it thousands of times. This one shouldn't be any different.

Stressing myself out is useless. A waste of precious energy that I'll need to get through this meeting.

To occupy myself, I pepper Bernie with questions. About Evelyn and their kids. Grandkids. All the things I should already know, but don't.

Bernie is funny, engaging and charming in that gruff way that street guys master by the time they hit puberty.

His stories make me laugh. The children and chaos. His daughter getting stuck on the roof. All parenting woes I've missed.

"Kids," he says. "They're a pisser."

I snort, absorbing the love he has for his family. "You're disgustingly functional," I tell him.

"Compared to the families you meet? Yes," he says, his thick accent a comforting balm on my fried nerves. "I'm grateful for it. Good kids. Never any trouble."

"Outside of the roof."

He laughs, runs a hand through his thinning hair. "Yeah.

Outside of that. I was so mad at her that day. They musta heard me yelling a mile away. Once she got up there, she was too scared to climb down. I had to call the fire department!"

Laughter pours out of me. "You didn't!"

"I did. I couldn't get her to move. The FD came over, raised the aerial ladder and got her down. If I wasn't so happy she was safe, I'd have killed her."

"How did she get up there in the first place?"

"Attic window. She thought it would be fun. She climbed out, realized she was three stories up and panicked. We were watching television and didn't hear her screaming. My neighbor banged on the door and said, 'Bern, do you know your daughter is on the roof?'" He laughs. "I'll tell ya, these kids. Nuts. All of 'em."

The doorbell rings and our laughter drops like a brick from said roof. My shoulders fly back. I check my watch. Noon. On the dot.

At least she's punctual.

Bernie and I both stand. I meet his gaze and he jerks his head. "This is it. You can still call it off. Go in the kitchen, out of sight, and I'll tell her there's a change in plans."

I shake my head, not even questioning my decision. "No. I've come this far."

It's more than that. It's about facing it. About pulling my head out of the sand.

Bernie moves to the door while I take a second, smoothing my hands over my jeans. Checking the hem of my summer cashmere sweater. I'd spent twenty minutes that morning deciding on clothing, opting against the cotton shirts that wrinkle the second I put them on and going for comfort. For something I won't be distracted by.

At a loss for what to do with my hands, I clasp them in front of me and watch as Bernie grips the door handle, his movements slow, contained as if waiting for me to speak up. Call the whole thing off.

"It's all right," I say.

Where the words come from, I'm not sure. I'm ready.

I think.

He gives the handle a tug, the door once again sticking. If I hadn't noticed Bernie giving the extra heavy push when we'd walked in, I'd consider it a sign. A message that meeting this woman and her child would do me no good.

But I saw it and there's an intense calm that washes over me. I don't understand it, but I don't have time for analysis.

"Hello," Bernie says, shaking me from my thoughts.

I shift my gaze to the petite—and incredibly young— brunette holding an infant carrier. She's pretty, with long, wavy hair that slopes gently over her shoulders. Like me, she's wearing jeans, but opted for a graphic T-shirt.

Leave it to Ryan to further flip me off by cheating on me with what appears to be a coed. A beautiful one at that.

We're an absolute cliché, my husband and me.

"Hi," she says, a tentative smile forcing its way to her lips. "I'm Tiffany."

Bernie steps back and waves her in. "Come in. Can I help you with your bags?"

"I'm good," she says. "Used to it."

She steps inside. A giant tote hangs over her right shoulder along with a bucket style purse.

Meeting my gaze, she halts just inside the doorway. "Wow. I'm..."

She peers back at Bernie, whose bottom lip pokes out, a habit I've noticed when he's puzzled.

Immediately, she turns back to me. "I'm sorry. I'm nervous. Had the whole thing planned in my head, but you're, well, you're *you*. A big star and, wow, so pretty and elegant.

Compared to you, I look like the easy waitress stupid enough to hook up with …"

She shakes her head. Hard. Tears fill her eyes and my therapist instincts kick in.

"Deep breath," I tell her. "No one looks like anything. We're two women in an awkward situation. That's it."

I gesture to the sofa. "Why don't you sit here? Can we get you anything?"

She eyes my ginger ale. "I'd love one of those. My favorite."

Great. We have more in common than our attraction to my husband.

Bernie heads to the kitchen and Tiffany eases her bags to the floor, then sets the carrier on the coffee table. She's positioned it facing her, blocking my view and I'm momentarily thankful. I'm still getting used to the coed, never mind the coed's baby.

"Oh, wait. Is it okay if I put her here? On the table?"

At a loss, I remain silent.

"It's fine," Bernie says, reappearing with another ginger ale and a glass. "That table is indestructible."

After placing the soda and glass on the side table, Bernie heads upstairs, telling us to call if we need anything.

What I need is to run screaming from this room. To stick my head back in the sand. Go back a few weeks, or a few months, when females named Laurel and Tiffany and Calle weren't part of my world and my biggest problem—I thought—was how to avoid turning my show into trash TV.

Now? Trash TV doesn't look so bad.

Coming from me, that's saying something. Something like it being time to walk away. Stop fighting. Stop racing to nowhere and chasing ratings.

Enjoy my life.

Avoiding even a glance at the baby carrier, I bring my focus back to Tiffany, who is still standing. "Let's sit."

"Thanks."

We both settle in, and I watch as she fusses with the diaper bag, unzipping it and pulling out a toy. A large rubber-looking ring with giant keys hanging from it. Then she grabs a bottle with a handy top that contains powder. Baby formula is my guess, but I'm hardly the expert.

"She's quiet," I say.

Tiffany nods. "For now. She fell asleep on the subway."

"You took the subway?"

The walk to the nearest subway station must be a mile. She lugged a baby and the bags all that way?

"My car is in the shop," she says. "I'm actually thinking about getting rid of it. I don't know. We live in Queens, so the subway is easy. I like having a car in case of an emergency, but parking in the city is a pain. It's good for trips like this one though."

She shrugs, clearly uncommitted to an answer, then leans forward, checking on Calle. A second later, she screws up her lips, trying and failing to hide a smile.

A mother's smile.

The one that comes out of nowhere and for no apparent reason other than that this tiny human exists.

I've seen it countless times on set. It's a bond. That mother-child thing that has fascinated me since my college days when I wrote a paper on superhuman strength in women when protecting their children.

She peers back at me, her big blue eyes twinkling and I can see it. Why Ryan fell for her. She's beautiful, yes, but it's more than that. There's a bright-eyed, youthful innocence about her despite the fact that she had an affair with my husband.

"Would you like to see her?"

Panic assails me, sending tiny shockwaves down my limbs. How do I even answer that? We're here so I must want to see her. Or maybe I just wanted to meet the woman—one of them— who derailed my life.

I mean, an affair is one thing. A secret child?

The tabloids will feast on me for days.

I lift my chin, let out a slow breath. "That's a complicated question." I hold my hand out, palm up. "We're here so, yes, I want to meet her. At the same time, I'm wondering what I'm doing."

She bobs her head. "Crazy as it sounds, I think I get it."

No, honey, you don't.

I must have made a face or winced or some other body language that tells my guest she's overstepped.

"That came out wrong," she says. "I'm sorry. I mean, it's weird. Us meeting. Without Ryan. I guess that's what I meant."

Lord, this is torture.

"Ryan," I say, "knows we're meeting. He couldn't make it today."

"He didn't want to come."

She poses it as a statement, rather than a question. "His opinion on fatherhood hasn't changed. He's uninterested."

It sounds harsh. It *is* harsh. I look away, staring at the windows and the peep of sunshine squeaking through the lowered shades.

I should be handling this better. I'm a professional. I know how to manage a situation. How to numb the sting. And yet, I seem to have forgotten.

Maybe the gift only works on others.

Finally, I gather my nerve, steeling myself as I stand and walk around the coffee table. From my vantage point, the collapsible cover on the carrier hides Calle's face. All I see is her body. Chubby arms and legs tucked into tiny leggings and a long-sleeved shirt with a giant strawberry on it.

Something inside me tears loose, rips right from bone and pain shoots straight into my chest.

This could have been my life. Lugging a carrier with an adorable baby girl in equally adorable clothes. Dresses and jeans and those little onesies that button up.

Or maybe a boy that looked like Ryan and wore jeans and baseball caps and Chuck Taylors. Did they even make Chuck Taylors that small?

I don't know.

I would have enjoyed finding out.

When Tiffany makes no move to lower the cover, I'm forced to do the one thing I absolutely don't want to do. If I want to see this baby's face, I have to sit next to Tiffany.

It's a curious thing, standing here, on the brink of facing an innocent child and knowing if she looks like Ryan, it will be seared in my brain. The image of the child he chose not to have with me.

Or maybe she'll look like her mother and not a hint of Ryan. That, too, is a confusing thought. Is it better to have a secret child who looks like my husband's mistress? Or one who's a clone of my cheating husband?

Time to find out. I lower myself to the sofa, keeping my gaze on the carrier cover until I'm firmly in my seat.

Then I do it. I look.

Baby Calle.

I draw a deep breath. There's something amazingly calming about a sleeping baby. There she lies, her tiny chest rising and falling, her bottom lip protruding, then retracting. In, out, in, out.

Her dark hair is silky, like Ryan's, the thin wisps held back by a tiny pink barrette. Her cheeks are full and her long eyelashes lie softly against her skin.

"I think she's dreaming," Tiffany says, pointing to Calle's still-moving mouth. "She does that when she sleeps. The babysitter thinks she's dreaming about drinking a bottle."

"She's—" My voice catches as a wicked mix of emotions clog me up. I clear my throat. "She's beautiful."

I'm not lying. This child is magnificent. Perfection in every way.

Of course, she is. She's Ryan's and his Golden Ratio—an ancient Greek mathematical formula used to measure physical perfection—score is a whopping 91.49 percent. We were drunk one night, measured his face and body and did the math. Sometimes, as I'm now realizing, it's a curse to be married to such a beautiful man.

Women simply can't resist him.

And he, clearly, can't be responsible enough, loyal enough, *committed* enough to resist them.

None of which has anything to do with the child in front of me.

I sit for a minute, taking her in. Her peaceful sleep that I haven't experienced in… I can't remember. Sleep, lately, has been a battle. A war between my brain and body.

But here's Calle, all sweet and vulnerable and perfect and all I want is to lean forward, snuggle into her softness and smell that clean baby smell.

Whatever that ripping sensation inside me was a few minutes ago happens again. My reminder, I suppose, that my career overran my life.

I blink, then blink again, willing my body to not give in. To not show the pain and heartbreak my husband has leveled on me.

How humiliating would *that* be?

Everything I wanted—theoretically speaking—sits right in front of me, but Calle isn't mine.

She's Ryan's.

And he doesn't want her.

Her eyes pop open. Just bam. Instantly awake. She peers at me with her mother's large blue gaze, her tiny eyebrows coming together.

"Hey, sweet girl," Tiffany coos and Calle's gaze shoots left.

Her mouth opens, a giant smile revealing perfect pink gums with one tiny lower tooth jutting out.

Oh, the cuteness.

She kicks her legs, as if the sight of her mother is physically too much and she must release the excitement. I laugh. I simply can't help it.

"My goodness," I say, "she might be the most adorable baby ever."

Tiffany leans in and tickles her daughter. "She might be."

Just that fast, Calle's face twists into an angry scowl.

"Oh boy," I say.

Tiffany reaches behind me, grabs the bottle. "We need to move quick."

Holding the bottle upside down, she unscrews the cap with the powder, then turns the bottle right side up and removes the nipple, pouring in the powder and mixing everything without losing a drop. She screws the cap back on, gives it a few vigorous shakes and shoves the bottle at Calle who reaches for it like she hasn't eaten in a week.

"You're good at that," I say.

"I know her habits. She's always hungry when she wakes up. Would you like to hold her?"

Hold her?

Um, no.

I pat my hands against my legs and stand, moving back to my chair. "Thank you. Not today."

If she's offended by this, she doesn't show it. She simply stares at her daughter, who is sucking on that bottle like a lifeline.

Time to get back to business. I reclaim my seat and look at Tiffany. "I'll be honest. I expected to come in here and meet Calle and, I suppose, go back to my life."

Whatever that life might be.

"Now," I continue, "I'm not sure how to proceed. Calle is Ryan's child. It doesn't seem fair to her."

Tiffany shrugs. "He told me from the beginning . . ."

"What?"

She shakes it off. Looks away and bites her bottom lip.

"Tiffany? He told you what?"

She swings her head back to me, and her eyes bubble with tears. "I'm so ashamed. I mean, I don't mess with married men. I don't."

"Clearly, you do." *Ach.* "I'm sorry. That was horrible."

"No. It's true." She lets out a snot-filled snort, gestures at Calle and digs in her bag for a tissue before blowing her nose. "*Clearly,* I do. I didn't know at first. He assumed I knew, which, hey, he wasn't wearing a ring." She shakes her head. "Anyway, he did eventually tell me. He was honest. Told me he loved you. That nothing would come of us. I knew the deal. I was in deep though. He was everything I thought I needed. He's just—"

Well aware of my husband's charm, I hold up a hand. "I know what he is."

"Anyway," she says, checking on Calle and pulling a small washcloth from her tote. "I wasn't trying to get pregnant. Believe me. I was on the pill. Took it every night. I still don't know how it happened."

"He could have used protection as well."

The realization hits that my husband lied to me about using protection and that his irresponsible behavior might have brought me any number of sexually transmitted diseases. Damned man.

I make a mental note to call the doctor about testing.

"True. We talked about…" She shakes off the thought, then glances at Calle. "Well, I just didn't see any other option than having her."

Abortion. Neither of us needs to voice it.

"After that," she continues, "he broke things off."

Great guy, my husband. He left a young, pregnant woman to fend for herself.

"He's been good to us though," she says, as if reading my mind. "Like I said on the phone. Whatever we need, he helps."

"As he should."

Again, she bobs her head, and the room fills with an awkward silence that is interrupted by the ticking of the damned clock and then a loud burp followed by a giggle from Calle.

Lord, who knew a baby could be that loud?

"Oh," Tiffany coos at Calle. "You're so silly!"

Despite myself, I smile. I don't want to like this girl, this *woman*. Or her baby.

Like everything else in my life lately, what I want doesn't seem to matter.

I lean forward, propping my elbows on my knees. "Tiffany, I'm not sure where we go from here."

"Me neither. I guess I was hoping Ryan would come. Calle will need a male in her life."

"I don't think you can count on him for anything but financial support."

"I guess I knew that, but never hurts to try."

"Calle shouldn't be punished because he's not emotionally available to her. Now that I've met her, I'd like to—"

What? What *do* I want?

I lift my hands, let them drop. "I don't know. I'd like to do something, but I need time to figure out what."

Time to ponder managing this without the press and social media vultures interfering.

I peer at her. "Until then, we need to keep this private. If people find out who Calle's father is, the paparazzi will hound us. They'll follow you and peep in your windows trying to get a photo. They're brutal sometimes. We need to protect Calle. *We* have to control the narrative."

"Of course. Absolutely. Shoot. I didn't think of that when I called your show. I figured it was, like, confidential."

"Well, luckily, the person who handled your call is kind. I don't think she'll be a problem."

"Okay. Good. I'm so sorry."

I hold up a hand. "Water under the bridge. Let's just move forward."

She bobs her head, her relief evident. "I'd like that."

For the first time, I'm realizing how brave this young woman is. The courage it took to come here, not knowing how I might treat her and coming anyway for the sake of her child.

"I'll call you in a few days. After I've had time to think and talk to Ryan."

"Thank you. I'm so grateful. I just don't want my girl to be alone."

It tugs at me. That word. Alone. Brings me back to my childhood when I was too paranoid to share secrets or talk about crushes. All that time refusing to get close to anyone.

"That won't happen," I say. "Now, let's get you both home. Does the carrier work as a car seat?"

"I'm sorry?"

"Bernie. The man who went upstairs? He's my driver. I trust him, obviously. We'll drive you and Calle home, if you'd like."

"Oh, that would be great. Yes. I can use it as a car seat. I don't like to do it without the base, but it's doable. Thank you."

"Of course. We'll take you home and I'll be in touch. In the meantime, I'll text you a number where I can be reached if you need something."

"Thank you. So much. I didn't expect you to be so nice. You should hate me."

I shrug. "Part of me does. I'm trying to put myself in your shoes. You fell for a man who has a way with people. When I was your age, I fell for the same man. We're human and he should know better. Plenty of blame to go around."

We drop Tiffany and Calle off at a tired two-story, aluminum-sided home just blocks from the subway station. According to Tiffany, she and Calle live in the second-floor unit and the landlords, a couple in their eighties, live on the first. No wonder the home has fallen into disrepair, with a single mother and a couple of octogenarians living under its roof.

I stay in my seat while Bernie walks Tiffany and Calle to the door. He's holding the infant carrier, completely relaxed. He's a grandfather. Probably accustomed to these tasks.

They climb to the top of the stoop where Tiffany digs through her giant tote, pulling out a set of keys before opening the door. The two exchange a few brief words and Bernie nods before passing Calle off. He waits for Tiffany to go inside and pulls the door closed before returning to the SUV.

"All good?" I ask when he snaps his seatbelt on.

"Yeah. She didn't want me to walk her up. Said she's inconvenienced us enough."

Dammit. I didn't want her to be kind. I *wanted* her to be a cold, unlikable snot. At least then I could run back to Ryan and lambaste him for tearing our lives apart with someone not even worth a conversation, much less having a child with.

"She's nice," I blurt, realizing how ridiculous that sounds.

He glances at me in the rearview and shrugs. "Seems like it. Reminds me of my daughter. She didn't sleep with married men —not that I know. But she's made mistakes."

"Meaning, I shouldn't judge her for sleeping with my husband."

"Oh, hell no. Judge all you want. I am. She can be nice and still screw up. That's all I'm saying."

I cock my head, pondering that. "I agree. Thank you."

"For what?"

The list is endless. Starting with allowing me to use his home for a secret meeting. "Being kind and *loyal*. And honest. You cut through the bullshit. Get straight to the point. I always know where you stand. In my business, you learn to appreciate that."

"Pardon my saying so, but your business doesn't sound so great."

I laugh, but don't find any humor in it. "There's a lot of truth there."

As we pull away, I glance back at the house, imagine Tiffany climbing the stairs, holding on to a polished wood railing as she lugs her bags and Calle along. Did my husband climb those stairs? Has he even been here? Sat on her furniture?

Rolled around in her bed?

Forcing that image from my brain, I face front again, focus on next steps.

"Back to the beach?" Bernie asks.

"No. The city. I need to speak with Ryan."

An intolerable forty-five minutes later, we pull in front of Ryan's office. Having been at the beach where it takes ten minutes to get to all my favorite stores and restaurants, I find sitting in traffic to be especially irritating. Particularly when I'm already in a mood.

Bernie hops out, hustles around the vehicle and opens my door.

"I won't be long," I tell him. "If I get delayed, I'll text you."

"I'll be around."

Translation: He'll either circle until I'm ready or double-park on a side street and sit in the car.

A born city man, he understands the workings of these streets. Once, I came from a meeting and found him double-parked with a police cruiser right behind him while he and the officer chatted.

I peer up at the dry cleaners next to Ryan's office. Being a nonprofit, they went for no-frills, subleasing part of the first floor of an office building that received a much-needed facelift.

Ryan, being Ryan, informed the landlord of all the reasons, including tax benefits, he should give them a break on the rent. They've been in the space nearly eight years and the rent hasn't gone up once.

That's my husband. Slayer of men and women.

Swiping the keycard Ryan gave me, I breeze into the office and stop for a quick chat with Amy, the receptionist.

Ryan's staff is under twenty people, half of whom aren't at their desks. Probably still at lunch. The others are on the phone or otherwise making themselves busy but wave a greeting as I stride down the row leading to the back wall where Ryan's assistant's desk is empty.

His door is closed. I knock once and turn the knob, cracking the door in case he's on the phone. Rude? Probably. But I don't have time to worry about it. Not after what he's done.

I stick my head through the crack and spot him on the couch that sits along the same wall as the door. He's resting his head back and his feet are propped on his coffee table, crossed at the ankles.

A blonde sits beside him, barely a foot away. Her back is to me. She's angled sideways with one leg crossed over the other and her skirt riding high on her thighs.

Fury, all that raging adrenaline, storms my body. My temples throb, my jaw joining in from the brutal gritting of my teeth.

I've just come from meeting his mistress, one of the two, and he's already lining up a third?

I let out a huffing laugh. It's that or I'll start screaming and make fools of all three of us.

They bolt upright and I step inside, closing the door behind me. The snick of the mechanism booms through the office.

"Becca." He launches to his feet and waves the blonde to the door. "I wasn't expecting you."

No kidding.

Before she slinks away, I slide in front of her. "In case you didn't realize it, he's married to the top-rated talk show host in the country. We're about to film a segment on his inability to keep his pants on."

"Jesus, Becca!" Ryan says.

The blonde's green eyes pop, and I hold my hands up, silencing Ryan. "Yep, we're doing it. Going public. Maybe I'll even decide to do a live show. We'll drag his affairs into the open. Let an entire *nation* know about the women he screws." I flash a faux bright smile, lifting my chin. "It'll be a sweeper. Massive ratings boon. I'd love for you to take part. Would you like that?"

The blonde angles around me, literally sprinting away and swinging the door open so hard it slaps against the wall. An idiotic sense of satisfaction rolls over me. I can't help it. So much is out of my control that I've resorted to horrifying behavior.

A woman scorned, indeed.

Truly, I have no idea what I'm doing anymore. The refined and reasonable Dr. Becca is MIA.

Wife Becca? She's had it with Ryan and his apparently insatiable appetite for women.

He pushes past me and closes the door again. "That was uncalled for. We were in a meeting."

"Please," I say, my voice sounding as tired as I feel. "I saw what you were doing."

"You *think* you know what you saw."

My fury slips away, leaving behind the rubble of my demolished marriage and my hopes for our future.

Slowly, I shake my head. "Don't gaslight me. You really have no shame. You absolutely disgust me."

There. I said it. Just calmly blurted it out as if reading the grocery list. Clearly, he's as shocked as I am because even as I wait for his outrage and passionate defense, he says nothing.

Somehow, his silence hurts worse than walking in on him as he groomed his next mistress. He's so guilty he can't even summon the energy to defend himself.

I'm a fool.

I squeeze my eyes closed, willing my emotions to get themselves together. In my mind, I envision a broom sweeping all that rubble into a neat pile to be disposed of later.

Then I face my husband again. "I met your daughter."

He winces. "She's not my daughter."

"If that's what you're going with, you've got bigger issues than I thought. She looks just like you. She is, in fact, perfect. Let's hope it's only your looks she inherits and not your lack of honor."

Moving to his desk, he sits and flips open a folder. "If you're done, I have work to do."

Good luck, pal. I'm not nearly through with him. "Your daughter doesn't deserve what you're doing."

"What I'm *doing*? I've supported her. I pay her health insurance. Tiffany's too."

"It's not about money. That baby needs a father. She deserves a family. People who love her. People who make her feel like she's not alone."

"Is this about Calle? Or you?"

Bullseye.

Being my only true confidant for the last quarter century, being the sole person I've shared my childhood loneliness with, my husband has gone for my jugular.

Bastard.

Weighty sadness settles on me, pressing down on my already fatigued body. "How totally beneath you. Then again, everything I've learned in these last weeks is beneath you. Or maybe it's not. Maybe it's simply who've you've been all along. I saw it that night in college."

He sits back, throws his hands in the air. "Oh, here we go."

"That night I caught you with that other woman. I put it out of my mind, bought into your story about studying. Down deep, I knew. But, silly me, I loved you. For the life of me, I still do."

"I don't know what you want from me."

I shrug. "The only thing I know for sure is that I expect you to give that child a father. Have a relationship with her."

"I can't believe you're saying this. You want me to have a relationship with my illegitimate child?"

Now the fury sparks again, kicking all that sadness to the side and energizing me. It'll be a short-lived burst, but it'll get me through. A blood rush blurs my vision, nearly knocking me off my feet.

Doing what I do, I've often spoken with spouses who've tried to describe a deep-rooted, murderous anger.

Before discovering Ryan's horrendous choices, I never got it. Not fully.

Never understood that kind of rage where you lose all perspective, all sense of right versus wrong.

Now, I could crawl over my husband's desk, put my hands

around his throat and grip so hard I'd snap his hyoid. Squeeze the life right out of him.

I grit my teeth again, focus on an unmoving Ryan. "Don't you *dare* call her that."

I have to leave. Just get out before … I don't know. I don't know what I'm running from, but nothing about this feels right or that it'll get us anywhere.

I spin and head to the door.

"Becca!"

I stop and turn back. "*Don't* scream at me."

"I'm not—"

"Shut up, Ryan. Just *shut* up. You need to get your act together. In two weeks, you're going on television and God help you, I have enough ammunition to make you look like the world's biggest idiot."

"Seriously? You're still planning on going through with that? With a baby involved?"

"You bet your life. I have staffers counting on me. Unlike you, I worry about other people."

With that, I swing the door open, just as the blonde did minutes ago, and make my grand exit, every eye in the place on me as I walk out. Head high, shoulders back.

I'm done screwing around.

CHAPTER 25

$\mathcal{N}$eeding fresh air, I opt to take the Snooty down the shore rather than have Bernie waste three, possibly four, hours schlepping there and back. He's done enough for today.

I don my wig and Jackie O. glasses and climb the stairs to the top deck of the boat. Sorry. My bad. The *yacht*.

It's a nice day and sitting outside in the sun will do me some good. Plus, the captain told me when I boarded that only one other person was on the upper deck. A win-win.

Upon reaching the top of the staircase, I find a woman seated in one of the cushioned chairs. She's reading something on her phone and doesn't spare me even a glance.

She's about my age, so I take a second to size her up. Long dark hair pulled into a tight chignon. Simple navy slacks and a white blouse are accessorized with a string of pearls. What looks like Gucci shoes lie at her feet and her blazer is folded over the backrest of the seat next to her.

After the day I've had, the champagne in her hand looks like a splendid idea. My soft heels click against the deck, and she finally peers up at me, her gaze locking on my blond wig.

She nods a greeting, but if she recognizes me, she's not letting on.

"Afternoon," she says. "Lovely day for a ride."

"Hello. I agree. The champagne is a pleasant idea."

"Champagne is always a pleasant idea."

Once again agreeing with her, I slip inside to the bar and order a mimosa from the bartender, a young guy in his twenties who always seems to be here. I pay for the drink, drop a ten in his tip jar and head back outside.

When the boat starts moving, I may have to retreat inside or risk losing my wig in the wind, but for now, I'll enjoy the warmth.

Rather than crowd the woman, I take the couch on the opposite side of the deck, set my glass on the table and my tote at my feet. Lacking energy for much else, I rest my head back, staring out at the Hudson and the commercial ferry boats and smattering of smaller vessels all carrying folks doing whatever it is they do midweek.

Me? It's been a helluva day.

First Calle, then Ryan and the blonde. Who'd have known my husband was such a shithead?

I lift my glass, silently toasting myself for living in oblivion for twenty-four years. How many people could pull that off?

"Cheers."

Before taking a drink, I peer across at the woman. She's holding up her glass. Obviously, she noted my toast to the universe.

I hold my glass a little higher. "Cheers."

We both sip our drinks and before lowering her glass, she tips it toward me. "You can take off the wig, Dr. Becca. It's windy and you'll probably lose it in a few minutes, anyway."

My disguise wasn't nearly as good as I'd hoped.

"We're the only two on board," she adds. "I checked with the crew when I got on. And, since I know who you are, no point in losing what looks like an extremely expensive wig."

Half relieved to be rid of it, I slide the wig off, store it in my tote and pull the pins from my hair.

"I guess the disguise wasn't so great."

The woman smiles at me. "Or maybe I'm just good at spotting wigs."

"Why is that?"

As the yacht departs, she digs into her purse for something—business card—and crosses to where I'm sitting.

"I'm Lilibet Humphries."

Humphries. I recognize the name, but it's swimming in my foggy brain. I take the card and stand to shake her hand. "Becca Matthews. But you know that already."

"Yes. And to answer your question." She points to the card. "I'm a divorce attorney with high-profile clients. Lots of wigs. Lots of press. Lots of amateur photographers trying to grab the money shot."

The money shot.

Lilibet speaks my language.

"The wigs I suggest my clients wear," she continues, "are from a boutique on Fifth Avenue. All handmade and not synthetic."

The same boutique where I bought mine.

"Ah," I say. "You give good advice. They're the best."

"They are."

I'm not necessarily in the mood for small talk, but meeting an accomplished, smart woman is never a hardship. Besides, ruminating over the wreckage that is my life isn't exactly productive.

"Have a seat," I gesture to the chair across from me. "If you'd like."

She moves back to her original spot, grabs her champagne

and rejoins me. "I have a summer home in Rumson," she tells me.

Rumson. A lovely town riddled with mansions that dwarf my cottage. The celebrity divorce business must be good.

Is it a bizarre coincidence that, after the day I've had, I'm meeting a divorce attorney? Is this the universe sending a message?

Could she be following me?

Now I'm just being ridiculous. Particularly since she boarded the vessel first and I made my reservation fifteen minutes prior to showing up.

I shake off the thought, concentrating on what might be my good fortune. "Do you believe in coincidences?"

She shrugs. "I believe there are reasons people are put in our path at particular times."

"It defies logic," I say.

"What's that?"

"That you're here right now."

"Not really. From May to September, this is how I get to work every day. The anomaly today is that I have a dinner tonight and left work two hours early."

"The further anomaly is that I'm usually at the studio."

She offers an easy smile. "Maybe we were just meant to meet."

Now, it's my turn to shrug. "Maybe."

Working on instinct, I reach for my tote, drag out my wallet and pull all the cash I have. Two twenties and four singles. Leaning forward, I hold the bills out.

For a few seconds, she stares at them, then seeming to understand, takes them.

"It's all the cash I have on me, but hopefully good enough for a down payment on legal advice."

What I want from Lilibet Humphries, I'm not quite sure. But

we're alone and she's literally been thrown in my path. If I hire her, everything I say is protected under attorney-client privilege, and I need to talk. To figure out my options. Am I, Becca Matthews, the miracle marriage-fixer, really considering divorcing my husband? Possibly. I'm confused and heartbroken and lost.

Maybe someone like Lilibet, with all the marriage issues she's seen, can help me sort it out.

She tucks the cash into her pants pocket. "We shouldn't talk here." She circles a finger in the air. "Security cameras. I don't know if they record sound."

Cameras. Should have anticipated that. "Thank you. I hadn't thought of that."

"You're distracted. It's not unusual. It's my job to protect you from that distraction."

"I'm not sure," I tell her. "What I want to do. Is that okay?"

"It's more than okay. I'm part attorney, part therapist. We'll talk and if I can help you, I will. You're the client and it's your money. We're on your schedule."

My schedule.

I like that. No pressure.

"Good. Let me do some thinking tonight and I'll call you in the morning. That work?"

"Yes. This dinner tonight will run late so I'm working from home tomorrow. If you'd like, you can come by. We can discuss it in the morning."

I nod and hold up my glass. "Here's to coincidences."

I ARRIVE HOME to find my mother's car in the driveway. Either she's had another fight with Dad and needed a reprieve or she's finally ready to talk.

Well, I don't have the energy for analyzing every detail of our argument. I apologized several times. I took responsibility. I don't intend to be beaten over the head with it.

Parking beside Mom's car, I glance around, checking for photographers who might ambush me. Not seeing anyone, I gather my tote and head to the front door half expecting someone to jump from behind a bush.

"Private property" is all I can think. It's a weird sort of balm to my embattled brain.

Dealing with paparazzi comes with fame. Mostly, I've been spared major intrusions.

I've been lucky.

I should have appreciated that more.

Fully focused on that luck, I slide my key into the lock and get inside without incident. My mother is curled up on the sofa, a book in her lap, her reading glasses perched on her perfect nose.

She looks exactly like what she is. A sophisticated, seventy-year-old woman who takes meticulous care of her body. On the outside at least. Inside?

No bets on that.

The unhappiness in her marriage could be shredding her organs.

I set my tote on the chair next to the sofa and prop a hip against it. "Hi."

Removing her glasses, she gently folds them and tucks them in the case. I know my mother. She's stalling. Adding a bit of drama by carefully placing her bookmark and closing the book before setting it and her glasses aside.

Finally she meets my gaze. "Hi. Hope you don't mind my being here."

"You know you're always welcome. I'm glad to see you. I've been …" I shake my head. "I don't know. Missing you, I suppose. I hate the way we left things."

She bobs her head, tears filling her eyes and I can't help it, I double-time my steps to reach her. I need to hug my mother. To feel her warmth and reassurance and love.

By the time I get there, she's on her feet and I throw myself against her, my mom who is a solid six inches shorter than me. I wrap my arms tight around her thin, bony frame and just inhale the familiarity of Chanel No. 5.

"I'm so sorry," I say. "So, so sorry."

"I'm sorry too."

Wait. Did my mother just apologize? The one who has, my entire life, maintained a steadfast reputation for moving beyond. Just marching forward. No looking back.

No apologies.

No discussion.

I step back, still holding her arms, refusing to let go. "I didn't mean to hurt you."

"I know. I'm not perfect, Becca. I probably handled that conversation all wrong. You know me. Never let them see you sweat."

"You were upset."

"Yes, but so were you. I made it about me."

That, she did.

I won't say it's okay. It's not. I needed her and she made herself unavailable.

"Mom," I give her forearms a soft squeeze. "I need to talk to someone. I need *you*. Can you help me?"

She blinks away a fresh bout of tears and bobs her head. "How about we order up some dinner and chat? Would you like that?"

"I'd love that."

I pull away from her, waving her into the kitchen where I grab the menu for her favorite Chinese restaurant. Plus, they deliver.

We decide on food, and I place the order before pouring us both a glass of lemonade I made the day before.

Settling in at the island, we swivel to face each other.

"Talk to me," she says. "How can I help?"

Starting from scratch, I put our argument out of my mind and lay it all out for her. Ryan's mistresses, baby Calle, the meeting that day and my husband's refusal to acknowledge his child. He might be financially supporting her, but make no mistake, he won't recognize her as his.

"And," Mom says, "you're sure the baby is his?"

"Positive. Not only does she look like him, he's confirmed that there's been a paternity test. I haven't seen the results first-hand, but Ry has no reason to tell me if he's not sure. After meeting Calle, I went to his office and found him with a woman behind closed doors."

At this, my mother rolls her eyes so hard it should knock her over. "Oh, come on!"

"I know! They were sitting on the couch in his office. Not doing anything, but the body language. I could tell. You know?"

Unfortunately, my mother nods. She does know and ... ick. My father is a good man. I love him. Desperately. But he's made mistakes. I simply chose not to acknowledge—emotionally speaking—those mistakes.

Not my monkey. Not my circus.

"Anyway," I say, "my husband is a cheater. Have I really been this blind? Not to have seen it?"

"Oh, honey, you love him. Unconsciously, you may not have wanted to see it."

"I knew we'd gotten comfortable. Maybe too comfortable." I shake my head, stare out the windows at the ocean. "I feel like an idiot."

My mother's head snaps back, and she pokes—poke, poke, poke—a finger at me. "Don't. You. Dare. It's *not* your fault. *He* did this. If he's unsatisfied in the marriage, he should have spoken up. And a baby? For God's sake, Becca, how could he do this?"

How indeed. I'm not above recognizing my responsibility in

this mess. Being too focused on my career and letting it rule my life, but Mom is right. He could have said something.

Could have sat me down, told me he needed attention.

Would I have changed anything?

I want to believe so, but being the host of a talk show is like feeding a large beast. There's never enough. It's always hungry and I'm only one person.

I let out a sigh. "I met a divorce attorney."

My mother's blue eyes sharpen, her shock obvious. "You're divorcing him?"

"It sounds crazy, considering what I do for a living. Plus, the network is running promos on the segments about me fixing my marriage. I honestly don't know what to do. But in an odd twist, Lilibet Humphries, a celebrity divorce attorney, was on the boat with me today."

Mom gawks, her mouth flopping open in a way that's nothing short of comical and makes me snort.

I'm laughing. How it's possible is a mystery, but it feels … good. A momentary respite.

"You *must* be joking," Mom says, her voice heavy on haughty indignance.

"I'm not. We were the only two aboard. She was right there. Sipping champagne. Almost as if waiting for me. Before I knew it, I handed her all the cash I had as a retainer. We're talking tomorrow."

"My goodness. You've been busy. Tell me about Calle."

"Ugh. She's adorable. I *hate* that she's so adorable. There's purity there. Like the world hasn't tainted her yet. Just looking at her made me smile."

Mom gives me a skeptical raised eyebrow.

"Even her mother," I continue. "Tiffany. She's nice. A young woman who made a stupid mistake. I resent her, but I can't hate her."

"What does she want from you?"

"She claims Ryan gives her whatever money she needs. She's alone. Estranged from her parents, which I can't imagine. Especially with an infant. She wants her daughter to have a family."

"I suppose we all want that for our children."

I wouldn't know.

I wanted children. Always have. Still do. No matter what happens with my husband, I know I need to have a baby. Maybe two if I'm still able.

One thing at a time.

"What now?" Mom asks.

"Question of the day. Ryan has no interest in meeting Calle, so I'm on my own there. Would it be weird to allow Calle and her mother into my life?"

"Of course it's weird. But she's an innocent baby. If you want to get to know her, that's your choice. As long as you're clear with Tiffany what the expectations are. That your kindness will only go so far."

I study her for a few seconds, running her comments over in my mind. "You mean no money."

Mom reaches for me. Sets her hand on mine. "I know your instincts are good, but this is an emotional issue. You may not see ulterior motives."

My father, in his infinite wisdom, calls getting conned a snow job. "Mom, I have too much at stake. I don't intend to be buried under a foot of snow. I'll make it clear all financial matters will go through Ryan."

She pulls her hand away, sits tall in her stool. "If this feels wrong to you, at any time, you'll have to back away. There's only so much you can do for people. You know that."

"I do. And I will. I'll go into it with an open heart, but if it winds up being a mistake, I'll remove myself from the situation."

"Good. Thank you," she says, "for trusting me. For confiding in me."

"Pfft." I wave her off. "You make me insane sometimes, but

there's no other person I trust more. Especially now. I'm glad we have each other." I jerk my head. "That we have this place."

She peers around, taking in the renovated kitchen and cozy living room. "Your happy place."

Yes. My happy place.

CHAPTER 26

I open my eyes, draw a deep breath and stare straight up at the ceiling where sunlight pours in over the tops of the shades. This, based on last night's weather report, may be short-lived. Rain expected by early afternoon.

Gotta get that run in.

I glance at the clock: 8:45. All this sleeping late is becoming a habit. In the past, I've found it beneficial to keep my same sleep habits each day. I'm less stringent on the weekends, but for me, it's better to stay in my routine. Otherwise, I have what Ry calls a sleep hangover.

Sleep hangovers make me crabby. Leave me sluggish and mentally anesthetized.

Like now.

I didn't even stay up that late. Exhaustion had taken hold by ten, Mom left, and I curled into my bed, dropping dead asleep for a few hours before the war between my relentless brain and fried body raged on.

The treadmill catches my eye. I remember a coworker, fifteen years my senior, telling me about ruler-wielding nuns at her Catholic grammar school. Bad penmanship? Whacked on the hand with the ruler. Late for class? *Whack.*

Today, those nuns would be in jail. Back then? Not so much. I glance at the treadmill again.

My version of a ruler-wielding nun.

Get going.

I roll over, set my feet on the floor, and sit for a second, pinching the meaty part of my thigh. Not too bad. I don't go for all that fancy testing that'll tell me what my fat percentage is. I know my body. Can feel the slight shifts here and there.

Lately, they're not so slight. Age is a brutal bitch. I fight and fight and fight her, but she's strong. And persistent.

I make a note to up my collagen intake, another weapon in my arsenal to keep my skin smooth and supple. HD television might be all the rage, but for me? I hate it. Every line, every sag, is in full-blown high def screaming, "Look at me!"

Time to go.

Getting to my feet, I make my way to the bathroom. After washing up, I hit the closet for running shorts and a tank, adding a baseball hat for good measure. Then I slide on one of my armbands that hold my phone and key while I'm running.

Sneakers on, I head out the side door, lock it and store the key in my arm strap with my phone.

On the beach, Danny stands at the foot of the shore, his bare feet soaked. Mug in hand, he's wearing basketball shorts and a T-shirt, his ever-present sunglasses in place. The back of his short hair is mashed, which I surmise is bed head that he appears unperturbed by.

That's the way to spend a morning. Simply easing into the day.

"Morning," he says.

I stop two feet from him, avoiding having my sneakers ruined in the surf. "Morning. What are you up to?"

"Eh. Bored. Figured I'd come outside. Maybe go for a walk. You running?"

Sure am. "Planned on it."

I tip my head back, soak up the warm sun and stillness. My brain is always engaged, dealing with a hundred things that really shouldn't matter but somehow do.

Now, here I am, marriage in the toilet and a secret baby that will, if word gets out, stir up attention that might flush my career down that same toilet.

No wonder I'm tired.

"Quit thinking, Becca. Won't do you any good."

I straighten up and peer at my neighbor, who holds his mug up in a toast. He's right. I need a distraction, something to occupy my mind and running won't do it. All running will do is give me more time to ruminate.

Why would I even want that?

I point down the beach. "Wanna walk?"

He gives me that look, the one over the top of his glasses. "What about your run?"

"Well, Danny, here's the thing. Maybe I'm sick of running. Maybe I want to slow down. Take a minute and figure out what I'm doing with my life."

"Wow. Didn't mean to open *that* can of worms."

I snort and give him a light punch. "Let's go. The company will do me good. Keep me from thinking too hard."

"Fine. I'm not sharing my coffee. Some things, a man can't do."

"Understood. We can stop at the coffee shop two miles down. I'll grab a cappuccino."

"Two miles? Holy shit."

"Two miles, Danny. Have I mentioned exercise is good for you?"

"That's four total."

"Excellent math skills. I think you can handle it. If not, I'll get you an Uber."

Bottom lip rolled out, he considers this a moment. "Deal."

I was kidding, but apparently he's amenable to the idea. If I do nothing else this summer, I'll get him exercising regularly. He has kids, particularly his daughter, who need him.

We head down the beach, passing two power-walking retirees and another couple I often see out here.

I wave and then stop to study a rock—white with gray streaks—that has washed up in the surf. Running doesn't give me the opportunity to pause and treasure hunt. I scoop the rock up, debate its merits and … yes, it's a keeper.

Danny holds his hand out. "If you don't have a pocket, I'll put it in mine. I'm used to it. Abby picks up all kinds of crap."

Handing him the rock, we continue down the beach, our pace leisurely, to say the least. Part of me can't stand it and wants to go faster. Get those endorphins really streaming. The other part? Gleeful.

"I made up with my mother last night," I say. "We had a long talk. I told her about the baby, and she helped me. I needed that."

I take another five minutes to fill Danny in on yesterday's events. Meeting Calle, possibly spending more time with her, busting Ryan in his office, the chance encounter with Lilibet.

Danny lets out a low whistle. "Lilibet is hardcore. She'll gut Ryan."

Ew. That sounds evil. Am I ready for that? "You know her?"

"Handled my second divorce."

"Your side?"

He gives me his over-the-sunglasses stare again.

"Ah," I say. "She gutted you."

"And my bank account."

"You said you're on good terms with your ex."

At this, he grunts. "*Now.* The months leading up to the

divorce were torture. Rectal exam gone bad. It didn't need to be that way. I'd have been fair."

I spot a shell. A pure white one with a chipped edge. Perfectly imperfect. I scoop it up and Danny holds his hand out, relieving me of my find.

"What if I'm not sure what fair looks like?"

Am I seriously talking about this with my neighbor? My mother would have a heart attack.

Danny, in a few short weeks, has become more than a casual acquaintance. More than the nutty guy next door. He's my friend. And that, despite the hell I'm living in, feels good.

"Frankly," I continue, "I'm not sure what *anything* looks like. How do I salvage my career if I divorce Ry? Part of my brand—and yes, I'm aware how disgusting this will sound—is my," I make air quotes, "thriving twenty-four-year marriage. Good or bad, the network has splashed us all over billboards and magazines."

I shake my head. Cheating was an aspect of his life that *he* controlled rather than the Dr. Becca machine.

I might be to blame for allowing my career to run my life, but I didn't make a fool of him.

Danny shrugs. "Your brand gave you a good life. Guessing there's no pre-nup?"

I scoff. "Please. We were broke when we married. After the money started rolling in, it seemed dumb to do a post-nup. I considered us partners. My success was our success."

Part of me, even the part that's ready to dropkick my husband, still believes it. Ryan's support over the years kept me sane.

Danny stops walking and faces me. "Do you love him?"

"I'll always love him. I'm angry at him. I might even hate him right now, but I'll never not love him."

"Fair enough. Can you get beyond the affairs? The baby?"

Ding, ding, ding. Give the man a prize. He's figured out the question of the day. "The affairs, maybe. I'd have to be convinced he could be faithful and that will take time. Years, probably. Calle? I'm not sure I could move on. Not only did he keep Calle from me, he's been paying child support. I deserved to know where our money was going. How could I ever trust him again?"

There's my answer. The one thing I'm clear on. "Whoa." I hold my hands up.

"What?" Danny asks.

"Before I left the office the other day, my EP asked me about putting Tiffany—Calle's mother—on the show. If we do, it exposes Calle, and that's not fair. She's innocent in this. But if we don't talk about Calle, if I can't trust Ryan, what's the point of these saving-my-marriage segments? I'm stuck, Danny."

"Take it easy. You're tackling too much at once. If you're not putting Calle on the show, go from there. She's your ground zero."

Ground zero. Yes.

If I start from there, I'll come up with a way to salvage my career and maintain Calle's privacy. Perhaps even get to know her a little. Why I want that, I'm not sure, but she's Ryan's child. Despite his transgressions, his daughter deserves a family.

No matter how dysfunctional.

As for my marriage?

I'll never get over this. Ever. The deception cuts too deep. Wounds like that? They leave scar tissue so thick the body never functions the same.

We can't go back.

The question is, how do move forward?

AFTER RETURNING from my walk with Danny, who managed to survive with minimal complaints, I toss my cappuccino cup in the recycle bin and pour a glass of water, throwing in some lemons from the stash in the freezer. Then I park myself on a bar stool at the kitchen island to make calls.

First up is Jenny and letting her know Calle and Tiffany are not an option for the show. This is one of my boundaries and it *will* be respected.

It's the joy of taped segments. We can edit anything out. Sure, I threatened the blonde in Ryan's office with a live show, but that was a bluff. All the way. I'd be a fool—an even bigger one than I already am, considering my husband's secrets—to do a live show with Marley at the wheel.

My conversation with Jenny is brief and although she's pleasant enough, understanding enough, professional enough, I know my EP and she's not happy. Borderline angry.

Too bad.

Life stinks sometimes.

Feeling at least somewhat productive, I dig Lilibet's card from my purse. I'm actually doing this. Calling a divorce attorney.

Just talking.

I let out a long breath, convincing myself it's only a conversation. An exploration. Fact gathering. That's all I'm doing. Sorting out my options.

Before I lose my nerve, I dial and wait as the phone rings and rings and—voicemail.

Shoot.

I leave a message asking to set up a meeting for the following week. Something preferably at the shore so I don't have to go into the city and risk being seen walking into her office.

A meeting next week gives me time to think. I peer out the sliders at the ocean where the sun still shines, but not for long. Dreary clouds stack up in the distance, creeping in. As a kid, I hated rainy days. Boring, I'd complain.

Even then I liked being busy. As a therapist, I now realize my childhood need for activity kept my mind occupied. Being idle meant time to think about my fear of oversharing with people. Back then, I spent most of my time with my mother. In the summer, we'd loaf around on the beach. I loved those times. Spending our days—sometimes into the evening—in our swimsuits, going back and forth from the house for snacks or magazines or books.

Perfection I never knew I had.

A vision of Calle and her bright smile flash in my mind. At only six months old, has she ever experienced the beach? The initial feeling of warm sand between her toes? The miracle of salty air?

I've thought about Calle since the second I saw those fluffy cheeks. Babies, somehow, even when they're the result of deception, make things better. They have an innocence unblemished by adult actions.

For someone who's built a career surrounded by impurity, it's a welcome relief. It's a sad reminder of what I've missed. The nighttime baths and snuggles.

The lack of sleep.

I didn't get any of that.

It's not too late.

Calle isn't mine. Never will be. But I'm only forty-eight and froze my eggs. A burst of fear-laced possibility pebbles my skin.

A baby on my own means a sperm donor and a life without Ryan. Before now, I'd have never imagined losing my best friend. At least, that's who I thought he was.

I lean forward and rest my head against the cool marble of the island. Divorce meant possibly losing my career. How could I go on being the super-fixer if I can't save my own marriage?

Sitting up again, I pause and just breathe. One thing at a time. That's all I can do. I have the next eleven days to sort out my feelings. Calle may be my ground zero, but my marriage hinges on whether I can move beyond Ryan's secrets. If we stay together, I'll have to get comfortable with Calle being in *my* orbit but not his.

I scoop up the phone again and tap the screen. Two rings in, Tiffany answers.

"Hi," I say, "It's Becca Matthews. Sorry to bother you."

"You're not. At all. How are you?"

"I'm okay. I have a question."

She hesitates for a moment. I can't blame her. The list of possible questions could fill a barn.

I pause. Consider what I'm about to do.

Ground zero.

Calle is where I rebuild. I sit a little taller and tip my chin up. I can do this.

"Becca?"

"I'm here. Has Calle ever been to the beach?"

CHAPTER 27

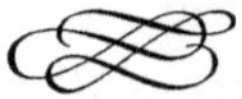

"*B*ubby! What the hell are you doing?"

On my knees in the sand, I look up, spot Danny marching toward me. It's ten in the morning and I've been up for four hours, my looping thoughts making me crazy.

At least it's a sunny, warm morning that promises to be a wonderful beach day.

Danny obviously thinks so too because he's wearing red board shorts, a white T-shirt and his signature Maui Jims. As he gets closer, I note the salt-and-pepper whiskers covering his jaw. He's normally clean-shaven so this scruffy look is … different. Not necessarily a good different.

Part of me is envious. He gets to walk around not worrying about paparazzi. Earlier, I saw one of the little bastards three houses down, lurking like a cockroach. The police can't throw them off the beach. At least I don't think.

I may need security on the beach. I'll worry about it later. Hopefully, for today, they'll think I simply have a friend and her child over.

Danny stops two feet from me, and I hold up two bendy rods. "You're a parent. You'll know how to do this. I'm putting up a beach tent. I did research and this one, hands down, is the best. I'm not sure how all these poles are supposed to go together."

His lips peel back as if I've asked him to eat worms. I'm guessing Danny isn't the handy type.

He holds up both hands. "Why do you need a tent?"

"Calle is coming over."

"Bubby."

At this, I laugh and drop the poles on top of the tent fabric, swiping sand from my hands. "After our talk yesterday, your comment about ground zero stuck. Calle *is* my ground zero. If I can't emotionally accept her, my marriage won't survive."

He tips his chin down, peers at me over his sunglasses like I've lost my mind. "So you invited her over for a play date?"

"It's crazy. I know. My intention was to float the idea. Let Tiffany think about me spending time with Calle. Tiffany works six days a week. Today is her only day off, so we're doing it. Having a beach day. Calle's first. And," I waggle a hand at the tent, "you know, babies have sensitive skin. I want to make sure she'll be okay."

Shaking his head, Danny grins. "Well, look at you."

"What?"

"A lot of people couldn't do this. Let this child into their home, much less their life."

"It's not her fault. I keep reminding myself of that. And let's face it, I'm not going to be able to have Tiffany around a lot. That's too much. If Calle can get comfortable with me, maybe she and I can have one-on-one time together."

Before I start thinking too hard and back out of this entire episode, I point to the mess on the sand. "Now, I need help with this stupid tent."

The two of us drop to our knees and I grab the directions.

"Have I mentioned," Danny says, "I'm more of a hire-someone man?"

"Too bad. You're helping me."

He paddles one hand. "I'll read. You assemble."

Deal. I hand over the tiny booklet. "Thank you. Not for this. Well, yes, for this. But, also, for being a friend."

"Eh. You're keeping things lively around here. And I like babies."

THREE HOURS LATER, I'm in my bikini—yes, I'm that shallow that I wanted my husband's mistress to see I can still rock one—and sitting in my beach chair beside the tent Danny and I assembled. Calle is inside, napping in her carrier with the zippered tent flaps tucked open so Tiffany can see her.

Tiffany is also wearing a bikini. A red one with teeny-tiny patches covering her full breasts.

Here I am.

Entertaining my husband's side piece who has a body that won't quit. Even after having a baby.

Go. Figure.

"She's a good napper," I say when an awkward silence drags on.

"She is. One to three o'clock is her usual time. If she gets off schedule, she's cranky, so I try to stick to it."

I file that information away. I may need it someday.

Tiffany settles back in the beach chair I set up for her and stares off at the ocean for a few seconds before coming back to me. "Why did you invite us here?"

Why indeed? My options are few. Anything but the truth will sound ridiculous. The *truth* sounds ridiculous.

"My neighbor," I point to Danny's house, "is divorced. He has kids. He's been my sounding board. By the way, he knows who you are. I trust him. He won't leak it." I wave it away. "I was talking with him yesterday about Calle and Ryan's refusal to meet her. As a result of that conversation, I thought it might be a good idea if I spend some time with Calle."

I'm not about to share with her how saving my marriage means getting comfortable with her child.

Too much information.

"Why?" she asks.

"Why what?"

She shrugs. "Spend time with Calle?"

"Other than the fact that my husband is paying child support and I have to learn to accept her?"

She screws up her lips. "I see your point. Do you have a plan? Not that I have any say."

"You're her mother. You have a say. I don't have a plan. Frankly, I didn't expect we'd do this so soon. I thought I'd run the idea by you and we'd think about it. It just worked out this way, which is fine. It gives us a chance to talk. Set some boundaries."

She peers at me, drawing her eyebrows together. "Boundaries?"

Did she think we'd do this without rules? "I'm a public person. I'd expect you to honor my—and Ryan's—privacy."

"Absolutely. I swear, I'd never talk to the press."

I believe her. If she were going to out us, she'd have done it by now. "Thank you. As I said during our first meeting, I'm not sure Ryan will come around. However, since he's my husband, I'm an extension of him and Calle is his responsibility. Which makes her part of my life. How much a part is the question. It'll take time for us—and I'm talking about you and me—

to figure out the boundaries."

"I understand."

Does she? I doubt it. I point to the tent. "Calle deserves to be loved."

Tiffany bobs her head again and her eyes well up. "She's such a good girl. She really is. I think that's why I was hoping Ryan would want to know her. So she'd have both a mom and dad."

"Maybe someday. I'm willing to try and figure out where we go from here. How she fits into our world. Maybe we start with visiting me a couple times a month. Would that work for you?"

"That would be great."

"I won't be a babysitter, but if you have an emergency, you can call. I'll see what I can do."

A gurgling noise comes from the tent and we both steal a glance at Calle. Satisfied her daughter is still asleep, Tiffany comes back to me. "I'm usually good with sitters, but I appreciate that. The lady next door, Val, has been awesome. She has kids. She gets it."

"You're resourceful. I respect that."

She shrugs. "I'm used to being on my own. Anyway, a couple times a month works."

I nod. "We'll start there and see where this goes."

"I HAVE EVERYTHING."

Tiffany hauls the diaper bag, her purse, another tote with their dirty beachwear and Calle's car seat base out the front door while I carry Calle, still in her carrier, to my SUV for the trip to the train station.

I suggested the ferry, but Tiffany balked. The train will be easier since she can hop on the subway once she gets to Manhattan. A ferry would require an extra subway transfer.

I'd offered to pick them up at the station upon arrival, but Tiffany had insisted on taking a car service rather than bother me. Going back, I'm the one insisting. She's a single working mother. The least I can do is save her some money.

"Yikes," I say, "that's a lot of gear."

"Life with an infant. You get used to it."

How she lugged all this stuff on the way down, I have no

idea, but it's not a shock. Over the years, I've worked with single mothers who have a superpower, another gear we kidless folks aren't blessed with, for functioning.

At the car, Tiffany drops all the bags in the driveway and climbs into the back seat, situating the base in the middle. "I like her away from the doors."

Understandable logic.

She takes the carrier from me, and Calle lets out a noise. It's a cross between a coo and, well, a growl and Tiffany opens her mouth wide, her face lighting up in exaggerated pleasure.

"Who's a silly girl?"

Placing the carrier on the back seat, she unbuckles Calle, scoops her out and holds her to me. Dumbfounded, I stand there while Calle, suspended in mid-air, kicks her legs and giggles, the sound knocking me from my paralysis and making me smile.

She really is adorable.

Tiffany nudges her chin. "Um, can you hold her? I need to strap her seat in."

Hold her. Okay. So not ready for that, but the ground isn't an option.

"It's okay," Tiffany tells me. "She won't bite."

At that, Calle offers another giggle. These two. Comedians, both of them.

Apparently, I'm doing this. Holding Ryan's child. I extend my arms, keeping my gaze locked on Calle's big blue eyes. If she screams, I'll lose my mind. I'll … I'll … I don't know what else I'll do other than take it as a sign that this blended family gig will never work.

Tiffany slides her into my arms, and I draw her close. Where should my hands go? When's the last time I held a baby?

Clearly sensing my struggle, Calle swings her head sideways, checking on her mother. Yep. Here it comes. I brace myself, waiting for the howl, the utter despair that comes with the coldness of a stranger in her mother's absence.

I have to get it together here. My PhD didn't prepare me for this.

Focus.

Calle watches Tiffany for a few seconds while I settle one arm under her rear for support and the other around her back. Okay. That seems comfortable. For both of us.

After ensuring her mother hasn't abandoned her, Calle comes back to me, our eyes locking. I slap a bright, exaggerated smile on my face. "Hello, pretty!" I coo. "Who's so pretty?"

I sound like an idiot.

She gives me a half-snort that I'll take as humor and call it a win. *Go. Me.* Maybe I *can* make this work. After a long few seconds of Calle studying me through squinty eyes, I shift her to my hip and she reaches up, touching my face, running her chubby little fingers down my cheek. Exploring. Her touch sends warm ripples down my body, soothing my fractured nerves. Babies. So sweet.

The snap of the seatbelt draws Calle's attention to Tiffany, who is tugging on the carrier, checking the fit.

"Perfect," she says. "Good and tight."

When she's done, she takes Calle from me, straps her into the carrier and then tosses the gear on the rear passenger seat before hopping in front. Total efficiency that impresses me.

Next door, the ever-diligent—and nosy—Danny is at his front window. I give a honk as we back out of the driveway and then wave, letting him know I'm on to him.

At the end of the block, I make a right and we cruise Ocean Avenue in silence. Something I don't mind. We're not friends, Tiffany and I, we're something altogether different that I haven't quite categorized yet. For now, we're two women learning to coexist.

"Are you sure you don't want me to ask Bernie to pick you up at the train? You have a lot to carry."

"No. We're good. I'm used to it. You've been really nice to us already."

Have I?

Who can tell in a situation like this?

I let the thought go. "Let me know if you change your mind. It's not a bother."

Even if Bernie can't do it, I could order her a car.

"Will do," she says. "Thanks."

Five miles in, I turn left off Ocean Avenue, drive two blocks and stop at the traffic light. Calle squeals.

"You're so silly!" Tiffany says, her voice overly excited for Calle's sake. "I love you, sweet girl."

Her words hit me a certain way. A certain way that sends my mood plummeting. Amazing how that can happen. Like a screeching halt. Just bam. Instant change.

Despite my attempts to be kind, I'm trapped in a car with my husband's mistress as she does this whole baby talk thing with their child. A baby I never had the opportunity to have.

I grip the steering wheel, concentrate on the road ahead. What's done is done. Me having a freak-out won't help me manage the situation.

I do my reasonable-Becca thing, reminding myself that she's a young mother who adores her child. It's not about me. It's about Calle.

Calle, Calle, Calle.

The light changes and I punch the gas hard enough that my head—as well as everyone else's, I'm sure—snaps back.

A horn blares. Truck horn. I swing my head right. An eighteen-wheeler blows the red light.

And is coming straight for us.

CHAPTER 28

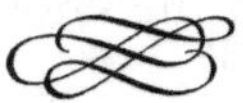

What happens next is something I've never experienced. A time warp where everything simultaneously slows yet speeds up. Confusion screws up my sensory perception, my body stiffening as I slam my foot against the gas pedal. For me, it's exactly like what you see in the movies.

The whole time-slowing-down thing? It's legit.

"Becca!" Tiffany shouts.

Her scream mixes with the blare of the truck horn.

The grill. No matter how hard I press the gas, the truck's massive grill comes closer and closer and then it happens. My brain dumps a mountain of cortisol into my system. Cortisol, one of my professors used to say, is the body's natural alarm system and right now? It's lighting me up, sending energy rocketing through my limbs.

I jerk the wheel—too late—and the truck plows into the side of my SUV throwing my strapped-in body sideways. All at once, an explosion of shattering glass flies from somewhere, Calle lets out a piercing wail and the airbags fly. Those suckers burst free, slamming against my face so hard pain shoots in all directions. I breathe through it and a nasty smoky smell assaults me.

What *is* that?

Calle.

Completely out of my control, my car is still moving sideways, the truck pushing us, the tires—mine or the truck's, I'm not sure—making a squealing sound that pounds my eardrums.

A guttural roar bursts from my throat as I grip the wheel, desperately trying to hold on. My foot. Not on the gas. When did that happen? The seconds, this utter hell, and the squealing of tires drags on. *Make it stop, make it stop, make it stop.*

My SUV finally rocks and comes to a halt. I sit back, blinking, waiting for the airbag to fully deflate. I'm almost too stunned to move. Neck injury. I could have one. Don't they say never to move someone with a neck injury?

Calle's terrified cries shatter my thoughts. *Calle.*

A blood rush blurs my vision and I blink again. *Blink, blink, blink.* No good. Everything is fuzzy and bendy and … whoa … going … dark.

"Ma'am?"

Someone touches me. A hand. On my arm. I jolt awake, jerk my head left—ow—and stare at a cop bending at the waist beside me. What the hell?

Accident.

We were in a car accident. My mental fog clears, the final moments before my blackout coming into sharper focus. Truck. Blew the light.

Terror comes back to me, and I slam my eyes closed. Please let it be a nightmare.

"Are you all right?" the cop asks. "You passed out."

Not a nightmare.

I take a second, draw a breath. The powerful odor of gas fills me, and I cough, trying to dispel the nastiness. I wiggle my fingers and toes and open my eyes, keeping my gaze straight ahead at the back of the front seat.

Whose car is this? I slide my gaze left then right. Police car. I'm in the back of a police car.

"I'm okay," I say. "I think."

And then … *Calle. Ohmygod.*

"The baby!"

"Whoa. Go easy. She's okay. We got her out."

I look back at the cop. "Tiffany? The woman with me?"

He nudges his chin, and I look to my right at the wreckage. The crumpled door where Tiffany took the brunt of the crash, the truck's mangled grill just feet away.

It's too much. I look away. Vomit hurls into my throat and I cough again, swallowing hard because I can't puke. Can't. Not now. Calle. Tiffany. I have to find them.

I peer out the side window where two paramedics load a gurney into an ambulance. An adult with dark hair is all I can see of the injured person. Is that? *Oh no.* I turn back to the cop. "Is she okay?"

"I don't know," he says, a little too honestly. "She's unconscious. They're taking her to the hospital. We got another bus on the way for you and your baby."

My baby? *My* baby?

"No," I tell him. "She's not mine. She's . . ." I point to the ambulance.

"Oh," the cop says.

"It wasn't my fault," I say. "The truck blew the light."

"Yeah. I know." He jerks a thumb over his shoulder. "We got a witness. Plus, he's on something."

Rage drowns out the sirens blaring from the ambulance with Tiffany.

Wait.

More sirens. Another ambulance? In the distance.

Calle.

I make a move to slide out of the car and the cop backs up a step, holding his hands out. "Slowly, now."

Never mind that. I need to find Calle. I get to my feet, and the street spins like one of the hand-tossed pizzas at Amico's. I grab the cop's arm.

"Let's get you back in my cruiser," he says. "Hear the siren? Ambulance'll be here any sec."

"Where's Calle? The baby. Where is she?"

He points to the side of the road where a woman who looks to be in her mid-twenties stands on the corner holding Calle's carrier like she's waiting for a damned bus and my feet start moving, bursting into a run across the intersection. Who gives a baby to a stranger? Or maybe she's not a stranger. For research purposes, I once did a ride-along with law enforcement. All I know is I need to get to Calle.

"Calle!" I holler.

The woman eyes me with a look that's more honey-you're-insane than the-baby-is-fine.

Finally, she holds up her free hand. "She's okay. Calm down."

Calm down? Who is this *kid* telling to calm down? Even if she is right. If I'm screaming, Calle will too. I'm a psychologist. I should know better.

We've just been through the first three stages of hell and I'm off my game. Sue me.

The woman turns the carrier and there's Calle, her big eyes widening when she sees me. That tiny tooth winks at me.

And then she holds her little arms out. Without thinking, I pop the buckle on the carrier and scoop her out, hugging her to me, inhaling that soft baby smell that instantly knocks back my stress.

She lifts her hand, touches my cheek like she did earlier and sighs. Sighs. Just a tiny gasp of air before resting her head on my shoulder.

"No, no, no." I gently tap her back. "No sleeping, baby. Not until we get you checked out."

I probably shouldn't have even taken her out of the carrier. Ach. I'm horribly inept at this.

But the no-sleeping thing? This, I know for sure.

I make a clucking noise and she peers up at me. Apparently, she likes that so I do it again. *Cluck, cluck, cluck.* The siren gets louder, and I turn just as the ambulance pulls to a stop beyond the wreckage of my SUV and the giant truck.

Seconds later, a middle-aged female paramedic approaches. "Ma'am? Let's get you and the baby in the bus. Can you walk?"

"My neck hurts, but I'm okay." I use my free hand to point to Calle who is eyeing the paramedic like she's a serial killer. "This is Calle. We need to check her first."

"Will do."

The paramedic holds my arm as we walk to the ambulance. "Are you her mother?"

"No. Her mother just left in the other ambulance."

She doesn't respond, and her silence sends a wicked flare up my spine. "Is she okay? Tiffany?"

"I'm not sure." She points to the back step of the ambulance. "Let's get you inside."

Ryan comes storming into my ER room, his posture immediately softening at the sight of me sitting up on the bed, still in the shorts and T-shirt I threw on after the beach.

Calle's carrier is safely tucked beside me. They'd wheeled a hospital bassinet in, but I shooed that away. I don't know a lot about parenting, but I do know Calle is comfortable in her carrier and perhaps the familiarity will help her stay calm.

After she was examined and the carrier checked for broken glass or any damage, she was placed back inside it. This also allows me to keep her close.

She's been sleeping for the last half hour, more than likely the stress of the accident and people poking at her, tiring her out. If Ryan has even noticed her, he doesn't show it. His focus is on me. On my face so intently it's as if he instinctively knows not to look to my right.

"Jesus, Becca."

He bends over, bracing his hands against his knees. "They told me there was an accident. Something about an impaired trucker and that you were taken to the hospital. I wasn't sure what I'd find." He lets out a hard breath and shakes his head before standing tall and pushing his shoulders back in that confident, star high-school quarterback way he has about him.

"I'm fine," I tell him, more than half-irritated that he won't even look at the baby carrier.

He has to know it's there. Has to.

Our eyes lock for a few brief seconds and I see it, the genuine terror, the tiny lines between his eyebrows that, a few weeks ago, I'd gently run my thumb over to smooth.

Back when I loved him.

Back when I thought he was someone he clearly isn't.

Considering he won't even acknowledge his daughter.

On cue, Calle lets out a half-sigh, half-cry and I peer at her, then gently rock the carrier, lulling her back to sleep. Her eyes are closed, her nose pinched tight. Is she dreaming? Pooping? Gas?

Internal injury?

Not being her parent, I don't know her signs. All I know is they need to check her again, just to make sure. Before I can hit the button to call the nurse, her features soften, and she falls back into peaceful rest.

I peer back at Ryan, still focused on me. If he's even looked at Calle, I'm not sure. I wasn't paying attention. Maybe that's been the problem. The reason he strayed from our marriage. He wasn't getting enough *attention*.

Well, he has a working brain. He should have spoken up.

Period.

"In case you didn't notice," I say, "this is your daughter. They've checked her and she seems fine."

He holds my gaze for a solid ten seconds, then slides a look at the carrier, the cherub nestled inside.

Then he comes back to me. Just that quick. No smile, no relief over her safety, no acknowledgment.

His own child.

"I came in the main entrance. There are reporters outside the ER. The hospital has a guard keeping them out. But they already know you're here. Someone must have recognized you."

My mind ticks back to the cop and the paramedic. The woman holding Calle's baby carrier. Doesn't matter. Someone talked and my phone blew up. I know this because before being whisked off to the hospital, I'd asked the cop on scene to get me my phone and purse from the car. Don, Jenny and Devin have all called. Along with a slew of other acquaintances and unknowns. I haven't spoken to anyone, but texted Jenny and Don, assuring them I was fine and would talk soon.

Buh-bye.

Danny called, too, asking if he should come to the hospital. So kind, my neighbor. I texted him, letting him know I was okay and would call him later. If things go south with Ryan, I may, in fact, need a ride home.

"I don't understand," Ryan says. "How is she with you?"

"I invited Tiffany to bring her to the beach. I told you I planned on getting to know her."

He gawks at me, his jaw flying open. "You invited them to our *house*?"

I hold up a finger. "Careful, Ryan."

I've never been one to assert the fact that I'm the breadwinner. That our lifestyle is due to my salary. I never found it necessary. Ryan has been my partner. My success is an extension of his willingness to travel this road with me.

Many men don't possess the self-esteem required to handle their wife being a star. I've been grateful for that. That after long days of taping, I didn't need to come home and feed his ego.

Right now? After all that I've learned, when he refers to the shore house as *ours*, it slices me open. Cuts right to the bone and reveals the rage lying in wait.

That house has been in my family since I was a child. If I divorce Ryan, you can bet it comes with me.

I'll get bloody before I allow him to take it.

He stares at me and then his head snaps back like he's been dropped into an alternate universe and still getting his bearings. "What's that supposed to mean?"

"It means, you're in no position to question anything I do." I hold my hand to Calle. "Case in point. The child you've been hiding."

An older man appears at the door. He's wearing blue scrubs and a white doctor's coat. He steps into the room, making eye contact with me and then Ryan. "Hi, folks. I'm Dr. Perkins."

We all shake hands. My gaze is glued to his face. To the sagging cheeks and vacant eyes that must come with years of being an ER doc. He has a presence about him.

A bad news presence that stifles the air, penetrates my skin, and steals every ounce of moisture in my mouth.

Instinctively, I rest my hand on the edge of the carrier, somehow wanting to protect Calle from the terrible energy.

"You're the family of Tiffany Ambrose?"

"Uh," Ryan says. "Not family." He gives me a quick sidelong glance. "My wife was in the car with her."

"I was driving," I add. "This is Calle. Tiffany's daughter. Is Tiffany all right?"

He glances at Calle, then brings his attention back to me,

those vacant eyes looking at me, yet not. He's staring right through me.

"She sustained massive injuries," he says. "I'm sorry. We lost her."

What did he just say?

"Wait," I replay his words. "She's ... *gone?*"

Dr. Perkins nods.

Such a simple movement, yet so cataclysmic. I swing my head to Calle and a mix of heartbreak and panic floods me, snapping my last nerve.

What now?

Ryan says something to the doctor. Something about family notifications. Tiffany being estranged from her parents. Arrangements being made.

Dear God. This sweet child will never know her mother. Probably won't remember the baby talk and pride over what a good baby she is. The endless love her mother poured on her.

Calle's mother is dead.

A guttural sound erupts from my throat, the agony breaking free. It's so brutally unfair.

"Becca?"

Ryan's warm hands cup my cheeks, and I relax into the familiarity of his touch. The comfort I've always found there. Just for a second, I close my eyes. Mentally erase the last few weeks and lock on to the night, months ago when he made the best tomahawk steak I've ever eaten. We sat at the island together while he playfully fed me bites and watched my reaction. My savoring it.

Foodie foreplay, he calls it.

And he's right. We made love after that meal. Right in the kitchen. For the first time in a long, long time, it was spontaneous and wild. Passionate.

Didn't even make it to cleaning up. Just dropped our forks and our clothes and went at it against the wall.

I want to go back to that night. Forget all that's happened. Beat the clock and fix our marriage before reality sets in.

Too bad I don't believe in time travel.

I snap out of my fog and jerk my head free of his hands. I don't want or need him touching me. Confusing me.

We have things to do. And, hello? There are reporters outside.

"We need to get out of here," I say. "Take Calle back to the city."

I slide off the bed, my hands still gripping the edge. Feet on the floor, I test my knees and equilibrium before standing on my own.

"Wait," Ryan says. "What?"

I step around him, grabbing my purse and phone. "What's to wait for? More reporters will show up and I've just been involved in a fatal accident involving the mother of your child. We have to get out of here. *Now*."

"We're taking the baby?"

Gawking, I shake my head. Shock. It has to be shock. "I need you to focus here, Ry. Of course, we're taking her. You want us to turn her over to social services? *You* are her father. The only parent she has left. She's your responsibility now."

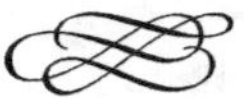

oordinating with hospital officials, we're allowed to sneak out via a loading dock on the backside of the building. Not a reporter in sight as I strap a pensive-looking Calle into a car seat a sympathetic nurse has let us borrow from her vehicle. The base to Calle's carrier is still in my car and the nurse has advised that it's safer to have a complete car seat—base plus carrier—rather than simply strapping the carrier in.

Another lesson learned.

Calle watches me with her big blue eyes, and I'm instantly thankful for the time we spent together this afternoon. At least she somewhat knows me and isn't screaming for her mother.

Her now dead mother.

Panic slithers inside me, curling my stomach into knots. I killed a woman today. Not me, per se, but I was driving and there's a certain amount of guilt that comes with that. Should I have double-checked the intersection before I stomped on the gas pedal? Was I too distracted?

I shake it off. Plenty of time later to analyze it. Right now, our focus needs to be on Calle and figuring out a way forward.

"Hi, pretty girl," I say, mimicking that same singsong voice Tiffany used.

I'm rewarded with a smile and that lone tooth bolsters my confidence.

Once I'm done securing the straps, I ask the nurse to check my work. She slides her fingers underneath the straps, showing me how to gauge the fit and then adjusts them.

So much to learn.

Then I hug her. Me. The unhuggiest person I know. But her compassion? Right now, when I'm so completely lost? It's a gift.

I promise the nurse a new car seat. At this point, I may buy her a new car. The minute I'm strapped in, I type her name into my phone—Chloe Conrad. My hand trembles. I sit back and close my eyes.

I'm spooked. A little jumpy. To be expected, I assure myself, after such a violent accident. After my world has suddenly and tragically been turned upside down.

Beside me, Ryan silently starts the car. He's not happy, clearly, but if he has ideas on how to manage this situation, he's not sharing.

"There's a neighbor," I tell him. "She babysits for Calle. She'll know her routine."

"You can't be serious. How long do you intend to keep this up?"

Summoning every bit of my already limited patience, I count backward from five. "Ryan, what are you not grasping about this concept? *You* are her father. Maybe not emotionally, but legally. You've established this fact by paying child support. And yes, we could turn her over to family services, let them find foster care for her until it's determined whether Tiffany's parents will help. I won't do that. No. Way. This child doesn't know those people."

"She doesn't know *us*."

He has a point. In an odd, tragic twist that puckers my skin, this might have been what Tiffany was concerned about. That Calle had people who loved her.

"She knows me," I say. "And I'm not turning her over to the state. Think of it this way, Ry, you run a nonprofit that helps families in crisis. What would your donors think if you abandoned your own child upon the sudden death of her mother?"

This seems to give him pause because the only response he offers is a sigh.

Whatever. I settle into my seat and stare out the window at homes and businesses. Anything but the road ahead. We pass Monmouth Park, the thoroughbred racetrack my dad enjoys visiting. Lots of fond memories there. Dad and I spending a day with me picking losers.

My luck must have extended to my choice of husband who, even amid tragedy, might turn his child over to strangers.

Did Tiffany have some sense she'd die young? Could she have known and wanted Calle to establish a relationship with him?

I don't know the answer. All I know is that Tiffany isn't here, and I told her that if she had an emergency, she could call me.

Well, it's an emergency.

My phone rings. I check the screen. Jenny. I swipe. Can't talk now.

Ryan changes lanes, roaring past a slower car and my temples throb, my nerves crackling. I've just been involved in a fatal crash and he doesn't have the decency to take it slow?

Calle chooses that moment to start screaming. And it's vicious. A shriek that bounces around the interior like an alien on the hunt.

"Jesus Christ!" Ryan roars. "What is she yelling about?"

I inhale and … yep. Diaper. "Take a whiff."

I crack the window, letting some air in while I come up with a plan. First, I've never changed a diaper, never mind having to do it in a car. Plus, with social media blowing up over my accident, I'm certainly not walking into some fast-food joint to use their bathroom and risk having someone recognize me.

Nope. This'll be a classified operation happening in Ryan's beloved BMW. I'll do what people do a thousand times a day and google how to change a diaper.

Find a video.

Change the diaper.

Easy.

SEAL team six of diaper changing, right here.

My ears are seconds from bleeding, given Calle's shrieking. How is it humanly possible for such a small person to make that much noise? I point out the window. "Pull into the mall. We'll find an out-of-the-way spot for me to figure out how to change her."

Once again, my so-called adoring, supportive husband gawks. How have I been so blind?

"Ryan," I say, the very last tendril of my self-control evident in the gravelly tightness of my voice. "Your best option right now is *not* to speak. I'm on the brink of a total breakdown, most of it due to your poor decision-making, so, pull this mother*fucking* car over so I can change your child's diaper!"

Calle, appearing to understand verbal cues, boosts her screaming another decibel.

"Great," Ryan says. "You're upsetting her."

"Ha! *That's* fantastic. Once again, it's everyone else's fault."

I'm so done. So, so done. Banged up, mentally strung out over a woman dying—dying!—with me behind the wheel, and now I'm fighting about a dirty diaper?

My life is toast. Gone.

Except, I'm alive. I survived that horrid crash and there's a reason.

I swing around, reach through the bucket seats and gently tap on the back of the car seat. Besides the seat, the nurse gave us a mirror she had draped over her rear seat. From my vantage point, I see Calle, mouth wide, face a desperate shade of red.

Pissed.

And Ryan is right. He and I hollering isn't helping. I clear my throat and focus on Calle. "Okay, honey," I say, giving my best effort at a soothing tone. "Sssshhhh. We're pulling over. We'll get you cleaned up and maybe a bottle."

I hope there's an extra one in that diaper bag. The cop—he must have been a parent—grabbed the bag from my SUV and sent it in the ambulance with us.

A fresh bout of panic fills me. I force it away. We're in a shopping mall. There has to be a baby store or pharmacy—something—nearby where I can buy some formula. I don't even know what kind Tiffany used.

Stay calm. That's all I need to do. Focus on next steps. I reach into the back, dragging the diaper bag between the seats, accidentally bumping Ryan and not bothering to apologize.

"What are you doing?"

"Praying there's a bottle in here."

I open the bag and rifle through it, getting my bearings. Diapers, wipes, a folding pad and ... *voilà!* One lone bottle, complete with powdered formula in the little storage area at the top.

"Thank you, Tiffany," I blurt, my eyes filling with tears as a storm of emotions ravages me.

Tiffany Ambrose destroyed my so-called happy life. Not her specifically, but her existence. The *reality* of her created a giant spotlight on my marriage where, from the outside, everything looked peachy. Underneath? Stage four cancer eating away at organs.

I set the diaper bag at my feet and swipe my hands over my

eyes, clearing the fresh tears. Later, I can break down. I grab my phone, go to my browser and search for how to change a diaper.

We can do this.

I can do this.

For Calle.

CHAPTER 30

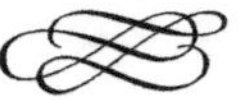

Diaper successfully changed, I sit in the back seat with Calle while she enjoys her bottle and Ryan drives. We stay mostly silent, me stewing and stewing and stewing as we make our way to Queens. Given that Ryan hasn't employed his GPS, he apparently has committed the route to memory.

How blind I've been, indeed.

"Have you met the landlord?"

He eyes me in the mirror. That would be a hard yes, I presume. It's probably good that they know him, but I'd still like to stab him.

"All right," I say. "We have to tell them what happened. And then talk to the neighbor. Figure out what we need to do for Calle."

By the time we pull up in front of the house, Calle is howling again, her screams piercing the quiet air. I unbuckle her, scooping her from the seat as Ryan hustles around to open the door for me. I scoot to the edge of the seat, working my way out of the vehicle, being careful not to clunk Calle's head on the door frame.

I don't know what this child needs. Demoralizing, at best.

Next door, a woman steps out onto the porch. Even from the distance, I sense her protective gaze on Calle.

Is this the neighbor Tiffany told me about? What was her name? I think back. Val. That's it. Cradling Calle against my shoulder, I head straight for the woman. "Hi. Are you Val?"

She nods, and my body instantly relaxes. So does Calle's. I feel it. That immediate release in her torso.

My first lesson in making sure I don't poison her with rotten energy.

Val quickly makes her way down the porch steps, the two of us meeting halfway on the sidewalk. She holds her arms out and I pass Calle off, watching as Val sways from side to side, cooing softly and rubbing Calle's back. "You're okay," she says. "I've got you. You're okay."

She snaps her attention to Ryan, still by the car, her gaze sharp enough to slice him in two. She knows him. No doubt.

Finally, she returns to me. "Are you Becca?"

I swallow hard. She apparently knows me too. "I am. Tiffany told you about me?"

"She said you were a nice lady." She peers up at Tiffany's house. "Kinda shocked she let you take her though."

Oh, God. I hadn't expected this. What it would feel like to tell Tiffany's friend about the accident. About Tiffany's death.

I clear my throat and meet Val's eye. "She didn't. I invited her down the shore with Calle. We had a nice day. I was driving her to the train. There was an accident."

Val's hand pauses on Calle's back. "Is she okay?"

Unable to find the right words, I shake my head and Val's eyes bulge. She steps back and wobbles, so I latch onto her forearm. The last thing we need is her going over with Calle in her arms. "I'm so sorry."

Tears well up as she peers down at Calle. Probably the weight of the situation landing. She sways again, back and forth, back and forth and when Calle looks up at her, she tilts her head, staring straight up at the sky. Hiding her tears, I suppose.

Pretending to check on Ryan, I turn away, giving Val a second to compose herself. I face her again, witnessing her magic as Calle lets out a heavy sigh and rests her head against Val's chest.

"She's had a day," I tell Val. "I don't know what to do."

Giving up on the sky, Val brings her attention back to me, her eyes once again focused. "Has she slept?"

"On and off."

"She's probably tired." Val peers at Tiffany's house. "Oh my gosh, all her stuff."

I summon Dr. Becca, the daytime talk show host skilled at controlling a conversation. "Val, this is a lot to absorb. Trust me, I understand. I think, for now, we need to concentrate on Calle. She's just lost her mother, and she's too young to understand. Let's try to keep to her routine as much as possible. Okay?"

Val nods. "It's too late for her to nap now. She'll be up all night. Let's keep her awake until seven. She's usually down by eight, but since she's tired, we might get lucky."

"Does she sleep all night?"

"Generally, yes. Tonight? Who knows?"

Understandable. As exhausted and achy as I am, I might be up all night. "Do you know who her pediatrician is? The ER doc said she's fine, but to follow up with her pediatrician."

"I have all that. Since I babysit, Tiff gave it to me. I even have her health insurance."

Health insurance. With Tiffany being gone, would Calle still even be covered?"

One thing at a time. Insurance is a nonissue right now. I'll just pay cash.

Val jerks her chin at Ryan. "Is he helping or just standing there?"

"Pretty much, just standing there."

"Figures. Sorry, but your husband is an asshole."

"Don't apologize. I get it. Believe me."

"I have a key to her apartment. Let me grab it. Did someone tell the Pekovskys? Her landlords."

"No. I guess, we'll do that while we're here."

In fact, I'll give that task to Ryan.

Val hurries back to her house in search of the key, and I angle back to Ryan. He's leaning against the car, one leg crossed over the other, arms folded across his chest and his head down.

What he's thinking, I cannot imagine.

I'm also not sure I care.

CALLE, trooper that she is, stays awake until 6:45.

I've sent Ryan back to Manhattan while I stayed with Val, gobbling up every ounce of her knowledge regarding Calle's care. Bath time, favorite toys and music, all of it while my aching body battles for respite.

Welcome to parenting 101.

Val returns from the nursery, joining me in the tiny living room. The apartment is in a typical row house. Living room, short hallway, two small bedrooms on one side, bathroom on the other and kitchen in the back.

Tiffany's home is cute in a shabby chic way. The furniture is well-loved and the cushions sagging. Whatever money Ryan has been sending isn't going to furnishings.

As if reading my mind, Val swivels her finger. "We bought it all at the thrift shop. Every dime goes to Calle. I used to tell her she could stretch a penny like taffy. I think she even started a small college fund for her."

"She was a good mom."

The words tumble from my mouth so easily, I realize I mean them. Tiffany, despite her mistakes, was a caring, supportive mother.

"Yeah," Val says. "She was. What's going to happen to Calle?"

I shake my head. "I don't know. The short-term plan is that we'll take care of her. I know Tiffany is estranged from her family. Do you know anything about them?"

"I know she'd rather poke her own eye out than let those people near Calle. I think that's why she went looking for you. You know, just in case? She was so used to being on her own, but she worried about Calle having someone." Val leans forward, clutching her belly. "How could this have happened? It's like she knew or something."

"You know, I had that exact thought."

She looks up at me. "Are you going to …?" She shakes her head. "Sorry. Not my business."

"Take Calle?"

"You don't have to answer. Like I said, not my business."

"It's all right. I think I'm still in shock. The accident wasn't my fault, but I was driving. I feel responsible." I lift my hand, waggle it by my head. "It's too much for me to process. I'm focused on Calle, so to answer your question, we're the obvious choice. Calle, I promise, will be taken care of."

Whether that means Ryan and I raising her, I can't know. Not yet. I need sleep. I need to talk to a lawyer. See what Ryan's rights are. See what my rights are. If I even have any.

And do I really want to raise the child my husband had with another woman?

Fatigue.

That's what this is. Total mental and physical exhaustion.

"Listen," Val says, "if you want to go, I can stay with Calle tonight."

No. I don't like that idea. If this turns into some kind of a legal battle with Tiffany's family, I want to make sure I'm not abandoning Calle on the first night.

Which means, since Calle is asleep in her crib, I'm crashing here tonight.

"Thank you," I say, "but that's unnecessary. I'd like to stay with her. Could I get your cell number though? In case she wakes up and I can't get her back down?"

"Sure. In fact, why don't I stay too? We'll double-team it."

No wonder Tiffany relied on this woman. Right now, she's my savior. My shoulders droop, all that tension and achy fatigue releasing. I lift my hands, covering my face for a moment as the day's events roar through my head.

Too much. It's all too much. I slide my hands down and settle them in my lap. "That would be great. You have no idea."

She glances down the hall. Instinctively, I know exactly what she's about to ask. "*Nooo*. I'm not sleeping in her bed."

That's all I need. Bad enough I'm even in Tiffany's apartment. Her bed? Never. I'd be awake all night imagining her and Ryan tearing up the sheets.

No, thank you.

"I'm good with the couch."

CHAPTER 31

*D*ay one of life with Calle starts with a bang.

Her howl rips clear through me and my eyes bolt open. Whoa. I blink, then blink again.

Still in my bikini, shorts and T-shirt from yesterday—damn, I need a shower—I scramble off the lumpy couch, getting to my feet, my muscles groaning.

It all—screeching tires, Tiffany's scream, the crunch of metal —comes back to me. Horrific thoughts that make my knees go soft and nearly buckle. I straighten up, holding on to the couch for balance as I get my bearings.

Keep moving. That's all I need to do. Take care of Calle and keep moving.

I take a step, noting stiffness in my joints. Back, legs, neck. Everywhere really. The ER doc had warned me about that. Told me to get plenty of rest.

Good luck there.

Particularly when Ryan is more than likely fast asleep in our bed when I barely managed a few hours. Even then, nightmares plagued me.

Calle is Ryan's daughter, and he simply left. Yes, I told him to go. Of course, I did. His bad mood—and energy—weren't helping and given the tension with Val, Ryan clearing out made things easier.

He did, however, text me a couple of times checking on us. Maybe he'll come around. I don't know and I'm certainly not counting on it.

"You good?" Val asks, rolling to her feet with the ease of a woman comfortable with crying babies.

"Yes. All good. What time is it?"

Val glances at her phone. "Six. Let's get her changed and fed and figure out what the day holds."

I head toward the nursery, rolling my shoulders and trying to work out the kinks as I walk. "If you can give me her pediatrician's phone number, I'll call them."

And then what? Am I going to take her to the doctor? The daytime talk queen will march into the pediatrician's office?

I guess I'll have to.

"You know," Val says, "I've taken her before when Tiff had to work. And, seriously, you were in an accident yesterday. You need rest. Excuse me for saying, but you look rough. Taking care of babies is like being on a plane. Put your mask on first. You're no good to her if you're tired. Besides, I know where I'm going."

Calle's wailing continues as I ponder Val's suggestion. I desperately need a shower. Maybe a soak in our tub for a few minutes while I work out some form of a plan. Mom. And Dad. They'll know what to do.

Then there's damage control. As of last night, all the networks were reporting on the accident, stating one fatality. An unknown female.

I make the turn into Calle's nursery and find her in her crib, tiny fists clenched, legs kicking and face flushed red. In short, she's pissed. I scoop her up. "The diaper must weigh ten pounds."

Behind me, Val is already pulling a fresh one from the changing table along with a onesie and some clothes.

"I'd like to change her," I say. "For the practice."

Val steps back. "Absolutely."

"Thank you. If you could help with the pediatrician, that would be great. I'll ask my driver to take you."

As soon as we get Calle squared away, I'll call Bernie. He'd phoned last night, checking on me and assured me he'd be available for whatever I needed.

Right now, I need him to get Ryan's child to the doctor.

An hour later, I leave Calle with Val and Bernie scoops me up from Tiffany's. He's freshly showered, his short hair still damp, something I'm wildly envious of at the moment. He eyes me in the rearview as we pull from the curb. Yes, I look a fright. Something he has rarely, if ever, witnessed.

"Becca, are you all right?"

No. Not even close. I settle into the back seat and with the smoky windows offering privacy, put my hands over my face. I have to breathe. Just take these next few minutes to quiet the chaos in my head. *Too fast.* Everything is moving too fast.

Tiffany. That poor girl. Her family. They must know by now. The police were going to notify them. Let them know Ryan had Calle. Do her parents even know Calle exists?

It's all too much. *One thing at a time.*

A shower.

That's easy. A shower and off to the studio for damage control. Later, I'll treat myself to a bath.

I check my watch. Val told me the pediatrician's office opens at 7:30. I'll call, make the appointment and let Val know the time. By then, I'll be back home for my shower.

"Becca?"

I shake my head. "I'm sorry, Bern. I'm not ignoring you. My brain is fried."

"Don't worry about that. What can I do?"

"You're doing it," I say, thankful for his calm presence. "I need to get home, clean up and head to the studio. I just texted Jenny to let her know I'm coming in. If I can get Calle into the doctor this morning, will you drive them, please?"

"Done. My wife will take you to the studio if necessary."

"Absolutely not. I'm not inconveniencing your family. I'll drive myself."

"The hell you will. Your doorman texted me. Reporters are camped out in front. We'll use your underground entrance."

Excellent. Just as I'd expected, the media swarmed. "Are the neighbors freaking?"

His nonresponse confirms it. Can't worry about unhappy neighbors right now. My mind drifts to Danny and I shoot him a text asking about reporters.

Tiny dots light up my screen. His immediate answer confirms mayhem at the beach. He's taking care of it. Probably the cops again. If only Danny could do his magic at the townhouse.

"My shore neighbor," I say to Bernie as I dial the pediatrician's office. "Danny? He's, shall we say, entertaining? I think I love him."

Bernie snorts. "What'd he do?"

"He hates people—any people—in front of his house. He's chasing off reporters."

"Good for him. I like him already."

A man answers at the pediatrician's office. I explain the situation and he squeezes Calle in, telling me to bring her over between 9:00 and 10:00. Perfect. Bernie can take me to work and then drive Val and Calle to the doctor. I hang up, shoot a text to Val asking her to call me when they're at the appointment so I can listen in.

We zoom up East Eightieth Street—well, as fast as one can zoom in Manhattan—and Bernie turns a block early, avoiding the front entrance of the building. He swings to the backside where a dozen reporters lay in wait.

"Get down," he says. "On the floor. They might see you through the windshield."

Doing as I'm told, I squeeze myself to the floorboard, my joints and muscles protesting the entire way. I hope Ryan filled that prescription for muscle relaxers for me.

The SUV turns and comes to a stop. Probably in the driveway waiting for the door to go up. Shouts from outside send my nerves crackling. Someone bangs on a window and I flinch.

"Vultures," Bernie mutters as the SUV lurches forward. "We're good."

I lever myself to my seat and peer out the back window where the garage gate has come down.

"No one got in," Bernie confirms. "I was watching."

He pulls to the curb at the underground building entrance, parks and leaps out to help me from the car. "Can you get upstairs okay?"

"I'm fine. I'll be quick. You can wait here or come up."

"I'll wait here. Make sure no reporters worm their way in."

"Thank you."

By the time I get upstairs, Ryan is already gone. Probably to his office. Avoiding me. Which is fine. I don't need to see him when I have things to do and his baby to take care of.

Panic hits like hot acid in my stomach. Poor Calle. She'll never know her mother. *Can't go there*. If I start thinking, I'll collapse.

I push my shoulders back and walk the last few steps to the bedroom. One thing at a time.

Forty-five minutes and a handful of calls later, Bernie has arranged for us to use the service entrance at the back of the network's building. This is part of his magic. He's befriended all the security guards by buying them meals and coffee and whatever else he can think of. All to prime them for moments like this. Moments when we need a favor.

I can't face the mob in front today. Cowardly? Sure. Do I care?

No.

Thankfully, we're able to pull straight into the building, the security guard closing the bay door behind us. The royal treatment today.

I jump out, hustle up the stairs and head into the hallway, out of sight, while the guard deals with letting Bernie back out.

All of this is the pain in the rear that comes with a scandal.

The guard escorts me to the elevator, where I thank him and assure him I can get to my office on my own. Anyone in the building is an employee or has been cleared by security at the entrance.

My luck being what it is, I get a commuter elevator that stops on just about every floor. People come and go, each of them making brief eye contact and nodding, before looking away. Fine with me. Thanks to my mother, Queen of My-Life-Isn't-Falling-Apart, I'm an ace at hiding heartbreak. I keep my shoulders back, my chin up, my gaze straight ahead until the elevator doors whoosh open at my floor. Excusing myself, I squeeze through the crowd and hustle down the hallway toward my office.

"Wow," someone says from the bullpen before anyone notices me. "We may have just crippled the internet."

"Welcome to Hell," I call in my faux cheery voice.

The heads of my producers and APs pop up over the half wall. In a twisted way, it reminds me of the Whack-a-Mole game I used to love to play on the boardwalk. Considering I was supposed to be taking two weeks off, they're all staring at me, wide-eyed with shock as a chorus of good mornings rings out. I keep moving. Not rushing, but purposeful. Routine.

If the staff sees me holding up, they'll do the same. The

Emerson quote I keep stashed in my top drawer swims in my head. *The speed of the leader determines the pace of the pack.*

Jenny appears in my doorway just as I reach my desk. "Morning."

"Good morning."

She takes a second, eyeing me in a critical way I don't often sense from my no-muss-no-fuss EP.

After a few seconds, she steps inside. "You okay?"

"I'm good. A little banged up. How are things here?"

"We're handling it. Tons of media requests."

I'm not surprised. My phone, too, has been blowing up. Calls from reporters I've worked with enough over the years to give them my number.

All of which I've ignored. I ease into my chair, taking it slowly and wincing only when my elbow hits the armrest. Drat, that hurts.

I shake it off and focus on Jenny. "I need to release a statement. Maybe do an interview with someone we trust. I'll talk to Don."

"The sooner the better." She smacks herself on the forehead. "Ooofff. That sounded bad."

"It's all right. I agree."

She's my executive producer. Not my therapist.

Before I can continue, she angles back, peering down the hallway, then coming back to me. "Oh, boy," she says, opening her eyes wide. "Ryan just walked in."

Just stop it. What the hell could he be thinking? I seem to be asking that a lot lately.

"My Ryan?"

Yes, I've just asked maybe the dumbest question in existence. As if there's another, kinder Ryan who hasn't lied, cheated and hidden a baby from me.

"Yep," Jenny says.

I nudge my chin. "Would you give us a minute, please?"

She disappears, off to do whatever she can to keep this ship moving before Ryan claims her spot in the doorway. Rather than have him stand there while the bullpen gawks, I wave him inside.

"Close the door, please."

I push myself from my chair—no easy feat, that—and come around the front of the desk where I lean on the edge. My husband, like a million times before, is barely two feet from me, and I feel nothing.

Maybe it's the pain meds numbing me. Maybe I've reached that level of anguish where my body refuses to take any more and is in battle mode, protecting me.

Whatever it is, I'm grateful.

Outside the glass wall, muffled chaos erupts from the bullpen. Two producers fly by my office, their AP's scurrying after them. Probably trying to keep the producers from cardiac arrest.

Social media channels are burning like wildfire with people interested in the woman who died in my car yesterday.

I hold Ryan's gaze for a long minute. My husband. My so-called best friend and confidant who's been in my life twenty-six years and is a mystery.

"This is a mess," I finally say.

"I'm sorry."

He should be. "We'll discuss it later. I'm about to call Don. Tell him I'll release a statement. Maybe even do an interview."

"An interview? Seriously?"

"We're already behind. The best thing we can do now is come clean. Admit everything and ask for privacy while we take care of Calle."

His head lops forward and a blood rush assails me. Given he's made no secret about not wanting to be a father, his shock shouldn't surprise me. Still, it takes every ounce of energy I have —which isn't a lot right now—to keep my cool.

I hold up a finger. "Your former lover died in a horrific wreck that your wife and child somehow miraculously survived, and you don't want to help said child? Your own flesh and blood?"

"Well," he pulls a hand from his pocket, circling it in the air. "You make it sound like I'm going to leave her at a firehouse. I'm not *abandoning* her."

"Aren't you? Who do you intend will raise her? You're her father!"

"I'm the sperm donor. All I did was send checks every month."

I step back, the words hitting me like a wrecking ball. Did he really just say that? "Who the hell are you?"

"Pardon?"

I let out a huff and don't give a damn how he feels about it. "How is it possible, all these years together and I don't know you? Not in the way it matters. Sure, you hate broccoli, and you like your underwear folded a certain way. Enjoy comedies and expensive red wine, but you lied to me. About everything. About wanting a family and noisy Christmas mornings with kids. That's why you said nothing."

Now he's the one shaking his head. "Sorry. I'm not following. What is it you think I never said anything about?"

"How about the fact that my career took over our lives and no matter how many times we had sex, I never got pregnant? And you stayed quiet. Didn't suggest adoption or fertility. You just let it happen. Let me lose my dream of being a mother. All because you didn't really want kids and wouldn't be honest about it."

Ryan lifts his hand, waves at my Emmys stacked like soldiers along the wall. "Look at your shrine. You were busy. And yeah, at some point, I realized that I liked not being tied down. It's not my fault your show took off."

"Oh no. You don't get to put this on me. I gave you everything. The big house, the snobby social scene. You love it."

He shrugs. "Who wouldn't?"

At this moment, the only thing keeping me from bludgeoning my husband with one of those Emmys is his six-month-old baby, who needs us.

I boost myself off the desk and jab a finger at him. "*I* don't love it! *You* are reaping the rewards of me killing myself."

The door comes open and Jenny sticks her head in. "Hey guys. Getting a little loud."

As if I give a *shit*. The Internet is flooded with rumors about me. My staff knowing my business is a nonissue compared to what I'll deal with outside these walls.

I jerk my chin at her, shooing her. Rude? Absolutely. I'll apologize later. Right now, I'm focused on Ryan.

Jenny retreats, closing the door behind her.

"I'm not doing it," Ryan says. "Interviews or statements or whatever the hell you're cooking up. I'm done with this crap."

No. He's not.

He starts for the door, and I finally face the truth. For years, he's been riding my coattails. Enjoying life while I worked and worked and worked and convinced myself that leaving daytime television was impossible. That I'd lose my entire career and the perks that came with it.

My train wreck of a life just broke any number of social media platforms and I'm still standing. Tension leaves my shoulders. My neck. My back. Just simply disappears in a hot second. Relief. That's what this is.

Clarity greets me like a warm morning sun at the beach.

I think about Calle's cherubic face. Her big blue eyes that, as much as I wanted to hate them because they were identical to her mother's, enraptured me.

Despite how she came into my world, I managed to somehow instantly bond with Calle, touched by her innocence.

Even now I don't understand it. Maybe it was the maternal instinct I'd brutally held at bay for years, but at that moment, I knew I'd never let the world crush that child.

And now I know that I can, and will, force Ryan to do the right thing.

"Hold it," I tell Ryan.

He halts and spins back. "You—"

"Be quiet. My career is more than likely over because you couldn't keep your pants on. We're done. We'll make a joint statement telling the world about Calle and ride this horrific wave until some other celebrity scandal eclipses us. "

"Hang on," Ryan says.

I spin around, ready to get started on my plan. "I, my dear devoted husband, am about to publicly admit that you're an adulterous scumbag. I'll refrain from telling millions of people you're abandoning your infant daughter. You're her father. You've been supporting her. If anyone else from Tiffany's side comes out of the woodwork, you'll get custody over them."

"Becca! Are you insane?"

If I am, I don't mind. In fact, this might be the first authentic thing I've done in years. I pick up the phone's handset, wave it in the air. "When I divorce you, you'll get a settlement that'll keep you in the lifestyle you love. You get the money, I get your child."

Ryan's eyes bulge, the vein at his temple expanding. Am I making this transactional? Is it in poor taste? Is it criminal?

Yes.

I am literally buying Calle. Being the materialistic person my husband is, it's the one surefire way to get his cooperation.

Phone still in hand, I press numbers on the keypad. "I never had children. I wanted them. If you won't do right by your own daughter, I will."

I tap the last number. "Devin will love this one." My voice carries enough disgust to fill a dumpster. "Airing my dirty laundry *and* accepting a baby my cheating husband fathered? Total money shot. The sweeper to end all sweepers."

My husband storms from my office while I busy myself leaving a message on Don's voicemail. Before I can even set the phone back in the cradle, my cell rings.

Val.

I scoop it from the desk and hold it to my ear. "Hi."

"Hi," she says. "I have you on speaker. We're with Dr. Conner. I've told her the situation." She pauses, clears her throat. "About Tif."

Her voice cuts out, breaking apart like crumbling brick. Poor woman. What was I thinking, letting her deal with this alone?

What kind of person does that? Maybe I'm no better than Ryan.

I shake it off. Plenty of time later to beat myself up. I'll somehow have to make it up to Val.

"Hello, Dr. Conner," I say. "I should be there in person. Val, I'm sorry I put you through this."

"I offered," she says. "I just didn't realize … Whatever."

"Ladies," Dr. Conner says. "There's no right way to handle this. All we can do is what's best for Calle. I've reviewed what the hospital sent and looked her over. She appears to be fine. Obviously, if you notice anything, take her straight to the ER."

Another bit of tension leaves me. Calle is okay. That alone is a win. I close my eyes and absorb the relief. "Thank you." I open my eyes, focusing on the glass wall. "Given the situation, once things calm down, I'd like to make an appointment to discuss Calle's health history."

"Yes. Good idea. Does that mean you and your husband will care for her?"

My husband?

I'm about to say no but catch myself. Until I speak to an attorney, it should appear that Ryan is co-parenting. He's her biological father. Without him, I'm just some random woman. No blood relation to Calle.

"That's correct," I tell her. "Calle will be taken care of."

I tell Val I'll call her in a little while to arrange picking up Calle and then hang up, lost in the myriad of thoughts scorching my brain. A knock sounds and I glance up. Marley stands on the other side of the glass. I don't know if I have the energy for her today, but it has to happen. I wave her in.

She closes the door behind her and marches straight at me, cornering the desk so fast, I barely have time to stand before she's wrapping her arms around me.

Um, hello?

For a few seconds, I'm stunned stupid. Literally don't know what to do, something that's clear given my arms are still at my sides.

"Becca, I am *so* sorry. This is horrendous."

Finally, I lift my arms, wrapping them around her, taking comfort in the last person I ever expected it from. I inhale the soft scent of her musky perfume and squeeze my eyes closed, fighting the punch to my chest and the tears stinging my eyes. "It is. But Calle—the baby—is my priority."

She backs away, holding me at arm's length. "That's good. Excellent."

"I was going to call you. About the segments."

She lets go of my arms and waves me off, walking back around the desk and taking one of the guest chairs. "Forget that. I came to see if you need anything. What can I do?"

Oh, wow. I sit back, take a minute to settle my mind and get my brain back into gear. What can she do? Hmmm ...

"I have a call in to Don," I say. "I'm in fix-it mode. My thought is that I'll make a statement and then do a brief interview. I'll come completely clean. That way I control the narrative. After that, I don't intend to speak to any media. And after everything that's happened, I need time off. In fact, I need more than the two weeks I had already blocked out."

Marley cocks her head. "Do you want my opinion?"

It wasn't my intention, but yes. Why not? She's not emotionally attached to the situation, and she has great instincts when it comes to the media.

I nod.

"I think," she says, "it's a smart move. Let the world hear it from you. They probably won't leave you alone, but it doesn't hurt to ask for privacy. With any luck, some reality television star will screw up and the trolls will move on."

Could I get that lucky? I sit forward, my back creaking, reminding me I'm pushing myself too hard the day after an accident. "If you're amenable, I'd like you to interview me for a morning show segment. Hopefully tomorrow. That gives us today to rough out questions."

Her head snaps back, her lips curling down. I've apparently surprised the unflappable Marley.

When she doesn't respond, I lift my hand, palm up. "What are you thinking?"

"I'm … huh … honored, I suppose, that you trust me."

"You're the only one around here I trust with this. I confided in you, and you kept it to yourself. I appreciate that. Anyway, for my show, the therapy segments are out. After this, Ryan will never agree to it. All I know is his daughter just lost her mother. We have Calle to worry about."

I shake it off. Thinking too much won't help me. I need to move forward. No looking back.

"We have a few weeks of shows in the can," I say. "I'll need more time off than that. My producers already have guests lined up for future shows. If you'd like, I'll propose to Don that you sit in as guest host on my show. Once we air all the canned shows, you'll do the ones we have lined up. That'll keep us on schedule, at least somewhat, and gives me time to adjust to this new situation. Would you like that?"

From her chair, Marley blinks at me. Three rapid ones. Blink, blink, blink.

Earth to Marley. I hold my hand up and snap. "Hey, you in there?"

She lets out a laugh, her face lighting up like Times Square. "Are you *kidding* me? You're handing me the top daytime slot and you want to know if I'd *like* that?"

"Well," I smile, "let's not get ahead of ourselves. I don't know if I want you to *keep* that slot. I just … need a break. You're the person I want sitting in for me."

"Considering you hated me, that's about the best compliment I can get."

"I didn't hate you. Our styles are different. Promise me you'll tone it down. Just keep my viewers happy. Can you do that?"

"Absolutely. I'll even check in with you every day for feedback."

"That's unnecessary. If there's something you need, call me. But I intend to focus on Calle. Jenny is terrific. She has this place so buttoned up, it'll be a no-brainer for you."

Marley's smile, all blinding white teeth, knocks a few pounds of stress from me. By entrusting her with my show, I've made her happy, and it gives me an oddly warm rush.

This might be it. That fuzzy thing called female friendship that's eluded me nearly my entire life.

Someone to seek help from.

Someone to trust.

Maybe my life isn't falling apart. Maybe it's just coming together.

AFTER MY MEETING WITH DON—HE spared me eight minutes—I swing by Jenny's office. She's in with one of the APs, so I ask her to drop by my office when they're through. I need to pick up Calle from Val's by noon and then what?

Buy a crib? Diapers?

Car seat.

We'll eventually need an extra car seat. One for Bernie's SUV and one for my car. As I'm walking, I do the one thing I'm constantly scolding Kaitlyn about. I send Val a text. Asking for advice on a car seat. She immediately responds with a link to one at a local store. A few taps later, I'm now the owner of a car seat I can pick up after twelve o'clock, along with the replacement seat for the nurse who kindly let us take hers.

Done.

Done.

Done.

Slaying it, baby. I sit at my desk, hit the mouse pad on my laptop to check emails. A knock sounds and I glance up at Jenny, striding into my office. Her pants and cotton shirt are, in typical Jenny fashion, beyond wrinkled.

She drops into her normal seat in front of my desk and smacks her notepad on her thigh. "What a freaking day. You doing all right?"

"Yes." I nudge my chin toward the door. "How's everything out there?"

"Eh. They'll be fine. They're worried about you. Afraid to upset you."

At this point, I'm not sure I can even feel anything anymore. I'm grateful for it. The numbness keeps me functioning.

"Please tell them they shouldn't be. We still have a show to produce."

Jenny nods. "I'll let them know. Devin called. And the PR people. Something about a statement?"

Boy, oh, boy, that pipeline is swift. They didn't even give me time to get to my EP and tell her myself. "Yes. I just met with Don. I told him I'm making a statement today. About the accident. Tiffany and Calle. Ryan being Calle's father. Everything."

Jenny lets out a long whistle. "Whoa."

"It's a lot. But we need to get ahead of it. If I come clean, the trolls will move on to fresh meat."

Her raised eyebrows indicate that I'm in Neverland. "Let's hope."

"The statement will go out this afternoon. I have to leave by noon, but I'll work on a draft. PR will tweak it and I'll sign off on a final before we send it out. Then, tomorrow, Marley will interview me on the morning show."

At this, Jenny's mouth flops open. "No way. Why not do something on our show? We could do a rush job and air it tomorrow."

She's irritated. I can see it. It's off-putting, to say the least. Yes, she's my EP. Together, we're responsible for keeping our show in the top slot. She sees the implosion of my life as a ratings grab. Part of me doesn't blame her. It's her job.

There's another part though. The human part that wants her to acknowledge what I'm going through. To recognize that I might not be comfortable with my personal crisis being broadcast on my own hour-long show.

Maybe more.

"The morning show can get us on tomorrow. Besides, I'm not doing an hour. The morning show segment is seven or eight minutes and I'm out. It'll be quick and brutal and I'll be done. No further statements."

Jenny tilts her head, puckers her lips. "You're the boss."

I sure am. "I can see you're not happy. I'm navigating this the best way I know how. I have to protect Calle and make sure everyone on staff stays employed."

At this, she pulls back, gives her head a hard shake. "What do you mean?"

"The second part of my meeting with Don was to let him

know I need additional time off. Probably the rest of the summer. Don't panic. I have a plan."

Jenny relaxes again, her body collapsing back into her chair. "Becca, we can't go on hiatus all summer."

I lower my hands. "I know. This morning, I spoke with Marley. I've asked her to sit in as guest host in my absence."

"*Marley*? I thought you hated her."

I flinch. Embarrassed that I let my personal opinions taint my staff's opinion of Marley. Hate might be too strong of a word, but for months I'd been dropping comments about Marley's abrasive style. My distaste for it.

"As you know, I'm not a fan of her aggressiveness. She's agreed to tone it down while guest hosting."

"Her fans will hate that."

"Probably. But she's a big girl. That's her decision to make."

"You're not afraid to let her take over?"

Actually, I'm terrified. But I have to risk it. Allow myself to be vulnerable and trust that Marley will do the right thing. That she won't disappoint me.

I let out a sigh. "There's only so much I can control. She's made an agreement. I hope she sticks to it. Anyway, Don is allowing her to take over for the summer. It'll help keep our current schedule in place. You, obviously, need to bring Marley up to speed."

Jenny nods and jots a note. "I'll call her and set something up."

Kaitlyn sticks her head in. "Sorry to interrupt."

Jenny turns and Kaitlyn peers at her. "Page Six is looking for you. Something about a follow-up."

Page. Six.

The Post's gossip column where news of Ryan's affair with Laurel Shelton was originally reported.

Interesting.

Page Six.

Only a handful of folks knew about the affair, and I'd assumed someone in marketing had leaked it. Now I'm not so sure. After all, EP's have their own contacts in the media.

I slide my gaze from Kaitlyn back to Jenny, who is still looking at Kaitlyn, but in profile has lost all color. An absolute bloodletting.

"They're calling *me*?"

Her voice is a bit too heavy with confusion.

Kaitlyn squints at her. "She said she's been calling your cell, but she's on deadline and needs a statement."

"I'll call when I get a minute."

Bordering on rudeness, Jenny turns from Kaitlyn, and meets my gaze for a long second.

Something is off.

I smile at my assistant. "Thank you."

"Of course. And I'm glad you're okay. Let me know if you need anything."

She goes on her way, and I focus on Jenny, my mind reeling. My EP has always been ambitious. A professional unafraid to push for excellence.

It's one of the reasons I picked her. It's one of the reasons we've been a great team for nearly fifteen years.

"Jenny?"

"Yes?"

"Did you leak Ryan's affair with Laurel to Page Six?"

CHAPTER 32

For the briefest of seconds, Jenny stares at me, her eyes darting away. Thinking. At least before she catches herself and realizes she hasn't responded. "I can't believe you're asking me that," she says, her voice full of haughty dismissal.

What Jenny doesn't realize is that I grew up with the master of haughty dismissal. "You haven't answered the question."

"I shouldn't *have* to. It shouldn't even *be* a question."

On this, I agree. The idea, in fact, sickens me. Twists my gut into a brutal knot. How much can my battered stomach take?

"You're right. I shouldn't have to ask. We've been together a long time. There's something to be said for honesty. And trust."

She stands. "I agree. Now, if we're done, I'll get to it with Marley."

"Not done. Page Six?"

She flaps her arms. "Why would I? What would I have to gain?"

"Our ratings spiked after that leak. You've been in this game a long time and knew what would happen. You and Devin speak often." I shrug. "Maybe he suggested it and you went with it."

"This," she says, "is ridiculous."

It sure is. "Tell me you didn't leak it. Look at me and tell me."

Again, her eyes dart right, away from me. Painful silence fills the space between us. It's quicksand, sucking me under. Somehow, in a matter of weeks, my most trusted allies have betrayed me.

Devastated, I shake my head. "Oh, Jenny."

She finally meets my gaze. "It's not what you think. *I* didn't tell her. Somehow, they got hold of it." She lifts a hand, rubs her forehead. "Probably someone from marketing. Page Six wanted a second source."

Before I can speak, she holds up a hand. "I told her I couldn't give her any information."

"And yet?"

"She bulldozed right over me. Asked if Ryan was having an affair. I wasn't going to lie."

Ah, we're playing that game now. "You didn't need to. No comment would have sufficed."

Times like this, my mother's twisted way of living isn't such a bad idea. Times like *this* prove her point about not sharing my business.

And what? I should go back to living life like my mother? Like how, just a few short weeks ago, I conducted myself? Trusting only Ryan—look where that got me?—and my parents. That life?

Not so great.

Lonely, in fact.

And now, with Calle to take care of, I'll need all the support I can muster. Still in my seat, I lean forward and tap the space bar on my laptop to fire it up.

"Becca," Jenny says, "please, this wasn't my fault."

"You could have protected me. You chose not to. Now I know what to expect. We're done here."

A few weeks ago, back when my career meant everything, back when I was reeling about my sinking ratings and my boss's displeasure, I'd have fired her. Made a helluva statement that discussing my personal business with the press won't be tolerated.

For the first time, I have bigger problems to deal with. I have a baby to care for and if I intend to have the summer off, I need Jenny here, running the show.

Helping Marley.

I log in to my laptop. Jenny is still standing behind the chair she just vacated, and I shoot her a glance. "Please leave."

Clearly receiving the message, my EP stalks out, leaving me with the revelation that she's been doing the one thing she was hired to do.

Deliver ratings.

No matter the cost.

And that just won't work for me.

BERNIE, being Bernie, insists on driving Calle and me to the shore. My new SUV, the dealership promised, would be in the driveway by dinnertime. The thing about having money?

Makes things easy.

On my way to pick up Calle, I called the dealer where we purchased my car, told him the situation and that the car was most likely totaled. I don't know this yet, but even if it isn't, I will never drive that vehicle again. Too much devastation attached to it. However, it saved Calle and I'll always be grateful for that.

For the new SUV, I signed documents sent via an electronic software system and I was done. All of which happened while Bernie drove me to the store to pick up Calle's car seat, where she is currently snoozing beside me.

I slide my gaze right and spy her doing that thing with her

lip when she blows it out. It's still the most adorable thing I've ever seen.

Dreaming, Tiffany had said. She does it when she's dreaming. Could it be just a week ago I'd spoken to Tiffany?

How the hell did we get here? Tiffany, no matter how I felt about her affair with Ryan, didn't deserve to be taken from her daughter. More than that, Calle didn't deserve to be denied her mother.

"You okay?"

Bernie is eyeing me via the rearview. I look away, peering out the window at the explosion of spring green on the trees lining the Garden State Parkway. All of them whizzing by. "I'm good," I say. "Just … I don't know. It's a lot."

"Sure is. Not to pile on, but how are you fixed for baby items at the shore?"

I swing my head back to him. "Oh, no."

"That answers that."

"Bernie, I don't know whether to curse at you or hug you right now. I didn't even think about a crib!"

I snatch my phone from the door's cupholder and find Danny's number. Please, please, please answer.

On the second ring, he picks up. "Bubby, where are you?"

"On my way down. With Calle. I need help."

"The cops are keeping the vultures off the street. You're good there. What else? Talk to me."

This, I have to believe, is what friends do. They rise up. No matter what.

"My house isn't equipped for a baby."

"*Alright, alright, alright,*" he says, the words flying at me through the phone. "Don't panic. I got this. I'll call my ex-wife. There's a ridiculously expensive kids' store she likes in Spring Lake. We'll go shopping. If she's not around, I'll go myself. Wave my credit card at the owner and get you some nice stuff."

What I'd give to see that? Too bad we can't be there for the show. "Call me when you get back to the house. I'll unlock the door from my phone. I think I love you," I tell him, relief washing over me. One less thing to do. "Obviously, I'll pay you back. I don't care what it costs. I need, well, I don't know what I need."

"How would you? I'm telling you, Becca, we're on it. One thing about my ex, she knows how to shop."

With that he hangs up, and for the first time in days, I laugh.

Beside me, Calle stirs, her face scrunching up. I freeze, hoping beyond hope, if I don't move or speak, she'll stay asleep. After a few seconds, her features loosen, and she lets out a long sigh as she retreats into her nap.

Baby sounds. I'll have to learn what they mean.

I ease out a long breath and sit back in my seat. I'm doing this. Figuring it out.

With help from my friends.

WE ARRIVE HOME TO CHAOS. Well, not chaos so much, but a living room crammed with stuff. Baby stuff. Boxes and boxes everywhere.

Gobsmacked by the clutter, I stand in the front doorway, Calle's carrier slung over my arm. At any minute, I'm expecting her to come out of her slumber and scream.

Danny is in the center of the room, hands on his hips. Sitting on the floor beside him is his daughter and a woman, his ex-wife, I presume, on her knees opening a box. She looks to be early forties with long silky, sable hair.

Danny paddles his hand at me. "It's not as bad as it looks. We're organizing."

The woman stands, shakes her head at Danny and laughs. "Times like this," she says heading straight for me. "I wonder why I divorced him."

"Hi." She holds her arms out. "I'm Kelly. Do you need help with her?"

I don't know where to begin with the help I need.

Gently, I slide the carrier from my arm, handing it off to Kelly. "Thank you. She's going to wake up screaming for a bottle any second. I have one in the diaper bag."

It's there thanks to Val, who set me up with three ready-to-rock bottles to tide me over until I got to the shore, where Danny and company had picked up a case of formula.

Danny's daughter hustles over to her mom, peeking at Calle. Her lips go wide, her smile and awe over Calle enough to melt me. They settle in on the couch just as Bernie enters, carrying the supplies Val had sent and a suitcase filled with Calle's clothes.

"Holy hell," Bernie says. "Major shopping spree."

"We melted the plastic," Danny says. "It's fun when it's not your money."

Whatever they spent, it'll be worth it. I offer introductions, point Bernie in the direction of the guest room to put away Calle's suitcase and I move to the kitchen to prep the bottle.

"Crib," Bernie says upon his return. "It's in a box. I can put it together for you."

"Yeah," Danny says, "they didn't have one assembled. I figured I could try. Even brought my toolkit over."

"No, no, no." Kelly laughs. "You don't want him doing it."

And wow. I like her. I snort and look back at Bernie. "Don't you need to get home?"

He shrugs. "Nah. We weren't doing anything. Besides, I put together all my grandkids' cribs. I'm the only one with the patience."

He retreats to the guest room while I stand in my living room, half stunned.

How did I get this lucky? It's all I can think. I'm surrounded by doers. People who know how to get things done.

Fast.

"Red alert." Kelly points at Calle's carrier. "She's waking up."

I finish mixing the bottle and nearly sprint to the couch where Kelly is already scooping Calle up, gently swaying side to side. She peers at me over Calle's tiny shoulder. "Would you like me to give her the bottle? Give you a second to get situated?"

A second. Just a few to breathe. Maybe wash my face and open a window. Let the ocean air drift in. These people. So … nice. Caring.

Finally.

The stress of the last twenty-four hours must be getting to me. Achy, tired and flat-out emotional, something catches in my throat, trapping my air. I have to relax. Just lean into this hell so I can get through it. I bob my head. "I'd love that. Thank you."

Calle goes into attack mode with her bottle, and I shift to Danny, who returns from the bedroom and grabs a box labeled Diaper Genie. "We can get all this stuff set up for you. You'll have to move the furniture around. Make room for everything. Bubby, I keep saying you need a bigger house."

Rolling my eyes, I playfully flip him off. Yes. I've given my neighbor the finger.

But he's right. Before, this was a summer cottage. My escape. Now? With Calle and all the supplies I apparently need for a baby?

I'll need more room.

Later. I'll worry about it later. Plenty of people raise children in fifteen hundred square feet.

Plenty.

I hold up a finger. "I can take the bed out of the guest room."

"And put it where?" Danny shoots. "You don't have a garage."

"I'll get a storage unit. Whatever furniture won't fit anymore can go there."

"Good," he says. "We'll put the bed in my garage for now. Get it out of your way."

"You don't have to do that."

"Yeah, I do. All hands on deck here." He holds up the Diaper Genie. "When she's done with her bottle, we'll show you how to use this."

"Danny," Kelly says, "is a fan of the Diaper Genie."

"Hey, good memories with it." He smiles at his daughter. "Listen, kid, stop growing up. You're breaking your old man's heart."

Now Abby rolls her eyes. "Daddy, you're not *old*."

Danny grins at her like a madman. One day, I want to be on the receiving end of a grin like that. One of pure, unconditional affection.

That's what I want. For sure.

I hold my hands out, gesturing to the boxes and bags that seem to eat up every available inch of space. "What can I do?"

Danny points to a pile of bags. "Go through those. Figure out where you want all that."

I grab a handful of the bags, ready to take them to the kitchen to unload, but something pulls at me. Stops me in my tracks. I turn back to my guests. Abby and Danny sorting through boxes, Kelly making funny faces at Calle while she downs the bottle. The only one missing is Bernie, who's already assembling the crib.

"Thank you, guys," I tell them. "This is amazing. I honestly don't know what I would have done without you."

Danny smiles at me with that warm, welcoming smile I've grown used to. "We've got you, Becca. You're not alone."

No. I'm not. For the first time in a very, very long time, I feel like I have found my people.

By midnight, I've been pacing the floor for hours. Calle is in my arms, screaming with a force no six-month-old should ever have the lung power for.

What's wrong with her, I don't have a clue. Overtired, is all I can think.

I know I am. Hell, I might start screaming with her.

I do another lap along the front side of the sofa. Danny and crew left four hours ago after clearing all the packages from the living room and getting me somewhat set up.

Calle had been fine, an angel even, when everyone was here and Danny's daughter occupied her by making silly faces.

Now? She's pissed. Epically pissed.

She *should* be sleeping. I followed Val's instructions to the letter. Getting her bathed—with Kelly's help—and fed and snuggled into freshly laundered sheets and her new crib.

No noisy mobile or sound machine.

Calle, I was informed, doesn't need distractions in her room. Just put her down and she'll go to sleep.

Not!

The bottle I tried quickly got knocked out of my hand. Clearly, she didn't want that.

I then set her in her carrier and gently rocked, but … nope. That brought on an even more blood curdling wail that turned her face the color of a ripe eggplant. Before scooping her back up, I checked her diaper.

Dry.

For kicks—and practice—I changed her anyway, giving her fresh pajamas. Who knew? Maybe she didn't like the ones I picked from her suitcase.

In short, I've done it all. And yet, unhappy Calle.

My head pounds, my vision blurring from fatigue. I was in a major car crash yesterday and I haven't had time to rest. I know I need to. I'll be better for Calle if I do, but how? How can I do that when I have to care for her?

A sudden, new empathy for single mothers fills me. I've interviewed literally thousands of single mothers and never fully understood their stress. Or their exhaustion.

Now?

I get it.

And I'm only on day one.

"What am I supposed to do?" I ask the room at large.

At the sound of my voice, Calle stops screaming. Just that fast. Boom. The silence is bliss and my body reacts accordingly, the tension breaking loose.

Calle lifts her head from my shoulder, stares at me for a good five seconds and howls.

I let out a sigh and ease onto the sofa. "Ssshhh, sweet girl. It's okay."

Really, it's not. Intellectually, I know this. She's lost her mother and that will never be okay.

She wants Tiffany. That has to be it. She simply doesn't understand where her mother went.

The screaming continues only now she lifts her tiny hands and places them on her head, her anguish so fierce it tears me apart.

"Girlfriend, we need help."

I stand and walk to the kitchen, scoop my phone up and dial Danny. No answer.

He's probably sleeping. God knows I would be. I hate to wake him up, I really do, but if I don't get Calle settled, I'll be useless.

Grabbing my keys and throwing one of the freshly washed baby blankets over Calle's shoulders, I walk out the front door where her wails shatter the peaceful night air.

I pull the door shut behind me, making sure the lock engages. I'll only be gone long enough to wake Danny and get him over here, but better safe than sorry.

I march across the lawn—he'll probably yell at me for that, but whatever—and ring the bell. "Come on, Danny. Please wake up."

The living room light goes on. Thank goodness.

I wait a few seconds, and the front door swings open. Danny stands there in shorts and a wrinkled blue T-shirt he obviously just threw on. His dark hair is mashed in all directions.

When Calle sucks a breath and lets out another wail, Danny squeezes his eyes closed. "Oy. I haven't missed this part."

On his doorstep, I sway back and forth, back and forth. "I'm so sorry. She's been like this for hours. I don't know what to do. I've tried *everything*."

"You missed the window," he says.

Wait. What? "What window?"

He waves me inside. "Kelly used to get mad at me if I let Abby stay up late." He pinches his thumb and index finger together. "We had a tiny window of opportunity to get her to sleep before she got overtired. A closed window is like purgatory. You're in it."

I tromp by him. "Nobody told me about a window. Val said seven thirty. That's what I went with. She's been screaming since you guys left."

"Yeah, you're in purgatory."

"Gee, thanks, Confucius."

He laughs, then shuts the door. "Lucky for you, my youngest son was a horrible sleeper. We'll try a trick that used to work with him." He waggles his hand. "Over there. On the couch. Lie down."

What the? "Lie *down*?"

"Do you want my help?"

"If it stops her from screaming? You betcha."

Doing as I'm told, I lie on the couch, being careful not to jostle Calle too much. My body nearly coos with relief as the soft cushions absorb my weight. She continues to scream and adds a baby version of a push-up into the mix by pressing against my chest and arching her back.

It's me. She's trying to get away from me. I'm not her

mother. Never will be. I don't even know anything about babies. Why should she want me?

"Okay," Danny lifts her, repositioning her to my left side and then pats her back.

"Ssssshhhh," I say, focused on keeping my voice calm while my fatigued brain works me over.

And then … whoa. Calle stops screaming. She's still doing a baby plank and I peer up at her. "It's okay, sweet girl. We're okay."

Her head lops forward and her locked arms go slack as she eases against me. Whatever this trick of Danny's is, it's working.

I snap my gaze to him and the triumphant grin lighting him up.

"It's your heartbeat," he says. "It reminds her of being in the womb. My son fell for it every time."

And, apparently, so has Calle.

My heartbeat. Go figure.

I make a move to stand and Danny holds up two hands. "Are you *insane*? She's quiet. Just stay there."

"I can't be here all night."

He shrugs. "Who says? Is your house locked?"

"Yes, but —"

"Let her fall asleep. Trust me on this. I'll get you a blanket and the two of you can sleep right here." He moves to the dining area, grabs one of the high-backed chairs. "I'll put these in front of the couch. Makeshift guardrail. If she slides, she won't go anywhere."

Already, I feel the stirrings of sleep, my body sinking, sinking, sinking into the cushions. "Are you sure this is okay?"

"I'm sure. You'll both get some rest."

Yes. Both of us. Calle and me. Figuring it out.

Together.

CHAPTER 33

*I*t's one of those days I'm convinced is straight from the gods. Eighty-five degrees, clear blue sky, blazing sunshine and zero humidity.

From. The. Gods.

Plus, it's midweek and the beaches are bare, the summer vacationers gone, the kids back in school.

Calle and I are on the beach under an oversized umbrella—I gave up on the tent—while she sits in a bouncer seat I picked up at the store where Danny bought all the baby furniture and supplies.

She loves the beach. Like me, something about the salty air and vast ocean seems to soothe her.

Plus, my parents are close by and she adores my mother. It's not a surprise, really. My mother has that way about her. All sunshine and blue skies even if they cover the storm clouds raging underneath.

I've come to realize that no matter how miserable Mom is, she will never leave my father. Or vice versa.

It is what it is.

It's also not a life I choose for myself. I refuse to stay in a marriage that's not working.

Across from me, Danny, in his usual swim trunks and sunglasses shakes his head. "Amazing. I don't know what you're gonna do in winter when you can't sit out here. Or open the windows so she can hear it."

That, like most things over the last couple of months, I'll deal with when the time comes. That's how it's been lately. Worrying about it when it happens. It's all I can do.

"Hello!"

I glance up at my deck where Marley stands, waving at us in a barely-there yellow bikini that appears to be working overtime keeping her boobs contained. She arrived twenty minutes ago, texting me from the driveway so I could unlock the front door from my phone.

"Whoa." Danny peers at me over the top of his glasses. "Have I mentioned I like big-breasted women?"

Such a pig. "Only about a hundred times."

One night six weeks ago, after a few too many margaritas, Danny and me? We had a moment.

A moment that thankfully passed quickly because as much as I've grown to care for him, to depend on his friendship, I don't feel *that* way about him. The way that makes us want to race to a bed together.

The feeling, we've both realized, is mutual.

I've heard it said that men and women can't be friends. I beg to differ. We're living proof.

Since that night six weeks ago, Danny has made no secret of his love for big-breasted women.

Marley? Right up his alley.

He's never met Marley in person and by the look on his face, the laser-sharp focus, I fear she might soon become wife number four.

At the bottom of the stairs, she kicks off her sandals, leaving them. This is the first time I've invited her here, and it took a bit of coaxing to get her to take an afternoon off, but we have things to discuss. Her future for one.

Before she reaches us, I peer over at Danny. "Would you mind giving us a minute? I need to talk to her."

He stands just as Marley reaches us. "Hey, gorgeous," he says, extending his hand. "I'm Danny."

Despite his being two inches shorter, Marley gives him a once-over, eyeing his expensive sunglasses and dark tan. "Neighbor Danny, hel-*lo*."

He flashes a smile that's a mix of boyish charm and knock-out confidence. Devastating, that smile. Now I understand how he convinced three women to marry him.

"Take my chair." He says. "I'll grab another. Besides, it's margarita time."

"Here we go," I say. "He makes the best margaritas."

"She's not lying," he adds, striding toward his house.

"Take it easy on the tequila," I holler. "I have a baby to take care of."

Marley eases into Danny's chair. "You didn't tell me Danny was cute. Even if he is shorter than me."

"Girlfriend, trust me. It won't matter. The way he was looking at you? You might be in trouble."

We share a laugh and Marley sits forward, tickles Calle's belly. "Hey you. I haven't seen you in a couple weeks. You're getting so big!"

I've been sticking to the shore house but heading into the city occasionally to meet with Marley about the show and with Lilibet, my crack divorce attorney who has Ryan so terrified he's basically agreed to all of my demands.

Our divorce may take a while, given our financial holdings,

but Ryan has kept to his word. I get Calle and he gets his lifestyle.

The truly sad part is that Tiffany's family had no interest in Calle, so the legal aspects of our arrangement weren't hard-fought battles. What people will see is Ryan and I sharing custody. In reality, it's me with part-time help from a nanny.

With the divorce in the works, my only other remaining issue is my show and staff.

When Marley sits back from cooing at Calle, I meet her gaze. "How are things with Jenny?"

Marley shrugs. "Fine. She's a good EP."

"She is."

I don't bother sharing that Jenny obliterated my trust. Somehow, it seems unfair. I've seen and interacted with her when I've ventured into the city for meetings, but our relationship is different. Cooler. More distant. Marley has mentioned this, but I explained it away, telling her I chose not to get friendly with my staff.

Hopefully, she received my unspoken message.

At first, losing Jenny saddened me. Another loss of someone in my circle. Maybe that's what needed to happen to get me peace.

Marley tips her chin to the sky. "I can see why you love it here. Stunning."

"I'm glad you could finally come down."

"Well, you know," she cracks a smile, "it's not easy. What with trying to satisfy your viewers. Damn, those people love you."

A tiny rush gives me pause. Am I being too hasty? Should I extend my leave? Maybe wait a couple more months?

No. No waffling. I wave her off. "You're doing a great job and you know it. You've also done everything I asked. Thank you. I appreciate you, Marley Ren."

"Wow. High praise coming from you. Thank you."

Marley, I've decided, will always be aggressive. Confrontational, even. However, she's balanced what my viewers want with her style and the ratings are holding. She's kept her word and over these last couple of months the bud of a friendship has developed. I'm hoping that bud will bloom.

God help me, I like Marley Ren.

Calle lets out another giggle and Marley cracks up. "She's so happy."

"She loves the ocean." I stare off for a few seconds and gather my courage before facing Marley again. "What about you? Are you happy?"

She studies me. "Sure. I have a great life."

Having lived that life, I know this to be true. In the beginning, I had it all.

Until I didn't.

"And what about with the show? Are you enjoying it? Even though I asked you to soften things?"

She snorts. "Soften. You're funny. Don't take this the wrong way, because I know you're coming back, but I love it. The chaos and drama. Watching your staff work. They're fantastic. Seriously, I told my agent to find me an opportunity for my own show after you come back."

Her own show. Bingo.

A wave crashes ashore, and Calle lets out a hoot. So cute, this kid. I glance at her, and she reaches her little arms out. I love when she does that. When she wants me to hold her. I scoot forward in my chair and lift her, placing her on my lap facing the sea. She rests her head against my chest and lets out a long breath.

"She's beautiful," Marley says.

That, she is.

I stare out at the ocean, think back on the last few months. The exhaustion and heartbreak. Getting Calle resettled—no easy feat—and adjusting to the slower pace.

"I've been thinking," I say. "About Calle and what she needs. What *I* need to care for her in the best way possible and be present for her. Ryan won't help, so it's on me."

I'm her mother now.

I've never said it aloud, but in Tiffany's absence, that's me. Surrogate mom.

Marley shrugs. "So, you work part time. You're the queen of daytime talk. They'll give you what you want."

I shake my head. "I'm done. You should take over the show. You have to keep Bernie though. That's my only request."

There. Said it. Just let it fly. Miraculously, it's not nearly as painful as I thought it would be.

Even the Bernie part. Somehow, I know he'll be taken care of because he and Marley? Two peas in a pod. When I decided to take the summer off, I loaned Bernie to Marley, who didn't have a regular driver.

Now, if my intention is to stay at the shore, it leaves Bernie without a job, and I can't have that. He's family.

Marley's mouth drops open. "Don't tease me."

I let out a snort. "I'm not. I'm tired of the network grind, Marley. It's all about ratings and marketing and keeping sponsors happy. Not to mention managing guests and staff." I pause for a second and look out over the ocean and then to Calle. "I enjoy the lack of chaos at the beach. Waking up and spending time with Calle makes me happy."

"Is it enough for you? Will you get bored?"

The question has plagued me for the last month. "Probably," I say. "But it turns out, I'm a good therapist. I got a call last week from an actress I've met a few times. Her marriage is on the rocks. She wanted to know if I could help them."

"No way."

"Yep. I had a session with them yesterday. In their home down here. They want to continue on. I'm excited about that. About taking the time necessary to help them."

"You want to go back to private practice?"

"Only part-time. Maybe a few hours a day."

She reaches her hand up and we do an air high-five which sends Calle into another round of giggles. I give her a squeeze and smack a kiss on her head. "You're so silly."

Across from us, Marley takes it all in. "I'm happy for you, Becca. Good for you."

"Thanks. I'm adjusting. I never thought I'd be divorced, never mind a single mom. It's an adventure."

"No kidding."

"So, if you want to take over the show full-time, I'll talk to Don. Give you total support."

Her mouth twists, and she shakes her head. Looks out over the ocean.

Sniffles.

Is she? Hold on just one second. Is tough Marley Ren *crying?*

I point at her. "Don't even tell me I've done the impossible and reduced you, of all people, to tears."

"Hey!" She peers back at me and carefully wipes her eyes so she doesn't smudge her mascara. "I'm human. And you just made my dream come true. I'm allowed to get a little freaking weepy."

"Is it safe?"

This from Danny, standing on his deck holding a tray of margaritas.

I look back at Marley. "Well? Do you want my job?"

"Bet your skinny ass I do," she says. "Thank you."

We both crack up and I wave Danny back to the beach. A minute later, he sets the tray on the little side table and walks back to grab an extra chair from the storage box under the deck while Marley, Calle and I sit quietly, taking it all in.

I've basically just quit my job, and it feels perfect.

Danny returns, sets his chair up and pours us all a drink. He hands off the drinks and holds his glass up. "What are we toasting to?"

"That's easy," I say. "To Calle and to friends. The gifts I didn't see coming."

The End

Thank you for reading *The Money Shot*. If you enjoyed Anne's writing, check out the following excerpt of **Risking Trust**, a romantic suspense by Adrienne Giordano (Anne's alter ego).

MICHAEL TAYLOR IS COOLER than ice under pressure. As CEO of a private security company, his job means protecting those at risk. But now Michael's the one in trouble—he's the prime suspect in his ex-wife's murder. To prove his innocence, he needs not just a few good men, but one smart woman. If she agrees to forgive him...

Read on to enjoy an excerpt of *Risking Trust.*

RISKING TRUST

BY ADRIENNE GIORDANO

Chapter One

"Mr. Taylor, do you want to make a statement?"

Michael remained still, his hands resting on his thighs, his shoulders back. He'd been in this Chicago P.D. interrogation room for the better part of an hour and hadn't said a word.

"Mr. Taylor," Detective Hollandsworth repeated, "your wife was murdered last night and you have nothing to say?"

Oh, he had a lot to say, the first being he didn't kill his wife, but if he'd learned anything running one of the nation's most elite private security companies, it was to keep his trap shut. "Not until my lawyer gets here."

An alien sensation settled on him. Shock? Disbelief? Maybe even sadness because a woman he had loved, a woman who had once been vibrant and fun and sexy, a woman who had grown into a greedy, unhappy wife was dead. Jesus. He may have wanted to end the nightmare of a marriage, but murder? No way.

In his worst bout of rage he wouldn't have done that to her. Sure they were finalizing a brutal—and costly—divorce, but money he had and if giving up some of it meant getting her out of his life, he'd do it. Simple arithmetic.

Right now, the only thing Michael knew was that these two detectives banged on his door at 8:00 a.m. to haul his ass in for questioning.

He flicked a glance to the two-way mirror behind Hollandsworth's head. The room's barren white walls and faded, sickening stench of fear-laced sweat made Michael's fingers twitch. He'd keep his hands hidden from view. No sense letting his nerves show.

The side door flew open and smacked against the wall with a *thwap*. Hollandsworth and his younger partner, Dowds, shifted to see Michael's lawyer storm in wearing a slick gray suit complete with pocket hanky.

Arnie Stark set his briefcase on the metal table. "Is he under arrest?"

"Not yet," Hollandsworth said.

"Do you have anything to hold him?" Arnie held up a hand and his diamond pinky ring flashed against the overhead light. "Wait. Let me rephrase. Do you have anything to hold him on that I won't shred in the next two hours?"

The room stayed quiet.

Arnie turned to Michael. "Have you said anything?"

"No."

The lawyer jerked his head without dislodging even one strand of his gelled gray hair. "Good. Let's go."

Thank you. Before Michael could move from his chair, Hollandsworth stood. "We're not done."

Arnie stopped in the doorway, spun around and said, "Charge him then."

Again the room went silent and Michael broke a sweat. The idea of being locked up scared the hell out of him. Hollandsworth's face took on the tight look of a balloon about to burst and Michael let out a breath.

Arnie pointed to the door. "We're leaving."

Once outside the police station, the late March wind coming off Lake Michigan slammed into Michael and he sucked in air as if he'd been without it for months. "I didn't do it."

"I don't care," Arnie said. "I'm your lawyer, not your priest. You want someone to hold your hand, I'm not your guy. You want someone to keep you out of prison, that's me."

Not that Michael needed a babysitter, but hell, he'd appreciate his lawyer believing in his innocence. Then again, this particular lawyer was the best in the city. Anyone living in Chicago knew that because he seemed to be on the news every other week touting another win.

"Keep me out of prison. What now?"

"We go back to my office and you tell me every disgusting detail of your relationship with your wife."

"Ex-wife," Michael corrected.

"Not yet she wasn't."

"It's on the four o'clock news," Mrs. Mackey said, pressing the button on the television remote.

Roxann tore her gaze from the declining numbers on the revenue reports and watched as the *Chicago Banner Herald's* longtime executive assistant, her hair teased and sprayed into submission, switched the channel from CNN to the local news station.

As much as Michael Taylor had wronged her, Roxann couldn't imagine him a murderer. Or maybe she didn't *want* to imagine him a murderer. "Has he been charged?"

"He's only been questioned. I heard from the newsroom that his lawyer got him out before he said anything."

"What about an alibi?"

"He says he was home alone. His doorman saw him go up."

Buildings have back doors.

"I can't believe it. I'd heard they were fighting over money and couldn't agree on a divorce settlement, but still, to kill her?"

Mrs. Mackey shrugged. "I always knew he was no good."

"Eh-hem."

Her assistant whirled to the office door and her head snapped back. Michael Taylor, the man who at one time had filled Roxann with unrivaled happiness, stood in the doorway. Her body went rigid. Literally frozen.

Twelve years ago he ripped her in two, carved out a chunk of her soul and left her emotionally obliterated to the point where she'd made her life so orderly there'd be no room for devastation. Ever.

She had yet to mend that wound.

How much did he hear? She shot out of her chair, sending the blasted thing careening against the wall. He stepped into the office and a tingle surged up her neck.

Michael.

Here.

Now.

"Sorry to interrupt," he said. The sound of his voice, resonant and edgy, had stayed with her over the years. A warm blanket on the coldest January day.

Then she remembered she hated him, despised him with a

fury that would level a city block. Her back stiffened, pulling her into immediate battle mode. What could he be doing here?

An explosion of something Roxann hadn't felt in a long time consumed her. She'd spent years preparing a speech that would reduce Michael to a sniveling lump of flesh. Now she had her chance. Twelve years of compartmentalizing. Twelve years of missing him. Twelve years of righteous anger. *Breathe. One, two, three. Stay calm.* Roxann imagined starting at her toes and rebuilding herself bit by tiny bit.

Michael continued to stare, his angular face resembling sculpted rock. She had loved that face. Not quite handsome, but rugged and intriguing. He wore his dark hair combed back and the style accentuated the few wrinkles around his eyes.

Mrs. Mackey glared at him. "How did *you* get up here? Did you even stop at the security desk for a visitor's pass?"

This man left Roxann with enough emotional ruin to fill Soldier Field and her assistant was worried about a visitor's pass? *Squeeze every muscle. More control. Tighter. Rebuild.*

She held up a hand. "He's here now. Let's not worry about the pass."

"I would have gotten a pass if the guard hadn't ignored me for ten minutes. What should really fry you is I made it up eight floors unimpeded."

"Should I have him escorted out?" Mrs. Mackey asked.

A little late for that. Roxann turned toward her desk. "No, but thank you. I'll handle this."

"But—"

Roxann eyed her. "I've got it. Thank you."

Mrs. Mackey offered Michael one last sneer before leaving. Any other time, Roxann would have laughed, but right now? Not so much. She ran a hand over the coil of hair tucked behind her head. Something told her this wouldn't be good.

"So," she said. "This is unexpected."

"That, it is."

The understatement of the century. If someone had told her Michael would be in her office today, she'd have stayed in bed. Sure she wanted the opportunity to skewer him for the destruction he'd inflicted upon her, but seeing him now, a successful businessman whose simple presence commanded the room, took her breath away. Yes, Michael had become better looking with age and according to the media, more dangerous.

She had wanted a life with him and over the years, as she watched from afar, the what-ifs tortured her. He had given himself to someone else, when all she'd ever wanted was for him to give himself to *her*.

For all the time spent obsessing over it, Roxann still couldn't determine why he had chosen Alicia over her.

In place of marriage, Roxann lived alone, worked like a demon and occasionally squeezed in dating men who never managed to capture her interest.

And Michael, the one man who had captured said interest was now suspected of killing his wife.

ALSO BY ANNE DANO

The Money Shot

Titles by Anne Dano writing as Adrienne Giordano

PRIVATE PROTECTORS ROMANTIC SUSPENSE SERIES

Risking Trust

Man Law

Negotiating Point

A Just Deception

Relentless Pursuit

Opposing Forces

THE LUCIE RIZZO MYSTERY SERIES

Dog Collar Crime

Knocked Off

Limbo (novella)

Boosted

Whacked

Cooked

Incognito

The Lucie Rizzo Mystery Series Box Set 1

The Lucie Rizzo Mystery Series Box Set 2

The Lucie Rizzo Mystery Series Box Set 3

THE ROSE TRUDEAU MYSTERY SERIES

Into The Fire

STAND-ALONE ROMANTIC SUSPENSE BOOKS

Crossing Lines

Deadly Odds

HARLEQUIN INTRIGUES

The Prosecutor

The Defender

The Marshal

The Detective

The Rebel

JUSTIFIABLE CAUSE ROMANTIC SUSPENSE SERIES

The Chase

The Evasion

The Capture

JUSTICE ROMANTIC SUSPENSE SERIES w/MISTY EVANS

Stealing Justice

Cheating Justice

Holiday Justice

Exposing Justice

Undercover Justice

Protecting Justice

Missing Justice

Defending Justice

SCHOCK SISTERS MYSTERY SERIES w/MISTY EVANS

1st Shock

2nd Strike

3rd Tango

STEELE RIDGE ROMANTIC SUSPENSE SERIES w/KELSEY BROWNING

& TRACEY DEVLYN

Steele Ridge: The Beginning

Going Hard (Kelsey Browning)

Living Fast (Adrienne Giordano)

Loving Deep (Tracey Devlyn)

Breaking Free (Adrienne Giordano)

Roaming Wild (Tracey Devlyn)

Stripping Bare (Kelsey Browning)

Enduring Love (Browning, Devlyn, Giordano)

Vowing Love (Adrienne Giordano)

STEELE RIDGE SERIES: The Kingstons w/KELSEY BROWNING

& TRACEY DEVLYN

Craving HEAT (Adrienne Giordano)

Tasting FIRE (Kelsey Browning)

Searing NEED (Tracey Devlyn)

Striking EDGE (Kelsey Browning)

Burning ACHE (Adrienne Giordano)

STEELE RIDGE SERIES: The Blackwells w/

TRACEY DEVLYN

Flash Point, Book 1 (Tracey Devlyn)

Smoke Screen, Book 2 (Adrienne Giordano)

Cross Roads, Book 3 (Tracey Devlyn)

Crash Course, Book 4 (Adrienne Giordano)

End Game (Tracey Devlyn)

ACKNOWLEDGMENTS

I often think writing a book feels a lot like parenting. It takes a village. Luckily, I have amazing people in my village.

An immense amount of respect and gratitude goes to my friend Dee J. Adams. Dee, thank you for sharing your years of experience in television production with me. I found the entire process fascinating, if not a little stressful.

Speaking of friends … thank you to my partner and soul-sister Tracey Devlyn for always being available when I need opinions or a voice of reason. I'd be lost without you!

To Kristen Weber, I'm so grateful you accepted the challenge when I tried a new genre! It's been an amazing ride that taught me so much. Martha Trachtenberg, your attention to detail is beyond impressive. Thank you for finding all those seemingly tiny details that threaten to derail my plot.

Elizabeth Mackey, you have once again crawled into my brain and somehow created the exact cover I dreamed of. Thank you for your ongoing patience and for sharing your exceptional talent.

Special thanks to Siiri Scott for your dedication to creating a fantastic audio book. You brought to life these characters I love so much and I'll be forever grateful.

Maureen Downey, thank you, thank you, thank you for everything you do. Without you, I'd get no writing done.

Much gratitude to Liz Semkiu, Sandy Modesitt, and Rochelle Howard for doing an early read on *The Money Shot*. I so appreciate your help.

Special thanks to my husband for traveling the publishing road with me and being patient while I chase my dreams. To my son, thank you for always making me laugh. I love you both more than I ever imagined possible.

A NOTE TO READERS

Dear Reader,

Thank you for reading *The Money Shot*. I hope you enjoyed it. If you did, please help others find it by sharing it with friends on social media and writing a review.

Sharing the book with your friends and leaving a review helps other readers decide to take the plunge into Becca's world. I would appreciate you taking a moment to tell your friends how much you enjoyed the story. Even a few words are an enormous help. Thank you!

If you would like to try my romantic suspense and mystery titles, you'll find them on my alter ego's (really, Anne is my alter ego, but don't tell her I said that) website at www.adriennegiordano.com.

Want to find out what's coming next?

Sign up for my newsletter

Follow me on Facebook and Twitter

Happy reading!

Anne

ABOUT THE AUTHOR

Anne Dano is a pseudonym for Adrienne Giordano, a *USA Today* bestselling author of over forty romantic suspense and mystery novels. Anne is a Jersey girl at heart, but now lives in the Midwest with her ultimate supporter of a husband, sports-obsessed son and Elliot, a snuggle-happy rescue. Having grown up near the ocean, Anne enjoys paddleboarding, a nice float in a kayak, and lounging on the beach with a good book.

For more information on Anne/Adrienne's books, please visit www.AdrienneGiordano.com. Anne/Adrienne can also be found on Facebook at http://www.facebook.com/Adrienne GiordanoAuthor, Twitter at http://twitter.com/AdriennGior dano and Goodreads at http://www.goodreads.com/ AdrienneGiordano.

Don't miss a new release! Sign up for Anne's new release newsletter!